WINGS
OF THE
MORNING

Julian Beale

for the love of Africa

WINGS OF THE MORNING

JULIAN BEALE

UMBRIA PRESS

Royalties from the sale of this book
are donated to registered charities
which support Africans in need.

Cover image: Shutterstock

Umbria Press
London SW15 5DP
www.umbriapress.co.uk

Printed and bound by
Ashford Colour Press, Gosport

ISBN 978-0-9573641-0-3

MAJOR CHARACTERS

THE OXFORD FIVE

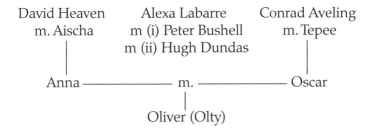

Pente   Kingston
Broke Smith   Offenbach

David Heaven   Alexa Labarre   Conrad Aveling
m. Aischa   m (i) Peter Bushell   m. Tepee
    m (ii) Hugh Dundas

Anna ————————— m. ————————— Oscar

Oliver (Olty)

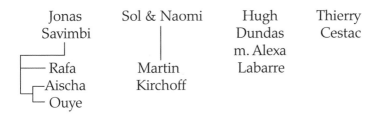

OTHER KEY PEOPLE

Jonas   Sol & Naomi   Hugh   Thierry
Savimbi   Dundas   Cestac
                   m. Alexa
— Rafa   Martin   Labarre
— Aischa   Kirchoff
— Ouye

If I take the wings of the morning,
and dwell in the uttermost parts of the sea;
Even there shall thy hand lead me,
and thy right hand shall hold me.

PSALM 139

OLIVER AVELING — 2021

Most people call me 'Olty'. I turn thirty today, the first of January 2021. I enjoy my birthday on New Year's Day. It wasn't so great when I was a child, but since reaching my teenage years, I've had a lot of fun with extra celebration after the partying on New Year's Eve. This year's a bit special of course: thirty is a major number and a dozen of us have planned a big bash for tonight. But I want to make a start on this project first. It's going to be a challenge.

I'm a diplomat by profession. I'm white, single, straight, solvent. I work with a great bunch of people and I'm lucky with my friends. I travel a lot, but I love coming home to this apartment with its brilliant view over the ocean. I have company from time to time, but there's no one really serious in my life.

I was born in England, but I've lived here since I finished school twelve years ago. 'Here' is Century City, Capital of Millennium, a country occupying a landmass on the West Coast of Africa as old as time itself, although our nation was born only twenty-one years ago today.

Millennium's struggle into existence is the kernel of my story, but there's a more personal element to it as well. Our country's founding president was David Heaven who's been long gone from life and much longer from that post. I was twenty-two when he died and I knew him a bit because he had been close to our family since I was a boy and he features in my earliest memories. He was gruff but kind, and to give him his due, he was a pretty good communicator with all age groups. Plus of course, David Heaven was for a while the *man* of Millennium and was therefore a significant figure. Until his death, I thought of him as an important family friend and after he had gone, I

1

simply thought about him less and less. I certainly had no idea that he was my biological grandfather, the father of my mother. So this news hit me like a thunderbolt.

A little over a year ago, I was spending a lot of working time in New York and I had a visit from a Frenchman called Guy Labarre. He's not a relative but our families have been intertwined over many years. Guy is a human rights lawyer and we did have a bit of business to do together, but that was not the reason to bring him calling. He bought me lunch and took the opportunity to hand over a letter written to me by David Heaven. It doesn't say much, just a simple message addressed to me in his handwriting which I recognised on the envelope.

'To my grandson, Oliver Aveling.'
The letter inside is not dated. It reads as follows:

'Dear Olty,
I do not know when you will receive this, neither do I know who will give it to you, but I leave it in safe hands and in confidence that it will reach you one day. I could not acknowledge you in life, but here is my legacy in death. Here is a record of my time and my efforts. There is untold history and there are unrecorded facts. Above all, Olty, I leave you my memories. I am certain that you will become the man who will make the most of them.'

There is no signature.

With this letter came a small suitcase, full of photographs, newspaper cuttings, memorabilia of all sorts. And there was a journal. I have one volume in front of me now. It's not a diary and it's hardly a memoire. It's not 'it'. There are eleven hardback books and the lined pages of all of them are filled with Heaven's neat handwriting. There's no concession to modernity. He might as well have drawn a pirate's map with a quill pen. There's no index, no summary and only a few of the photos are dated. But

2

the journal is compelling and I was hooked from the moment I started to browse.

It's recorded history that my grandfather started a revolution. He raised an army and planned an invasion. He came in from the ocean with three ships and three thousand people in the small hours of the new century. He aimed to take over an established sovereign state and to replace it with a new country, a new order and a new society. Human engineering on a grand scale.

It's people who shape events on this planet and the personalities which drive the people are formed from background, relationships, opportunity and sheer damn fortune. It's the 'humanity of history' as my grandfather calls it somewhere in this tome of his. Mostly, however, he keeps his emotional side in check. He writes in facts and figures and dates. He uses terse language, abbreviating his inner feelings.

I could have tidied this up and published his journal as a posthumous autobiography. But I wanted more. I wanted flesh on the bones of his sparse account and so I have spent the past year in research and conversations with survivors of the era.

This is an extraordinary story of momentous times. It starts with a relative of my family friend Guy Labarre – his Uncle Michel.

MICHEL LABARRE — 1963

On the evening of the fourth day, the young man standing on tip toes accepted that his death was imminent and found that he was quite looking forward to it.

When he was snatched from the hotel, his first reaction had been disbelief larded with a sheer, raging terror. He liked to talk as tough as any red-blooded young man when a bit taken in drink and surrounded by his mates, but that would have been in Paris or in his home city of Limoges. Out here he was in strange territory, without the familiar points of reference and he had felt both excitement and isolation from the moment he had stepped off his direct flight from France into the arrivals hall at Niamey International Airport in the Republic of Niger.

Michel Labarre was twenty-three years old with a reasonable degree in chemical engineering from the University of Sorbonne. He came from a quality family, possessed of money, status and standing. He was an enthusiastic sportsman, a good looking, fun-loving young man, with a lively and likeable personality.

The oyster of Michel's world was opening up as he arrived that day from Paris. He was joining, as a management trainee, a substantial French conglomerate in civil engineering called Georges DuLame & Cie which had global interests but especially in the former French colonies of West Africa. Newly recruited university graduates could expect to spend at least half of their first three years on short term postings overseas, and for most of them, this was a significant attraction of the job.

Michel was therefore one of a kind and he relished the chance, following his inaugural stint at the DuLame training centre outside Nanterre, to cut his teeth on some proper work in Africa. For the first couple of months, the company's well established practice was to apply a regime of strict acclimatisation. The young men, and there were precious few women of any age, were required to knuckle down to big company discipline, to work diligently and to get their bodies used to the extreme climate with its 40 degree heat. They must tolerate the sometimes dodgy food and accept the basic accommodation. The incentives were that expatriate life offered decent money, infrequent but long leaves, and satisfaction for the Beau Geste spirit if that turned you on.

Michel loved it all. He liked the work, liked the heat, liked his fellow workers be they French or Nigerien, especially liked the feeling of accomplishment that he was doing something different, and doing it well. The French management at the DuLame compound took to him also, congratulating themselves that they had an asset in Michel Labarre, all the more impressive as he came from a pretty toffee-nosed background. And all his colleagues appreciated his ability to keep up with the pace of beer when they had a night out in the bars and dives of Niamey, especially as he was something of a musician and could play a reasonable guitar even when several sheets to the wind.

That single talent led to his undoing. A group of them finished up one night at La Chatte, a lively club in the red light ghetto, notorious for its innovative band which was delighted to welcome Michel into an impromptu jamming session at which his playing ability shone out as brightly as his face whilst the drinks poured down and the heat of pressing bodies mounted. It was during a beer break that he talked rather loosely to the double bass player who encouraged Michel in his account of learning to play the guitar at his exclusive school in France and applauded him for working hard in the Sahara despite obviously coming from a pretty wealthy background. Michel was well past picking up any danger signals from this trend of conversation and his new friend took care that their little talk did not include the other members of Labarre's group from the company.

Half an hour after that, the girl arrived. She might have been from Mali or perhaps from Mauritania, but she was actually a

Senegalese and strikingly beautiful — tall, very slim, angel face and totally poised. The entire package was white hot sexy, and Michel was overboard when she came straight over to talk to him. She gurgled with the claim that word of his excellence had reached her from her friends in the band and she just had to see him perform. She delivered that line with such clear innuendo that Michel felt as if he had been that kicked in the groin.

A little more music was played and a good deal more beer lowered before the senior DuLame man announced that their group was leaving. That was an absolute instruction. No one got left behind, certainly not Michel Labarre with his hormones pumping, but the girl , who called herself Salacia, managed to whisper that she could not say adieu and just must meet him two nights hence in the main square of the city at 6:30 pm, and that he must come alone.

The following day was a Sunday and Michel spent it in a fever of indecision mixed with lust. Company instructions were explicit. No employee to leave the compound without a pass and never alone in the evening. But Michel knew, like everybody else, that the wire perimeter was holed like a Swiss cheese, that many of the inhabitants went out from time to time and that the African workers in the camp brought their own women in through the selfsame holes. So practicality was not an issue. But then there was risk assessment, and he made a steadily less objective job of this as his animal instincts drove his brain south.

Monday was therefore passed with the electricity of planning and anticipation, with the enticing body of Salacia ever dancing before his eyes. He finished his work, showered, grabbed some cash and slipped out of the compound. He picked up a flea bitten cab immediately which was surely a good omen and was in the square by 6:20 pm feeling relaxed and sure of himself. She would be pleased to see him and he paused by the fountain to light a cigarette with luxuriant pleasure.

Salacia was indeed delighted to see him. She had a good feeling about this one, but you still needed the proof that the fish was on the line. She was sitting at the back of an open fronted cafe across the square, hidden by the awning overhead and pleased to see her mark exhibiting the body language of nerves drowned in expectation. Now she whispered a final instruction to her companion, a huge man in a flat white cap which obscured a little of his beard, unusually luxuriant for an African, and then she rose to slip away, lithe in her sea green dress with the skirt just a bit too short. Minutes later, she could be seen approaching Michel from the other side of the square having circled around. The big man shook his head. She was almost too sharp and sexy this one, but she knew her business and made more money more easily than any of his former partners. Plus she liked a bit of rough and brawny occasionally, so no way was he going to complain about taking orders from Salacia.

Meanwhile, Michel was in heaven. This gorgeous girl was treating him like manna from heaven, a little decorous kiss on his cheek, smoothing his hair, compliments on his appearance and her finger nails skittering down his arm in a gesture of welcome and possession. Supremely sexy.

She slipped her arm through his and led him away out of the square into the main street and towards the misnamed Hotel du Parc, which was nonetheless the best establishment in town. As they walked, she explained that she worked for the Foreign Service of Senegal, she had flown in a week ago on a visit mixing business with pleasure and that she always stayed in this hotel. Michel was entranced and questioned none of this. They went into the foyer, in which he felt instinctively that he should be discreet if not furtive, but Salacia continued their conversation uninterrupted as she waited for her key, saying that their plan should be to go and listen to some more music, but first perhaps, a refreshing drink and a little relax. She looked demurely at him with a twinkle in her eye which would have debauched a monk.

Upstairs in her spacious room, she poured him a cold beer, lit a cigarette for them both, kicked off her shoes and slipped gracefully onto the double bed, patting the sheets alongside her in invitation. Michel put down his glass and moved towards her, his throat, despite the lager, already dry with expectation.

'Cheri', she invited him calmly, 'I think you should first remove your clothes ... just like me'.

She smiled encouragement as she let slip the dress from around her neck and lay back in the middle of the bed, hair spread out, breasts high, nipples thrust in excitement, legs ajar, the whole marvellously naked. She held out her arms to him and Michel stumbled awkwardly out of his trousers, almost tripping as he simultaneously ripped off his shirt. In his fevered state, he didn't notice the lift whirring to a halt on their floor, neither did he hear the door to the bedroom being gently opened, nor sense the large man with the white cap enter with a silence which belied his bulk. But at that moment, Michel might not have noticed a rampaging bull — he was one himself. With a groan of delight, he got onto the bed and leaned forward to rest his belly against Salacia's knees which she had drawn up into her chest. Michel supported himself on his arms, his hands palm down on either side of his lover. Classic missionary stuff, he had time to think to himself as he pushed forward quite gently and was thrilled to feel her knees begin to part before his thrust. Nirvana, here we come, he thought.

But in an instant, his every instinct turned from slaking lust to fighting panic as he seemed to levitate in a manner which defied all his senses. Michel was suddenly powerless, overcome by extraordinary strength. One large human hand gripped his throat so he could gurgle but not breathe. Another slipped between his legs and gathered all his rampant genitalia in one massive grip which would have made him scream if he could have used his larynx. He felt himself being swung effortlessly into the air, the same two hands in the same two places, but now he was being held upside down and then lowered into a heavy hessian sack with fumes which drove the breath from his nose as he started to choke. But neither hand released its hold until Salacia, who had snatched the bag from under the bed and opened the neck to receive its human burden, pulled tight a drawstring which laced the bottom of the sack around Michels's down-stretched neck so that the giant could pull out his hand and permit the cord and the fumes to stifle any cries which the captive might make. Without delay, the big man stood on the bed, lifted up Michel by balls and body and thumped him head down on the wooden floor. The lights went out for Michel.

The giant and Salacia looked at each other. There was a prevailing silence, with only the normal sounds of street and public building to reach them. White Cap had a sheen of light sweat on his upper arms but his breathing was steady and normal. Almost effortless work for him. But Salacia was snorting and throwing her head about, cascades of glittering black hair whirling around her shoulders and her limbs trembling as if in trauma. White Cap recognised the symptoms, not of fear or crisis but of battle lust and he proposed the remedy with one uplifted eyebrow. She nodded at him. Michel lay like a donkey's dumped burden. White Cap scooped up Salacia with one arm and released his jeans with the other. He chucked her on the bed, face down, bottom up and pulled her roughly back onto him. She cursed at him to go harder. He grunted and went at it. He was over in a minute, she was dressed in two more. They left the room without a backward glance, the hessian bag and its unseen occupant slung casually over the giant's shoulder. He passed through the lobby with a direct but unhurried gait whilst she lingered briefly at reception to pass over an envelope which made good a prior agreement. They joined up again at the front door and walked into the car park to retrieve a battered Nissan pickup. Salacia drove. White Cap tossed the sack with casual abandon into the load bed. He got in beside her and they drove off without a word.

Michel Labarre came to briefly around midnight but lapsed in and out of consciousness during the early hours and it was not until the African dawn came blazing up around 6 am that he was able to take any stock of his position. It was not good.

Vision for him remained very faint. He was being held in the middle of a warehouse which permitted scant daylight through its few dusty windows. Worse, he was still inside the heavy, musty sacking and his head was splitting from its treatment the previous evening. It took him some time and freshly rising panic to understand that although there were no bindings on his limbs, he was still trussed like an animal for market as he remained upside down, one drawstring still around his neck at the bottom of the sack, and a second below his feet, thus sealing him in a hessian tomb. He struggled with a desperation born of horror and this action made him swing. He fought his claustrophobia and regained just enough self control to work it out. The sack was suspending him from some fixture above, but he had no means of knowing at what height nor whether there was any sort of help within earshot. He tried to shout, but the resultant noise was feeble and blanketed. The effort also caused him to suck in more dust and he started to choke, causing yet greater panic. Mercifully, this led him to pass out again and he spent the next few hours in a state of semiconscious delirium.

Meanwhile, there was progress of a sort. At 5 am, a ragged urchin had scrambled through one of the holes into the DuLame compound and, as instructed by Salacia, who remained at a safe distance sitting in the old pickup, left an envelope under a heavy stone at the door to the main administration block. It was addressed to the senior French executive of the company. Inside was a message from a fictitious revolutionary group demanding a ransom in CFA francs for the safe return of their captive whose battered and unconscious face was quite recognisable in the poor photograph enclosed. Cash payment was to be made according to precise instructions within forty-eight hours or Labarre would be executed.

By 9 am, the telex lines to the DuLame Headquarters in Lille were chattering and by the end of the day, it became clear that retired Colonel Joffrey Labarre, a wealthy man in his own right and with considerable experience of the African colonies, would personally underwrite the price of his son's return. With a speed and pragmatism of which the French are most capable when roused, the details were arranged and a note left out for collection by another small boy, which requested an extension of twenty four-hours simply to get the cash together and to parcel it as instructed.

Salacia relayed this to Paulus, the personable double bass

player from the club La Chatte who had provided the brains and the organisation behind the kidnap. He ordered an agreement to the extension. He had anyway been planning for it. Meanwhile, they were to keep young Labarre safe but scared, not fed but watered, secure from any possibility of escape and Paulus did not want to know where they were holding him.

The other parties to the agreement were content if not happy. DuLame management did not want to rock any commercial boats by running for help to either the Niamey Police or the Niger Government. Colonel Labarre knew best and would pay for his preference to be respected. Payment would be made and young Labarre recovered. He would have to leave Niger immediately and the employ of DuLame just after that, but the parents would get their first born back – very severely chastened but nonetheless intact.

Whilst this process took its course, Michel's circumstances improved, if only a little. On that first day, he returned to some normality just after noon, had the beginnings of a further panic attack but fought it down and was just starting to think through the desperation of his position when he heard a heavy footfall and felt his sacking prison being first lifted and then lowered roughly to the floor. The strings were untied, the material pulled back and the unaccustomed light battered his brain. He was hauled to his feet. He made out the all too familiar features of the giant above him as his arms were swept together in front of him and bound palm to palm by White Cap using insulating tape over which he placed a heavy rope tied in a noose. The big man thrust a plastic bottle into his mouth and upturned it, waiting almost patiently while Michel choked and gurgled to get some of the warm and dirty water down his throat. Then he threw the end of the rope over the rafter from which Michel's sack had been suspended and heaved until the prisoner was obliged to take his weight on his arms or to stand on his toes. The rope was secured to a stanchion in the floor.

Michel was looking around as Salacia came sashaying out of the shadows, a slight smile playing over her sexy features, another slinky dress, long legs, long black hair. The nightmare returned to him and he felt simultaneously a terror at his prospects and humiliation at his filthy nakedness which he could do nothing to hide. She came right up close to him and gripped his head in her two hands.

'You were never too attractive,' she said, 'and you'll look and smell horrible by the time we're finished. But you'll be alive at least. So do as you're told. No shouting or you go back in the sack. No complaining or Claude here will beat the shit out of you. And he'll enjoy it'.

Behind her, White Cap gave a slow, broad grin, full of infinite menace. She looked into Michel's face for a long time until he could no longer bear her gaze and he dropped his eyes in abjection. Only then did she turn on her heel and walk off into the darkness of the building's extremities.

And so began for Michel Labarre a terrible test of endurance which had brought him, four days almost to the hour after his abduction, to a point of suicidal despair. By day, they left him roped up to a height at which he could choose to give some slight respite to either his arms or his feet. But not both together and increasingly he came to stand on tip toes. At night, they placed a stool by him on which he could climb to rest and try to sleep vertically, overcome by exhaustion until he fell over or was disturbed by the rats which crept out of the shadows to sniff around the droppings from his increasingly nauseating body and even to nibble at his feet. They kept him alive on water only. He saw only Claude whom he once asked for something to eat to be rewarded with a kick in the groin and belt welts to his back and buttocks. Sometimes, he thought of home and wept. He tried to keep his hopes alive, knowing that he was worth money and that money would be found and paid if only the communications would work.

Michel could not know that they did work, and pretty smoothly in the circumstances. The delay stretched beyond the deadline, but Paulus was not fazed by that. An intelligent man, well educated in Kinshasa, he had spent some years living in France. He knew the systems and could read the characters. He had seen the opportunity and acted decisively. But this was a big job — the largest which they had pulled together and as soon as they had the cash safe, it would be time to move out. It would be best to be on his own for a few months, give the band a rest, let Salacia go back to a little whoring in the expatriate community somewhere, encourage Claude into more body building. While for him — well, perhaps a trip back to France would be good. He was relaxed.

But then it all went horribly wrong.

The ransom sum was assembled and packaged as demanded. It was delivered to the petrol station and truck stop on the route out of Niamey towards the border with Mali to the north. Inconspicuously parked amongst the big vehicles, Paulus could see the drop made, just another 45 gallon oil drum amongst so many others, and he could see Claude arrive five minutes later to collect the drum with the big red stripe and sweep it into the back of the old Nissan whilst Salacia waited at the wheel. They did as he had told them, and went to the pumps to buy fuel so that he would have some minutes to see if there was any suspicious car looking to follow them. Nothing and no one. Salacia and Claude drove out of the truck stop to circle the city back towards the warehouse where Michel was hanging from his rope, shortly to be released to find his way towards help and home, filthy, naked and lost whilst the three perpetrators and the rest of the band would make their way quietly from the city, dividing their takings and then go their separate ways.

But as Salacia drove at modest speed with Claude beside her, she put an alternative scheme to him which he liked very much indeed. They had done all the work and taken all the risks. Why share the profits and why anyway on such an unequal basis as Paulus proposed? As a partnership, they felt confident together. She the style and brain, he the unstoppable bulk. But they had to be ruthless, with nothing left behind to assist either Paulus or the authorities. And thus was sealed the fate of Michel Labarre.

They drove the pick up into the warehouse and shut out behind them the waning sunlight. Michel was unmoving and looked at them through a face masked with the pain of standing on his toes. Salacia walked right up to him, just as she had done when she left him three days before. She wrinkled her nose at the smell but managed a sexy, secret smile. Michel was far gone in fear and exhaustion, but he opened his eyes as she stroked him gently and gazed at her as she stepped back a pace, lifting her arms above her head, pushing her hair out onto her shoulders, striking a provocative pose with one leg cocked in front of the other. Michel was never conscious of White Cap circling behind him.

'Well Monsieur', said Salacia, 'most men say that I have a body to die for. I hope you agree?' She smiled as Claude broke his neck from behind with the speed and indifference which a farmer might use on a chicken.

Claude stuffed the corpse of the young man into the sack in which he had arrived. He put this next to the oil drum with the red stripe in the load bed of the pickup, and then took the wheel himself as they drove sedately out of the city towards Ouagadougou, capital of Upper Volta. Eighty kilometres later, and by now in complete darkness, Claude took the body in its sack and carried it a further kilometre over rough desert ground away from the road and there abandoned it in a slight depression in the ground.

Claude returned to Salacia with the keys of the car in his pocket. You can never be too careful. But probably, they did not go much further together. Not only had they made an enemy of a brighter man, but they had also made a serious mistake. Paulus had no cause to suspect them, but he was ever cautious. Thus, they had collected the drum with the stripe as he told them, but that was not the drum with the money. Paulus himself had awaited their departure from the fuel station before moving in to find the correct article and even now he was counting the money to share with his confederates. But two of them would not now dare to return.

The body was never found. Over time, decay and vermin stripped away the flesh, whilst the searing sun and desert wind bleached the bones. There was never to be Christian resting place for Michel Labarre, and it was to be many months before his family could accept that he was forever gone from them, and in circumstances which they would never know.

DAVID HEAVEN — 1943 to 1965

David Charles Heaven was born on the 9th May 1943, the youngest by six years of four children. His father, Lawrence, was the headmaster of a boys' boarding school in the home counties of England to the west of London. Running a school may have been a worthy occupation during the war years, but it was a hard and thankless task for a man who felt jilted of his opportunity to join up and see some action.

As he grew up, David had difficulty in establishing much of a relationship with his father who was austere and preoccupied with his own disappointments. In school time, the boy tended to merge as a statistic into the crowd of responsibilities as David started his education, quite literally, at home.

David's three older siblings were all girls, which served to increase the already considerable age gap. Almost nothing is recorded about these sisters, and not much more about their mother Esther. There seems to have been no sense of family. No Christmas together, no birthday celebrations, no holidays, no wedding announcements. Most significantly, no photographs of the individuals, still less the family as a group, saving one only of a school assembly showing David, just discernible in the back row with his father looking stern in the middle of his teaching staff.

So, a rather sad childhood and an unpromising start in life, yet many people have risen from beginnings more different and difficult. At the age of thirteen, David went on to school at Lancing College in Sussex where he prospered in his work and especially on the sports field and the running track. But as for earlier years, there is scant record of social activity and of course, an absolute absence of family events.

In 1962, rather older at nineteen years and some months than was the norm for those days, David went up to Oxford University to read history at Brasenose College. Behind him, he left those shallow roots and slight beginnings. Oxford and the society he kept became overnight his home and his heartbeat.

David Heaven made the most of his time at Oxford and loved all of it. He worked quite hard out of enjoyment as much as duty and took a creditable degree. He socialised, debated, became an enthusiastic club man and was active if not outstanding in his chosen sports. He lived life to the full. He drank and dined and womanised. He became like a sponge in his eagerness to soak up the benefits, the warmth and the experience of all the relationships which could be persuaded to come his way. He was making up for lost ground in earlier years. Very seldom did he feel any sense of abiding commitment. He was fulfilled by just working his way around the smorgasbord of life. He was well spoken, but no snob: he had a bit of money, but was not flash with it: he was not bad looking and was easy company: he had a sharp sense of humour and was apparently game for just about anything.

And so he flirted with everything which crossed his path, and in later life he thanked his stars and a rather remote God that he had not been irretrievably hooked or damaged by any of it. Looking back, he could see that all the experiments with bookmakers and poker players, with dodgy booze and nameless drugs, with women both wanton and weary, and once, disastrously, with a cultured chorister, all this frenzied activity had been as for a child on a first outing to the sweet shop.

David made four significant friendships at Oxford, one woman and three men.

First, there was Alexandra Labarre who was a little younger than the rest of them having come up early to university to escape the aftermath of a family tragedy which was never articulated. Neither age nor gender could hold her back. Alexa — as she liked to be called — was of Anglo French birth and a most magical girl. She had stunning, ethereal looks and a most

16

beautiful figure, the highest quality wrapping for a razor brain and a diamond core. Being bilingual from childhood, it was perhaps too obvious that Alexa should be a language specialist but she nonetheless distinguished herself. Her French father Joffrey travelled extensively in South America and spoke both Spanish and Portuguese whilst her English mother Elizabeth was an authority on the churches in Venice and thus fluent in Italian. Alexa was competent to masterful in all these languages, but trumped her parents' aces by taking Russian at Oxford. She was extremely talented but wore her ability lightly and was ever marvellous company. David enjoyed a tide of laughter with her and endless, provocative debate on any subject. Never once did he look like winning either the arguments or access to her bed, and perhaps he loved her all the more for it.

The three men batted in no particular order. Rupert Broke Smith, who came to be known to one and all as 'Pente', was a gentle giant of a man who entered the priesthood immediately after leaving Oxford and abandoned forever the study of physics which had won him an exceptional degree. Pente had a background not dissimilar to David's. He was the lonely, only child of ageing parents who lived in a remote part of Herefordshire, eking out a living in the rare book trade. Pente was schooled locally, and had hardly been beyond Bristol until he surprised everyone by gaining entry to Oxford in considerable style. He was the brightest of David's contemporaries and would have succeeded in any subject. Pente was tremendous company too. A huge beer drinker and an energetic party animal, he was an impressive rugby player reckoned to have missed a Blue only through insufficient training. But during one vacation, he vanished for six weeks into the Hindu Kush and returned with the 'call' from which he never wavered. He was no Holy Joe, did not tax his friends with the strengths of his vocation and was in no way a lesser companion. He may have been a little better behaved, but he still drank a great deal and laughed even more as he became overnight a man with a mission and a faith.

And the sobriquet? He won it at the seminary which he

attended for an introductory course following his return from India and the story always warmed David despite his natural disregard for most men of the cloth. It went that his fellow students suffered just so much of his fondness for mixing pickled onions and pints of bitter with explosive results to his digestion before they nicknamed him 'Pentecost' to recall another rushing, mighty wind and of course, the abbreviated version became his for a lifetime.

Then there was Conrad Aveling, born to be the successful soldier which he duly became. Conrad was the youngest child of the four sons and two daughters produced by General Sir Anstruther and his Lady Vivien Aveling. The family lived in baronial style in a vast and ugly mansion located in a village only just outside Oxford. On first acquaintance, Conrad seemed a bit quiet for David's taste, but it became quickly apparent that he was simply withdrawn from his overwhelming family. His mother was of towering personality, a physically dominant woman who was said to have given birth to one of her brood only hours before returning to the hunting field. All the Avelings, boys and girls alike, were large and brave. Conrad was the exception in that he had a brain as well and with it came a waspish sense of humour.

During their first year at Oxford, David was invited to spend a good deal of time, weekends and summer evenings, at the Aveling pile of Barrington Park and he grew increasingly to value Conrad's companionship. The rambunctious family atmosphere was so completely different from his own experience. There was always activity, sometimes close to chaos, but set against a prevailing background of relaxation tinged with a faded elegance. Conrad's siblings seemed to drift comfortably in and out of his life. Their father, the jovial General, had achieved war time distinction and retired to manage his land from the draughty old house, but it was generally accepted that he was forcefully guided by his imposing wife. Lady Vivien could be a battle axe, but wise and thoughtful too, as David learnt from his very first visit to the Park. Once she had recovered from mild astonishment that he had never sat on a horse or held a gun, Lady Vivien had managed to draw from him more about his early life and distant family than he had ever previously confessed.

'She's a shrewd old bat, my Mum', Conrad had spoken of her lovingly,'and we all owe her more than we can say or she would accept. She holds our team together, no question'. David had found himself quite moved: this sort of family experience was completely new to him. It made a deep and lasting impression.

As the Oxford years progressed, David became close to Connie Aveling. They had shared interests in sporting, carousing and the politics of the day. But while David was undecided on a future career path, Conrad was entirely committed to the army, although unusual at the time in having opted for university rather than going straight from school into the army. Connie had a relaxed good humour and a wry turn of phrase, but he kept a close counsel and it was hard to read where his thoughts were turning. This led David to an increasing concern that Conrad's similarly lustful pursuit of Alexa Labarre was more successful than his own, but Connie would give nothing away. And then again, it often seemed that her favourite was Pente, but at least he came to put himself out of the chase. Whatever else, it was all a lot of fun.

When they came down from university, Conrad went to Sandhurst and then to take up his commission in the Rifle Brigade where his military career was soon to prosper. He and David kept in close touch to further a friendship which built on the diversities of their interests and lifestyles. Conrad was a man of perception which he inherited from his mother and nurtured in the shabby grandeur and windy corridors of Barrington Park.

The third man was an exception in every respect. Kingston Horace Offenbach was different in age, nationality, religion, politics and colour. An unusual man to be found at Oxford University in the mid 1960's, King Offenbach was born in South Carolina in September 1938. He had one brother less than a year older and their father abandoned his small family when

Kingston was three months old. His mother was left high and dry with two tiny children, no money and precious little support from her family. But she was an intelligent girl with guts, looks and the determination that she would do right by her children. She managed to succeed, but not without further heartbreak. Her elder son had been a sickly little boy from birth, and she lost him to pneumonia just before his third birthday at a point when she had no reserves of energy or money to buy him the drugs which might have saved him. She had retreated from his pathetic little grave, vowing that that she would channel her every effort into raising his brother. King rewarded her by exceeding her wildest expectations, becoming in due time an outstanding student who worked his way through secondary education and exhibited such promise that he was taken into US Government Service under which sponsorship he won an excellent degree and then was sent to the UK to do a postgraduate thesis at Oxford. Now, at the age of twenty-six, this was the first time that he could not make his monthly visit back home to his mother's small house in a small town.

King Offenbach was older than the undergraduates with whom he shared life at Oxford and he had little in common with any of them. In addition, he was a self-effacing man, much more inclined to listen than to offer opinions. Despite his colour, King had a talent for melding into the background, present but not accounted for.

King's course at Oxford was for one year, and David first met him one gloomy evening in November 1964. He was running late for an appointment with his tutor as he rounded a corner in his college and collided with the unbending Offenbach frame. To make matters worse, David assumed him to be a tourist visitor or a new member of staff and had been less than polite.

From such an unpromising start can sometimes grow the strongest relationships. People would say of Offenbach that he stood a little apart from the rest of them by reason of his age and others would cite his colour, his Deep South accent or his religious fervour. Or could it have been the 'transatlantic flavour' as one Don famously labelled a prejudice for which he could find no other name.

It was Pente Broke Smith who became closest to Kingston Offenbach, and even he talked of deep and still waters. Pente remarked one day to David, 'I know this is being pretty pompous, but I reckon that on a spiritual level, King will always keep a bit back. He has this compulsion to hold onto his reserve. But of course that personality trait is cranked up further by his profession.'

David looked at him with surprise.

'What profession? He's a student like the rest of us. Just a little more mature, that's all. Oh, and a bit darker too!'

'Dimwit', rejoined Pente as they walked together, 'no David, you're missing it. Our Kingston is on the CIA payroll and has been since he was at school, I shouldn't wonder.'

'Balls,' said David, but he had his doubts even then.

David, Alexa, Pente, Conrad and King: a group of friends drawn into a coterie which was recognised by their many colleagues and contacts throughout the university — so much so that someone dubbed them the 'Oxford Five', a collective which they were all happy to embrace and to retain down the years to come.

There was another man too, in his own way just as vital an ingredient, but he was not at Oxford and was about as different to David Heaven as could be imagined. Perhaps that's why it worked as well as it did. In the long vacation of David's second year, he joined a party of bright young characters to spend a month on the Riviera near Menton. The arrangement was as might be expected. One fellow undergraduate blessed with plenty of money and some good connections is keen to acquire a wider circle of friends and thus a house party is assembled.

They swam, sailed, caroused and gambled. Towards the end of the holiday, they were returning from a casino outing when one of the party's cars, with David at the wheel, was in a minor traffic jam collision with a sprightly sports car driven by a young man of about his age. Damage was minimal, there was no police involvement and hardly any delay. But the following day brought a telephone call for David from the other party, politely asking him over for a quick drink to deal with some insurance questions. What the hell, David said to himself, and went. That was the introduction to his first employer who was to become also his business partner, mentor and a much valued friend.

Unlike some of his companions in Menton, it troubled David not at all to sit down in the company of a Jew. Martin Kirchoff was also on holiday, and during the couple of hours they spent together in the lobby of his smart hotel, they found an instinctive enjoyment in each other's company. Martin had a sense of fun which he tried to keep under tight control but which David was able to tease out of him. He was transparently entranced by the vision of an undergraduate lifestyle and presented himself as a sort of social thoroughbred yearning to escape from a commercial carthorse existence — but only occasionally since he was so deeply committed to his business aspirations. For his part, David was stimulated by Martin's status as an emerging entrepreneur. It seemed to David that this guy was already embarked on life with a capital L, whilst his own existence was dilettante in comparison. It further appealed to David that Martin was in partnership with his father. The image of a dynasty fired his imagination.

They concluded their form filling and exchanged contact details but parted without a plan to meet again. Yet each took away the firm expectation that there was more to come from this chance encounter. They were right.

JOSH TROLLOPE — 1965

David Heaven's graduation day on 13th July 1965 was significant also for Rory Trollope as it was the date of his birth. Rory was pugnacious from conception, a kicker and a puncher in the womb. He gave his mother a hard time of it in the Pretoria hospital where Rory came into the world. She lay in the hot and foetid cot staring at the fan above her head beating vainly at the successive waves of pain which broke about her.

This was not Moira Trollope's first experience of labour, but it was infinitely the worst of her three pregnancies and was bearable only because she could feel the living child within her whereas the previous two births had resulted in stillborn girls. But the monster about to emerge felt all too like a man with a demanding nature. She bit her tongue and ground her teeth against the astonishing pain, determined that she could and would get through this to triumph in her healthy son but she did so wish that his father Josh could have been there with her, or at least within call. Instead of which, he was lost to her, hundreds of miles to the north somewhere, a soldier of fortune fighting in some squalid little war in which he had only two interests — to stay alive and to pick up his mercenary's pay with which to establish a home and hearth for his wife and child.

Josh Trollope had come late to marriage and to any thought of settling down. A career soldier, he had joined the British Army straight from school and the elite Grenadier Guards had enveloped him as a member of their lifelong family. Josh had seen action in Normandy after D-Day and had remained in the thick of it until the end of the War. He had gone on with his Regiment, serving as much overseas as at home, steadily increasing his status with the passage of time and the building of experience.

He had been a senior NCO serving in Germany when he met Moira five years previously. She was a South African over on a working holiday and they had fallen for each other in a style which had amazed Josh's mates. Moira's father had land in South Africa, but he was widowed with no son to take it on and he himself was running short of strength and morale. Josh and Moira paid one visit to the farm, in the process using up much of their savings and his accumulated leave, but it was worth it. For Josh, seeing was believing and understanding, so he returned to hand in his papers, taking an immediate chance to leave the Guards after twenty years of loyal and productive service.

He was now just forty years old and on the day of his son's birth he was lying prone, silent and sweating behind inadequate cover in a small village many miles northeast of Libreville, capital city of the republic of Gabon. In 1965, all this region of West Africa remained under the colonial influence of France, but it had become destabilised by the bloody war which had been raging in the Belgian Congo since the early sixties. Josh knew a fair bit of the history. He was too good a soldier not to take an interest, but he cared very little as to who would win. He had been able to see at the outset that this conflict was all about possession, not politics and certainly not principles despite all the high flown language and the international debate.

When Josh and Moira had disembarked in Durban after their emigration voyage, he had seen newspaper advertisements which sought trained and battle experienced soldiers to sign on as mercenaries. The logic of a short term engagement was compelling. They did really need some capital to take over the farm and to plan for the future.

So within weeks of arriving to settle in South Africa, Josh was on the move again and back into soldiering, but now as a mercenary in the Belgian Congo, a member of the force working to re-establish the charismatic Moishe Tshombe. Trollope signed on with the English speaking 5th Commando led by the legendary Mike Hoare and stayed with him through most of the Simba war until Hoare's retirement in December 1964. By then,

Josh reckoned that he had put by enough in savings and was more than ready to move on to his new life on the farm with Moira and her father in the background to help.

But then came the baby. A few days of unexpected leave started the bulge which was just showing on Moira by the time of his contract termination. When he returned home to the farm, there was news that the baby was fit and strong in the womb, but the final stages were expected to be testing. Moira was going to need expert and expensive help to deliver the infant so they must invest much of their nest egg in the best medical care they could find and worry about replacing the money later.

And worry he did. Josh was preoccupied when he went into a bar in Pretoria during the Christmas period and bumped into a friend from way back in his British Army days. Barry Bingham was established as a soldier of fortune, and as it happened, looking for help. He had little difficulty in talking Josh into one last tour which was to be with the private army of a character who called himself General Moses Samson. This self appointed general, whose birth name was never discovered, was recruiting a dozen white officers to manage the efforts of a rabble which he referred to as a battalion, and his objective was brigandry, pure and simple. Josh was to come to tax himself for being so quick to commit, but he was seduced by the lure of enormous money for a short and dirty contract. There was neither time nor opportunity for Josh to meet Moses Samson in advance. He simply relied on the version of events as set out by his old mate Barry Bingham and although Josh was mindful of Barry and had taken several pinches of salt with his story, it still remained a long way wide of the mark of reality.

Samson claimed to be the leader of a recessionary tribal group occupying a small wedge of territory in the extreme south of the Central African Republic, seeking independence from the colonial government installed in the capital city of Bangui. In truth, Samson was after much more than this. He aimed to annex a small corner in the north west of the vast country which was then the Belgian Congo. Samson was not the only privateer to see the opportunities to be afforded under the convenient cloak of civil war and he was at least as cunning as any who tried. His target patch of ground was something of the size of Switzerland and it was not so much the land which took his fancy as the valuable minerals beneath it, especially the iron ore which the French had been extracting from two mines in this region for the past decade.

Profiting from the unsettled politics of the day, Samson had approached the East Germans who, fronting for Moscow, had been prepared to advance him some funding. With this help, and his own powers of persuasion, he had contrived to recruit his modest team, no more than 500 strong and some materiel. Most of his fighters were hired guns who brought with them their own motley armaments. In a gesture towards some military professionalism, he was recruiting a few white mercenaries, but this was also to make his insurrection the more newsworthy in Europe and the United States.

Samson raised his force in Cabinda in northern Angola, right by the Congolese border. He then took his men further north by a cheaply chartered tramp steamer and disembarked in Equatorial Guinea, a tiny country with a lawless reputation in which he could buy an unopposed reception for modest price. From there, the column had marched and driven in a ragbag of vehicles almost due east with an outline plan to pass swiftly through the extreme north of Gabonese territory en route to their end objective, a few hundred kilometres distant.

Barry Bingham and Josh Trollope were late to join the force, and Barry had insisted on first passing through Libreville to collect fifty per cent of the contract price up front which was the deal he had struck with Moses Samson. It was enough for signing on and starting up. There were all sorts of reasons why the balance might never get paid.

When Barry went sick, he and Josh had been in Libreville for twenty-four hours, just long enough for them to pick up their money from Samson's bag man and get it safely into the French banking system. It was over an evening meal before their onward journey that Bingham collapsed without warning, literally into the soup. Josh knew enough about Africa's sicknesses and malaria in particular to speculate that Barry would be lucky to survive this attack, never mind catching up with 'the army of Moses'.

This left Josh in a difficult situation but not with a decision over which he hesitated for long. He knew that he couldn't return the money to a nameless man who had long since vanished and he couldn't hope to hang on to it and bail out without the risk of Samson's retribution overtaking him. He would never be free of that worry and besides, he would be condemning Barry to an unpleasant end if the malaria didn't get him first. And then there was another aspect. If Josh went ahead and did some of Bingham's job for him, he could count on picking up a fair proportion of Barry's pay as well as his own.

So Josh stuck to the plan even though he was sorely hampered by being alone and unable to communicate easily. He rendezvoused at dawn the next day with a one legged guide and they travelled north together by native bus, an interminable journey which gave Josh the chance to practice extravagant explanation in sign language and pidgin of what had befallen Barry Bingham. He was not confident that his companion either understood or believed him, still less General Moses Samson whom they met more or less on schedule two days later in camp outside the little bush town of Mbornou.

There had been an unending tirade from Samson, delivered in a mixture of language and dialect of which Josh could decipher hardly a word, for all that the message was clear enough. White mercenaries were expensive and unreliable, especially if they came from South Africa. They were there only to exploit the poor and downtrodden blacks, but they should be careful now as the day was dawning for the new Messiah, Moses Samson himself, and all this announced with much beating of breast, rolling of eyes and jiggling of his little goatee beard. Samson cut a physically small and insignificant figure, but there was no denying his presence and the inspiration which he aroused in his fervent followers. A true rabble-rouser, Josh thought to himself as he suffered this performance which was interrupted from time to time by an immense Belgian mercenary who was on hand to provide a limping translation. In some response, Josh made the most of his own attendance despite the sickness of his partner before lapsing into a surly silence.

This interview with the great leader constituted the whole of his welcome and introduction into the army of Moses. It was made plain was that they were behind schedule and they broke camp before dawn the following day, moving off to the East in a straggle of unlit vehicles down the rough track. It was three hours later when the crisis struck, but it didn't take Josh unawares. His every sense had been warning him from the moment when he had walked into this outfit that a moment of truth was approaching, the only questions being what and from which quarter.

First they stopped and then they sat. From his vantage point beside the driver in the elderly Mercedes truck which had wheezed its way up the track, Josh could see in the full daylight that his vehicle was about two thirds down the line. The column ahead wound up a shallow incline and there was a gathering way ahead by the lead vehicle, a similar truck to his own with its squat, blunt bonnet lifted. Presumably some sort of breakdown. After a twenty minute delay, brilliant for mobility tactics he thought ruefully and all the better for being in wide open country, Josh saw the big Belgian start to descend the track on foot. As he approached, he acknowledged Josh with a jerk of his head and shortly afterwards, Josh heard him bellow to a Frenchman who was riding shotgun in a Land Rover further to the rear. Josh waited for them to come up to him. There was some delay while they exchanged conversation. He could see them from his cab as they talked. They knew each other well, he decided, well enough to work together, close enough to be discussing something from which he was to be excluded.

Finally, they walked up to his truck and Josh nodded to his driver before descending to join them. The three walked together to the head of the line and there made out a group of a dozen or so gathered around the lead truck which by now had its bonnet mostly closed again and the engine on tick over. The assembled company included all the white mercenaries, an assortment of Africans who served as Samson's personal staff and of course the General himself, apparently spitting tintacks and fulminating enough to make his spray fly.

Plus one more: a powerfully built black man, completely naked, bloodied back and buttocks. His head, neck and arms were pinned beneath the bonnet of the Mercedes truck on which two soldiers were seated, casually raining further blows on the unprotected torso beneath them. The prisoner was flinching, jumping and scratching his feet in the dirt as he fought for purchase from which to ease his position. His discomfort would owe less to the beating than to the under bonnet heat on his face and hands. Josh Trollope had seen this form of bush stocks treatment before.

As Josh and the other two mercs arrived at the scene, Moses ceased his harangue to boot his captive between the legs and then turned to Josh, at the same time snarling at the Belgian to come forward. Not that much interpretation was needed. Josh could pretty much write the script himself, but he settled himself in a casual pose, hands on hips, allowing the tirade to sweep over him and ignoring the stumbling translation whilst he thought furiously.

The theme of the Moses speech was that the captive was a Nigerian, an Army deserter presenting himself as a mercenary. He had been assigned to travel at the front of the convoy to be on hand for the General in case they met English speakers. He had been caught rifling through papers, no doubt looking for cash and saleable commodities. Just now under questioning, he claimed to know you, Mr Trollope. Probably nonsense, but just to be sure, you grill him a bit more and then finish him off. Enough time wasted already.

It was just as Josh would have expected, and the real version said 'this poor sod has been singled out as a means of testing you whom I don't know and don't trust. Nor do the mercs standing around you who can probably do the job without you and will certainly enjoy your money, so don't look to them for any support. Don't forget also that I'm paranoid, must show that I'm the only boss around here and that I can treat my black guys as expendable if it helps me to impress you whiteys.'

Even before Samson's high pitched sermon was finished, Josh was moving slowly and deliberately over the couple of metres which separated him from the truck. He placed one hand on the wing of the vehicle and gestured with the other for one of the soldiers sitting on the bonnet to climb down. It was a moment of challenge. Josh locked eyes with the brutish, slovenly figure who held his gaze for a full minute before he dropped his face and slid down, encouraged on his way by a barked instruction from Moses. His departure permitted Josh to raise the bonnet a shade and to jam his water bottle into the gap. Then he crouched to see, dimly, the face inside which was by good fortune turned towards him. The heat inside was terrific and he could make out some of the welts on the man's arms caused by contact with the metal and rubber of engine components. The soldier's breathing was laboured and his eyes rolled, but this seemed to Josh to be more in fury than in pain. Josh Trollope was a fighting man and in that instant he recognised one of his own. Josh wanted out of there and he had just found a fellow traveller.

Josh spoke just above the engine beat, allowing its noise to muffle his words from the big Belgian who had moved up to stand next to him.

'Name and rank?'

Immediate answer.

'Nugumu, Patrick, Suh. From Cross river, Nigeria. Ten years Nigeria Army. Staff Sergeant, Artillery. Last posting with Maiduguri Frontier Force. Retired with honour. Suh.'

The voice was strong through the pain. The Nigerian was trying to form a bond with his only possible salvation and Josh thought to himself: no choice now, must risk it and use the surprise. And then, as always, came the tightening stomach muscles and the slowing of time and events as they passed before him, the two harbingers of action.

He responded.

'I'm Trollope, ex Grenadier Guards. You ready for action on my count of three?'

A fierce nod in reply. Josh stood upright and turned to Moses Samson who was still standing there with the Belgian at his elbow. Josh spoke slow and clear.

'This man's an Ibo. He'll be treacherous and a liar. Clear and lift the bonnet. Turn off the engine. I'll finish the job'.

He turned back towards the truck and drew his handgun from the pouch at his belt. He was slow and deliberate in his actions. The big Belgian did not trouble to translate: he didn't need to. Moses chattered. The engine silenced. The second guard came off the bonnet and started to lift it. Josh called a soft 'THREE', shot the guard in the head, grabbed Moses Samson's scrawny neck in the crook of his left arm and threw the gun at Patrick who came out of his trap like a greyhound. The Nigerian caught the weapon smoothly and jammed it straight into the Belgian's neck.

There was the brief benefit of shock and surprise and Josh had to use it fast. He had no trouble in holding the general and now he pulled the revolver from Samson's belt and ground the barrel into his right ear, there for all in their little group to see plainly. He practically lifted the little man off his feet and frogmarched him towards his own command vehicle, another tatty Land Rover only five metres away with the driver standing by the door and goggling. Patrick followed with the big Belgian who was not going to die needlessly for anyone.

A smooth changeover by the Land Rover, with Josh and the naked Patrick working as if they had trained together. Samson thrown in the pickup rear, with Patrick sitting on top of him and crushing his face to the floor, one huge hand around the neck, the other still covering the Belgian who stood large but relaxed in a clear exhibition of 'not my fight'. Then Josh was behind the wheel and driving, at Patrick's instruction, back down the track.

'Must go that way, Suh. Go gentle. I play dead.' They bounced back past the convoy, past men who could have been dangerous but who in their ignorance of what had been causing the delay were bored and inactive except to note that rough justice had apparently been meted out.

As they cleared the column and built up some speed on the track, Josh considered their next move. There would be swift pursuit once they had sorted themselves out. Not from loyalty or love, Moses Samson would have earned little of either from black or white. But money, that was a different matter. Samson had raised and financed the expedition. He was the banker and the paymaster. Without him, the motley force had no purpose and no reward. That's why they would pursue and they would be deadly, especially the white mercenaries. And that's why Josh Trollope braked the Land Rover to a stop in a shower of dust and turned in his seat. Patrick too had worked it out and moved off Samson who sat up, choking and spitting. Without a further word, Josh shot him cleanly between the eyes with his own gun. Patrick tipped the body over the tailboard and onto the track for the 'army of Moses' to find. Then they drove on in silence and made best time back to Mbornou.

And there it might so easily have ended. Just another little African punch up, characterised as much by incompetence as violence. There was no further pursuit. Josh and Patrick dumped the Land Rover just outside the town and walked into the centre with Patrick garbed only in a form of loin cloth which he had fashioned from a large rag in the toolbox. Once there, Josh funded a brisk search for some other clothes and a quick meal before lying in cover to watch their back while Patrick found them a bush taxi in which they completed a direct journey to Libreville, arriving after nearly sixteen hours of bone shaking travel, punctuated by the odd breakdown.

Barry Bingham had died less than twenty-four hours after Josh had left him at the hospital, as he learned from the French doctor. Cremation had already taken place and the doctor handed Josh an urn of ashes together with a little bundle of documents and effects which were the only residue of Barry Bingham. Josh had no idea of the deceased's family or responsibilities, but he accepted this small burden which included a notarised bill of transfer under which Barry's pay for this last, shambolic operation passed to him. Josh handed a significant sum in cash to Patrick before they parted at Libreville airport, promising to stay in touch.

Josh Trollope flew home to his farm, his wife, and his new born son. He never took up arms again. But life's lottery casts a long shadow. Patrick Nugumu continued as a soldier under the influences of both choice and circumstance. Quite shortly after this little incident came the outbreak of the Biafra war in Nigeria, which he survived on the losing side and thereafter he gained the distinction of a mention in Frederick Forsyth's account of The Dogs of War. Later by far, when age and experience had honed his fighting judgement to its full potency, would come his most productive struggle, to be waged at the shoulder of Josh's son Rory Trollope whose father had plucked him from a grubby death some thirty-five years earlier.

SOLOMON KIRCHOFF — 1965

Before the end of 1965, just a few weeks after Josh Trollope's little skirmish in Africa, David Heaven was looking for a job. He was no different to a million other graduates. He had vague notions of what he wanted to do with his life, but was surer of what was not for him. He was certain he would not join Pente in the church, nor to go soldiering with Conrad, nor follow Alexa into banking. Medicine, the law, accounting or insurance — he couldn't get excited by any of these. He did know that it was straightforward commerce which sparked his interest. He wanted to start something, nurture, build and sustain some form of enterprise which would remain a fascination to him. By the middle of November he was in London, dossing down with friends, doing some interviews and trying to tighten up his thinking despite the attractions of much partying.

He was conscious of going too slowly, and thought he might look for advice from his old chum Martin Kirchoff, with whom he had kept passing contact since they had met in Menton. Destiny, however, intervened before he could make an appointment. His father Lawrence died, a heart attack which dropped him stone dead on the sparse turf of the school rugby ground in the middle of a match for which he was the referee. He was just sixty-eight. David was surprised to find himself badly affected by his death. Father and son had become closer over the past year and as Lawrence had been delighted with David's degree, David had come to form a respect, if not a warm love, for his father. He admired how Lawrence had stuck at his role and responsibilities, but it was a shock to discover the impoverished state of affairs which he had left behind. Finances had been strained by David's time at university and this reality added sharply to his need to knuckle down.

David also sensed that without Lawrence, there would be little further contact with his mother or his sisters. He did not blame them, especially not the latter with whom there had been such scant connection since childhood, but he felt a finality when Esther announced to him shortly after the funeral that she intended, 'after a suitable interval', to go and settle in France from where she would provide a point of contact in due course of time. From this cold announcement, David gathered that there was another man and another existence for her. It says much about this emotionally dispersed family that he apparently did not enquire further and it seems likely that mother and son never met again.

Approaching Christmas 1965, David was living very cheaply in a remote outpost of London's western suburbs and pushing coins into a telephone box in order to make contact again with the Kirchoffs. He received a warm welcome and was invited to visit Martin's office one day in Christmas week. David travelled on the tube up to Bayswater, filled with an excited anticipation which he could not explain to himself.

At first sight, the business of Kirchoff and Son did not impress, being housed in a small, nondescript building sandwiched between two large Victorian houses which had been converted into flats. Once inside, however, his opinion altered as he took in the planning and the style with which the single storey with mezzanine had been laid out to make the most of the space and the natural light, such as was available on a December afternoon.

Martin showed him around, introducing him to three girls at work at their desks spread comfortably around the open plan area, and then settled David in front of his own table which groaned beneath telephones and files in piles. They had not spoken since David graduated so Martin was keen to hear details of the lifestyle after which he had yearned. Then David told him of Lawrence's death and the ensuing conversation underlined for both of them the gulf of difference between their respective family circumstances.

As if on cue, the front door burst open to admit a great woolly bear of a man who interrupted them with a cry of greeting. Solomon Kirchoff was a real charmer and an enormous extrovert, expansive where his son was diffident and as outrageous as Martin could be shy. The three of them settled to conversation, starting with a reminiscence of the original meeting in Menton when Martin collided with David's car. It seemed that the incident had caused Solomon huge amusement and he was still chuckling now as they sat together. David thought his humour must be pretty easily aroused but then spotted that the real cause of Sol's pleasure was that this silly accident might lead to a new friendship and a widening of Martin's world. He chided himself with the arrogance of this thought but it stayed with him as the evening fell and he was drawn by the vitality of Solomon Kirchoff into revealing more of himself, his current circumstances, his hopes and aspirations.

By now, it was sometime after six o'clock and the girls in the office had said their goodbyes and left for the evening. The big man rose from his chair and beamed down at them. He was not very tall, but was built like a barrel with great arms, legs and head all in similar proportion and topped off with a beard which fell to his chest. Had that been white rather than streaked black, he would have answered perfectly to the popular vision of Father Christmas.

'David', he announced ponderously as if commencing a speech, 'David, I have so much enjoyed meeting you and I would like for us to speak again soon. I do believe that we could be of help to each other, but first, you must let me think a little further.'

'Thank you, Mr Kirch....' David started his reply but the old boy cut him off.

'David, you must call me Sol just like the rest of the world does — even including Martin unless he is really upset with me', this said with a guffaw as Martin rolled his eyes towards the ceiling, 'and secondly, you owe me no thanks as already we value your friendship'. He glanced at his son whose look said to David that he agreed with the sentiment but wished Sol would ease up on the drama language. David understood and his smile said so.

They remained frozen in this tableau as Sol's smile embraced the younger men. Then the moment was broken by the sound of swish over carpet as the front door from the street was opened. Two men had entered and now stood together without a word, their eyes fixed on Sol. The larger, who was black and very large indeed, looked to be West Indian. His companion was white, slim, smartly dressed with highly polished black brogues and holding a small umbrella. It was he who took the lead. David took them to be customers or colleagues in the business, arrived for a pre-planned meeting, and he sensed this was his moment to leave. He turned to say his farewell to Sol, but was shocked to find that he had become another person. The great shambling bulk had been instantly diminished and reduced in every way. The shoulders hunched, the beard wobbled on his chest, his hands washed at each other but could not disguise their tremble. When he spoke, his voice emerged cracked and reedy, so different from the booming tones of earlier.

'Mr Riley and Mervyn' he squeaked, 'You're a little early today gentlemen. No doubt it's Christmas arrangements, but I can accommodate you. Of course I can. Please follow me.'

And with that he led the way up the spiral staircase which was located at the extreme end of the building, leading up to a reasonably sized meeting room which completely occupied the mezzanine area. Martin had showed it briefly to David and explained that they seldom used it except for client visits, so David assumed that these two represented some important business. It was certainly a performance to get up there, with Sol and the huge Mervyn struggling to negotiate the stairs.

David continued perplexed by the dramatic change in Sol, the more so because Martin was now definitely moving him towards the front door and himself acting in an anxious manner.

As they stood together in the open doorway, Martin spoke.

'Thanks for coming, David. It's been good to see you and we must make another plan. I can tell that Sol is definitely doing some scheming.' There was a forced joviality as he gesticulated with some wild movements before going on, 'what about New Year's Eve if you're around that day? We'll be back at work, so come up for some lunch and maybe we'll all have something more to celebrate in the evening'.

Even as Martin was speaking, they could hear clearly the sound of raised voices from the upstairs room, Sol in agitation and an aggressive note from the white man, Riley. Immediately afterwards, there was a crash against the inside wall followed by two or three thumping noises, unmistakeable to David as the sound of blows to the body. He grabbed Martin by the arm and spoke urgently.

'Who are these guys, Martin, and what are they doing to Sol? More to the point, what are we going to do about it?

'Please, David, just leave now. I'll be able to handle it OK.'

He held the street door wide in invitation. His voice was tremulous but his message was clear, so David walked out and set off down Westbourne Grove, leaving Martin to duck back into the building. David stood on the pavement for a minute or so in uncomfortable indecision before he started to move away. But he had gone only a few strides before heard the door of the Kirchoff building slam shut again, and turning, he saw the unwelcome visitors. They were coming towards him. Riley was in the lead, Mervyn in close attendance with a small bag in his ham like fist. They were unhurried as they approached. It seemed to David that they would simply walk on by, but Riley stopped short and fixed him with a gimlet eye. Without warning, he jabbed a short, hard blow from his gloved left fist deep into David's stomach. He dropped to one knee on the pavement fighting for breath. Riley bent a little from the waist and hissed into his ear,

'Not your business. Keep it that way.'

Then he was walking on, steel capped shoes ringing in the cold evening air.

David gave himself some recovery time. It was as much the shock as the pain. Then he walked straight back into the office. Martin must have heard the door and came clattering down the spiral stairs. Sol remained out of sight, up in the meeting room.

'Sorry,' said David with a wan smile, 'but they thumped me too on the way past. So now I think I should know a bit more.'

Martin looked dishevelled and agitated.

'Christ,' he said, 'let me just see to Sol.'

Whirling round, he disappeared upstairs and David sat on a typist's chair and listened to the muted tones of conversation above him. Martin came back, looking no less disturbed. He slumped into the chair at his desk and loosened his tie. His hands were shaking.

'Sol needs his medication. It's his heart you see. I'm going to get him home to Naomi who will handle it. Give me half an hour and I'll be back. I agree that you should know more and Sol insists on it. Can you manage here on your own?'

'Of course I can.'

David sat and watched without comment as Martin carefully manoeuvred his father down the awkward stairs and through the main office into the street outside. Sol was ashen and trembling all over. A taxi or hire car had pulled up outside; Martin must have summoned it. David heard the doors slam and the vehicle pull away. He got up then, closed and locked the front door and wandered around the office while he waited. He felt numb and confused. What the hell was going on here?

He got his answer during the remainder of that evening. Martin was good to his time estimate and returned in another cab. He proposed they walk to a restaurant where he sometimes had lunch. It was still early for evening traffic in the bistro and they had the place almost to themselves. They sat at a table in the window, ordered pasta and a bottle of Chianti.

By this point, Martin had recovered himself and was more composed. David could see that he was less nervous, but still agitated and that stemmed from embarrassment. He confirmed this in his opening comments as they waited for their food to arrive.

'Riley and Co. They've been onto us for about six months now. It's a protection racket and they've targeted a good few businesses around here, including this restaurant, I think. It's unpleasant, but we can afford it if we have to. And we must. Sol gets really badly affected as you've seen and if truth be told, I'm not much better myself. Taken together, we are really a thug's dream.'

Martin paused there and gave a sheepish grin. Then he continued.

'Actually, David, I suppose I'm grateful for that incident happening today — while you were with us I mean. You see, I'm keen for you to join us. I'm sure you and I would work well together and Sol agrees but he just wants a bit more time to think the thing through. That's fair enough and I predicted his reaction. I was also sure that before there could be a commitment, you'd need to know more about our history and where we come from in every sense. I wanted to take my time about that. I tend to keep the past buried and when I tell you about our background, you'll understand why. But Riley's visit means that I can't delay. I've got to lay it out now. All I ask of you, David, is that you keep what I'm about to say to yourself — even if it puts you off any further association with Sol and me. Is that agreed?'

David was relieved to notice that Martin's confidence became stronger with every word of this introduction.

'You have my word', he said with a brief nod.

Martin started with the family history, speaking of Sol's parents and their simple life in a small village community located midway between Lodz and the Baltic port of Gdansk in Poland. How Sol had been a bright pupil who married Deborah, his childhood sweetheart and greatest friend. How the young couple moved to Warsaw for Sol to take up the offer he had won from High School to enrol for a degree in Economics. Some years of living close to the breadline finally rewarded with an outstanding result which gave Sol the chance to move again, and this time a much greater step. To Germany and to an appointment with a Government ministry in Berlin. The year was 1935. They prospered, working hard, becoming fluent in the language, living frugally, managing to send home a little money for their families and to build up some reserves for themselves. Deborah was able to work, but then found herself pregnant and their daughter Natasa was born in November 1937.

At this point, David could anticipate the tragedy about to unfold. He could imagine a devout, hard working couple, content to be self effacing as they built their lives, enhanced their security and determined to ignore all that was going on around them.

Martin did not dwell on the detail of what happened next, but his biting summary was all the more effective. Deborah and Natasa were removed by the police for 'resettlement' during the early weeks of 1941 but Sol was retained at his job in the Ministry for a further year. It was explained to him that his work was valued and in recognition of his contribution to Nazi Germany, his wife and child were being kept safe and well. Precisely what became of Deborah and Natasa is a story which can never be told. They simply disappeared, and Sol saw neither again after his final glimpse of their faces at the window of the bus which took them away.

It was almost a relief when the end came for him. He was picked up when it was judged that the value of his work was worth less than the burden of employing a Jew. He was jammed into a train holding thousands and transported to Dachau.

Martin ordered coffee and they smoked in silence. Then David asked,

'How did Sol survive the Camp?'

'By becoming as close to indispensable as it was possible to be. He managed to get work in the Camp commandant's office, work that was relevant to his skills and qualifications. All the concentration camps had to submit up to Himmler's level what I guess we would call today a business plan, with details of how they were performing against target. The work was meat and drink to Sol. He knew far more than the Germans at Dachau what was required and he was bloody good at it. But of course, the "product" — what else to call it? He was dealing with a profit and loss account which depended on his fellow prisoners who were being harvested. What items of value did each leave behind, right down to teeth and hair; how to turn possessions into marketable assets; how to dispose of the unwanted remains. Sol has erected strong barriers, but deep inside him, there's a despair which won't die before he does.'

'Yes.' David was absolutely at a loss for words.

'And there's more,' Martin continued, 'in his job, Sol had help from other inmates — prisoners who were assigned to him for work in typing, filing, that sort of thing. None lasted very long, but there was one woman who was especially competent. Ironically, she wasn't a Jew, but a Romanian gypsy. Anyway, she worked well and became a good friend. She had a daughter with her and I guess that touched a strong chord in Sol. The child was eleven or twelve and she came to help Sol whilst her mother was too sick to work one day. The girl was pretty enough to attract the attention of one of the soldier guards and he made a grab for her. He held her down across Sol's desk, bawling at him to get on with his figures whilst the child was being violated in front of his eyes. Sol broke the habit of a lifetime just that once. He got out of his chair to fight back. It wasn't much of a fight: a fit young soldier against a broken down Jew. Sol got knocked senseless and the soldier completed his rape. He called in his mate who did her as well. Then they slit her throat. And then they woke Sol up and started in on him. They took turns to knock him about a bit more before they castrated him with a pair of office scissors. Then they made him get rid of the body of the girl and get back to work himself.'

The nausea which this horror produced in David made him miss the further significance of the story but it came to him in a rush as he saw Martin staring at him. Martin spoke without waiting for the question.

'No, of course I'm not his son and it's just a coincidence that we have our similarities. But he is the one and only father figure in my life. I respect him and I love him plus I owe him a great deal. You see David, I have no idea who my natural father was and neither has my mother, Naomi. She was in Dachau too, and being young and quite pretty, she was much in demand. How else was she to survive?'

He looked appealingly at David as if to seek approval for behaviour under circumstances which are unimaginable except to those who were forced to endure them. David stretched across the table and put his hand briefly on Martin's shoulder. It was an instinctive gesture made both to acknowledge the anguish and to thank him for sharing it. Then he said,

'It's a desperate, tragic story, but thank you for trusting to tell me. I guess you don't often speak of it.'

'You're right. Only once a year. On our Day of Atonement, my mother Naomi, Sol and I, we stay home alone and just sit with each other, sometimes saying nothing for hours on end, sometimes talking trivia. We find there is no catharsis to be gained from sharing memories of that time, it's just enough to be still together.'

David was moved by this and said so. Then he added 'Please tell me what happened next. How did you get from there to here?'

'Well, to keep it brief. Sol and Naomi survived Dachau until the camp was liberated by the Americans in 1945. They'd become very close and it made things much easier to pretend that they were man and wife with me as their son. Also, Naomi is Austrian, so we went to Vienna until Sol applied successfully to bring us here. We arrived in London late in 1947 and we've been here ever since.'

David had plenty more to ask about, to burrow deeper into the relationships and understand more about the business, but he decided that he would hold his peace for now.

'You get back to them, Martin. I'll settle up here. I'll probably have a last drink and then head for home, but I'm looking forward to being back on New Year's Eve.'

The two shook hands and Martin left David in the bistro.

A while later, he was walking back to Bayswater tube station, his mind a maelstrom of thoughts and emotions.

DAVID HEAVEN —1965

The following evening, David was returning to his poky flat but turned into the local pub for a drink. There in the bar, he found a welcome surprise as the familiar face of King Offenbach beamed at him over a pint of bitter.

'Where the hell did you spring from?' said David, 'and anyway, how did you find me? Or is this all by chance? Whatever, King, how good to see you!'

'Do I have to answer all the questions at once,' drawled the black man 'or how about I go ahead and buy you a drink so we can start talking from there?'

They took their drinks to a side table and sat facing each other. David was trying to remember when they had last met and thinking that it must have been here in London at one or other of the post graduation bashes.

King anticipated the question.

'The last time I saw you, David, you were very much the worse for wear in that club off Covent Garden, trying to remove from one of the dancers what little she was wearing. With your teeth as I recall.'

David didn't even have the grace to blush.

'I just hope she enjoyed it as much as I'm sure I did, but honestly I don't remember too much about some of those wild evenings. I've come down to earth since.'

'Sure thing,' King smiled ruefully, 'well, I guess I got home about mid-September and pretty much straight back to work. But the good news is that my chief has lined me up for a job in Europe, and as of a couple of days ago, I'm based in London out of our Embassy. I'll be here for six months or more, so it looks like I get to spend Christmas and most of next year in my

44

favourite city. And since you're wondering, I'll tell you right off how I came to find you.'

But David had already worked this one out and answered in one word.

'Pente'.

'Right on', said King, pointing an elegant finger, 'that's how I tracked you down. Plus I've got to tell you straight off that Pente reckoned you might be able to put me up. Just for a night or so while I'm waiting for the Embassy to allocate me an apartment.'

'Sure. It'll be a real pleasure. But I've got to warn you that my place is small and scruffy. I'm hoping to move in the New Year, but I've had a few things to sort out. That's mostly because my father died suddenly a couple of months ago.'

'Oh gee, David, I surely am sorry to hear that. You were close?'

'No, not so much, except for during what has turned out to be the last year of his life.'

'Yup. Family matters can surely be quite a challenge,' King replied and then to change the subject he enquired, 'Tell me other news, David. I know you're pretty tight with Conrad. How are things for him?'

And so they went on to talk — people, places and events. After an hour or so they left the pub and went for a meal at a friendly Italian restaurant just round the corner. They ate in a peaceful corner, fussed over by Sergio who insisted on choosing a menu for them and telling them to take their time. It was an excellent ambience to encourage two normally reticent characters to bare a little soul. King Offenbach started it.

'David,' he said,' I guess you know I keep pretty close contact with Pente and the first thing I want to say to you about that is thanks!: it was you who introduced us shortly after I arrived in Oxford.'

This was true. David remembered the occasion of getting a group together in the pub one evening to meet 'the King', and Pente had certainly been amongst them. But it was hardly a big deal, and he said so.

'Sure, I appreciate that,' King went on, 'but it's become a bigger deal since, definitely for me and I think for Pente also. No, it's nothing like that,' he chuckled as he saw David's eyes start to widen. 'Jeez, but you Brits drag sex into everything,' and he waved away David's protests, 'let me concentrate on expressing this.' He paused to take a pull at his drink.

'I guess you could say that Pente has become my spiritual adviser as well as close friend and confidant. So that's the big thing you started. You see, religion is pretty damn important for me — after all, I'm a boy from the wild wastelands of Carolina. I guess it's both bred and beaten into me by way of a difficult family background and also it troubles me that what I do for a living seems a fair way towards being at odds with the scriptures. I've got to say that good ole Pente has a way with his words and his analysis both, so now I've gotten the habit of touching base with him on a regular schedule, just to chew the fat a bit and to run a few ideas past him. Plus there's a reciprocal too. The only doubt which troubles Pente about his calling is that he's not exactly a natural for turning the other cheek. As you know, David, he can get awful steamed up about things and then his notion of Christian justice gets to come a bit under the heading of brimstone.'

David kept his silence as King picked up his glass and drank again. Then he continued.

'David, I do need to be quite straight with you now about something which Pente guessed the first time we talked and which I know he mentioned to you. It's true. I do work for the US Government, specifically the CIA and yes, those guys picked me from school and bankrolled my education including my time at Oxford. Telling you this is no indiscretion. It's not going to get either of us shot though it's not something I advertise. But I figure it's important you know.'

There was a silence between them before David took up the conversation.

'Well. There's a bit to think about here, King. First thanks for saying your piece. I'm pleased to hear how you and Pente work for each other, plus I endorse all you say about Pente's character and intellect. I'm sure you have a calming influence on him when needs must, but frankly, I'm amazed how Pente can keep himself quiet when he feels he must. He may have guessed your profession, but I told him he was talking rubbish and he didn't put me straight. That's loyalty for you and I admire him for it.'

David paused to light up before he continued. 'But look, King, it's great news that you're stationed over here for a while. Will you be in London throughout?'

'No, not the whole time. I'll be making some trips into Africa from time to time. The project is joint with your guys, and I can say that it involves finding out more about drug cartels operating into both Europe and the States. I'm part of our Africa team as I speak some of the languages well enough, and because it's a little easier for me to blend into the background there.'

King gave his charming, languid smile and David laughed with him.

'Is it dangerous?' he asked, 'a pretty stupid question I suppose.'

'Well actually, David, there's mostly danger when you stop believing that it might be there, if you follow me. Research rather than confrontation is the phase we're on right now, and anyway, it's not all wasting and women in the Service.'

David sensed the reticence and was not surprised to find himself politely dismissed. They went on to talk of other things and to reminisce happily together over their days at Oxford. Then King asked him about his plans and David tried to explain his vaguely formed conviction that Sol and Martin Kirchoff represented the future which he wanted to pursue.

'Makes sense to me. I can see that this sort of outfit and the international aspect would be a real good outlet for your energy. A few centuries back, I reckon you'd have given Sir Francis Drake a run for his money.'

Over coffee and a second bottle, David said that he was going to the Avelings at Barrington Park over Christmas and invited King to stay in the flat as long as he wanted.

'Of course', he added, 'I can always ring Connie and get you along too. I'm sure he'd be delighted and God knows, they've got enough space.'

'Thanks and I'd like to, but I'm arranged already. I'm off to

Amersham or near to. My contact at the Embassy, Mark Leary, has fixed for me to be with him and his family. He's a buddy from way back and we work together. I'll give you his details and he can always reach me when I'm overseas. Pente's got the arrangement too.'

'What about your apartment?'

'They say I can move in before the New Year, so if you're around, come over and see the glories of the US of A in Grosvenor Square.'

David was happy to do just that and he rang King as soon as he returned from the Avelings, offering to go round to help shift some boxes. But before he left his flat, he had a call from Martin Kirchoff.

'Are you still OK for New Year's Eve, David?'

'Absolutely.'

'Great. It's just the timing. Sol and I wondered if you could come over earlier in the day. We'll have lunch together and you get off after that. I'm afraid Sol has had another contact from that Riley guy, and he's insisting on coming in early afternoon to talk about arrangements for the New Year. I don't want our time together to be spoilt by that visit and there's no need for you to be involved.'

David was quiet for a few seconds. He was minded to say a lot in reply but he told Martin that he would be happy to arrive at lunch time.

'We can take it from there', he said and they hung up with a note of relief in Martin's voice. David had no intention of leaving early. If he was going to join this little business and its owners, he was going to earn his keep from the first. Whilst resting between packing cases, he laid out the situation to King Offenbach and asked if he would be willing to come along with him.

'I'm afraid it's New Year's Eve', he said, 'and I'll quite understand if you can't make it.'

'No problem for me. I won't get put to work for a couple of days yet and I'd be happy to help sort things out for your friends. You know, we get a whole lot of this protection racket business in the States, and you'd be amazed at the number of Mom and

Pop stores as we call them, which will put up with any amount of abuse. I understand why, it just makes me mad as hell at these sleazebags.'

'I'm relieved, King, and grateful already. But I suppose we need some sort of plan how to handle things.'

'Hell, no', King chuckled, 'my advice is to play things off the bat and you'll find the right way'. It will come to you soon as you get started talking to these guys. I'll keep a back seat, but remember you'll have all the backup you need.'

So it was that when David turned up again in Bayswater at around noon on New Year's Eve, he was accompanied by a tall, lithe black American whom he introduced as a friend from Oxford days, just over in London on a business trip. Martin received this news with equanimity. Sol, in full character, turned on his most boisterous welcome and was as genially dominating as before, but David wondered how much he was dreading the arrival of his next visitors.

They had lunch together as a foursome in a nearby pub, exchanging small talk, returning promptly to the office. As the afternoon wore on, Martin responded to a request from King to show him something of the firm's export financing systems and David was surprised to see King absorb himself in the detail with evident relish. He himself was then rescued by Sol, who beamed at him and announced that this was their opportunity to have a little talk in private. He led the way up the spiral staircase and they entered the upstairs meeting area which seemed larger than David remembered. They sat facing each other across the table which centred in the room. Sol became suddenly earnest and produced from under his arm a well used folder which he announced as being the source of all necessary information on Kirchoff and Son.

'Davy', he said, 'the guiding principles of any business, be it ICI or a market stall, is that you must have a product which people want to buy, and secondly, you must cherish your customers. Everything else flows from these two commandments. Now in our case, you might think that the product is to be found within these pages', and he riffled through a kaleidoscope of ploughs, tractors and trailers interspersed with endless obscure widgets. 'But it's not. All these products are important for sure but for us, Davy, our business is the total service which we provide to bring these things to our customers all over the world.'

David felt patronised. 'Sol,' he replied, 'I already know that your business is in export trading. You don't have to make a mystery out of it.'

'Fair enough and I stand rebuked,' he shot back with a disarming grin, 'and yet that's my very point. I don't seek to make a mystery. I just want you to understand my philosophy, which is that if you look after the customer, he will in turn look after us.' He laid emphasis on that final word, 'us', and then he sat back in his chair to look David in the eye. Both of them knew what was coming next.

'Davy', he said, 'I'm going to suggest that it's time for both of us to take a little gamble. You need a job. You don't really know what. You have been imagining that you will go to work one day for some big shot colossus where you'll wear sharp suits and eat one day in the senior staff canteen. You've never dreamt of throwing in your lot with some little Jewish outfit. What will the family say?'

'I don't have a family.'

'Sure. I know that. And I didn't say it to offend. But you know what I mean, Davy. You come to work for Kirchoff and Son, and tongues will wag. No?'

'I understand what you're saying well enough, but I'm not troubled by that. I've always had to buck a few trends. What I don't know is why you want me. I'm untried and untested. What is it that I've got to offer?'

Sol said, 'We need help, Davy. We need some more firepower. Look here,' and he bunched himself forward on his chair, 'we have an excellent small company which is set and ready to expand. But I'm growing a little old and tired before my time. There's reason for that and I'm content that Martin has told you about our family history. I can't go on as I am forever.'

There was a silence between them, a lull over which

washed the background rumble of the conversation which was engrossing Martin and King and the rattle of the secretary's typewriter. Finally, Sol continued.

'And there's another matter which is all to do with Martin. I'm glad you know already that he's not my son in the strict meaning. But in terms of love and companionship, he's everything to me. Even so, Martin is his own person. He has his own characteristics, his own skills and his own strengths. He's an individual. I can't do without him, but equally, Martin can't replace me.

He needs help you see. He needs the courage and confidence which flows from having a friend and confidant to share the triumphs and tribulations. But also, Davy, this business has to have a lead salesman, a champion who will get out there to proclaim our cause and to shout about our qualities. Of course, Martin is himself one such quality, but he will never say so, not to himself and much less to a customer.'

It made sense. David could see that there was a role for him in this burgeoning enterprise, and the prospect gave him a surge of excitement. He was hugging this to himself when he became conscious that the background noises downstairs had fallen quiet. He glanced at Sol and took in the quantum change which again engulfed his host. Sol became the instant nervous wreck, pushing himself to his feet, pulling his jacket about him, moving with crabbed and hurrying steps to the head of the staircase whilst running shaking hands through his hair. David remained seated as he listened to Sol's small feet pattering on the stairs and heard his obsequious greeting as he descended into the view of the visitors.

'Gentlemen, good afternoon. A pleasure to see you as always, Mr Riley and of course also Mr Mervyn.'

'Who's this?' Riley's well remembered voice responded with quiet venom as he jerked a finger in King's direction. Sol's flustered reply came in a higher than normal pitch.

'Oh, just a working colleague from the United States. Here for a few days. He'll excuse us I'm sure. Why don't you come upst...' and his voice trailed off as he realised that he had left

David there which would require more explanation.

At that moment, an unexpected confidence calmed David: what was it that King had told him? Something about the right way coming to him. Perhaps it had. He rose from the conference table and stepped down the stairs with as much poise as the awkward spiral permitted. Riley and Mervyn stood dominating the room. Smart, professional and infinitely threatening as before. The highly polished shoes winked at him again. At their side, Sol fluttered, shifting his feet and dabbing at his beard. Martin sat upright and motionless behind his large and cluttered desk. The three girls were wide eyed and frozen, one standing by the bank of files, two sitting at their desks. In front of Martin, with his neck turned in mild curiosity, the King lolled in a visitor's chair, entirely relaxed. He had put on a pair of heavy, horn rimmed spectacles which gave the aura of the remote intellectual to his long, lank frame. He was in his shirt sleeves, his jacket thrown around the back of his chair.

David stepped up to stand toe to toe with Riley and to look him in the eye. They were of much the same height. Riley spoke to him.

'Didn't I warn you last time? This isn't your business. Just get out of here and take the black with you. I have things to do with this man here', he gestured dismissively at Sol, 'I don't need interruptions.'

David stood his ground, his self confidence growing with every millisecond. He sensed Mervyn stiffen in anticipation. David needed to stretch this defining moment and willed himself to wait, to stand there motionless and unspeaking. Only the scuffing of Sol's shoes, marking time on the floor, broke the silence.

It seemed an age before Riley lost the initiative by speaking again.

'Last chance,' he said. 'Leave. Both of you. Now.'

Cue at last for David and he found that he could speak calmly and without tremor in his voice, standing tall and placing his hands on his hips.

'Wrong,' he said, 'it's you two to go. Immediately. I'm in

charge here now. I don't need you or whatever other scum stand behind you. Just bugger off.' And he reinforced his challenge by staring into the gimlet eyes of Riley, ignoring the antics of Sol who was leaping like a flushed partridge.

A look of incredulity flashed across Riley's features before he recovered to push his face closer to David's.

'You don't know who you're dealing with, my friend,' he hissed, 'but that's OK. I'll give you a lesson you won't forget. Mervyn.'

This was an action command. Mervyn moved into motion with a speed surprising in such a big man, taking one step backwards to give himself more room and putting one hand into his jacket pocket to come up with an obscene looking cosh, black leather covered, a foot and more long yet looking lost in his giant paw. He raised it high, committed to wreak mayhem and pain.

But he achieved neither, except to himself. There was really no contest and afterwards, David was to feel almost sympathy for these two hapless, small time thugs. The King came out of his chair like a striking black snake, moving with a speed and fluidity which took Riley and Mervyn completely by surprise. The villainous cosh had hardly started its descent towards David's head before King was there, catching Mervyn's arm with one hand, plucking the weapon from his grasp with the other. He thrust the cosh into the gaping pink mouth of the big man, twisting it to produce a shattering scream as the teeth broke and simultaneously using the massive body weight as a pivot against himself so that Mervyn was turned and dumped flat on his face on the floor with a crash which shook the desks and filing cabinets. King showed him no mercy. He pulled Mervyn's right arm up behind his back into the near vertical, placed a foot on the barrel neck, selected the little finger and simply pulled back on it until the snap could be heard by all in the room to be followed by renewed bellows of outraged agony. One of the girls added her own scream, her eyes open like moons and her hand rising to cover her mouth which yawned open in shock. Sol skittered, pulling at his beard. Glancing sideways, David could see Martin still sitting upright behind his desk, rooted to the spot. King just stood there, casually holding down his vanquished opponent. He looked at David as if for further instruction.

There was something of a play here and David found that he could slip easily into his role. He addressed his aside to King as if from commander to hired gun.

'Don't damage him further for now.'

Bringing his face up again to Riley who had not moved an inch, he went on.

'Now. You've heard and seen. I'm running things here and there's no room for you. Take your baboon and get on back to your boss. Tell him to leave me and mine alone for good, starting right now. Or someone is going to get properly hurt. Understood?'

They stood with eyes locked for a few seconds before Riley broke the contact and David knew he'd won. Riley turned aside, mumbling to himself in a message of reassurance.

'Yeah, well. This little outfit's not worth the trouble anyway.'

He gave Mervyn a nudge in the ribs with his polished brogue. King released the ham like wrist and stepped back. Within another minute they were gone, Riley leading the way, followed awkwardly by the huge Mervyn, blood dripping from his mouth and his damaged hand cradled in front of his great belly as he bumped his way through the door frame.

Left alone, the owners, staff and friends of Kirchoff and Son looked silently at each other until Sol could bear it no longer and let out a wild whoop of triumph before sweeping David into a great bear hug.

'I've found a new recruit,' he bellowed to the world at large, 'and a second son!'.

Looking over Sol's shoulder at Martin, David was amazed to see him applaud this outburst. The three girls looked shocked and relieved while King beamed like a midwife completing a successful delivery.

It was a good moment for David. That day and hour was the start of it all for him.

THE OXFORD FIVE — 1970

The first day of a new decade saw all five of the Oxford contemporaries pass through London's Heathrow Airport.

The first to arrive was Kingston Offenbach who had flown overnight from New York. He was sorry to have cut short his Christmas visit to his mother but duty called. He released the belt on his Pan Am seat, reflecting that London had now become more home to him than New York. He looked out of the small window at lights flashing in the dark, cold dawn and realised that he was looking forward to getting back into this miserable climate.

King liked London and he liked its people, but the real lure lay in the job. Part of that was down to good fortune — tasks and timing which spelt opportunity — but also, he was damn good at it. Over the last few years, the growth of traffic in hard drugs had become a pressing problem for the US Administration, threatening security and costing millions of dollars. For America, most of the problems came from the south, from the continent of South America via Central America and through the Caribbean. Therefore, the efforts of the CIA and complementary organisations were concentrated in that direction. If King had been a member of that team, he would never have gained the experience and seniority which he now enjoyed. The European region had been seen as less significant, but during the last two years, things had changed with drugs being trafficked through North Africa. This was the opportunity for King and he made the most of it with his ability and characteristics. Despite the colour of his skin, still unusual for Europeans moving in his circles, King built a reputation and acquired respect. His technical credentials could not be questioned and his analytical skills stood out sharply. He was a good listener and could do so in reasonable French and a little Spanish. But what most noted was his calm, his composure and his ability to work with others. The added bonus was that drug supply sources in Africa were critical and there was no other member of the team who could blend into that background as he could.

The plane doors were open now and the King was moving. He carried only hand luggage and was intent on getting into his office at the American Embassy. The following day, he would chair the first meeting of a working committee including delegates from Great Britain, France, Spain and Portugal. He wanted to be well briefed and prepared and that meant no recovery sleep from his flight over. The tall, lithe figure slipped quickly through the quiet airport and was soon lost to view.

King would have loved to have dallied a few minutes to catch a cup of coffee with David Heaven and Conrad Aveling, but he had no way of knowing that they would be in Heathrow that day. David had spent another Christmas with the Aveling clan at Barrington Park and was now off on his travels again. He had lost count of the number of times during the last five years when he had passed through Heathrow en route to wherever, but he had never lost the appetite for this itinerant lifestyle. He relished the flights out and relaxed on the trips back. He had found his true metier and he was contented in his work.

And they were succeeding. Kirchoff and Son was no phenomenon. There were several similar companies in England which were busy metamorphosing from colonial trading houses into manufacturers' export agents. The oldest could trace their origins from the days of the Raj and the times of imperial expansion, but during the 1960's the famous wind of change was blowing strongly. New-found political independence for the previous colonies brought changes to the commercial scene so that many of the former brokers in Europe developed into providing an export service for manufacturing companies which were keen to expand into new markets across the world.

This was the business sector for Kirchoff and Son. Sol had

seen the opportunity. He had moved steadily to establish the business in helping to sell products with which they could identify and to places of which they had some knowledge. They installed themselves quietly and built up their business in slow and measured style, the warm flamboyance of father contrasting productively with the conservative care exercised by son. Sol's contacts, together with his natural flair, were the drivers to their expansion and equally valuable was Martin's reserve and determination to temper daring with prudence.

David Heaven's arrival had contrived to strengthen the characteristics of both father and son. David loved the international scene and discovered in himself a natural ability for languages and became quite fluent in French with a reasonable ability in Portuguese. He was always interested, without being pushy, in the business of others and was ever alive to how Kirchoff's could expand their business base. Sol and Martin were amazed by the number of new clients whom David had introduced from unlikely beginnings — stray conversations on aeroplanes or in the single hotel bar of some remote town in the wilds of Africa.

At the same time, David was conscious of all that he did not know, especially about matters which tended to bore him for all that he recognised their importance: the detail of accounting and the legal provisions of contracts. Such things were Martin's world and so it was that the two young men found it easy to play to one another's strengths while the bond of friendship developed to the point when each could anticipate the thoughts and reactions of the other.

They spent a good deal of time together, both embraced under the paternalistic umbrella which dear old Sol rejoiced to hoist over their heads. There were a few social occasions, but their home lives were widely separated by custom and distance. For the past three and a half years, David had been living in London's Parsons Green. He had bought a nondescript house, indistinguishable from its neighbours, quiet, self contained and reasonably generous of space with a bit of a garden which gave him pleasure. As with most things in his life at that time, David had consulted Sol before making the final commitment.

'Get on and buy the place Davy,' Sol had said without inspecting the house, 'that part of London will take off in value over the next few years. All those young and smart people with money have already gone through Chelsea and are infesting Fulham. Where are they going to go next? Right up that street of yours and others like it you can be sure.'

On the first of January 1970, David was established now, enjoying his work, his lifestyle, his friends, his house and garden. He had a spasmodic love life which, as he admitted to himself, could only be just that for as long as he continued to be too selfish to commit himself and too absorbed in his business which was the centrepiece of his existence. It might sound pretentious, but he really did believe that they were building a dynasty. And right now that required him to spend ten days in the African States of Mauritania and Mali. It would be an extended visit although not by much. He was leaving London sooner than planned simply because his old friend Connie Aveling had been summoned to travel to Singapore two days in advance of schedule and David thought that he might as well accompany him to Heathrow.

Conrad had a similar commitment to his own career. He had followed his father into the Royal Green Jackets and quickly settled into regimental life, first at their home base in the UK, followed by a posting to Germany. He drew some military attention for his useful combination of brains and brawn. He was bright, with a special ability to think clearly whilst under pressure. He was no dummy as a linguist and developed as a competent communicator. And then there was the brawn. Conrad enjoyed his sports and played most to a better than average ability so it followed that he kept very fit, even as judged by the standards of his peer group. What was unusual was his exceptional strength. He stood just a bit above average height and had a build to match, but by some quirk of nature, his power to weight ratio was way above the norm with a devastating strength in his upper body and arms. This combination of brain and body made for a useful asset and Conrad was pulled back early from Germany to be assessed for secondment to the special forces. The British SAS in the late sixties was all the more effective for its anonymity.

By Christmas 1969, Conrad had spent a year with the SAS at its home base in Herefordshire, learning a hard trade and honing his skills. He had now received his marching orders to join a unit based in Singapore which operated throughout the region. A dose of malaria had cut down one of his colleagues already in post, so Conrad's travel had been speeded up, bringing forward his departure date and interrupting his Christmas leave. He was not complaining, but he was quiet in David's car as they drove up together to the airport from Barrington Park. David knew his old friend well enough to recognise that this withdrawal was Conrad's way of getting himself prepared for action. He understood and asked no questions. He dropped Connie outside Terminal 3 for his long haul flight and they took leave of each other with a typically understated farewell. David drove on to leave his car in a long term park and take a bus into his terminal for a European destination. It was then about 3 pm.

After checking in for his flight to Paris, David found another surprise awaiting him. He moved easily through passport control, browsed briefly in the duty-free shop and went in search of a cup of coffee. In the self service restaurant, his eye was drawn to a huge figure, shapeless in a dark brown monk's habit and slouched over a table on which rested a plate of sandwiches and a mug of something. No two people could possibly look like that, David decided and he moved up to place a hand on the monk's shoulder.

Pente Broke Smith whipped his head round with surprising speed and goggled at him in momentary disbelief before springing up to tower over David and sweep him into a great bear hug embrace.

'The Lord must be smiling on me to start the New Year', Pente boomed in a voice to startle nearby onlookers. 'David Heaven.

How very damn good to see you! And just where are you off to?'

David extricated himself from the encircling arms, and grinned back.'Nowhere for at least an hour', he said,'just let me get myself a coffee and I'll tell you more.'

When they were both seated and still smiling at each other, it was David who spoke first.

'Golly, Pente, it must be eighteen months or more since I saw you last. That's about right too. You came and spent a couple of nights when they had let you out for a week to come down to London. But I thought you were now in Africa, nobly suffering somewhere: wasn't it in Madagascar?'

'You're right. It was and it still is. I'm just on my way back there now. To Paris in an hour or so and then on overnight to Antan.' David didn't need to be told that Pente was referring to Antananarivo, the capital city.

'Well that's a good start. I'm for Paris too, and then on to Nouakchott, so we've got plenty of time to catch up on a bit of news. What a shame though. I've only just left Conrad whose now in Terminal 3 on his way to the Far East. His own version of Onward Christian Soldiers.'

Pente guffawed, 'You don't say. Well that is a pity. I haven't seen old Connie for years — hardly since Oxford. Is he getting on OK?'

'Yes he is, really well. Now part of the tough eggs brigade, and revelling in it. But tell me how things are going for you.'

There was a pause as the big man took a giant swig from his tea mug and David knew he was getting ready to set out his stall. Pente hunched his shoulders, drew in a mighty breath and removed his enormous tortoiseshell spectacles which he polished on the hem of his habit as he started to speak.

'I've got to say that it's a matter of mixed fortunes, David, and I'm really not sure that I'm going to make it in this calling. I was just mulling it over when you tapped me on the back.'

David was unsurprised by this dramatic candour. Pente was always one to wear his heart on his sleeve. He waited for him to continue.

'When I was staying with you, I think I must have bored you with stories of my early days in training.' Pente gave his familiar, lopsided grin.

'It was hardly boring,' rejoined David. During two long evenings, Pente had scarcely drawn breath in regaling David with his experiences in the remotely located Northumberland monastery, the home of his Order in which he had spent two years preparing for the priesthood.

'Well anyway, it's got a lot tougher since then.' Pente drank some more of his tea and then fumbled in the folds of his vestment and came up with a short and very black cheroot which he preceded to light and blow all over David who coughed his objections.

'Surely that thing constitutes a weakness of the flesh, Pente, mine if not yours. Are you allowed to smoke it?'

'Oh sure. Nothing in the rules of either God or man which says no. There aren't many smokers in the monastery and we're pretty careful as to where and when. No, I'm afraid that this weed has been the least of my failings while I've been a Novice.'

David looked up sharply as he caught the thread of serious comment. Pente removed his spectacles and massaged his face with one huge hand.

'Frankly', he said at last, 'I've been having real trouble with my faith. When I saw you last, I would have made light of it if I mentioned it at all and honestly, I thought I was just going through a learning curve which my mentors told me to expect. But lately, it's become more deep seated and now I'm questioning whether I was right to take my vows.'

Pente sat back in his chair with a deep sigh, but David knew him better than to interrupt and waited for him to resume.

'Do you remember, David, that during our first two years in training, we all spend a six month period away from the monastery. You might think of it as a stint of practical experience to leaven the mixture of learning, routine and theory.'

'Yes', David replied, 'of course I remember because when you were with me in London, you had just returned from your time away and you were en route back to Northumberland. You were in South Africa, weren't you, outside Cape Town somewhere?'

'That's right. But what I didn't tell you was that I'd been sent home early. I was judged to have failed in my time down there, and was required to return to the monastery to do a load more study. Plus I had to put myself into solitary confinement for a whole month, to search my soul and to test my faith in order to find within me greater humility. I just scraped through the monks' second test, and in June I was sent out to Madagascar to less politically sensitive surroundings. It is here that I have a final chance to prove myself in their eyes. And incidentally, I've only been back now for a few days because my old Mum, bless her, has just died so in addition to everything else, I am pretty distressed at leaving my father who is now nearly ninety and all on his own. But you didn't know either of them.'

David replied, 'that's so and I'm sorry that we've never met, but even more so for you in having to leave him. That's very tough on you. But look, I believe I understand all you're saying, but you'd better spell it out for me.'

Pente stubbed out his noxious cigar and returned David's gaze as he resumed.

'When we were all together at Oxford, the sudden conviction that I wanted to spend my life in Holy Orders was a marvellous sensation in many ways, including the simple feeling of certainty: of decision made and never to be regretted. Oh, I knew there would be plenty to cope with along the way, no small discomfort and sometimes a bit of ridicule. But I had no qualms, you see, I was just completely sure from the very first that my faith would remain rock constant and utterly impervious to temptation and influence. But now? Well now I'm really not so sure. I'm afflicted by doubts and the more I'm bullied, the more those doubts multiply. To be honest with you, I am naturally a little rebellious and not really the typical aspirant for our Order. In training, I have chafed at some of the restrictions and requirements which strike me as petty and anachronistic, exactly the sort of Pharisee rules which our Lord would have debunked in short order.'

David couldn't help himself. He said nothing, but could not prevent a smile spreading across his face. He could well imagine that Pente's opinions would not have thrilled the authorities in their cloistered surroundings where life would be lived by long established rules and customs.

Pente went on speaking.

'These are relatively little matters and we must rise above them. The greater problem is the feeling that I'm misplaced and the pivotal issue for me is all about life in Africa. Our Brotherhood is dedicated to missionary work. The Order is well established in both Kenya and Tanzania, also in South Africa and of course, we have the small mission in Madagascar. In all these places, we believe that our role is to improve the standard of life and the quality of spirit.'

'So where's the problem? You can surely identify plenty to be accomplished.'

'Of course. But my problem, David, is that it's all about politics rather than God's word. The whole Order is consumed with the battle against apartheid in South Africa and anyone who is seen as being insufficiently committed is taken to be unreliable at best — or even some sort of heretic.'

Now David was really engaged.

'So where do you stand with your conscience, Pente? Is this not one of the burning questions of the new decade?'

'I agree', said Pente, 'but I also think that there's more to life in South Africa than a struggle between black and white. Furthermore, I'm certain that the entire continent south of the Sahara can't be judged simply by what's going on in the extreme south.'

'Do you mean that you churchmen shouldn't get too involved? That you should devote yourselves to God and avoid getting your hands dirty with life in the raw?'

David had intended to provoke, but as soon as the words were out of his mouth he knew he'd gone too far. Pente started to turn puce at the perceived affront and David made to apologise but he was way too late and made to suffer with a stinging rebuke which half the lounge in the terminal could hear. But at least it encouraged him in the vision of good old Pente in full flow and he did enjoy the absence of priestly language as Pente completed his tirade.

'Don't you dare sneer at me and mine or I'll kick your balls down your throat, you miserable, exploiting capitalist!'

Mercifully, Pente stopped for breath at this point and reached for another foul smelling cigar. David took advantage of the lull to remark mildly,

'Well I can at least see that your good brethren must have been gaining some fresh ideas and different language.'

They looked at each other and simultaneously burst out laughing, just as it had been with lively debates in days gone by. Pente said,

'I guess you deserve an answer to your question, and it's this. I do believe the Church should be involved in politics. Put another way, I don't see how any individual, group or organisation can possibly engage in work of conscience and calling without being political. That's life as the Almighty created it, and we must all get on and accept it.' He waved a great paw as David sought to interject, 'but actually, that's not my point. What bothers me is whether the obsession of breaking apartheid and replacing it immediately with black majority rule is either sound or in God's plan for us to pursue.'

He gazed intently at David for a second or two before concluding, 'I don't know what you think, knowing Africa as you do, but I can tell you that my views attract very little sympathy within our Order.'

David struggled with his reply, making several false starts before he was able to express himself clearly.

'Just as a gut reaction, Pente, I will say three things to you. First, you must have real courage to be holding such a view and articulating it within your community. I admire you for that and I can imagine what pressure you provoke from both your colleagues and your conscience. Secondly, you can count on me as an interested listener. I love travelling in Africa, but the plain fact is that I'm just a bird of passage. It takes a lot of time and patience to get to know even one country, let alone the whole continent. That said, I must say that wherever I go, it does seem that the great majority is being taken to the cleaners by a very small minority and the rest of the world seems neither to recognise this nor to care too much.

'But finally Pente, I ask you to hang on in there. I honestly believe that the best way to deal with your worries is to keep them to yourself for a while. Let a bit of healing time flow over the whole question of where your personal faith is trying to lead you. Use your remaining time in Madagascar for what it is, an opportunity to explore yourself. That's my advice, and for what it's worth, that's what I'm doing. To be frank, I don't know whether or not I'll keep working in this area for life. My instinct is that I will, because every time they open the plane door in Khartoum or Kigali, I feel that I've come home again. Wonderful places and wonderful people, but oh my word, do they ever create a shambles.'

David rose and started to collect his few belongings together.

'We'd best get going and get seated together. Let's return to this weighty subject in a few months' time because I need something a bit more flippant on the way over to Paris.'

'You're right,' Pente said as he heaved himself to his feet, 'I'll start by telling you about my first funeral which really did turn out a dead loss ... Ho Ho!'

They walked away together, unaware of how much help they could have been right then to Connie Aveling, sitting in the neighbouring terminal building and wondering about the fifth member of their Oxford Five who was only yards from him.

Conrad had been happy to arrive early at the airport. He liked to be organised; he was not yet an experienced traveller and had never been further East than Cyprus. He was therefore content to make his way slowly through the departure formalities, eventually to take up a lounge seat near the gate from which his Qantas flight would depart in the early evening, calling at Frankfurt, Bahrain, Karachi and Singapore where he would disembark, allowing the plane to continue via Darwin to Sydney.

He was sitting there, reflecting on a happy Christmas and the promise of this crucial posting. He was not concentrating on his crossword and kept on looking up in distraction. That is how he came to see Alexa Labarre, who was apparently inspecting a bookstall in the company of a large black man. Connie was mesmerised by the sight. Alexa had been his first love and she remained among his most precious memories. But they had not seen each other since university, and of course he hadn't expected to see her now. There was something else. It was Alexa ... and yet it wasn't. Could this be another girl, a complete stranger? There was something about her wandering gait, a slightly brittle, almost tarty look to her which was so unlike the Alexa of his past. He was spellbound, and being cautious by both nature and training, he settled to being inconspicuous as he studied the couple.

THIERRY CESTAC — 1970

The traffic was light. It was barely mid-morning on New Year's Day. He was comfortably settled in the rear of his opulent Mercedes, watching the final outskirts of Paris give way to frozen countryside as they took the main highway south and west towards the Dordogne. His chauffeur, Olivier, was at the wheel. Cestac did not attempt any conversation, being occupied with his private thoughts and a review of his position. He was satisfied enough with the night's work and relieved to have the package out of his hands. He was glad of the instinct that it was the final deal for him. His conviction was strengthened by the colossal profit he was making, but it was time to move on. He had already started to do so. The new business was very attractive although he sensed it would be short term. The income was excellent but the competition was intense and growing ever more ruthless. Cestac could not shake off the nag of concern which had hit him that morning as he left his apartment and looked up the street He had seen the Citroen parked fifty metres away with a tell-tale, fine plume from its exhaust rising in the cold, early morning air. He neither looked nor lingered as Olivier held the door of the car for him, but he had snatched a glimpse of two figures in the front of the Citroen and was conscious that the driver had killed the engine. Was that coincidence, or had the occupants been sitting in patient wait for him? He didn't know, but he was not going to challenge the natural, furtive cunning which served him well. He would go to ground for a few weeks in his country cottage near Bergerac and would sniff the air carefully before he emerged and returned to Paris. In addition, as he told himself, it had been a hard couple of months. He could do with the rest.

Thierry Cestac was a complete, gold carat villain, concerned with serving no one but himself, dedicated to his luxurious lifestyle, titillated by causing pain and discomfort to others. He had been brought up in the southern French city of Pau, nestling beneath the Pyrenees. He seemed predestined to make his way through the diligent practice of any number of black arts and his first motivation had been to escape a life of provincial ennui. His father was a diffident civil servant and his mother a simple girl from a remote farming community. There was no indication in their gene pool to explain the talents and temperament of their son, and whatever influence his mother might have brought to bear on him was lost as she developed cancer whilst carrying him and died within a year of his birth. An unmarried aunt helped to raise him, a large woman as dominating as her brother was weak, and she thrashed away at Thierry both physically and mentally without any consciousness that she was making a bad situation worse. As Cestac turned fifteen, all he wanted was to escape his stifling surroundings, and there came the day when he packed a bag, walked to the station and caught a train to Paris. He never returned, nor had further contact with his father.

When first in Paris at school boy age, Cestac had been severely tested. He knew no one in the capital and he was short of money. He was helped by the pressures of the time. These were mid-war years in German-occupied Paris and neither individuals nor the authorities had much time for stray teenagers. To help him, Cestac had his wits which were considerable and his morals which did not exist. Within a month of arrival and living in a cheap doss house, he contrived to be picked up by a seasoned old roué, a sixty something year old pouf who was an established literary critic and lived in some style in the Latin Quarter. Cestac was happy to be used in whatever way pleased the old boy, who became unreasonably devoted to him, admiring his brain and natural guile, insisting that he complete an excellent education at the expense of his patron. Cestac stuck to it for ten years, recognising the value of all he was gaining from studies, qualifications and life experience, whilst at the same time building his own circle of contacts. By the age of twenty-five, he had achieved the dominant role in the relationship and then came the night when his carnal exertions achieved such a result that the old chap expired from heart failure. Cestac was gratified but not surprised to find himself the beneficiary of a considerable will. This was not a windfall. He had worked for it. Now he set himself to make the best use of his legacy. His life strategy was simple. Be wealthy, be secure. Exploit the weaknesses of others. Be calculating. Be cruel, because you enjoy it.

Comfortably settled, Cestac moved carefully. He avoided the commonplace criminal fraternity. He was not interested in robbery. He would not get involved in financial fraud and would not have anything to do with kidnap and ransom. He was determined to work alone. He was available to befriend the lonely and wealthy if there was the chance for substantial gain, but he was no longer offering his body as part of his attraction. His insistence on what he would not do came to pay dividends sooner than he had expected. Moving freely in the twilight criminal world of the 1950's, Cestac found that he could do well as a kingmaker who could put people together. If an introduction clicked and a consequent scheme succeeded, he would earn nicely, and if not, then he got nothing. But this way his bona fides became clear and respected.

Later, his strategy started to pay huge dividends as the world moved into the swinging sixties. This was all about sex. Cestac had been quick to see the opportunity offered by changing attitudes. A small number of wealthy people with extravagant tastes now felt empowered to go out and buy the sort of entertainment which had hitherto been unavailable except in their wildest imaginings. Cestac set out to be the purveyor of dreams, assuring absolute discretion in return for stratospheric fees. He got involved in providing girls and boys and children and even animals. He became known within this warped community as the man who could arrange, and this soon moved from France to an international client base.

By 1965, Thierry Cestac was dealing with the English, the

Spanish, Scandinavia and Russia. Not with the USA. He had his chances but did not pursue them. He had a recurring suspicion that his privacy would be threatened so he kept his distance. Then there was the Middle East which became a dominant source of business. There was no shortage of money of course, but it did surprise him that there was such a demand for his services. He had assumed that religion, practices and penalties would annul the attractions of all he had to offer. But he was wrong, and happy to be so.

During the second half of the 1960's, Cestac prospered mightily in the white slave trade. This was an ill-defined term. There was a trade, but not in slavery as such and not all the victims were white. The transactions revolved around the kidnap and delivery to those whose taste and wallet qualified them, of humans of both gender, various ages and any colour suitable to meet the cravings of the client in question. The victim was unconscious of selection, not consulted in advance and not expected to survive for very long. The traffickers operated with caution, fearful on the one hand of the international authorities and on the other of clients claiming dissatisfaction with menace as their appetites were temporarily reduced. And occasionally, there were the relatives of victims, hell bent on any form of revenge. The suppliers protected themselves through checks and cut outs and Cestac was the best at this management control. He did not meet or speak to a single one of his end users. He used a number of intermediaries with whom he kept guarded contact as he trusted none of them. He employed 'mules' as companions to ensure safe delivery of the merchandise to the client. This was the most delicate and risky aspect of the transaction but Cestac developed it into a fine art, calculating the combination of calming drug, deceit, bribery and blandishment required to ensure that the captive went willingly to a chilling fate while he was counting his profits.

It was thus that Thierry Cestac had moved over twenty-five years from bored child through teenage villain into an evil maturity. He was always a loner. He had great wealth and lived with every comfort at his disposal. But restraint was his style.

The gap yawned between his true personality and the way in which he presented himself. He was probably psychotic but it would never have occurred to him to consider the point.

Cestac was now taking stock of the present and considering his future. The swinging sixties had passed and international standards for the sexual norm were shifting. This was sure to lead to a reduction in demand for his specialist talents and he felt it beneath him to compete in a dying market. And then there were fresh opportunities, of which the most significant lay in drugs, especially heroin. He was doing some good business in arranging supply at a fabulous profit to some of the smart set in Paris. But he was wary. This was not a product which he could source himself. To obtain supply, he had to negotiate with two brothers of Bulgarian extraction with contacts through Turkey into Afghanistan. They were savage men, unreliable and unpredictable. At the other end of the chain lay the using punters, men and women who lived too close to the world of Cestac to permit him to relax in the anonymity he cherished. He was also sure that the drug trade was set to blossom and grow. This would lead to reduced prices and reduced margins while the whole business would become increasingly more cut throat and less exclusive. Not at all right for him.

He needed to plan for his next development which he had already identified. The post-colonial independent states of Africa seemed to him to have great potential. In almost every case, the new rulers were hugely wealthy, entirely corrupt and eager to indulge themselves in all manner of mischief. He could help them with the supply of arms, the provision of mercenaries, with purchasing property and establishing hard currency reserves. And, of course, with obliging them with any extreme of personal foible.

This was going to take some time and concentration, but first, he would rest up and relax during the first couple of months of this new decade. With this decision made, Cestac put his head back on to the leather luxury of his fine car. He slept as Olivier drove on towards warmer and quieter surroundings.

KINGSTON OFFENBACH — 1970

At 4 pm on New Year's Day, it was almost dark in London and King was still at his desk in the American Embassy. The building was mostly deserted and he was surprised to hear his direct line ring, then pleased to recognise the gruff, smoker's voice with the heavy accent.

'Keeng? You are there?'

'Yes, Victor, I'm here. It's good to get your call.'

They had a short conversation and agreed on a plan. King sat back in his chair and reflected that this was going to cost him the early night he'd been planning but it would likely be worth it. He got on well with Victor Sollange, Sicilian born, a well-respected officer in the French Security Service and a key member of the international team which would meet tomorrow. Victor was already in London, staying at a hotel in Victoria and King joined him there just after 6 pm. They went to a wine bar in Elizabeth Street and sat in a quiet corner to talk over coffee and some house red.

Sollange started the conversation, speaking slowly in his guttural French. He wanted to talk about the latest developments in Paris. About twelve months previously, the two men had met for the first time when King visited Victor's office. It had not been a comfortable occasion. Sollange had been reluctant to receive King and wary of sharing information with a black American arriving from London. But King had been at his gently persuasive best. He knew it was vital for him to build a constructive relationship with this man. It was the French who knew most about Africa, and Victor Sollange was their top man, with priceless experience and an impressive record. It had taken King a further two visits to persuade Victor that the CIA was serious and had something to offer. Specifically, he had provided Victor with valuable details on the Brothers Grimm and their heroin supply routes of which much was known in Langley. In response, Sollange opened up with his knowledge of how South American cocaine was coming into Europe via the continent of Africa.

The Brothers had been allocated a suitable codename. They were wealthy, well known and viciously ruthless. They were content to be assumed as Bulgarian, but had in fact been born in Turkey and had spent time as guest workers in West Germany before slipping into France. The Grimms were not the only suppliers to French users, not even the biggest, but they had the greatest notoriety and were the fastest growing in coke distribution. Sollange had selected them as his prime target and he had fresh news to share.

'I can confirm the Grimms are working with Thierry Cestac,' he announced 'we had a positive sighting just this morning.'

King raised his eyebrows but said nothing. Sollange lit himself a fresh Gauloise and went on.

'I must give credit to young Geslin. He's not been with me for long and I told him to take New Year off. But last night he went round the clubs they visit, got lucky at the third and saw them leave around 3 am. Geslin followed and they parked up in Rue de Constantine — a very chic area. They sat there until 7 am, heater running from time to time. My man froze his balls off fifty metres up the street and watched them. Then Cestac appears. He has a young blond guy with him. They separate, Cestac gives his overcoat to the blond and then gets in his car which is chauffeured up to him. Blond walks up the street and climbs in with the Brothers Grimm. Both Cestac's limo and the Grimm car vanish, but in different directions. Geslin doesn't have the horsepower to follow either of them, so he goes to look at the building. They're apartments, very high value. Cestac's name doesn't appear but one bell push is marked 'Enterprises Pau', so that'll be him.'

Sollange reached for his glass and lit another Gauloise. The eyes beneath their bushy brows twinkled across the table as he continued.

'Cestac must really matter to the Grimms. Why else would they spend New Year's Eve sitting in a car waiting for him? Cestac is cunning. I confess we didn't know he has a place in Rue de Constantine but it seems the Brothers had the road if not the number. My guess is they want to take Cestac out of the picture. He has the contacts in the smart set and they want his middleman profit. They figure to get him off guard and alone — then it'll be a painful end for M. Cestac.'

King interrupted, 'I follow you, Victor, but you've said nothing about Cestac's partner — this blond guy.'

'Him. Oh shit, King, I've no idea, but you can be sure that he was no sort of business partner. And I do mean 'was'. The Grimms took him off assuming he's in on the act, they'll have sweated him a bit, found he knows nothing, then they'll have wasted what was left of him and our colleagues in the Gendarmerie will be fishing him out of some canal in a day or so. Cestac works alone and trusts no one. He's way too smart for the Grimms and I bet he sniffed something this morning. So he sent off the blond as a diversion to give himself a bit of time. He'll be back. They must owe him product so he'll be back ... and with muscle behind him. What we must do now is watch and wait. We've got a good chance to roll up the network and get our hands on some of the using clientele too, and they'll be a high profile bunch you can be sure.'

'I'd sure like that,' said King, 'but if you're right Victor, what was the blond doing there? Is he a boyfriend? Is Cestac a queer?'

Sollange laughed, 'God no. Cestac certainly likes the girls and he likes variety too. So, I reckon that Blond was the cabaret for the evening.'

Seeing the look of puzzlement on King's face, he went on, 'Sorry. I didn't mention that Geslin saw three people coming out of that apartment. Cestac, Blond and also a girl. No doubt they'll have been partying most of the night and she went off with Cestac. Perhaps he dropped her home, but I don't think so.'

'What d'you mean?'

Sollange lit yet another Gauloise and spoke through a stream of smoke.

'Cestac sells flesh. He supplies live bodies to order, a few pretty boys but mostly beautiful girls. He has customers in Europe and the Middle East. He finds and fattens the product, then delivers it to his pervert of a client who will have a mountain of money, but no morals or mercy. Not a pleasant business, but it's the slave trade of this century and it's a strictly one way ticket for the poor souls once he's got his hands on them. They never come back. Not one.'

King grimaced in sympathy. 'I've heard speak of it, but never been involved in that field.'

'And won't now, I think. It's a dying business. No doubt Cestac sees a better return from peddling powder and pills to those who have the money and brains to know better. But it looks like Cestac is going out on a high note. He's sent out a girl this morning from Paris — an absolute stunner.'

King shrugged. 'But this is a guess, right?'

'It's more than that, my friend. You see, I gave myself a bit of extra time at Orly today before my flight and chatted to my friends there in customs and police. Thought I'd check if Cestac went through today. They let me see the manifests and it didn't take so long: light traffic on New Year's Day. I couldn't find Cestac's name, but I recognised another. Georges Eboli. A big black guy. He's small time, does cons and scams, quite a smooth operator. I was interested because he's run errands for Cestac before so I dug a bit deeper and found that Georges left Paris today to travel to London, then connecting onto a flight this evening to Bahrain. And he's travelling with a lady. I got the passport details as you should know about him. Eboli claims he was born in Cameroun but who can tell. French passport now and he's been living in Paris for fifteen years. Have a look where he's been in the past twelve months. Twice to Conakry and once to Sao Tome: both on your possible transit points for South American drugs, yes?'

King reached out to take the paperwork which Sollange had dug out of his pocket. He looked at the handsome black face and glanced at the guy's personal and travel details which were summarised beneath. Efficient staff work, he thought. He was about to lay the document aside when Victor spoke again.

'Have a look at the girl too. I'd surely love to see the rest of her. I reckon Cestac has groomed her for some sick bastard. Now Eboli is playing delivery boy and there's not a damn thing to be done. She's old enough and wise enough. If she goes of her own accord — well then she goes. But I doubt she'll be coming back.'

He gave a Gallic shrug as he continued, 'anyway, King, it's not our affair. Now I suggest that at tomorrow's conference, we don't mention ...', but he broke off there as he realised his audience was no longer listening.

King Offenbach felt a long shiver pass down his spine as he scanned the second sheet which Victor had passed to him. There could be no doubt. He knew that face so very well and the details of her passport confirmed it. Alexandra Celeste Labarre.

There was a long silence. King sat motionless with his eyes fixed on the photo of Alexa. Inwardly, he was in turmoil with thoughts cascading over each other. They were interrupted by Victor who leaned forward and said,

'Don't tell me. You know the girl?'

King just nodded and then he gave Victor a concise little run down of the background story.

Sollange remarked, 'Life can indeed be a bitch. I really don't know what you can do, King, but you don't have much time and you better get going. I'll see you in the morning.'

King nodded his thanks as he left. He was lucky with a cab and was back at his desk in twenty minutes. He grabbed the phone and started to work contacts, not helped by the day or the time. By midnight, he knew that Alexa and Eboli were on the regular Qantas flight to Sydney which went out around 2100 every evening. Their destination was Bahrain and they would now be sitting in mid-air with three and a half hours to go.

King dialled again and was lucky. His old buddy Mark Leary

was at home for the New Year and abandoned a family dinner to listen. At the end, Mark said laconically,

'It's a bit of a challenge, King, especially with the tight timing. But then again, you're in the right shop. Communication is pretty much the name of our game.'

After which, things moved pretty quickly. Some important strings were pulled and a succinct message sent at 0216 GMT 2nd January to the captain of Qantas Flight 002 in level cruise towards Bahrain.

King Offenbach could do more then. He went to bed and forced himself to sleep.

ALEXA LABARRE — 1970

She was sitting in the departures lounge of London Heathrow Airport, Terminal 3. She kept repeating this dull, factual information to herself because it made her feel that she had not quite lost touch with her own sanity. She was very tired, overcome with sleepiness and every few minutes she would start to nod off. As soon as that happened, she would be gripped by a panic attack which made her sit bolt upright and gasp for breath. She found she could regain some control by restarting the litany 'I am sitting in the departures ... etc' and in due course she would go through the whole process again. And again. Except that the whole cycle was taking longer. I'm getting worse, she told herself. I'm losing touch with reality. I need help.

Alexa was about to turn twenty-six. She was christened Alexandra Celeste, the names chosen to reflect her Anglo French family. From baby days and childhood into her teenage years, Alexa trailed behind her an unending stream of superlatives which increased with her adult independence. She had brains and beauty, charm and character, poise and personality. She was fine, flirtatious, sometimes feisty, always feminine. She had the lot, her many friends would say of her, but they could not call her a rich bitch. She was wealthy indeed, but apparently never a bitch despite all the benefits bestowed upon her. Alexa was schooled first in Limoges near to the small chateau which had been home to her father Joffrey's family for successive generations. When she was thirteen, her English born mother Elizabeth's influence sent her to boarding school in England and it was from there that she went straight up to Oxford University.

Alexa prized the independence which Oxford and England made possible. In 1963, her brother Michel had disappeared whilst serving his commercial apprenticeship in Africa, and no trace of him had ever been found. The tragedy had almost destroyed the Labarres. They had always been a close group, the parents happy with each other and both were international, influential and involved. Their children, three to include Alexa's younger brother Bernard, were all touched with gold and had enjoyed an idyllic childhood with the expectation of a fulfilling life before Michel dropped out of sight.

They were all changed forever, but Joffrey was shattered by the experience and tortured that he would never know the full story. He hired an expensive investigator who vanished into Africa and reported back with the likely conclusion that Michel had perished because thieves fell out. But there was no proof and nothing left behind.

While Joffrey and Elizabeth struggled to accept this finality, they were locked together in a dungeon of grief, guilt and frustration and as they served their sentence, the relationship with their other two children suffered. Alexa dealt with this estrangement by going to build her life around Oxford. After she won her degree she was still anxious to preserve her independence and accepted a job offer from a London city bank. Two years later, she was offered a move to their Paris office. It was good that she was closer to Limoges, but not too close and she settled down to enjoy her career and the Paris lifestyle.

By the autumn of 1968, all was pretty good for Alexa except that she was working long hours with too little time for her friends and not much of a love life. But that changed just before Christmas when she attended, on behalf of the bank, a reception at the Chilean Embassy where she met Thierry Cestac.

He was better than a breath of fresh air. After fighting off too many dreary bankers and immature suitors, here at last was a man of abundant style and savoir faire. He was fortyish and established. She was unsure of his profession, which mattered not a jot to her. He was older and wiser, with time, charm, conversation and a real interest in her. He was fun to be with and won the instant approval of her friends. She was delighted to be invited into his bed and fulfilled by what happened there. Alexa fell in love and under the spell of this cultured, handsome man with the long face and aquiline nose which she chose to describe as aristocratic.

They were together regularly throughout 1969 and Alexa's confidence in their relationship grew without check or concern. Thierry was the man for her and she was never as happy as when in his company. He was kind, thoughtful and endlessly entertaining. He was an energetic lover and imaginative with it. The manner in which he used toys and diversions fired her libido to an extent which sometimes shamed her, but never enough to complain and still less to stop.

During all the progress of the year, it would have been inconceivable to her that Cestac had a different agenda: that he was all the while preparing her for sale. The background story was unprecedented. Cestac had received an approach on behalf of an end user client in the Middle East. The man had bought two girls from other procurers, but neither had lasted more than six months. When the initial thrill was satiated, he resorted to pleasuring himself with such violent treatment that both girls had died at his personal hand.

The client was now prepared to pay without limit if Cestac could find for him a girl of exceptional physical attraction, but also one of breeding, character and brains. She was to be a toy that the client could not break too easily and would remain the challenge which his warped ego demanded. The task energised Cestac, all the more as he had just met Alexa. He recognised her worth immediately. She was pure gold. He set himself to turn her into a million dollars of income and the ultimate stimulus for which he was ever seeking.

He devised a development programme which relied on his natural instinct to go slowly and with caution. He knew that Alexa was special and would take time. He knew also that the client's need and budget would be heightened by waiting for the very best. But finally came the time in late November 1969 when Cestac was satisfied that she was ready and the client was desperate. It was time to close the deal, and Cestac agreed to delivery in the New Year.

Alexa, of course, knew nothing of this duplicity and evil. But she did feel bloody awful. She sat there in the Heathrow lounge and the world around her seemed to be spinning off its axis. Physically, she alternated between nausea and shivering with either accompanied by a splitting headache. Mentally she felt much, much worse, but she lacked the experience to recognise the symptoms. She was already in trauma. The worst of it was the confusion. Alexa simply could not get a grip on what had happened to her during the last twelve hours. She remembered some things quite clearly but then others seemed to lose focus and the chronology was never as it should have been.

She was fixated by her last sight of Thierry. He had introduced her to this huge black, Georges, who was to accompany her to London and then on to Bahrain but she had hardly responded to Eboli's graceful bow as he turned aside with some small talk for Thierry. She had suddenly felt tearful and lonely. She had never been to Arabia and the prospect of twenty-four hours in a hotel waiting for Thierry to catch up with her was scary. But why? She knew the plan. Thierry had an important business meeting in Frankfurt: he was going there today and would join her by flying out tomorrow night. She was troubled and Thierry seemed to understand. He broke off from Georges and came to cuddle her, whispering endearments and saying he would soon be with her and they would fly on together to Singapore. Quite his normal, considerate self and she felt reassured. He said that she must take the sleeping pills which he had given her. They would give her a good rest on the long overnight journey to Bahrain. She smiled bravely. Then he said that she and Georges should go on through customs and he must run for his plane to Germany. She allowed Eboli to shepherd her through the formalities and then she looked back over the barrier. But Thierry had gone: he had left. It seemed to symbolise abandonment that he had not troubled to wait just a few minutes more.

Other flashbacks danced in her head. It had been a great party but she had no memory of who had been the host, where it had been, who else had been there. She remembered accepting drinks which Thierry described as 'just a cocktail' and with one of them some powder in a twist which he had encouraged her to sniff. When they left at whatever hour after midnight, there had been another man in the back of the car with them. He was young and blond. Russian, so Thierry had told her, and a friend. She spoke to him in his own language and he mumbled a reply in a coarse accent as he concentrated on getting a hand up her skirt.

When they left the apartment that morning, Thierry was distracted by something in the street and he simply dumped the blond instead of dropping him on the way to the airport. What had all that been about? Perhaps it had been to do with what went on during the night. She had a horrifying vision of herself greeting the dawn by making oral love to Thierry while she was being screwed rigid by the nameless young Russian.

And now she felt bad, must look worse and was intimidated by the huge Georges who tried to sound smooth but smelt of cheap Cologne and would not leave her side for a single minute. He had even insisted on standing outside the Ladies when she went there an hour ago. That thought brought back the nausea. Alexa stood up abruptly and put her hand to her mouth. She said something about la toilette to Eboli. He nodded and kept his seat, but his eyes followed her across the lounge. She was feeling distraught. She must simply lock herself in and refuse to come out. 'Thierry himself will have to come for me' she was thinking, and at that moment, she saw Conrad Aveling, sitting by himself and reading a newspaper. He didn't look up.

Alexa got herself into a cubicle, sat down and shivered as she thought. 'Connie? Could it really be him? Why was he here? Perhaps she could ask for advice. Perhaps he could find Thierry for her. Surely he could at least get her away from Georges'. Then the nausea returned, followed by a fresh attack of panic in which she was convinced that the roof was coming slowly down on her head. She sprang up and fled out of the Ladies.

CONRAD AVELING — 1970

By the time they started calling forward passengers Conrad had been keeping careful watch for ninety minutes. He couldn't work out Alexa's condition. She kept her gaze down and her hands were constantly picking at each other or running through her hair. When she got up, she seemed startled and her movement was crabbed and nervous, not the elegant stride he remembered. The big black guy was constantly with her and watching her. Conrad bided his time. Alexa might resent an intrusion and if she was in trouble, a bald approach might let her companion spirit her away before the riddle could be unpicked.

But then she banished any doubt from his mind.

At Oxford, they had been lovers for a while and were extravagantly discreet. When with friends, she used to communicate a private message with a toss of her head and an arched eyebrow which meant — stay with me. Five years later at Heathrow, the first class queue was overtaking economy and as Alexa moved past, she turned her face to him. Conrad was shocked by the look of nervous pain, but he didn't miss her message as the eyebrow arched.

The passengers filed into the aircraft. They left on time and made a brief stop in Frankfurt to take on fuel and a handful of passengers. Two hours later, with the aircraft at cruising height and dinner served, Conrad sat in his window seat with two Australian neighbours who filled their seat pockets with beer cans and the cabin with smoke. They got up for the washrooms and Conrad slipped out to look for a cabin attendant. He picked out Max, the steward with a mincing step, and asked diffidently if he could visit the flight deck. He had chosen well and soon Conrad was following the tightly trousered bum through the curtain into First Class with its suitably expensive calm. He had time to notice that Alexa was in a window seat on the port side with her companion next to her.

Max tapped at the door of the flight deck and after a word of introduction, stood aside for Conrad to pass into the small, cramped space lit by the subdued orange glow of innumerable instruments. A large man in the captain's seat turned to hold out a hand.

'Welcome to the sharp end, Mr Aveling. I'm Peter Bushell and my colleagues tonight are Keith Curtis,' this with a wave to the First Officer who smiled a greeting, 'and beside you there is another Peter — Pete Grimes, who I hope knows where we are right now! Not much room in here I'm afraid, but it's always nice to have a visitor. Have you been in a 707 before?'

'Only once', said Conrad, 'but I have spent time in various helicopters and a fair few Hercules.

Actually, I'm a Captain too, but different and junior to you, Sir,' he produced his military warrant card and handed it to Bushell, adding 'I'm travelling to join my unit in Singapore. I believe I've got a problem. It's nothing to do with my job, but it is urgent and I need your help.'

The Captain stared at him and the other two assumed wary expressions. Finally, Bushell said, 'Well you're in here now so you'd best say your piece, but keep it short and don't move around. I don't care for deception on my aircraft.'

'Quite,' responded Conrad, 'I apologise but I felt I had no choice but to contact you this way.'

He went on to provide a concise summary of the background and the current position. There was a long pause when he had finished and the aircraft seemed to hang in space whilst digesting the information. Captain Bushell broke the silence.

'So, the bottom line is that you think an old girlfriend who just happens to be travelling on this aircraft just might be in a bit of trouble and that she just could be some sort of victim of the big black guy whose with her, even though right now she's slumbering like a baby in one of our first class seats. Is that about it, and what do you expect me to do with this story?'

Before he could answer, Pete Grimes piped up to comment.

'Better check it out, boss. We've only just had the abduction risk lecture.'

Bushell ignored him and said to his First Officer.

'Keith. Nip out and do a cabin tour, would you? Take your time and make it at least fifteen minutes. Give me a chance for a bit more of a talk with Captain Aveling here.'

'It's Conrad'.

'OK,' said Bushell, 'and Keith, if this is for real, I don't want the big guy alerted, so grab hold of young Max and put it about that it seems Conrad and Pete were at school together way back so they're going over a few old times. Tell Max to come back and collect Conrad when time's up.'

'She'll be right,' murmured Keith Curtis as he slipped out of the flight deck door, pulling on his uniform jacket as he left. Outside, he paused to smile at Miranda Longman who was in charge of first class and busy in the small galley area.

'Just going to do the rounds,' he whispered to her, and then in a louder voice which could be heard by first class passengers, 'I'm leaving the Captain a bit of space. Amazing coincidence but the passenger who just came up with Max knows Pete. Childhood mates. I've left them swapping stories for a while.'

He winked and moved on slowly up the central aisle of the aircraft. He saw that Alexa was dozing and maybe had the look of a girl a bit spaced out, but under the circumstances, he might be imagining things. By her side, the large man called Georges Eboli was very awake and watchful. He definitely did look tense, like a passenger with a fear of flying. Curtis smiled encouragingly at him and walked on to draw back the curtain into the economy cabin which he knew to be pretty much chock full. New Year's Day would not be every traveller's choice, but on these flights they topped up with assisted passage emigrants: if you wanted to start a new life, you went when you were told. Curtis kept relaxed as he chatted easily to passengers. It took him more than five minutes to reach the rear of the aircraft where he found Max and gave him the Captain's brief. Max nodded and glanced at his watch.

Meanwhile on the flight deck, Conrad was being grilled by Qantas Training Captain Peter Bushell, a veteran of flying and travel, also a shrewd judge of character. Connie told all he could about Alexa: her family, her history, their time together and what he knew of her doings over the last few years. He left nothing out but kept the account short and sharp.

They were interrupted by a sharp intake of breath from Pete Grimes as he digested a radio message. He jotted a note and passed it to his Captain who slumped back in his chair as he read it. Conrad steeled himself.

The Captain said, 'I'm going to read you this, Conrad, at my own initiative. It's from Qantas Flight Control at Kingsford Smith Airport Sydney, and therefore my boss,' he added laconically, 'and it reads BE AWARE. INFORMATION RECEIVED AND BELIEVED RELIABLE INDICATES FEMALE PASSENGER LABARRE FRENCH NATIONAL NOW ON AIRCRAFT DESTINATION BAHRAIN IS ABDUCTION VICTIM REF SI QS18H874NOV69. MAY BE LINKED TO MALE PASSENGER EBOLI AND/OR FRENCH NATIONAL NOT TRAVELLING CESTAC. RECOMMEND INVESTIGATE/ACT AT YOUR DISCRETION WITHOUT RISK TO AIRCRAFT OR ROUTE. BE AWARE. MESSAGE ENDS. OK. Well, I don't know how or where they got this, but it sure as hell supports your story. Now ...'

He broke off as the door opened. Keith Curtis was back. Bushell handed him the note.

'Christ Almighty,' he said softly as he finished, 'this is going to be bloody complicated'.

Bushell replied, 'let's take a couple of minutes to think this through, Keith. It might help us to concentrate if you explain it to Conrad who must be pretty confused.'

'Isn't it obvious? We have to speak to Alexa immediately and then take her on with us to ... well Singapore I guess and from there get her heading home.'

Keith Curtis answered him.

'No, Conrad, it's not that easy. I'll lay it out for you. You're right we need to get the girl in private and let her speak for herself. But remember. We've got suspicions, but zero proof. We have no warrant for action, we're not any sort of international police force and we're not dealing with a passenger who's underage or with a mental deficiency. She's not drunk or dangerous, no sort of threat to the safety of this aircraft. She's a paid up first class passenger and she's travelling with a guy who looks pretty damn competent. Assume that Eboli is well in on this and knows the ropes and his rights, he has brains and balls and Alexa is one big meal ticket to him. He's not going to admit to anything, plus he'll be a canny bugger. I bet even now he's just a bit worried about you being in here. He won't like anyone or anything that's different — routine to him spells normal equals safe and sure. If he gets a sniff of what he believes is trouble, he'll drug her up so she can't speak to us and he'll pull the big sob story that she's travel tired and sick.'

Conrad tried to protest, but Keith cut him off.

'Just hear me out. First off, this route is vital to Qantas. We fly it every day of the week, every week of the year and in both directions. Second, there's range: we can only go so far without stopping to refuel. We have to have a staging post in the Middle East and for us, that filling station is Bahrain. Third, Bahrain is past being a suburb of the Poms' colonial empire. They make their own rules now. In particular, we can only disembark passengers in Bahrain. They don't allow us to pick up new fares on stopover and we can't take on further someone who is pre-booked to get off. If you want to do that, you've got to get out, check in to Bahrain, do all your formalities and then start over on a new flight and with a different airline. You can fly in with our mob, but you can't fly out.'

He paused long enough for Conrad to respond.

'OK, I understand, but surely if we, or rather, if you brief the authorities in Bahrain, won't they permit an exception for an emergency?'

Keith Curtis gave him a wry smile, but allowed his Captain to take up the commentary.

'Conrad, if you imagine how much money and risk someone has invested in this abduction attempt, it's a hop of logic to guess that he must have heaps of money and a barrel full of influence. He'll have experience, power and passion. Sum it all up, this aircraft has to land in Bahrain and we've got to follow their instructions. At the same time, there's some guy down there who will be determined to get his hands on the flesh he's paid for and will have the clout to make sure we can't stand in his way.'

Conrad Aveling thought furiously to find a way out. He said,

'I understand. But you haven't said we now give up and simply chuck her out?'

'Too right,' Bushell replied immediately. 'Look, first priority is to get you talking to Alexa and hope she can talk back. She's a lucky lady. There was someone out there to send us warning, there's we two who know how things are done, plus she has you on board and no way the bad guys could have planned on that.'

He gave Conrad a hard look before continuing, 'I don't expect you to give me detail, but I reckon you're not quite the straightforward soldier. Maybe have a bit of specialist training which could be of use here?' He raised an eyebrow and Conrad responded with a positive nod.

'OK,' said Bushell, 'How do we get close to Alexa? Do we try Miranda and go for a bit of girly chat with Conrad in the background?'

Keith Curtis cut in immediately.

'Not that. Too many uncertainties and it leaves the black guy alone and worrying. No, better to take him out for a while and Max can do that a treat. He helped me a couple of months back with some over drinking rowdies.'

'Fair enough, Keith, I'll go with that. What do you say Conrad?'

'I trust Keith's judgment.' Conrad meant it and he could not have chosen a better comment.

'Pete,' said Bushell turning to his Navigator, 'go out and find Max. Tell him to come up here in ten. No longer.'

'Will do, Skipper, and we're now one hour, thirty-five out from touch down.'

The flight deck door closed behind Grimes as Peter Bushell addressed the other two.

'Let's make our plans. Conrad, we need to brief you on Bahrain International Terminal. I'll hand over to Keith for that. He knows the place much better than I do. And make sure you listen bloody carefully. While you're in there, we won't be able to help. We'll be so far behind we won't hear the band playing.'

Time past quickly. Max joined them and Conrad was impressed by his calm ease as he took in his instructions. There was just time for a brief handshake and a murmur of good luck, then Conrad was following Max back into economy. He scrambled into his seat beside the Australian farmers who were now snoring.

Max turned on his heel and returned up the aisle, entering the first class galley with a blown kiss and a cheery greeting to Miranda.

'Sorry about this love', he announced, 'but Captain's orders'.

Max swept up a tray holding a bowl of soup. He added a large glass of red wine and bent down to release the lace on one of his winkle picker shoes. Then he burst out of the galley and advanced a few steps up the aisle, gaining speed as he went. Then he proceeded to 'trip' over his loose shoe, depositing his tray and its contents all over Georges Eboli.

Eboli sprang up with an oath, his crutch burning from the hot soup, his crisp white shirt and expensive Hermes tie ruined by the explosion of best Australian claret. The neighbouring passengers looked appalled as Max struggled up from the floor, distraught and gesticulating his apologies. Miranda appeared with hot towels and comfort. Eboli was persuaded into the galley while Max fetched some replacement clothing. As they disappeared, Alexa felt a firm hand on her shoulder and looked up to see Conrad. He beckoned, she followed with Miranda behind as all three processed right to the back of the plane. They stood inside the rear galley and Alexa fell into Conrad's arms with a gasp of relief.

He held her tight to him but wasted no time. They had little of it. He spoke into her ear and his voice came to her, soft, familiar, calming.

'Alexa, what's going on here? You're in some sort of trouble, yes? I didn't imagine it? You did send me our message?'

'Oh yes, Connie, yes I did and thank God for you being here. I feel just bloody — all spaced out and confused. I know I've been on drugs, but I couldn't tell you what. The big black man I'm travelling with, he's taking me to Bahrain to wait for Thierry before we go on for our holiday in Singapore. I'm excited about that.'

Her voice started to slur and drift away, but she caught herself and shuddered within the encirclement of his arms.

'There's something wrong, Connie. It's all such a mess. I don't just feel ill, I feel frightened.'

She shivered violently, but with a sudden mood change seemed to relax as she added, 'but I don't feel scared with you. I always feel safe with you.'

She slumped again as if she was falling asleep in his arms. Conrad recognised the symptoms. Some form of barbiturate which was keeping her either side of consciousness. He shook her slightly, and pressed his fingers into her upper arms.

'Don't go to sleep on me, Alexa. Just two more questions and then you can rest again until we get into Bahrain. First thing, has your companion given you a pill, or a drink or any injection since we left London?'

'Yes, Connie, but only two,' her voice was back to a slur, 'just my normal pink ones while we were in the airport — and maybe there's been one more since.'

'OK,' Conrad kept his voice reassuring; 'now I'll tell you what to do when we're in Bahrain Airport. Listen very carefully. It's simple, but you must do exactly what I tell you.'

'Alright then, Mr big, important man.' She drew back and smiled at him, then threw her arms around his neck and pressed herself to him provocatively. Conrad did not resist: he knew that this was his only chance to get through to her. He hugged her more tightly to him and whispered one simple instruction over and over again. Then he held her a little away from him and put one hand gently under her chin, making her look at him.

'Repeat what I've told you to do.'

Alexa fixed him with huge flirtatious eyes and did so. She was word perfect. He was relieved, but far from certain sure that it would stick. He made the decision to leave it at that. There was too little time and too many risks in trying for more. But he did ask a final question.

'When does your friend arrive — the man from Paris — Thomas did you say?'

'No. Not Thomas. He's called Thierry. Thierry Cestac. He's always reliable. He'll be there.'

This was the crowning proof. Certainly she was spaced out and definitely scared. But 'Cestac': that was the name in the message from Qantas HQ. The crisis for Alexa was real. Conrad looked past Alexa at Miranda standing there behind them. He mouthed a message.

'Confirm up front. It's genuine. We'll act as planned. Now, please take her back.'

Miranda took over and steered the comatose Alexa back to her seat. Georges Eboli was just in time to see her settling in as he appeared in some clean but unflattering clothes. He sat beside her, demanding to know where she'd been. But the girl was genuinely out of it by then, incapable of coherent reply. Georges scowled and tried to stop worrying. He could not shake off a feeling of disquiet. Finally, he stood up and leaving Alexa to her sleep, he paced up and down the full length of the Boeing jet, sometimes pausing and peering at his fellow passengers. He saw Conrad, stuck away inside his burly farmers, and recognised him for the flight deck visitor. He doesn't look too threatening now, thought Eboli to himself, not pressed in like that and snoring with his mouth open. Just another geeky air freak, Georges decided and returned more confidently to his seat. Conrad watched him go through slitted eyes and was glad to recognise a little spring in the black man's step.

The pink of an Arab dawn began to penetrate the cabin and the passengers could feel the slowing of the aircraft. They heard the familiar tones of Captain Bushell as he announced their imminent arrival into Bahrain. At the controls, Keith Curtis was flying the plane and he spoke to Air Traffic Control. Qantas QF 002 on time and on plan. All would be ready for them, he was reassured, ninety minutes on the ground for refuelling and cabin cleaning. Passengers disembarking in Bahrain to leave the aircraft first. Then all others to the transit lounge. Only those with Transit Pass or Flight Crew permitted to re-enter the aircraft. No joining passengers permitted. All the usual drill, but it had never sounded so ominous.

Conrad caught a view of sea, sand, scrub and black tarmac unwinding beneath them before the slight jolt of a smooth landing, the noise of engines in reverse thrust, the effect of braking. Then came the slow process of turn and taxi while they listened to Keith Curtis with more details of arrival, temperature and local time.

Quite some delay, and then the doors opened front and rear. The passengers started to file out, stepping down to the parking apron and gasping as the temperature hit them. Conrad took his place in the line, and received his yellow transit card from a Bahraini airport official, a fixed smile of welcome on his face. He followed the flow of fellow passengers towards the terminal building. Eboli and Alexa were already out of sight but he was expecting that. First class carries its privileges, but he could see no sign of a welcoming party actually on the tarmac which had been one of his fears. They had yet to start unloading the hold luggage. It was essential to their plan that this process should take longer than normal and Keith Curtis had promised a delay.

Conrad walked into the transit lounge and made directly for a spot which gave him a clear view out over the apron towards the parked Qantas jet. He pulled a paperback novel from his pocket and settled to read it. He had about an hour to wait.

He would have been relieved if he could have seen Alexa. She was standing quietly beside Georges Eboli as he made polite conversation to a diminutive figure beside him. The small man had approached them as they were waiting by the luggage area. He made a charming self-introduction and flashed a beaming smile at Alexa. He was Mr Riaz, Comptroller of your host's household, delighted and honoured to welcome you both, responsible for all arrangements for your comfort and entitled to the special airport pass which he was now exhibiting. Alexa noted this old world gentility, touched a little with self-importance. Mr Riaz was determined to put them at their ease, offering drinks while they waited and apologies for the delay. Outside, he had more staff to help, plus a van for the luggage as well as the limousine in which he would whisk them to the fine house which awaited them less than an hour's drive away. What a magical setting it enjoyed, Mr Riaz rolled his eyes dramatically: quite beautiful and almost new. They had been in occupation scarcely a year, although he had himself been in his position as Comptroller for much longer. A Pakistani by birth, he had been living here for almost ten years. Mr Riaz was in Arab dress which suited his small stature. He wore a full beard, neatly trimmed. He kept his small feet pressed closely together, his hands clasped in front of him. Alexa found him innocuous, even engaging and she began to wonder if this whole thing was not a false alarm, whether perhaps Thierry might appear at any moment, flashing his elegance. With a slight smile on her lips, she unconsciously struck a pose and ran a hand through her shoulder length ash blonde hair. This caught the attention of Mr Riaz who turned the full beam of his admiring attention on her, murmuring how truly entranced his Master was going to be to meet her. Something in his bland words and the rapacious flash in his dark little eyes sent shivers down her spine. She was suddenly afraid again. She tried to push down the panic and listened to Georges express his regrets that he was so unsuitably attired due to the idiot steward on the plane. Mr Riaz smiled encouragingly.

Conrad could only sit and wait. He kept his head in his book and managed to read the script and turn the pages. The clock in his head ticked round towards their action hour. After fifty minutes on his uncomfortable plastic sofa, Conrad snapped shut his book, stood and stretched before commencing a casual wander closer to the big windows. His timing was perfect. He watched Keith Curtis descend the front mobile steps, walk round under the inner port engine, and pause to remove his cap and scratch his head. This was the cue to go.

Conrad made his way towards the door marked 'Toilets'. He didn't hurry, neither did he meander. Beyond the entrance was the expected division between 'Men' and 'Women'. He entered the gents and locked himself in the middle of five cubicles. He looked up to see a simple roof made of plastic panels carried on a lattice framework which would not bear weight. But just below the roof and securely mounted to the block wall in front of him protruded the solid iron stanchions which supported the lavatory header tank. There was no pedestal, but a white tile surrounded hole in the ground. Nothing daunted, Conrad gazed up at the right hand stanchion while he composed himself and relaxed his muscles. He crouched with his head turned upward and his eyes fixed on his target stanchion. He came up out of this squat position in a long, fluid leap, right arm punched vertically above his head so that at the top of his jump, his hand locked around the stanchion. He relaxed for a moment, swinging in a gentle arc around the pivot of his arm which took his body weight without effort.

He went on then, bringing up his left hand onto the second stanchion and pulling himself higher, using legs and knees to gain purchase from the solid downpipe which ran from the cistern to the ground. Then he could position his left arm along the top of the cistern to take his weight and provide balance while his right hand explored further upwards. The roof panels rested on their frame. He pushed up the one above him and manoeuvred it onto its neighbour so he could move his right hand to grasp the top of the breeze block wall. From there, he used his strength to haul his body through the gap and into a crouch on top of the wall, which was solid but narrow. He removed the adjacent roof panel giving access to the cubicle on the other side of the wall. He slipped through to swing from the brackets in reverse procedure to his ascent. He dropped to the floor, flushed the cistern and adjusted his clothes.

So far, so good. Conrad left the cubicle, finding that he was alone in the gents' block. He made his exit, merging into the wider entrance and on into the arrivals hall. Ten yards in front of him was a writing shelf set at standing height with piles of landing cards. Conrad made for it with a confident walk.

The place was hardly bustling. No other flights had landed that morning, and Peter Bushell had given him the passenger count, only twenty-three including Eboli and Alexa, of those leaving Qantas in Bahrain. He could see various groups of uniformed officials around the large hall and at points between, plain clothed cleaners shuffled lethargic mops. All the arriving passengers had completed immigration, heath and police. He could see them in a group at the extreme end of the hall with the tall black figure of Eboli prominent amongst them. Further away, he could see a group standing behind the Customs barrier, likely a welcoming party with two tall men of European descent and one woman. Also a fourth figure who stood out: he was immense in stature and bulk, swathed in Arab dress.

Conrad left the desk and moved towards the group of passengers. He willed Alexa to turn and face in his direction. Sight of him was to be her trigger for action, to follow the single, simple instruction he had given her in the plane. As he walked, he eyed the gallery above and at the back of the hall. It seemed empty, but the sole occupant had been careful to conceal himself in the shadows of a supporting roof pillar. He was a man of above average height and slim build, impeccably dressed in a dark suit and carrying a small crocodile attaché case. His wealth was apparent in every detail. His fine features and dark complexion revealed his provenance from this region. His rapt attention was concentrated on the vision who was Alexa. He was shuddering as he watched her every move and expression. Thus far, she exceeded his expectations. The client made the colossal effort to retreat to the staircase which would take him down to the front of the airport, through the crowds of merchants and beggars and welcome wishers and on to his chauffeured car which would follow the limousine to his secure villa.

Standing by Georges and listening to Riaz continue his chatter, Alexa was taut. She had so often turned her head to look that she dare not do so again. But she must and finally she did, then blinking and looking again to be sure in her tortured mind that it really was Connie standing there, out in the open and studying some piece of paper in his hand. Alexa put a hand up to her mouth and swallowed twice, stifling a sudden urge to scream with relief. She felt bile rising in her throat. She saw the luggage approaching and was inspired to speak.

'Georges', she said, 'I've been standing here long enough and I feel hot and tired and grubby. Fetch me that small case of mine please, and I will go to the Ladies to tidy up a bit.'

Eboli started to protest but Mr Riaz chimed in to support her and to demonstrate his proficiency in French as he declared it a good idea which would cost them little further delay. He turned to summon help with the raise of his elegant little arm. Immediately, the single woman and the huge man detached themselves from the welcoming committee and were waved through the barrier by the customs official.

Conrad viewed this with concern. It amounted to three against one with Alexa as baggage. He could manage, but he did want to keep it discreet and it didn't help that he was now the only obvious passenger still milling about whilst the others collected their bags. He withdrew again to his writing table and began to scribble furiously. Alexa was the first to pass him, followed by the white woman minder who looked East European, fit and strong, not to be underestimated. Mentally, Conrad christened her Olga. Just a few steps behind came Georges Eboli, toting a suitcase and puffing as he walked. By his side paced the colossus whom Conrad named Black Beauty. Close up, this guy bothered Conrad less. He was big, but too bulky and looked far short of fit.

Conrad slouched after them into the common entrance to the washrooms, walked down the hallway and entered the Gents. He found Black Beauty pacing the floor while Eboli stood in front of a basin. The three of them were alone. Conrad caught a glare from Beauty as he stepped up to the urinals, then a shorter stop before a basin before making his exit. Eboli would be five minutes more and expecting Alexa to take longer. Conrad had time, but not to waste. He stood for a few seconds in the common hallway, appreciating its gloom and reckoning that the watchers at the customs barrier would have trouble in seeing him. But they did know that he had gone in there and they would be watching to see him come out again. Action time. He hunched his shoulders, giving himself a slight stoop as he crossed the hallway and pushed open the door to the Ladies, hesitating as he entered.

All the cubicle doors were open except one: Alexa must be behind it. Olga was standing to his right, resting her back against a line of basins with mirrors above. She gesticulated to tell him he was in the wrong place and should be across the hallway. Conrad gave her a befuddled nod and turned to the entrance door which he had allowed to close behind him, pushing at it when he should have pulled. Olga gave a grunt of exasperation as she pushed herself away from her basin rest and moved to grasp the door handle, to get rid of this oaf as soon as possible.

Standing beside her, Conrad struck. His left hand moved to join Olga's on the door pull while the right circled behind her head. With all the force he could muster from this short take off, he swept head and door together. Olga gave a grunt of pain and he could feel her stunned. She might have passed out but he couldn't take the risk. He took her sagging weight in his arms, spun her round and ran her head first into the tiled wall opposite. Bloody mess, inert body.

He let Olga fall to the floor and crossed to Alexa's cubicle, knocking lightly.

'Open, Alexa, it's me.' He heard a sob of relief mingled with fear as the bolt scratched back and the cubicle door swung open. Alexa was sitting there on her throne, fully dressed, knees pressed together, feet wide apart. She looked up, tears starting to stream down, shoulders hunched and shaking. He could take in the signs easily enough. Alexa was collapsing. He stepped forward and lifted her into his arms. He held her tightly to him and whispered quietly, sounding calm although he was wound like a spring with the urgency of their timing.

He said, 'Just do exactly what I say and we'll be fine.'

As if on cue, the entrance door behind him hissed and he whipped round to see Black Beauty enter. Conrad was never to know what had alerted the colossus to check on his partner. It didn't matter. The big man took in the sight of Olga in a crumpled heap, Aveling and Alexa embracing. He drew a knife from beneath his robes and rushed straight in, the huge bull figure threatening to eclipse them. Conrad felt relief. Beauty should have retreated to raise the alarm, and then they would have been in real trouble. He pushed Alexa away and she flopped back on her loo seat, looking out on the scene through eyes as wide as saucers.

Conrad jumped forward to meet the assault, twisting his body and ducking his head as the vicious knife scythed just above him and folds of Beauty's robe swept across his face. He smelt rancid body odour as he kicked out sharply, connecting with the Arab's knee which collapsed under the hurtling weight. Beauty was face down on the floor, sliding past Alexa's cubicle, screaming fury and hardly hurt with his knife still clasped in his right hand. Conrad whirled round and kicked him twice more in the side of the head, aiming for the ear. He dropped onto his back, broad as a boat but flabby beneath his knee which he settled under the back of the neck. Ignoring the outstretched arm which flailed vainly with the knife, Conrad linked the fingers of both hands through the beard and under the chin. He used his strength to pull back sharply against the pressure of his knee. The resulting snap was instant and audible to Alexa. Episode over as reflexes juggled with the big body in its dying and the knife clattered onto the tiles of the floor.

Alexa was catatonic. He took her by the arms and stood her by the door of the adjoining cubicle. He hefted the big body from the floor and hauled it into Alexa's cubicle to lie draped over the pedestal. He fetched the much lighter weight of Olga and dumped her face down over Beauty. Back out to fetch Alexa, pushing her in front of him and telling her to stand still and close her eyes. He bolted the door behind them and climbed over Beauty's body to stand on Olga, from which height he could stretch up to reach the roof panels. Their exit became simply the reverse of his entry. Move a panel, up onto the breeze block wall, move another panel. Now for the tricky bit. Alexa still stood motionless below him, her eyes screwed tight shut, rigid with shock. Conrad slipped back down to stand beside her, lifted her with his arms wrapped around her knees until he could place her feet on Olga's back. He stretched to push her face towards the wall and held her there with one hand while he scrambled up beside her. He forced her hands around the cistern pipe and went on up himself, turning on top of the wall to balance on his stomach, the lower half of his body sticking through into transit whilst his arms dangled down towards Alexa. He could just reach her and she managed to place one hand in his. Then, for her, it was like going up in a lift.

He dropped Alexa onto the floor on the other side and steered her before him out of the cubicle. To his relief, Miranda was there and waiting, poised between the run of basins and the exit door. She was ashen, her hands clinging to the handle of a small Qantas crew bag which she ripped open, pulling out a uniform and shoes. Alexa was motionless, perhaps the best help she could have given them. Conrad pulled off her smart Paris dress and Miranda struggled her into the uniform, lifting one foot at a time to get on the shoes and finishing with the airline cap crammed on her head.

Miranda linked her arm tightly through Alexa's and carried the flight bag. She opened the door, looked out and nodded to Conrad. He moved in front of the two girls and left the Ladies, moving in a diagonal across the transit lounge to distance himself from them before walking up behind the few passengers who were waiting to go through onto the hot tarmac. He reached into his pocket for his passport and transit card. Behind him, he heard the click of the girls' heels on the tiled floor. Miranda was chattering brightly. They hardly broke step as they passed through the separate barrier reserved for crew members.

Conrad passed out of transit and walked under the broiling sun to the aircraft. He took his turn, climbed the steps and settled back into his seat beside the Aussie farmers. He closed his eyes but remained electric inside. He had hoped to spirit Alexa away, not to rub out a couple of objectors in the process. If they found the evidence quickly, they would keep the aircraft on the ground and take their time with a search. Conrad balled his fists in his lap, forced himself to stillness, longed to hear the distinctive whistle of four jet engines spooling up, willed the Boeing to start moving.

Back in the arrivals hall, Mr Riaz had waited after Eboli and the girl walked off with their minders. He knew they would take some time, but after ten minutes he felt a pricking concern and moved quietly to check things. He walked nimbly on his small feet down the length of the hall, bowing politely to various officials as they stood at their posts. He reached the lavatory block and went into the Gents to find Georges Eboli looking renewed. Mr Riaz complimented him gravely and asked about Jamil, 'the large man who accompanied you down here.'

Georges looked at himself in the mirror as he gave a final tweak to his tie.

'I heard him leave when I was shaving a few minutes ago. I imagine he's waiting outside'.

'Very good,' said Mr Riaz, 'I will await you in the hall.'

He stepped back through the entrance with alarm bells going off in his head. He crossed the corridor and pushed open the door to the Ladies. The empty room yawned at him. One cubicle was closed and locked against his push. He looked around and saw Jamil's knife discarded on the floor. Riaz gasped, took a firm grip on himself and started to compute in his very sharp brain the most likely explanation and the best course of action now open to him.

He went back into the hallway and allowed the door of the Ladies to swing shut. At that moment, Georges Eboli emerged into the hall.

'I have found Jamil,' Mr Riaz said calmly, 'a policeman has informed me that he was satisfied you had all you required and he went to morning prayers. He will rejoin us shortly. And now, I will accompany you and we will pass through customs together. Then, Mr Eboli, you will have truly arrived in Bahrain.'

'Surely we must wait for Miss Labarre.'

'Oh, you are too late for that. It is rare indeed for a lady to complete her toilette before a gentleman, but it has been so on this occasion. She returned to our group and I have already escorted her through.'

Mr Riaz beamed at Georges, who shrugged and resumed his walk. He was feeling restored and confident. The two men carried on their way to the customs post. When they stopped for Eboli's documents to be checked, Riaz spoke to one of the two European men waiting at the barrier and then he turned to Georges.

'Please proceed with my staff who will escort you to our limousine, Mr Eboli. I will delay you only a few minutes, but I must pay my respects to our Airport Director before I leave. It is our custom, you know.'

Georges nodded, content to follow his porter and a gaggle of retainers as they made their way towards the smart cars parked in the reserved lane outside the terminal building. Mr Riaz crooked his finger at the tough Russian named Gorki, and together they walked quickly back to the lavatory block and into the Ladies. The closed cubicle still held its secrets but Gorki made short work of the door and the grim burdens lying across the pedestal were exposed.

Mr Riaz was a resourceful man. The basic explanation was obvious. No time to waste now in working out the details. The girl must by now be back on the plane and whoever had helped her, probably that guy with the landing card, must be there with her having taken out two of his prime assets. The priority was to stop the departure. With the plane anchored to the ground by red tape and edict from Air Traffic Control they could sort this out, secure the girl and go to work on her accomplice: there would be time to see if Eboli had been in on it. But once Qantas took off, proof, retribution and the 'product' would be gone forever and there would indeed be hell to pay from his Master.

All of this whistled through his head. He gave Gorki a simple set of instructions. Stay here, do not move or let anyone in under any circumstances. Wait for my return. A curt nod in response and then Riaz was scuttling off on his short legs. He knew exactly what he was doing. He couldn't issue an order to the airport management. He didn't have the blood or the breeding, not even the nationality. He had the brains, however, and he knew where to get the clout. The Master was qualified and well respected too, even by those who knew him well enough to overlook his peccadilloes.

Mr Riaz knew exactly where to find him. He would be in the upstairs gallery, concealed behind a pillar, pawing the ground and just waiting for her to walk the last few yards into his clutches. Mr Riaz sprinted up the stairs and was horrified to find he was wrong. The watching point had been abandoned and the Client had sought out his car and chauffeur, relocating into the public car park from where he could monitor progress unobserved.

Mr Riaz dashed out of the terminal in search of the Master's car. He expected to see it right outside but there was no sign. Desperate and despairing, he cast his net wider and finally located his Master's Cadillac. As he scuttled towards it, he heard the thunder of engine power and looked up to see the Kangaroo symbol sail over his head. Mr Riaz stopped to vomit on the scorching tarmac. Allah alone knew what would happen next.

It went worst for Georges Eboli. They did not believe his protestations, nor did they wish to. Georges succumbed to merciful heart failure about a week later in one of the dungeon cells beneath the Master's remote villa. He first endured relentless physical abuse and degradation, much of it orchestrated by Mr Riaz who was desperate to redirect the incandescent wrath of his deviant Master.

On the Qantas jet, Alexa was in a state of gibbering collapse. They drugged her and cuddled her, but had neither the knowledge nor medication to provide lasting assistance. Peter Bushell took a critical personal decision. At Karachi, where they handed over to another crew, he chose to leave Keith Curtis and the rest. He continued as a passenger in the aircraft, watching over Alexa and sitting by her all the way to Sydney.

Conrad Aveling left the plane in Singapore, on plan and on time. He was horrified by Alexa's condition but he had no skills to help her now, and no one to whom he could turn. He had to trust Peter Bushell. He said nothing of the Bahrain incident to his brother officers and the men of his unit. He did, however, take the first opportunity to ring home. He had one task for his mother and she acted urgently. Lady Aveling got hold of David Heaven to say he must tell Alexa's parents that she was in Australia, to be contacted through Peter Bushell — number provided. The Labarres were mystified but quick to comply. Two days later, they flew from Paris to Sydney.

Kingston Offenbach also spoke to David, and filled in the background of his chance involvement. He would not say more, except to comment on the providence which had placed Connie in the right place at the right time.

And in France, in deep Dordogne countryside at the end of February, Thierry Cestac was feeling well fed and rested. He returned to Paris and to his house in the Latin Quarter. There was no message from Georges Eboli. There was no message from Alexa Labarre. He contacted his banker and confirmed that no final payment from Bahrain had reached his account. Cestac was nothing if not a realist. The absence of news spoke volumes. Something had gone wrong or just maybe he had been double crossed by Mr Riaz. Whichever, he could do little more. He might get the chance of revenge on Riaz, but the girl and Eboli were gone forever. It was a pity about the money.

DAVID HEAVEN — 1970

November of that same year was a watershed month for David. He spent nearly three weeks in southern Africa, starting in Mauritius where he signed a contract with a sugar cane company before travelling on to Johannesburg. There, he went to see Piet Soldemeyer as planned.

Soldemeyer was a middle man, his outfit even smaller than Kirchoff and Son. He had good connections in the mining sector and he wanted supply out of Europe for materials handling equipment. The introduction to him had come via a mysterious figure from Sol's past, a man called Gluchamheig whom he had met 'on a train'. This Glucky was in costume jewellery but had a chance to get into industrial diamonds, importing from Piet Soldemeyer — except he knew nothing of import/export which is where Kirchoff and Son came in. There was huge volume and money at stake, hence Sol's excitement.

Piet turned out to be about David's age, maybe a few years older, and they got on well enough together. They spent a couple of days talking through the basic business, eating and drinking together in the evenings and David had started to wonder when they were going to get to the diamonds when Piet had broken it to him over a late night whisky. It was all to do with people way up north in South West Africa.

'I've set it all up for you, man. You can check it out for yourself and report back properly to your boss and the diamond buyer guy, Glucky isn't it?'

David nodded as his eyes wandered round the crowded, noisy club in which the thumping music was keeping their conversation discreet.

'Only take a week or maybe less. Meanwhile, I'll be seeing

the mining guys here so we can talk some turkey when you get back and then you'll be flying on home with a fistful of orders.'

He didn't wait for a reply, getting up to push his way to the bar for more drinks. David wasn't going to argue. He was excited by the prospect of this trip into the unknown and anyway; it sounded necessary if he was going to get any further with this diamond business by which Sol was setting such store.

Next day, he took a flight from Johannesburg to Windhoek. He was met by the character Piet had told him to expect, a great bull of a guy who introduced himself as Klaus Wallisch and took him to a small hotel for that night. Wallisch was taciturn on the short drive, saying that he would explain more during the long journey they had to make the following day. David should have a quick meal in the hotel and get an early night. He must be ready to leave at 6 am. David wasn't. He woke at midnight in a muck sweat and knew he was going down with a fever. With luck, it wasn't too bad, he told himself and nothing he hadn't experienced many times before in Africa. He had pills and potions with him. He would just need fresh water and time in bed. They would be delayed, but too bad.

That wasn't the reaction of Wallisch when he crashed into his room at first light. He was in a fair state as he took in David's condition and he made for an intimidating sight. With much swearing and frustration, he finally conceded that David could rest up for the day but warned they would have to drive all night to regain the schedule. He was calmer, however, when he returned in the early evening to find David better, but still pretty weak. Wallisch remained insistent that they had to go, but he gave David plenty of time to get his things together and he followed this with an outline brief as they sat over a cup of tea before leaving.

Wallisch seemed surprised that Piet Soldemeyer had said so little. He was silent for a moment, then gave a grunt as he ran horny hard hands over his grizzled, clean shaven face and scalp before speaking with his heavy, Afrikaans accent. He gave David a concise background, concentrated on politics and mostly on

SWAPO — the South-West Africa People's Organization. It was loosely formed in late '66, he explained, and had developed into a fully fledged guerrilla group with a clear agenda, nothing less than full independence from South Africa.

'You can read all that in any library,' said Wallisch, fixing David with his gimlet eye, 'what you won't find is how organised SWAPO is already, and how determined. The South Africans don't want to launder their linen in public, but they're fighting an increasingly tough war and the name of their game is to stop arms getting through to us. And I do mean 'us'. SWAPO isn't a Black African movement, it's mixed race and I am myself a member of the Command Council, in charge of the north of this territory which will be called Namibia when we've won'.

David felt a chill on his backbone which had nothing to do with fever. He realised that he was being given information which this man would kill to protect and Wallisch gave a bleak smile of understanding before continuing.

'We're expecting a long struggle. We've got the men, and we've got the women we need: we've all got commitment. But we have to keep chipping away. Right now, we're just a thorn in the side of the South African defence force and we have to become a proper combatant. We can't do that with hunting rifles and Bushmen blowpipes. We need some serious weapons which we can't get from the South, but we can bring in from the East coast through friends in Zambia. Then there's the money. If we could pay in blood, we'd manage. If we could pay in Rand, then not so hard: we can rob and extort enough. But that won't do for you guys. We know you operate only for US dollars. So we started thinking and came up with another idea, and that's why you're here now, Mr Heaven: to meet the man who may be our partner and paymaster for us both.'

David opened his mouth to respond. He was horrified: Wallisch clearly believed that Kirchoffs were is the arms supply business, and was acting, presumably, on information received from Gluchamheig via Piet Soldemeyer. David needed to put him right, but instantly he realised that he couldn't do that.

In that snap summary from Wallisch, he'd been given facts which put him at big risk. If he tried to take himself out of the picture, well, that's exactly what would happen to him. So he temporised, asking how Piet came into this.

Wallisch allowed himself another brief speech.

'I was born in the Steilrand Mountains,' he said, 'outside a small town called Okauwe. My family trekked up over a hundred years ago. I took on running our farm when I'd just turned fifteen with my grandfather to guide me. My father was burned to death in his tank with Rommel at Torbruk. The Soldemeyers too have history in these parts. Piet's brother ranches outside Rundu near the Caprivi Strip which gives access to Botswana and Zambia. The property can support only one family so Piet went south to live in Johannesburg. Piet's a fully paid up member of SWAPO so he's valuable to us as a resident in the heart of the enemy camp. But he has to be careful. If discovered by the authorities, he'd be straight down to the interrogation centre and he wouldn't come out alive.'

David made to ask more but Wallisch cut him off.

'Time to go. I'll tell you more on the way.'

There were thirteen in the party, including David. Wallisch had two other whites with him and nine blacks. All were armed to the teeth, and had little to say to David or to each other. They travelled in a ten ton ex-military truck, a Mercedes four wheel drive. One of the whites drove and David was put in the cab alongside him for the first stint. They made good time, heading just about due north. There was no tarmac outside Windhoek but the dirt road was wide and straight. There was hardly any other traffic and the driver slowed for nothing except to light another cigarette. There was no conversation.

Promptly at midnight, they stopped for a break. Somebody brewed tea, there was a container of sandwiches and strips of biltong — dried meat. Four of the blacks, with help from the driver, got stuck into refuelling the truck from jerry cans. David wandered into the bush for a call of nature. No one took notice. There was nowhere to go. When he returned to the group, there was time for more conversation with Wallisch. They had a cup of coffee together, leaning against the front bumper of the truck as it stood foursquare in the middle of that dusty track.

'We're driving into Angola, Mr Heaven, and you should know something about what's going on there. Portugal may still be running the country but there's a resistance group now. It's called UNITA and led by a man named Jonas Savimbi. He founded UNITA six years ago to rise against the Portuguese and win independence. Right now, he's not achieving much more than to make himself a nuisance but he's come a fair way in a short time. He's built a following and quite an arsenal. He's got most of this by ambushing the Portuguese military and plundering the Benguela railway which carries supplies, money and diamonds.

'SWAPO and UNITA have things in common. Neither of us is after the territory of the other. We both want ownership of where we already live. We both need arms. Savimbi has plenty of money and can get more. But he has no supplier contacts and no one to train his people. As I've told you, we in SWAPO lack finance but we can guarantee supply and training. So there's our deal. UNITA funds, SWAPO buys, delivers and trains. Savimbi is the bagman and you need to meet him.'

The time had ticked round to 1 am. They climbed back in the truck for a further five hours, finishing on bush tracks and slower going. The other team were already at the meeting point. There were a few more of them, maybe two dozen in all, but scruffier and less well equipped. They had squashed into three old Peugeot pick ups and a Land Rover. The rendezvous was in a grassy depression and all around there was the same view clear to the horizon. Miles of empty bush land, no habitation, endless scrub waving in the breeze with a few stands of trees dotted about. David couldn't even make out the track which had brought them in: he felt like a first explorer.

The two groups stood looking at each other, about fifty yards apart. It seemed like a stalemate. At length, the door of the Land Rover opened and Jonas Savimbi emerged. It couldn't have been anyone else. He was a big man, six three or four with a heavy build and the power of his personality was immediately obvious to David. He strode over with a broad grin on his face and gave a warm welcome to Klaus Wallisch. Then he turned to David, offering thanks for coming and apologies for the inconvenient location. The experience was surreal to David, standing there and thinking that charisma is an overworked word, but Jonas Savimbi had it in spades.

They didn't dally there for long. Savimbi was wearing a form of battle dress and he produced an immense cigar which he lit while Wallisch went through a weapons wish list which filled three foolscap pages, highlighting some items in a commentary to Savimbi and passing each page to David. It was easy to guess what was coming next. Savimbi fixed him with a magnetic stare as he spoke in perfect English.

'Now Mr Heaven, please provide us with an estimate of the price of such a shipment.'

David knew he dared not prevaricate and he replied confidently.

'I need to do some detail work, of course, and it will depend on the means of payment, especially if we are talking diamonds. But I'd say between three and five million. US dollars.'

There was no immediate reaction from either Savimbi or Wallisch. David just stood there, the pages of the shopping list hanging from his hand and the anxiety mounting at the gamble he was taking. In truth, he hadn't a clue, didn't even know the purpose of some items specified but he reckoned that he had to bluff it out. There was no way that he wanted to be returned to Wallisch, exposed as a fraud. He was remembering also what Wallisch had told him in advance. If first impressions rested well, Savimbi would invite him to his bush Headquarters for more discussion and would arrange for his journey back to South Africa.

The seconds passed and David could feel the sweat break on his face. He willed himself to stand straight and still: his relief must have been palpable as Savimbi issued his invitation with a broad smile and a pat on the back.

Wallisch was quick to depart with his men. He had a quick handshake for David, saying,

'Good so far, and we'll depend on your conversation at his camp. You won't see me again, but go to Soldemeyer as soon as you get back to Jo'burg. He'll be waiting for you and will know what to do next.'

Then Savimbi walked David to his Land Rover and they left immediately, one of the pick ups in front and two behind. The bush grass was long and the vehicles much lower than the Mercedes truck, so David could see nothing except the narrow track which took them northwest and deeper into Angola. The journey took a couple of hours.

Savimbi's camp came as a surprise. It was bigger and better organised than David had expected, with a number of substantially built bungalows spread out at random. They stopped at one which was Savimbi's house and office in one. It was brick built with a thatched roof and a wide veranda running all around. A water storage tank stood up behind it, and there were tended flower beds on either side of the steps running up to the front door over which was pinned a flag with the UNITA emblem. Inside was a large living room, a dining table placed centrally with armchairs and a couple of sofas scattered around. In one corner stood a huge desk which faced out towards the front door and Savimbi went straight to it. He motioned towards a corridor and David went down it to see bedrooms and a bathroom which was clean and reasonably equipped with towels and running cold water.

He returned to find Savimbi talking to a visitor in khaki drills, sitting erect in one of the two upright visitors' chairs arranged to face his desk. Savimbi waved a great paw to welcome David into the second chair and he found in front of him a tray with mugs, a jug of hot water, instant coffee, powered milk and sugar. He made his own while Savimbi and his lieutenant talked.

That detail set the pattern for a long day of visitors appearing to sit and talk. Each conversation was terminated by an abrupt sweep of Savimbi's right hand across his desk. That was the signal to leave. All those who came in were men, most in military dress, two together in civvies who seemed to be petitioners for something while all the others were there to report. There was one white man who left a small bag open at the throat to show diamonds.

In the early afternoon, they ate a cold lunch together, served at the table by an elderly woman. They talked, but not a word about the possible business to be conducted. Instead, Savimbi spoke about his background, his childhood and education by missionaries, his time at medical school in Lisbon. David said little, listened much and made no enquiry as to what was to happen next. This seemed to pass the test.

At about five thirty or so, with sunset coming on, Savimbi dismissed his latest visitor and rose from his chair. He walked around from behind his desk and David tried to get up to join him but he was wobbling and put a hand on the desk top. Savimbi looked at him.

'Wallisch mentioned that you were unwell on your journey. It's not behind you yet. Get a good night's rest before you go on. You're welcome here and I've got medication.'

David tried to argue but Savimbi cut him off, saying with a smile, 'I know best. It is I who has the medical qualification.'

So David went down the corridor to one of the empty bedrooms, popped a couple of pills and fell gratefully into bed. He slept for nearly fifteen hours straight. The house seemed quiet when he woke around 9 am, but after showering he walked through into the main room to find a scene almost unchanged from the previous evening. Savimbi was sitting behind his big desk and engaged in yet a further conference, this time with an African smartly turned out in suit and tie with a pigskin briefcase standing beside him. Savimbi broke off to welcome David, explaining that the African had also stayed overnight and was shortly to return to Luanda. Then he waved David to the table which was set for breakfast while he returned to his conversation in Portuguese. David sat and waited until an excellent meal was produced by the same elderly woman. As he finished, so also did the session around the desk and the African came to say a polite goodbye before Savimbi accompanied him to the door.

His host returned, 'a gentleman that one, and a rising star. But he'll have to be patient in waiting for his chance. Just like me.'

David, with a mug of coffee to his lips, let his eyes frame the question and Savimbi smiled.

'Him? He's from Mozambique where he leads FRELIMO which has the same sort of ideals and objectives as we do here. We have very few opportunities to meet so we have to make the most of them. He and I have been talking for most of the night. His name is Samora Machel.'

Jonas Savimbi seemed to have inexhaustible energy and he still wanted to go on talking. But after a night of strategic conversation, he was disinclined to go on with supplicants and detail. Instead, he escorted David around the extensive camp before they returned to sit in easy chairs on the wide veranda. Savimbi talked throughout in fluent English, using idioms which were remarkable given that he had never lived in an English speaking country.

'You must be wondering why I'm baring my soul to a guy from a different continent and culture,' he said interrupting his own flow,' and one reason is that I never miss the chance to give a lecture and advertise my point of view'.

He gave a great bellow of laughter and leant forward to bang David on the knee.

'More important, I'm sure I recognise a companion in spirit. You're like me, David, you like to soak up information and be prepared to have it change your mind'.

Then came the political history lesson. Savimbi spoke freely about the courting tactics of the great powers, the USA, the Soviets and increasingly China. He gave fascinating detail of how UNITA was approached by the big guns with offers of help in many forms provided he was prepared to dance to the donor's strategic tune. It was riveting to hear about proposals which had been put to Savimbi and others of his stamp and stature across

Africa: in the East, in the Congo, in Ethiopia and in Zambia. It really was neo-colonialism in the raw.

David asked him, 'what do you want to achieve here in Angola? Not what you expect, but what you want.'

Savimbi looked at him sharply.

'That's a shrewd question. There's a big difference between those two. I expect a win for UNITA, that's for sure. We'll get control of this country and say goodbye to the Portuguese. What comes after is tougher to predict. Angola is a wealthy country, but ironically, it's the wealth which gives us the problem. Post independence, they'll be many Angolans who'll want to grab their share and then all the bickering and infighting will start. I'll have a distracting struggle to control some people who'll want to build their own power base and fortune.'

He paused to take a pull at the soft drink beside him and looked out at the view over the savannah country which surrounded the camp. Then he continued,

'Of course, David, there's a chance that I'll become corrupted myself and develop into a grasping megalomaniac. After all, that's been the route for a few African leaders already and there'll be more to come this decade.'

'Why do you say that?' David asked him.

'Why? Well it's simple, you see. It's bred in us.'

'I don't understand what you're saying.'

'OK,' said Savimbi hunching himself forward in his chair as he gazed at David, 'it's like this. If you look at this entire continent and then leave off all the national boundaries, what do you see? I'll tell you. It's one place, one people, one culture at least from the Sahara on South. Of course there are great differences in topography, in climate, vegetation etcetera. And of course there's an uncounted number of peoples and dialects. But there's a common denominator which is that we are all tribal and we have been over generations past. If you're born an African, it's imbued in you that you are a member of a tribe. You can expect fulfilment, but based on membership rather than meritocracy. You see, we Africans are incredibly enduring. We're hardy, patient and long suffering. We don't ask for much: the means and the environment to sustain a life of dignity and adherence to long established practice. We expect a boss, a leader, an elder to map our path and we're content to do as we're told. We certainly don't appreciate a Soviet style hierarchy, but we're not too persuaded by democracy either. We don't want to be converted, recreated or developed. We prefer to get on with life according to the customs of our fathers' fathers. We wish the rest of the world would mind its own business rather than obsessing with ours and we especially dislike being pawns in some mighty power play which offers us nothing, however it plays out.'

Savimbi smiled his great beaming grin. 'And so, incidentally, I'll go on accepting blandishments and hand outs from all and sundry. I'll make the right noises in grateful reaction. But behind all the diplomatic bullshit, my agenda remains just that: my own'.

'And how do you summarise that,' David asked.

'That brings us back to your question, what do I want. Well ok, first I want the Portuguese out of Angola. Not so much because they colonised and elevated themselves to the top of our pyramid. It's more because they've been so bad at it: hopelessly cruel, disrespectful and incompetent. When they're gone, I want to bring about change, but a complete shift, more bold and fundamental than you'd expect. I don't champion the 'Angola for the Angolans' dictum. No. My vision is to enlarge our community, to invite other nationalities from East and West and any colour under the sun to join us here.

'Why? Because we have space and my God but how much we have. We are blessed by nature with all we need or want: you name it and Angola has it. We can develop to everyone's benefit but we won't do it for ourselves. It's not that our people are incapable — it's back to those tribal inclinations with which we are born. Obey, make do and manage, do as your forebears have done through countless years. No less, but no more either. I don't believe that any edict or political imperative will change that attitude. We need, you might say, some fertilizer and cross pollination to improve the crop.'

Savimbi went on to speak of other things. He was a compulsive communicator and had the need to be nurtured by conversation. He was well informed about world affairs and international politics in particular. He seemed fascinated by speculation on what might happen to Europe. Was there the prospect for some form of integration in the distant future? Would a shared antipathy towards the Soviet Union speed this process? He appreciated the power and ability of the United States, but despaired of finding an American who had any true understanding of Africa. He despised the Portuguese but he loved the country and had been at his happiest while living in Lisbon. He admired the British: they were haughty and insensitive, but they knew how to manage things. Interspersed with all this global talk, he found time to ask more about David's life, his background and his family which Savimbi found alien and incomprehensible. He asked about work and Kirchoffs: from David's description, he believed he would get on famously with old Sol.

Then the sun was going down and it was time for David to go. They got up together and went through the front door to stand on the veranda. Beneath them on the dusty road, a car was standing, a much travelled VW Beetle with both its doors open and a driver standing by it, dressed in slacks and a colourful print shirt.

Savimbi turned to David and explained that the car would take him to the fishing port of Mocamedes, a journey of about four hours but quite good going and with no security problem. Not with this car and driver, he said and repeated the comment in local language at which the man in the print shirt laughed. In Mocamedes, Savimbi went on, he would be handed on to members of the family who would put him up overnight and transfer him to a fishing boat in the morning. There would be a voyage of about thirty hours south to Swakopmund where someone from SWAPO would take care of the paperwork and take him to Windhoek and on to Johannesburg. He finished by saying,

'Thank you for coming, Mr David Heaven. I have enjoyed your company and admired your behaviour. You would be welcome again. I hope that we will do business together, but I understand you must return to Europe and speak to your partners. Please pay my respects to Mr Kirchoff and to Mr Gluchamheig. And please take with you a clear memory of this place and of the people you have seen. We are still only small, but we are already much larger than we were. The cub is fit and growing: the mature lion is coming.'

Suddenly they were gone, churning up the dust as David wondered if he would ever have another chance to spend time with this magnetic personality.

The African night fell within an hour of their departure and David became drowsy. He felt lightheaded, perhaps a remaining touch of fever, but he was warm under a blanket which the driver had thoughtfully pulled from the back seat. The two of them had no common language, so no conversation was possible. The little VW ploughed gamely through the sand on the track which was thick in places and needed the good judgement of the driver to keep them moving. It was pitch black, with no light of habitation to see and no other vehicle to greet. After two hours, they stopped on a rocky outcrop to refuel from a smelly jerry can and there was warm water from a leathern bottle. David slept deeply as they went on, and woke up much later, disturbed by the noise of washboard dirt surface beneath their wheels and the lights of a huge, onrushing truck. He stirred himself to take note, gaining a cheery grin from the driver. Another forty-five minutes, and they were running through the suburbs of quite a large town. It seemed incongruous to see a traffic light and a divided main road with hibiscus growing in the tended earth of the central strip. Then they were turning off into a series of broad, tree lined residential streets before they pulled into the crescent drive of a large, two storey house. The driver smiled at him again, tooted his horn and turned off the engine.

Immediately, the imposing front door of the house swung open and light from inside flooded out and onto the steps, down which ran a young man with a hand raised in greeting. He opened the door for David and announced in English.

'Welcome to Mocamedes, Mr Heaven, and to the house of my father whose name I must not mention here'.

David returned the greeting. He shook hands and looked for his small bag but the driver had moved faster and was standing in wait with it in his hand, his beaming grin wider than ever.

'Please call me David,' he said, 'I am delighted to meet you and to be here.'

'Sure. It's a long and dusty road but no one knows it better then Jaou here. You've been in good hands. Oh and I forgot to say, I'm called Rafael, but normally known as Rafa.'

'OK, Rafa. Please thank Jaou for his excellent driving and for making me so comfortable. He did a great job.'

Rafa translated in a volley of words, and Jaou squirmed with pleasure at the compliments. Then all three moved up the steps and into the house. They entered a spacious hall, with wide stairs placed immediately in front which mounted in two flights to the first storey. David caught a glimpse of a grand room off to their right, then his host was taking his bag from Jaou and leading the way upstairs. They went down two bisecting corridors before stopping at the entrance to a large bedroom. They entered together and David found it comfortably furnished, with a bathroom off and a massive, wood framed bed placed centrally under a fan which was revolving slowly. There were windows flung wide onto the garden and he picked up the scent of the sea. He felt tired again and the huge bed looked comfortable, but Rafa said,

'I'll give you thirty minutes to shower and change. Let me know if you need to borrow any clean clothes. Otherwise, just be casual and leave any washing by the door. It will be done and back to you by morning. Come down when you're ready and we'll go out to dinner. It may seem late to you, but we'll be just on time here. After all, we are sort of Portuguese and we keep Mediterranean time in these parts!'

With that he was gone and David was left to wonder what

next as he shaved, took a welcome shower and put on his only remaining clean shirt and jeans. He was on time as he left the room and went down to find Rafa waiting for him in the hall.

Jaou drove them again but this time in a much larger car, a big American barouche which purred imperiously through sparse traffic towards what was evidently the centre of Mocamedes, and then on to the beach side where there were the welcoming lights of several restaurants, all apparently humming with clientele.

As they entered Rafa's choice, a cry went up from a long table at the back, set to look out over the beach and with a party of about a dozen already in situ with bottles, glasses and some form of starter food. There was a rapturous greeting for Rafa and a polite welcome for David. It was a young party, no one older than him except for one man with a lined face and thinning hair plus a pepper and salt goatee beard. He has to be French, thought David to himself as at he took a seat between the beard and a pretty girl. She gave him a lovely smile and said her name was Lila before resuming her conversation with a couple sitting across the table. The beard was indeed French and introduced himself as Benoit. He was good company with English to much the same standard as David's French, so they laughed a lot. Benoit explained his background over a huge intake of the cold, light rosé which washed down their first course of fresh sardines with a green salad. He originated from Brittany, had spent time in the French Merchant Navy and developed an expertise in diving which won him an expatriate job in Mocamedes where he had lived now for ten years. He mentioned that he was aware of David's passage through, and would be putting him on the fishing vessel which would take him south the following day.

'You'll be OK with those guys,' he said, 'I know the skipper well and he's got a good crew.'

Between courses, other members of the party came to exchange a little banter with Benoit in his Portuguese which sounded pretty basic to David. During these interruptions, he tried to talk to Lila but she was preoccupied with the couple facing them and had very little English and no French. He was enjoying himself despite this, the food, the flowing drink, the conviviality and the strange sensation of feeling at home in a city which he'd never heard of before. His instinct told him that this was a group of friends who met quite often at this or similar establishments. It was a gathering of local society, maybe the younger generation of the movers and shakers in the community.

Rafa waved to him from the top of the long table and David noticed for the first time the two girls sitting on either side of him. They were twins — incredibly and exactly identical. He found himself staring for longer than was polite. Then he saw them stand up as one and move around the table in his direction. He got up to meet them.

One said, 'We thought it was time to come and meet you properly as you are our guest overnight. I'm sorry we were not at home to greet you, but we hope our brother Rafa looked after you properly.'

The English was almost flawless, betrayed by just a slight and beguiling accent. Her sister spoke with equal perfection.

'We're happy to welcome you to our home, David, but sorry you can't stay with us longer.'

'The regret is all mine,' said David with heavy gallantry, 'but I hope I'll need to come back. Will you have a drink and tell me all about life here in Mocamedes?'

They nodded as one and the three of them move to an adjoining table with their glasses. David scooped a full bottle of wine from the tray of a passing waiter.

When the three had sat down, David raised his glass and asked,

'Who am I drinking to?'

'I'm Aissata', said the girl on his left, 'but call me Aischa.'

'And I'm Ouye.'

'Aischa and Ouye' said David, 'what elegant names. So there are three of you with Rafa?'

'Well yes,' said Aischa, 'Rafa is our full brother. You've been with our father but sadly, we can't introduce you to our mother as she died three years ago. She was Irish and came to southern Africa in search of a wild life in every sense. She found that with our father who more or less grabbed her off the roadside as she was trying to thumb a lift north. But I don't think she ever complained. Our father has other wives but our mother, who was called Maeve by the way, was his chief wife and his favourite.'

'How did she die?' David asked the question impulsively and then felt ashamed that it might have sounded insensitive.

Ouye replied, 'she had a malarial attack and it moved suddenly to her brain. We were in deep bush at the time, but honestly I think it would have been fatal anyway. We miss her very much, all three of us, but she had already done so much to start us off in life.'

'And now you live here in town?'

'That's right,' said Ouye, 'we two and Rafa. We've been here for nearly five years. We came in from the bush life at our father's insistence to finish our education. Aischa and I have just joined our brother at the university here from High School. It may not be for long. The plan is for Rafa to go on to medical school in Lisbon, which is what our father did, but it might be a problem to arrange.'

'Yes, of course, I can understand that. I imagine it must be difficult for you to see much of your father.'

'You're right!' The twins burst out in precise unison and then collapsed in giggles.

'I'm sorry,' said Ouye, 'we do so much together that sometimes we say the same thing at the same time! But you're right. The better the campaign goes for our father, the more difficult for us all to meet. He's always so busy too, and not just with work. He has another three wives and ten children — all much younger than us. But we do get together from time to time, and of course we support him as best we can. So we try to work hard and keep a low profile here in Mocamedes.'

David wanted to lighten the conversation, so he waved a

hand at the high spirited party all around them.

He remarked, 'It doesn't seem too low profile to me'.

The girls laughed with him, and it was again Ouye who went on to explain.

'Actually, in this town David, you would stand out much more and especially at our age if you were not to be seen out and about. We're a very sociable and fun loving group.'

As if to prove her point, some of the party members at the main table spilled over to join them. Two couples to whom David had not had the chance to speak previously and he was impressed with the command of English shown by all of them. Probably they were keen to practise, but he hoped they were enjoying his company too. More food was delivered to the two tables, the wine flowed, the participants moved around in conversation.

David was enjoying himself. He knew that he was drinking too much, especially having been swallowing pills to ward off a return of sickness, but he felt confident and in control, flattered that he seemed to be accepted as contributing to the general entertainment of the evening.

Benoit joined him again, asking 'What do you think of our twin beauties?'

'I think they're absolutely stunning,' he said, 'and not just good looking either. They're great company and fun to be with.'

He meant it. But it was certainly true that Aissata and Ouye were very beautiful indeed. He would have liked to have met their mother, or anyway to have seen a picture of her. The girls benefited from the mixed blood of their parentage. Their colour was a striking cafe au lait, they had a marvellous bone structure with a deep forehead, slightly concave cheeks beneath prominent bones, piercing eyes quite deep set in their sockets and a retroussé nose, but if all these came from their mother, they must thank their father for their mouth, wide, warm and welcoming. It was in that feature that David could see Jonas Savimbi so clearly.

He realised that he was musing in the singular, but that

was another point. Look at Aischa and you looked at Ouye. Their likeness was astounding: two outstandingly elegant and feminine girls with poise, style and dramatic figures. I'll start drooling in a minute, he told himself sternly, and turned back to renew his conversation with Benoit. But even as he did so, Aischa reappeared by his side and before she could say anything, he put the question to her which had formed his reverie.

'How can you two be told apart?' he asked her.

Aischa put her hands on her slender hips and smiled down at him.

'We dress differently,' she replied sweetly, 'otherwise, you would struggle! Now come over here and talk to Rafa for me. Ouye and I want to come and see you off at the harbour tomorrow, and he's being difficult about it'.

She led him away from Benoit who bowed his head in acknowledgement of the superior invitation. David followed the gliding form, graceful in her full length deep maroon skirt surmounted by a deliciously tight fitting top, to where Rafa was still holding court at the head of his table with Ouye taking a seat beside him, her print blouse tucked loosely into tight white jeans which set off her impossibly long legs.

They partied on. In time, David came to meet almost everybody in the group, and was struck by the warmth of welcome and apparently genuine interest in his provenance, why he was there this evening, when he would be returning. It often happened as the evening wore on that he would find himself back in the company of Benoit, whose conversation was very entertaining. He was sitting with him again when Rafa came up to announce that it was time to head for home.

'After all, David,' he said, 'we've all got to get up in the morning, but no one more than you'.

They made some noisy farewells, the bill was somehow settled, and David found himself back in the car park, pleasantly the worse for wear. They did not wait for long before Jaou reappeared with the car, and David was placed beside him in the front whilst the three siblings lounged behind as they drove through almost deserted streets to the large family house. It was 1.30 am.

They bade each other good night and arranged to breakfast at nine before going to catch the boat. Rafa was worn down by his sisters into agreeing that they could come. He guided David to the door of his room and left him there with wishes to sleep well. David undressed and showered, amazed to note that the clothes he had dropped on the floor were already returned, clean and ironed. The fan over the large bed continued its steady sweep. He stood by the open window for a few minutes, savouring the smell of the sea. The city slept. Somewhere close at hand, a dog barked plaintively. He left a light burning in the bathroom, took a last batch of his pills, and feeling lightheaded from the effects of either the medication or the party or both, he sank naked into the middle of the blissfully comfortable bed and fell instantly asleep.

It was as dark as before when he woke suddenly and the face of his luminous watch told him that it was just after three in the morning. He felt tense. Something had woken him from a deep sleep and he could not locate the cause. The fan droned on, the dog still barked intermittently, he lay silent and unmoving as he tried to work out what had disturbed him. At last, he raised his head slowly from the pillows and had the immediate sense that the door of the room had opened. His anxiety increased. He was fully awake, suddenly poised for fight or flight, whichever.

And then a voice spoke from the darkness by the bed head.

'It's true. You can't tell us apart if we are dressed the same ... or not dressed at all.'

Then there was the rustle of the sheet above him, moving as two slender forms slipped into the great bed, one on either side of him.

For a fleeting instant, strange reactions chased each other through him. Relief that he certainly did not need to either fight or fly, panic at what Rafa would say, much greater panic at what Savimbi would do. And then a marvellous calm as the four arms closed around him and Ouye whispered in his ear.

'This is very forward behaviour. We are not normally quite this naughty, but you're fun and not here for long, and most important, we do not get many chances to try out an Englishman.'

After which, of course, he was just twenty-seven, red blooded, slightly drunk, slightly drugged, to hell with anyone else and to hell with any consequences.

The four arms concentrated into ten fingers marching deliciously across his body, soft mouths alternated with nipping teeth, perfect, pliant breasts danced tantalisingly before him and the moonlight through the window caught the waves of hair cascading halfway down a naked back. The sensuous long legs surrounded him, beneath him, above him and finally encasing him. Yet still there were muffled giggles and endearments, even the feeling of a bit of a scorecard being composed and compared. Above all else, there was a sense of fun.

If this was not paradise, David had just the time to think to himself, then it was as close as he would ever get.

He had woken alone, the twins having slipped out in the grey dawn as silently as they arrived. They left the house on schedule and farewells at the harbour had been warm, but decorous. Sad but happy, he watched Mocamedes recede into the distance and dozed for most of the voyage south. The remainder of the trip back to Johannesburg had been uneventful and now it all seemed like a dream, to be wrapped up and treasured, brought out for review from time to time.

Back in London, however, there had to be confrontation. David went straight from the airport to Westbourne Grove to give Sol and Martin a carefully edited account of his experience.

'Savimbi was right about the journey. That was exactly as it happened. I flew back into Jo'burg and had a last talk to Soldemeyer. I made no commitments about the arms list, but I have a mass to do about stuff for the mines. Now I'm here and you two know what happened. I'm open for questions of course but I do have a few of my own.'

David stood up from his chair and moved to pour himself another coffee from the pot standing on a side table. Behind him, Sol clasped troubled hands behind his neck and Martin chewed his pencil. It was for Sol to explain to them both, and at last he stared to speak.

'It seems that I should apologise to you boys, and by God I need an apology and an explanation from Glucky. I've told you that I met him on a train and I did: it was taking us both from Berlin to Dachau. We were together in the Camp, but we lost touch afterwards. Then here in London, I bumped into him again, but only about ten years ago and that was at Lancaster Gate tube station if you can believe it. Since then, I've seen him every six months or so and we've talked of this and that — old memories and such like. You can imagine. But we've not spoken about business, not really. He said he was in the rag trade — mostly cheap jewellery and I never questioned further although I knew he had a smart address. And he never mentioned the arms business, and I know why. I told him I'd never go near war again or anything to do with it. I've seen too much already and suffered from it. I'm suffering still. I guess Glucky got word of a fat opportunity in our part of the world of which he knows nothing and decided he'd try to get my help without asking first. He'd have known my reaction.

Well, let's forget it boys, and I'm sorry to have put you through it, Davy. You must have handled yourself well to get out of there. But Glucky has lied to me and fooled me. That's his mistake as he's lost any chance of that business now, and my friendship with it. But I'll get even yet. He owes me now.'

Sol's voice drifted away. He was sad and diminished. David could understand why.

He spoke again. 'I hope you'll excuse me if I leave now. I need a bit of time to myself.'

'Go, go,' Sol bellowed, 'you deserve a break.'

David went. It was good therapy to walk and think things through. He passed through Kensington Gardens and went on swinging down the pavements of Chelsea and Fulham towards Parson's Green and home.

ALEXA BUSHELL — 1971

In September, Alexa married Peter Bushell, twenty-one months after arriving in Australia.

It was a marriage of convenience, but also a successful union which brought contentment to them both although they knew that death would part them sooner rather than later.

On 'Alexa's flight' as he thought of it, Peter had known that he was approaching an early end to his career. A year previously, he had sought advice in Sydney about the persistent tingling in his hands and forearms which had started to trouble him. He was told this was probably the onset of multiple sclerosis and the diagnosis was confirmed by a leading authority in Harley Street, so Peter knew he was heading home to tender his resignation from Qantas.

That was important, but not urgent. It was the state of Alexa which was screaming critical as the aircraft cruised over the Arafura Sea and entered Australian airspace before putting down at Darwin to refuel. Peter was sitting with her at the back of the plane in an area screened off for crew rest and he was willing her to last the final hop to Sydney. They were taking advice from his brother Mark who would meet the plane on the tarmac at Kingsford Smith and meantime, all he could do was to keep her going by guess and by God.

Alexa's condition was deteriorating. She couldn't or wouldn't speak now, but she gibbered constantly. She moved around in her seat, tossing her head about, occasionally giving out a high pitched keening sound. Once, when they were in some turbulence, she sprang up with a chilling yell and Peter had to restrain her physically. She was at her best when curled into a foetal position but even then she shivered no matter how many blankets he put over her.

Peter knew she had been lucky, even if she was now almost wiped out. Lucky that someone had sent that message, lucky that Aveling was there for her, lucky they had got out of Bahraini airspace. She was luckier still that he now had help for her from within his own family.

Mark Bushell was his only sibling and about ten years younger, in his mid-forties. Mark was a psychiatrist. He had trained in general medicine and studied further at the expense of the Australian government. Enlisted in their Army Medical Corps, he had spent time in Vietnam and emerged as a specialist in post-traumatic stress disorders. The brothers, different in appearance and professions, had always been close despite the age gap, a natural friendship enhanced through the tragedy of losing both parents in a car crash when Mark was still a schoolboy. He had grown to be a big, cuddly man. He was much darker than Peter, habitually in need of a shave. He had a great crop of curly black hair, ran easily to overweight and wore heavy horn rimmed spectacles. He had a marvellous humour always at the ready, and spoke in an irreverent, typically Australian style at odds with his profession. But in the dawn of the seventies, Mark Bushell stood at the forefront of international expertise in the treatment of severe mental disturbance and Peter felt a profound relief as his brother took over at Sydney Airport, emanating calm and care as he helped Alexa into the private ambulance which stood on the tarmac. If anyone could help her, it would be his younger brother.

Peter went off to handle the paperwork and make his own phone calls. He spoke to Joffrey and Elizabeth Labarre in Paris and they came running to arrive at Alexa's bedside two days later. They were shocked to the core by the zombie state of their only daughter, whom they had last seen as a clever, beautiful and composed young woman, if a little wilful. Alexa had been placed in a private clinic in North Sydney, to which Mark Bushell was one of several consultants. At that point, she had no idea who she was, where she was, whether she was alive or dead, not even sure which she wanted to be. She was heavily sedated, fundamentally damaged. She was unconscious and uncaring. She did not recognise her parents but actually shrank from them.

Mark Bushell kept his consulting rooms in the city, in Pitt Street, but he lived at Castle Crag on the North Shore with his wife and two children. He spent much time at the Clinic which was convenient to his home and the day before the Labarres flew back to Paris, they sat together in a small lounge close to Alexa's bedroom, where they were joined by Peter. Elizabeth asked Mark when they should return to see their daughter.

Mark knitted his brow and steepled his hands as he answered, 'Look, Elizabeth, I'm buggered if I know. I'm only the shrink around here you know.'

They all had a laugh, even Peter who heard it coming. He knew his brother's style of giving confidence to anxious relatives. Mark continued,

'The best way I can put it is this. If Alexa had been seriously injured in some accident and I said to you that she was on life support, then you'd understand, right? She wouldn't be able to survive without machines taking over the vital functions until she became fit to fly free again.'

Joffrey Labarre nodded at him.

'OK', resumed Mark, 'then what I'm asking you to appreciate is that Alexa is now on life support. It's necessary, not for her body but for her brain and that's the most complex element of what makes us all tick. The medication I'm giving her is cutting edge stuff, plus I'm experimenting as we go. It's supporting her, but only to the extent of keeping her reasonably calm. That's just the start of getting back her sanity and any sort of normality, like the rest of us. I'm sorry, but I can't tell you yet how long this stage will continue. I can't even say if it will succeed. Alexa is very damaged, very traumatised. She has panophobia which means she's suffering terror and blind panic attacks which are way beyond the experience of the rest of us.

I'm putting this to you in such stark terms because you have to understand if you're going to help her later on. Alexa is in very deep trouble, and I don't know if she can come through this. But if anyone can help her through, I believe I can. So all I ask of you is to trust me, and to trust Alexa herself. If we can do this thing, we'll do it together. And remember, I'll never bullshit you. I'll always tell you how I see things. Right now I'm saying fly on home, stay in close contact, plan on being back in six weeks or so. Otherwise, just hope and pray.'

Joffrey Labarre felt shattered, and yet perversely a lifting of his spirits. Here was honest to God truth. He didn't feel inclined to ask for more.

'We'll see you in six weeks to the day, Mark. And thank you.'

He swept Elizabeth up in his arms and guided her away on their first steps back home to France. They returned in mid-February as planned and went on travelling regularly between Paris and Sydney during all that year. In the interim periods, they spoke every Friday to Mark who gave them the unvarnished facts. He had to report that Alexa's progress was patchy and spasmodic. She veered from suicidal to aggressive to lucid: huge mood swings and instant changes of mindset. She would encourage Mark one day only to have the most savage regression on the next. He felt both challenged and depressed. Deliberately, he matched her vagaries with his own stark differences in approach. Sometimes he would be all tea and sympathy, consoling her as the victim of monstrous abuse, but in other conversations he would be very tough, reprimanding her for being unable to find the courage to confront her demons.

Over Christmas, Alexa had a visit from her younger brother Bernard and Mark saw that his presence was a therapy. He managed to drag Alexa from her listlessness to share memories of childhood days in the chateau outside Limoges, to talk even of their long lost brother Michel, sometimes even to laugh a little. That was a start and by the time Mark was again with Elizabeth and Joffrey in March 1971, he was able to give them positive news.

'Look,' he said,'you're going to see a change in Alexa this trip. Somehow we've found a trigger point. Something has tripped a switch in her mind and she is now saying, acting and believing that she can get her life back. Honest to God, I don't know whether that is due to the medication or to my sessions with her. Whatever, I'm sure that Bernard played a part. Best guess is that we were able to keep her going whilst she found the key for herself. It's extraordinary what the human brain and spirit can accomplish, but they need the surroundings which give them the chance to recover themselves. Look back to the First World War and you'll find shell shock victims who did make it back to mental stability, but not while they were still in Flanders.'

The Labarres recognised that Mark was making light of his own professional efforts. They were uplifted by the improvement in Alexa and even more delighted when they returned in April, exchanging the early scent of spring in Paris for bright autumn colours in Sydney. They could sense their daughter coming back to them, a bittersweet contrast to the homecoming which had never happened for her brother Michel.

Mark told them, 'She's turned the corner, no question. But there's something else you should know. My big brother Pete is often here to be with her. He's part of the therapy for Alexa, and I've got a professional and personal involvement. His own sickness has really got its claws into him. In many cases, MS means a gradual deterioration over a long period. But for some, it can be a real aggressive son of a bitch and Pete is seriously affected. He's completely out of Qantas now and he'll never fly again. He still drives although I'm not so sure he should. His reaction time is way down. His speech is sometimes a bit slurred and he's just about always using a stick to help him walk. But with all this, Pete hardly lets a day go by without coming to see Alexa and to be brutally honest, I think it helps her to feel she's moving forwards while someone near and dear is getting worse. That's the brain for you. Anyway, you see and judge for yourselves.'

They were all together in the North Sydney Clinic to talk it over a few days later: Joffrey and Elizabeth, Alexa looking slight and thin but showing a bit of her former self and Peter also, physically diminished, but with the spark still in his eye. Mark led the conversation.

He judged that Alexa was well enough to leave the Clinic. He was concerned about a possible relapse but the big leap back into a normal, independent life needed to be made at some point and he reckoned that further delay might make the transition even more testing.

'Not to go into all the boring medico details,' he said in his breezy style, 'but it would be good as gold for Alexa to go home now, great to spend some time in Paris and excellent that Bernard will be around. Then there'll be all your mates to catch up with and I hope you'll soon feel like getting back into some sort of work. This is all the stuff of getting your own life back, and I'll be cheering you on from here.'

He paused to beam at them all from behind the woolly black eyebrows and the huge spectacles.

'The only problem I have with the whole scenario is that I won't be right at hand over the first few months while you're finding your way.'

The Labarres nodded but kept silent as they grappled with these thoughts. Alexa crossed and re-crossed her elegant legs, a sure sign that she was working to control a rising anxiety. It was then that Peter spoke up.

'Perhaps Alexa could come and live with me for a few weeks. That way, she would be re-establishing her confidence but would still be just a few minutes away from you, Mark.'

'That would be just brilliant for me,' Alexa said before the others had time to react, 'I'd like to do that.'

Mark nodded in sage agreement, a distant look in his eyes hinting that this was the very thing which he had been hoping to stage manage without suggesting it himself.

And so it was arranged.

Alexa and Peter had their problems of health and the future, but money was not an issue for either of them. Peter had been a Qantas employee for years, with a senior and well paid position at the time of his enforced retirement. He was also a widower, having lost his wife to cancer. She had been a country girl, an heiress from Victoria. Children had never happened and neither had felt the need to ask why. Together they had bought a large and luxurious apartment, located in prestigious Double Bay and enjoying a spectacular view over Sydney Harbour. It was a home for romantics and companions, but not for young children.

At the Clinic that April day, there was no need for further discussion. Joffrey and Elizabeth could see the practical benefits of this interim stage and happy that their daughter had the confidence in this man to go and live alone with him. There were no proprieties to be observed but it was still quite a development given that her whole crisis had been precipitated by sharing a luxury penthouse with another man in another city.

Alexa moved across the Harbour Bridge two days later and her parents returned to Paris the following week. Elizabeth carried an intuition which she kept to herself, the feeling that although her daughter was saved, she would not be coming home any time soon.

By the end of June, Peter was a little weaker, Alexa a great deal stronger and in truth, it was she who proposed marriage to him as they sat together on the balcony early one evening with the mid-winter sun still playing on the waters beneath them.

They married in September on a little island which stands out in the harbour, approached from the exclusive suburb of Vaucluse. It was a celebration made better by the gathering from far and wide. Mark played host in boisterous form and many came from the Clinic, men and women who had become friends with Alexa during her long stay with them. Her parents flew in with Bernard, accompanied by old family friends from Limoges and Paris.

David Heaven arrived from London via Mauritius where he linked up with Pente Broke Smith. Pente insisted that he couldn't afford the time or the cost of travel, but David would have none of it. He battled with the monks and put a hand in his own pocket to ensure that Pente was with him. King Offenbach surprised them all by appearing unannounced.

Conrad Aveling was then near the end of his tour in Singapore and he arranged to reach Sydney a day before the others. He wrote in advance to Alexa, proposing a quiet rendezvous and the chance to give her his own news. He came to the apartment in Double Bay and she invited Mark to be there with them.

The first sight of Conrad standing in their doorway was too much for Alexa's composure — her Connie of old, friend, lover and saviour. She fell into his arms in a flood of tears with the nearly forgotten panic of Bahrain threatening to return in assault. But the comforting bulk of Mark was there beside her and there was distraction from her insecurity in the look of shock on Connie's face. He saw behind her in the hallway the ravaged face of Peter Bushell who was a shadow of the dominant figure which remained in his memory.

At last, Alexa made a supreme effort to extract herself from Connie's arms, using both hands to wipe her streaming eyes and to push back her hair into some semblance of order.

'It's very sweet of you come,' she said shakily, 'both of you.' She knew who was with him, she could see the slim outline of a girl turned sideways and pretending to study a picture on the wall, someone who was now a vital component of his life but not a part of their history. Alexa felt embarrassed for the girl and ashamed of her lack of welcome. She smiled and spoke the name before Conrad could start in on a formal introduction.

'Antoinette.'

The girl turned to face her with a wistful, slightly timid smile. Alexa knew that they were not far apart in age, but Antoinette looked so much younger, little more than a school girl. This was her lineage. She was of mixed race, Asian European. The combination helped to give her a winsome beauty, but she had a background as tough, and even worse than Alexa's own.

'Alexandra,' came the reply, 'or may I call you Alexa, like everybody else?'

And then the girls were in each other's arms in a warm embrace which both knew would last a lifetime: instant friends.

The wedding party gathered and celebrated. They were together for two days and it was an interlude touched with magic as Sydney's best weather smiled upon them. The Oxford Five huddled together to agree that this was a reunion dinner which should be repeated whenever possible. Looking back, they could see that Alexa and Peter's wedding party was the start of a new phase in their friendship. As Pente remarked, it was 'like Enid Blyton's Famous Five growing up a bit.'

DAVID HEAVEN — 1973

David's birthday in May was a bright and breezy in London and he was all thirty and enthusiasm as he strode up Piccadilly with Martin Kirchoff, puffing at his heels with a developing fretfulness. They were on their way to inspect some property which just might be an answer to the difficulty which was threatening the expansion of Kirchoff and Son. Ever the optimist, David was seeing the problem as a glass half full and for him, the future was entirely rosy. Their business was booming and he was now both a director and a prime mover of its affairs. He enjoyed an excellent relationship with Sol and especially with Martin. They were indeed foils for each other. Martin was the guardian of their commercial security. No detail of a proposed new deal or expense ever eluded his watchful eye, but he was content to leave to David what they both referred to as the 'visionary stuff', which encompassed all the marketing of their services to European based exporters.

David and Martin were good friends but outside of the office they saw little of each other. From time to time, David would spend an evening at Martin's house in outer Highgate. His wife Ruth combined an aura of charm with a mischievous sense of humour, and David enjoyed her company. During these comfortable occasions, they didn't talk about the business, but David would tell them more of the places he had seen and the people he had met. The conversation would run to Ruth's agenda. In truth, she had more interest than her husband in the ways of the worlds which he encountered across Africa. David had lost none of his enthusiasm for travel, but now most of his trips were return visits so there were sights and sounds which he took for granted until prodded by astute questions from Ruth. She made him describe the experience of arriving in Mogadishu or hitching a lift on a decrepit old DC3 aircraft between Kinshasa and Bujumbura. She tried to tease out of him news of where and when he might have met a suitable woman to make an honest man of him. He would laugh and try to brush her off, but when it was time to leave, Ruth would tell him that she must check out any girl whom he might have in mind. And kissing her goodnight, David would insist that he could not risk such a thing. There was no lady out there up to Ruth's high standards. And Martin would laugh with them, the contented laughter of a man who had the life and companion that he wanted.

Sol Kirchoff remained very active, if a little quieter. He was more distant from the transactions of the moment but his sense for strategic development remained sure. Six months previously, he had started to tackle a major problem. They had long outgrown the modest offices in Westbourne Grove and rented overflow premises with the inevitable result that they were too often in the wrong place for each other. They looked for a single base into which they could consolidate, but all the possibilities proved too much, too far or too difficult.

And then from somewhere, Sol had managed to conjure up a contact who knew someone who needed a favour and he in turn knew of spacious accommodation at a prestigious address which was going unaccountably cheap. David never did establish the full background story and he knew better than to ask. But on that morning, it didn't seem to matter much as they were shown around the top two floors of a building with which he and Martin fell instantly in love. The interior on offer had fallen on hard times, but as ever in property, location and potential is all and they were persuaded by their hearts over the doubts which persisted in Martin's head. For David, this place was the best birthday present which he could have imagined.

It took them over three months to complete the deal, to legalise their tenancy agreement and to move in with bag and baggage. At the beginning of September, the business of Kirchoff and Son was relocated to the lofty, higher floors which were reached by an ancient lift or muscle-building stairs. But they were in a magnificent building which was reflected in its imposing address — 100 Piccadilly, London.

Ten days later, David flew into Lisbon having spent the previous week in Mauritania and Mali. He was there to meet Alves Gomes, a charming, cultured man in his mid-forties with whom they were in partnership for the market of Angola. David had found him on a visit to Luanda the previous year, and they got on well. Alves was now taking a holiday to catch up with family and friends in Portugal and had invited David to call by.

They spent most of two days together, discussing the business potential in Angola which was significant but difficult. David worried about getting an adequate infrastructure in Luanda and Gomes agreed, confirming that recruitment down there was hard, with endless red tape imposed by the colonial authorities. They worked out a plan and agreed that David would visit Luanda in four months. In the meantime, good luck and go with God as Alves told David as he left him in his hotel for an evening on his own before flying back to London in the morning. David continued to sit in the bar, and ordered himself another gin and tonic, wondering how he could get himself on south to Mocamedes. It would be over three years since his trip through South West Africa to meet Jonas Savimbi at his bush camp. He smiled happily at his memories as the waitress came up with his drink.

David lit a cigarette, twisting in his chair to prevent the breeze from the window extinguishing the flame of his old Dunhill lighter. Suddenly, he was transfixed. There was a man standing at the entrance to the bar and David could hardly believe his eyes. But the guy smiled knowingly at him and there was no doubt: here was Rafa again. David waved in welcome as Rafa strolled over to his table.

'Wow. What a pleasure to see you again, Rafa,' he said, getting up and stretching out his hand, 'this is a huge and happy coincidence. Sit down and let me get you a drink.' He noticed that the waitress was already on her way.

'It's huge and happy, David, but no coincidence. You've been set up by our mutual good friend, Mr Alves Gomes!' And he beamed his familiar grin.

'Who cares? It's just so good to see you. But how come anyway?'

Rafa ordered himself a mineral water and sat down before he replied.

'It's simple really. Alves and my Dad go way back together. Alves is a bit older but they were both studying at the same time here in Lisbon and they became friends. They still meet when they can which is not too often. The last time was down in the bush outside Lobito somewhere. Alves was talking business and mentioned the name of your company. My father forgets nothing, so said that he knew of Kirchoff and remembered your visit. Then Alves said you guys are working together and my Dad sent a message to say hello. I'm living here right now, at Med school like he was.'

He paused and smiled before going on, 'there's someone else you'll want to see more than me and she's right here too.'

Rafa put out his hand in a theatrical gesture and David turned again to the door of the bar. Standing there was Aischa: or was it Ouye? Whichever, David stood as the girl walked over to join them. She put an arm around his neck and pulled him into a welcoming embrace.

'It's lovely to meet again,' she said softly, and then added with a mischievous twinkle, 'and I'm Aischa.'

The three of them laughed simultaneously and then the loyal waitress was running back to take another order. Soon they were deep in chatter. David was transported back to that magic evening in Mocamedes with the atmosphere of fun and relaxed companionship. They both plied him with questions. How was the business going? How was life in London? Where had he been travelling? Had he been back to Angola? Why had he not been in touch?

All this, David sensed, was lovely and gentle sparring. He had the certain feeling that they already had the answers and knew more of his recent life then he knew of theirs. He signalled for more drinks and while he was occupied, brother and sister jabbered companionably at each other in Portuguese, speaking too quickly for David to follow. He thought he picked up that Rafa was working a night shift at the hospital and would shortly have to leave. David felt a guilty pleasure that he would be left alone with Aischa. He took a moment to sit back in his chair, fumbling to light a cigarette as he studied her in profile.

She and Ouye must be twenty-two now, no longer the twinkling teenagers of Mocamedes but poised young women, at least to judge from the sister who sat beside him. Aischa was looking fabulous, a picture of composed elegance. In contrast, her brother bounced around in his chair, a bundle of nervous energy and gloriously rumpled in his casual shirt and shorts, large feet thrust into tennis shoes without laces. Aischa was alluringly smart in a lightweight beige dress, deceptively simple, fashionably short so that it rode up on her deep golden thighs. The top two buttons were undone and the third struggled against the swell of her breasts when she leant forward to pick up her glass. David reflected that they were not obviously brother and sister except in that marvellous deep honey colour. Then Rafa was leaping to his feet, bending over to give Aischa a kiss and turning to David with his hand outstretched.

'Great to see you again, David and sorry I've got to dash off. Aischa will give you my number and on your next trip, promise that you'll leave time for us to have a whole evening together.'

'For sure, I will Rafa, I'll look forward to it. But good luck and take care of yourself for now.'

'Well I can't get into too much trouble right now,' Rafa chuckled as he turned, 'being a medical student doesn't leave much time for anything else, let me tell you. Still, I'll be qualified in a year's time which will be good news for everyone except my patients'.

David and Aischa laughed with him as he left the table and they caught a last glimpse of his arm waving as he left through the hotel doors. Then they were alone together.

David glanced at his watch. It was just 9 pm and although still early by Lisbon standards, a reasonable time to go to dinner. David signed for the drinks bill and they set off from the hotel together, Aischa's arm thrilling as it slipped through his and guided him down a maze of side streets to a discreet restaurant which appeared rather small and cramped on entering, but opened out at the back into a spacious garden in which tables were set out at random. They chose one near to a fountain which was gurgling softly. They ordered an aperitif and sat back to study the menu. David hadn't noticed that the establishment was Italian but he couldn't have been less worried by what he was to eat. Aischa evidently knew the place and he was just relaxed and happy with the ambience, eager to pick up the thread of their earlier conversation, to find out more of what she was doing with her life, to get news of her father and her sister.

The garden tables were far from full and quite shortly, the maitre d' appeared. He was a saturnine man of medium build, smart in a dark blue dinner jacket. He had a welcoming smile for Aischa and he gave a slight bow as he greeted her.

'Good evening, Senora Gomes. How nice to see you again. And good evening Sir. What may I bring you. Our veal is particularly excellent today.' He spoke in English with a heavy accent.

Aischa smiled calmly back at him as she made her choice from the menu. David felt as if he had been kicked by a mule, but he pulled himself together and completed their order, adding a bottle of white wine which he chose almost at random. Then they were alone again and David hitched himself forward on his seat trying to think of words to cover his confusion and embarrassment. But Aischa leaned forward across the table, putting a finger to his lips.

'Just relax while I explain a few things to you,' and as David froze in anticipation she went on, 'it's true. Alves and I are married. We have just celebrated our first anniversary and we're in Lisbon for me to meet some of his friends and family members. We return to Luanda next week and soon after I will go south to spend time in Mocamedes at my father's house which you may remember kindly.'

She said this with arched eyebrows and heavy meaning. You little minx, the thought raced across David's mind as he struggled to find a suitable reply, but he was still speechless as she waved her forefinger gently at him and continued,

'David, things are not so straightforward. Alves Gomes is a

person of substance in Luanda. He's a a man of some wealth and status. He's a good friend of my father, although that's a relationship which remains discreet. But he is also over twice my age and while I enjoy his company, he's not what you could call a romantic figure for me.'

She paused long enough for David to interrupt and he spoke stiffly.

'That may well be, Aischa, but he is now also my business partner in Angola. It's really not proper for me to be squiring his wife around town on the quiet.'

Aischa burst out laughing, holding a hand to her mouth and shaking her head.

She said, 'Oh Lord, what an Englishman you are and what a marvellous, old fashioned expression. How lucky am I being — squired around!'

There was flirtation in her voice as she laughed at him.

'It's a fair comment I reckon', David said huffily, 'but go on then. I'm all ears.'

'OK. Well when Alves proposed marriage to me, he was really putting forward a business proposition. You see, he wants to maintain his position in the Colony, but also to become better established here in the home country. Alves could've been a politician. He's a perceptive man and keeps himself very well informed. Also, he is ... well conscious of his position and what people expect of him. So his proposition to me was that we could share his money and possessions, but also the connections which both of us enjoy although they span different generations and different centres in Angola — mine in the south as you know, whilst his base has always been in Luanda. Neither of us is well known in Lisbon, but we are a socially acceptable couple and we'll get there in time. Then of course, there's my father. Right now, he's a renegade and his friends are damned alongside him. But that would change overnight if he achieves his ambitions and Alves believes that his time is coming. So basically, Alves approached me with the idea of a partnership, an idea which he had discussed with my father and received his blessing. And to be quite fair to Alves, he did include in his little talk with Papa the proposition that we would lead a married life which would be 'fulfilled in its temporary separations' as he put it.'

David paused with his glass at his lips and narrowed his eyes to pose the question.

'Alves meant that we should have what they refer to these days as an "open marriage", in which both parties are free to make their own romantic liaisons provided that such are conducted discreetly and without damage to the marriage contract.'

David was profoundly shocked. Of course he had heard of such arrangements, had even known of a couple, but it seemed weird to him that Aischa, with all she had to offer, should settle for such second best. He didn't say that. Instead, he asked a much more obvious question and felt himself a fool when he heard the answer.

'I don't understand, Aischa. Why would you be prepared to let your husband to go off chasing other girls?'

'Not girls, David. Boys.'

'And for your next question,' said Aischa, 'what's in the bargain to attract me? Well there are two things. The first is that Alves has Portuguese citizenship. He was born and baptised in Lisbon and went out to Angola as a baby with his parents. His father died a long time ago, but he used to be a big land owner in the southern highlands. It was while Alves was growing up in the bush that he met my Papa. Anyway, this means that as his wife, I have equal rights and a Portuguese passport, so I can move and live here in Lisbon if I choose to. There may come the day when I'll need to do that. Secondly, I was not quite the free agent that I might have been in the suitable marriage stakes, because ...' she broke off and looked at him with a different sort of appeal in her eyes, 'well because I have a child, you see. And she needs me.'

This was indeed an evening for surprises David thought as he watched two waiters threading their way over. There was a lengthy pause as they were served and by unspoken agreement, they didn't speak again until they were half way through the excellent food and David was refilling their glasses.

Then he said, 'Thank you for telling me all this, Aischa. You were always deliciously frank.' They both laughed as he went on, 'tell me about your child. A girl, you say. How old is she and what's her name? Don't talk to me about her father or you'll make me jealous.'

'She's called Anna and she's nearly eighteen months old: a beautiful baby although I say so myself, and I adore her. Don't worry yourself about her father. He's an admirable man but he can't to be part of her life. It's complicated.'

Aischa pushed away her plate and pressed her napkin briefly to her lips. He thought he could see tears in her eyes as she looked at him.

'Please give me a cigarette, David.' She pressed her hand over his as he held a flame for her and then they sat back and looked at each other. They maintained a warm silence as their plates were cleared and a simple dessert placed before them. They ate it to the friendly accompaniment of the fountain, content just to murmur to each other about the quiet beauty of this peaceful garden in the heart of the bustling city. It was not until they had coffee and a liqueur that they returned to serious conversation.

Aischa told him more about Anna, the stage of development she had reached, the old and devoted nanny to Aischa herself and to Ouye who had come out of retirement to help care for her. They moved onto politics and the developments in Angola, the frustrations of the people, the actions and inactions of the colonial power, the aspirations and lifestyle of her father and his surprising obsession for his granddaughter for all that he been able to visit her only once or twice. This brought them back to matters of family and the one question which had been hovering on David's mind. Again, Aischa seemed to divine his thought and her answer came from her unbidden tears even before she could articulate the words.

'Ouye,' she said, 'you want to know about Ouye, don't you David. She's dead, you see, dead and gone and I believe I'll never stop crying over her.'

Suddenly she was quite cross with herself, moving brusquely to find a tissue in her handbag to dash away the tears on her face. As gently as he could, David probed for a little more detail.

'What happened ... an accident?'

'Even more stupid and avoidable. It was a purely feminine

problem, much bleeding and pain. It shouldn't have been fatal, but it happened when we were out in the bush camp visiting our father. That place is remote as you know. It's also pretty basic with a small female population and they're all very simple women. My father himself did the best he could for her, then we decided to make a dash for Mocamedes, but we were too late. She died on the journey there. So we returned to the camp where poor Ouye is buried. Papa was completely distraught and I don't think he'll ever get over her death. And as for me, well she was my twin, my sister, my irreplaceable friend.'

David took in the ravaging pain on Aischa's face. Instinctively, he rose and pulled his own chair around the table so he could put an arm around her. He said nothing whilst she sobbed. Soon, she pulled herself upright and smiled at him.

'You do bring out the worst in me, Mr Englishman. I'm making an exhibition of myself and ruining my makeup. Ouye would be furious. She always was a great one for keeping up appearances.'

With that, she disengaged herself from him, rose and vanished into the restaurant. David was left to order another coffee and to ponder on the cruelties of life and a persistent feeling that there was more to come.

When Aischa reappeared, she was revitalised and looked entrancing. She seemed to glide over the garden towards him, moving from sorrow to seduction with each stride of her long legs as the faint lighting caught their golden sheen. She dropped a kiss on the top of his head as she regained her chair and she sat forward in a thrusting pose of invitation.

'Well then,' was all she said.

David took his cue, 'and where will my friend, your husband, Mr Alves Gomes be right now?', he asked smiling at her.

'He informed me earlier that he will be entertaining this evening ... and all night'.

'And where does he expect you to be?'

'Well sleeping with his friend of course. I do hope you're not going to let me down?'

David's answer was a barely muffled growl as he called for their bill.

THIERRY CESTAC — 1974

Cestac had prospered during the last few years and was well pleased with his circumstances as he sat out the quiet month of August in Paris. He had made an exit from both the sex game and the drugs business. The first was dying its own death at the turn of the decade. He still regretted that his final foray had ended with only partial success. Even so, he had pocketed half a million US and managed to keep a client on side. Late in 1970, the redoubtable Mr Riaz had got back in contact. He reported that the last girl — and how supreme she would have been — had somehow made her escape. It was assumed that M. Eboli helped her and they questioned him so severely that he expired.

'Not my responsibility' was Cestac's response and Riaz agreed, confirming that it was an episode behind them and enquiring if they could now agree on a fresh contract for similar merchandise to be located and groomed in advance. Cestac declined, but he did pick up a rough and brazen type, a girl from Tunisia who went eagerly and without an escort. Cestac collected grateful thanks and a further hundred thousand. He heard no more from either Riaz or the girl.

More satisfying still had been the denouement to the drugs affair and his perilous relationship with the Brothers Grimm. As Victor Sollange had prophesied to King Offenbach, the Paris gendarmes pulled the remains of the young blond Russian from the bank of the Seine during the third week of January 1970. He had been dead awhile from unpleasant injuries, but not long in the water. The police could not identify him; however they could manage a just less than gruesome photo of the face which was circulated to invite public response, hoping for help in locating a missing person. This came to Cestac's attention. The fate of the

Blond was of no surprise or concern to him, but he did recognise an opportunity.

Cestac had good connections into the Paris police and he chose his interlocutor carefully. Between them, they set up a cut out for Cestac and selected as intermediary a lowlife, inadequate con artist who was persuaded by a few hundred francs to make a signed deposition to the police. He said he had seen the Blond early on New Year's Day getting into a car in Rue de Constantine. He happened to have noted the make and the number. This fingered the Grimms and the police moved in on their apartment in a squalid northern suburb of the city. The Brothers were unconcerned to be taken in for questioning. There were no forensics to be found and their heroin house was miles away. They told the police that they had parked in Constantine for a party at a nearby club and had given the Blond a lift on their way home. God knows who he was, but he seemed pleasant enough and was grateful for the ride. Fair enough, the detective told them, but to finish matters please come with us to the morgue and confirm ID. The Grimms piled willingly back into the Black Maria which had brought them in for interview.

Sollange and his team stood off to observe all this. Geslin, his assistant, was again on the streets and watching. His boss did not want to move until they could place the Brothers and Cestac together. They never got that chance. The Black Maria moved sedately until it reached the Peripherique, at which point the driver switched on his lights and siren, losing Geslin's old Peugeot within a minute. The police vehicle moved at speed and unchecked until it halted an hour later in the forest of Montorency, North West of Paris. The Grimms remained locked inside for the duration. They were concerned but unscathed. Not for long. Waiting for them was a small party from Soviet Russia, tough men and known to the late Blond, who had been powerfully connected in his home city of Moscow. He must have been so, in order to have gained funds and exit permission for a holiday trip to France, to say nothing of his introduction to Thierry Cestac. It was Cestac who had provided him with entertainment and more recently obtained the information to enable his death to be avenged. The driver unlocked the doors of the van and the burly men moved in. They removed the Brothers without difficulty and tied them to separate trees. They started their chain saws and cut the Grimms into small pieces, without troubling to kill them first. They left the pieces behind and abandoned the van. Its driver had long departed. Cestac's chauffeur, Olivier, knew when to make himself scarce.

This violent end left Cestac free from the threat of the Grimms, and it gave him the keys to their kingdom. He sold their remaining stock to his smart clientele at enormous profit. Afterwards he left the drugs trade, sooner and better rewarded than he had planned. Sollange was apoplectic and devoted himself to finding the mole in the gendarmerie. King Offenbach was merely disappointed. Both knew it was the end of only one battle in their war.

Cestac returned to the Dordogne and gave himself a few months break. Later that year, he started to move in the new direction. He made an extended trip through Francophone Africa, observing conditions, taking in the local politics, building his first contacts on the continent. It was twelve months later before he engineered his first deal, but he didn't mind the delay. He had plenty of money. He looked for much more, but with interest in every meaning of the word. It all looked very promising. The arrangements which he made for some senior army officers in Uganda with assets grabbed from the Asians kicked out by Idi Amin made a good start for him, but they were nothing compared with the influence which he was now wielding to cater for the weird demands of President Bokassa of the Central African Republic. There was real power here as well as unlimited money. In addition, there was the allure of high quality villainy, his ultimate aphrodisiac. Cestac sipped his coffee as he sat at a table outside a favourite Bar and let the August sun beat down on him. He was well content.

CONRAD AVELING — 1975

He climbed into his car and drove slowly towards the main gates of the Regimental headquarters. He was going home, but also leaving another, and doing so with a heavy heart. Conrad had resigned his Commission at the required time before this June day. He was sure he had made the right decision but that didn't make the point of departure easier. He returned a last salute at the guardroom, and swung his car out onto the main road. He felt better. The challenge was awesome, but it was good to be underway.

He had a forty minute drive ahead, a meander through the country roads of Hampshire to the thatched house which he and Tepee had been excited to find within their budget. They were settled there with the three children: Peter and Oscar, the twin boys of ten and their young sister Camilla, Conrad and Tepee's child, rising three and spoiled by her two big brothers.

The journey provided him with a chance to reflect. He was happy with his memories, of which the best were of the two years spent in the Far East. He'd been anxious when his Qantas flight had left him in Singapore, nervous at his first meeting with his fellow officers and soldiers, still more worried that his bloody actions in Bahrain would be revealed. But no word had ever been spoken and he relaxed further when he got news that Alexa was safely in Sydney.

The work during those two years was always varied, always demanding, bloody at times and boring at others. The British Naval flag still flew and there were skirmishes and clandestine operations in which the specially trained forces were involved: some tough soldiering and he had enjoyed every minute of it.

The day which had changed his life came in early June 1971.

Conrad and his team had just finished an assignment in East Timor, attached to an Australian force, and they returned for a few days leave in Singapore. Connie was trying to develop his watercolour painting. He was less than brilliant, but he did enjoy it and it was good for relaxation. That day, he took his box of brushes, his easel and canvass and paints, and he set up a position at the edge of a small flower market just off Marine Parade. It was a pretty enough spot, always bustling with activity which actually made for more privacy. If you wanted to be inconspicuous, it was best to get in amongst a crowd of people who had more pressing things to do than gawp.

He was working on a couple of outline sketches when he noticed a girl standing a few yards away. She was holding up her bicycle which had an enormous wicker basket attached to its front forks and a sort of trailer hooked up through a gooseneck attachment to the saddle post. There were two small boys squatting in the little cart. The girl was giving him a quizzical look with the touch of a smile playing around her mouth. He could see that she was slim and unusually tall for an Asian. She was very beautiful indeed. She was also a pain and a distraction. Conrad steeled himself to start preparing his paints and palette. He knew she would be gone when he turned to look again. She was not. She was unmoved. But now she did brush a lock of her long black hair from her eye and spoke to him across the small distance that separated them.

'Good morning, Sir. You must think me very rude to be staring, and I am interrupting you which is even worse. I paint myself and it's not a help to have onlookers. I'll leave you in peace, now. You've picked a good spot.'

She flashed a full smile at him and gathered her skirts as she prepared to mount her bike. Then Conrad committed a cardinal error: he talked back.

'Ah well, if you're a fellow artist, you better come and have a look.'

'Maybe later, if you're still here. I've got my hands full right now.'

Conrad found the determination to get absorbed in his creation, and was pretty pleased with the result: four hours later, he started the process of cleaning up. Suddenly, he was aware of the girl's reappearance, standing straight and tall beside him and staring intently at his day's work. She took a pace back and puffed out her cheeks in concentration.

'Not too bad,' she delivered her verdict, 'really not bad at all ... except perhaps you might want to try...' and she went on with a clipped critique which implied that she would have managed a superior job herself. But it was delivered in sunny tones, a little trace of accent which sounded European to Connie's ear and delightfully mischievous.

'I'm sure you're right', he said, 'and I bet you're as expert a porter as a painter. Would you like to help me carry some of this stuff?'

There it was. The start of a love affair which he was sure would last forever.

She was born Antoinette de Brue, the only child of a French Army officer and his Cambodian born wife. There might have been siblings to follow, but Major Pierre de Brue was on the staff of General Navarre and he was one of the seven thousand Frenchmen who fell at the battle of Dien Bien Phu in 1954, when Antoinette was four years old.

Her mother, a gracious lady who could trace her origins amongst ancient Kampuchean nobility, took the child and returned to her native town of Kampong Som on the Bay of Thailand, better known as Sihanoukville. She did not remarry but eked out a precarious existence funded by savings and some irregular income from fine needle work at which she was adept. Her brother helped by providing for Antoinette's education. Their life in this provincial town continued calm and quiet for twelve years until the tranquillity was shattered in 1965. By the time Conrad had come to know these bare bones of early life, he and Antoinette had met on two occasions, once more in the flower market where they discussed painting, and once when they walked on the beach, accompanied by the little boys.

Then Conrad returned to work and was fully occupied for ten straight days with preparations for a possible mission to Burma. On his first free day, a Sunday, he had gone looking for her and finally found her in the market. This time she was alone and they went for cup of tea before going on to an early dinner. She was in no hurry and he assumed it was her day off.

Over dinner, Connie asked for her address and a phone number. He was pleased to recognise the name of her road and she jotted the numbers on a scrap of paper pulled from her bag along with her keys. These were on a ring with a plain enamel badge marked with two initials entwined together but still clear as 'TP'. He asked her about them and she paused in her writing to look at him.

'Oh, that's my nom de plume, or my nickname as you would say. It came from my father. When I was little, I couldn't say my own name. 'Antoinette' was too much for me, so I used to say 'Toiny' and he converted that into 'toni'. He would sit in the evening on our veranda while Mama was getting supper and he used to say it was our time of day: Toni and Pierre together.'

'I've got it,' cut in Conrad, 'and that became just TP. Yes?'

'You're right. TP. Since then I have lengthened it again and call myself Tepee, so everyone thinks I was born in a wigwam!'

She laughed at herself and blew him a little kiss as she went back to her writing. Conrad felt his heart turn over. Tepee finished her note and he asked her to continue with her story.

'Normally I find all this pretty hard to speak about, Connie, but with you ... well it seems easier to talk: that's because you're quiet too and I think you keep a bit back, just like me.'

She paused and looked at him, but Connie didn't reply. Soon, she continued.

'I'm lucky: I had a very happy childhood although there was sadness lingering in the background. That's because of my father. My mother yearned for him the rest of her days and she resented his death in a pointless cause. But she bottled that up and put everything into all that was left of him ... and that was me. I had a terrific relationship with my darling Mama. We never had a cross word that I can remember, not even with me as a teenager. She was a marvellous woman, good fun and wise company, always immaculately turned out with a sort of serene poise. I don't know how we managed financially. I knew we weren't rich but I wasn't conscious of the strain on her and that got worse when my uncle died suddenly.

But even so, she somehow managed to make life secure and settled. I enjoyed growing up in Kampong Som and I loved our little house which Mama kept so perfectly. When I turned sixteen I was happy with life: happy at High School, doing OK to good, lots to do, plenty of friends. They were girls mostly, some boys too, but not boyfriends. I was not exactly naive, but not experienced either. I suppose it was a quiet and provincial life, but I was content.'

Tepee paused in reflection for a moment and Conrad saw her eyes mist over. Then she pulled herself more upright and shook her head briskly before going on.

'One evening I was going home after school and then a netball game. I was a bit late and had to run for the bus. If I missed it, I knew there would be an hour's delay so I cut through a side street to save time. I had left the game in a rush so I was still in my shorts and a little blouse, with my long uniform skirt rolled up in my bag. That way I could run quicker and I was always pretty quick. Long legs, you see. Racing down that street, I felt really good. I could have gone faster than the bus.'

She smiled at him, but there was painful memory in her expression as she continued.

'I never made it to the bus stop. Suddenly, the door to a scruffy little bar opened right in front of me and figures were pouring out past the tables on the sidewalk. I didn't dare dodge into the road. Instead, I tried to dash between the tables and the wall of the bar. I didn't try to stop, although I should have done. I've often thought about that since. Anyway, I didn't and that's how I came to run straight into this man, knocking him into a table and falling headlong myself. The next bit is all confused for me but I know there were three guys in this group, all European and all drunk. I'm pretty sure they were short stay visitors in our town. In those days, there were few holiday makers but sometimes workers on a break by the sea. Always men, some pretty rowdy, probably down from one of the mines in Laos. These guys were rough and tough. They had drunk too much and were out on the town looking for more booze, for women and for any sort of action. They must have thought they had found it all at once, and my struggles to get up and get away only made it worse for me. I don't think I screamed once. Probably there wouldn't have been anyone to hear. It was a quiet street and they'd be no questions asked in that awful little bar. I was still fixed in my mind on getting to that bus. My silent struggles excited them, my blouse tore right open and my shorts rode even further up. They became animals.'

There were tears streaming down Tepee's face and she sat hunched over the table. Conrad registered that her language was harder. There was worse to come. She made a big effort to look him in the eye as she went on and he was determined to hold her gaze.

'The three of them picked me up and one clapped a great sweaty hand over my mouth and nose. I could hardly breathe. I was kicking and struggling. I knew where they were taking me. There were plenty of unoccupied places in that part of our town. They kicked in the door of this house. The room was empty except for rubbish and a great roll of sacking on the floor. The guys were shouting at each other and giggling with excitement. They dropped me on the floor. I was choking and gagging, just trying to get my breath back. When I did, I wished I hadn't. It was gloomy in there but not dark and I could see all three of them. They showed no hesitation and no mercy.'

Tepee broke off again and wiped her face with the back of her hand. Conrad stayed motionless and did not shift his gaze from her by one iota. He had to see this out with her.

'They raped me, Connie. They chucked me on the ground and they raped me and used me and attacked every part of me for their gratification: all three in turn. I don't know how many times and I don't know how long it went on for. Finally I was left alone on that sacking, bloody, bleeding and devastated. But also, I had aged about ten years in one nightmare. Less than an hour before, I had been a schoolgirl, just growing up like a million others. Of course I knew about my body and that I was attractive to men. Of course I knew all the facts of life in theory. Of course I laughed and joked about sex with my girlfriends. But I had only ever kissed a couple of boys who were more nervous than I was. I was a virgin. I had never even started to make love to anyone. All that magic experience was still to come. And now three ugly strangers had stolen it from me. They fucked away the last of my childhood.'

Tepee's head drooped. Tentatively, he stretched a hand out towards her, and the strength of her grip rewarded him. Connie was good at waiting and they sat together there in silence, hands clasped across the table. Tepee moved first. She removed her hand from his and stood up, tall and graceful, beautiful even with her face ravaged by tears and her long black hair disordered. She still managed her golden smile as she spoke softly.

'I will go to the Ladies, and I may be quite a while. When I come back, could we go for a walk on the beach please?"

Connie just nodded as she turned away and he sat back to light himself a rare cigarette as he called for his bill. They were walking hand in hand for over fifteen minutes before Tepee took up her story again. She suddenly looked up at the moon rising over the Straits, gave that familiar shake of her head, and launched straight in again.

'Somehow, I got myself home. Not on the bus or in a taxi. I was too ashamed for that. I walked all the way. I only had my shorts and they wouldn't do up properly. My blouse was in tatters and my bra had disappeared. I found a filthy old tee shirt at the back of that room and I had to frighten off a big rat before I could get it.

Mama was standing in the hall. She took one look and must have guessed. I collapsed in her arms. The rest of that night and the next few days remain a blur for me. Mama helped me to bathe and get into bed. Our doctor came round and examined me all over, left a load of pills and potions, promising to return the next day. I don't remember his further visit, but I'm sure he was good to his word.

It was ten days later when the next disaster hit our house. I had slept all through the night, which was a first, and I woke feeling a bit better. I looked at my watch and found that it was nearly midday, which astonished me. Normally, I would always hear my mother rising at 6 am. But these are not normal times, I thought to myself as I lay in bed. Perhaps she's gone out and left me a note. I went downstairs to our small kitchen which was as neat as ever. There was no message. I climbed the stairs again and went across the landing into my mother's bedroom. Mama was there and still in bed. As soon as I looked at her, I knew she was dead.'

Tepee stopped abruptly in her tracks on the sand and turned to face Conrad who, as before, held her gaze and said nothing.

'I don't know if you can understand this, Connie, but it's a funny thing about shock. You sort of get used to it. Here I was facing a much greater ordeal than even the rape. I was alone and frightened and very, very sad. I adored my mother: we were so close and such good friends. I should have gone instantly out of my mind, but I was quite calm. I walked out of her room and out of the house. I even locked the front door behind me. I went to the doctor's surgery and asked the receptionist lady if I could see the doctor urgently. She knew what had happened to me. It was only a minute or so before I was with the doctor and he came with me straight back to our house. I half hoped that we would find my mother out of bed and her normal self, but of course that was not to be. The doctor examined her body for some time while I waited downstairs. Then he came to me and explained that she had a heart attack in the night. He believed she had died in her sleep. He was distressed, but perhaps I had not known that he had been treating her heart condition for some years. He would start to make suitable arrangements, and I must come and stay with him and his family for the time being.

But I couldn't do that: not yet. I couldn't leave my mother lying there on her own. The doctor was very understanding and came to spend that night on the sofa while I went to my bed and slept with my door open so that I could look across to Mama's room and hope this was a passing nightmare. Quite early the next morning, they sent a van to remove her to the funeral home. Our neighbours either side came out to hold me and we all cried together as she left our house for the last time. I asked to be left alone in her room for an hour or so and then I would go to them. But I didn't do that. After a while, I changed into my best school uniform and left the house quietly. I still felt calm, just terribly detached as if I was watching my own life from somewhere far away. I walked to the bus stop and started the familiar journey to school. I had no trouble in getting there and I went straight to see the Girls head teacher. She was a really nice lady. She was popular with all the students and she had good advice to give you if you asked for it. So I asked. She was terrific. She hadn't heard from my mother after the men attacked me, just had the message that I was sick and at home. So this news about the rape and about my mother's death came as two complete and terrible surprises. We talked together for ages and she telephoned our doctor to tell him where I was. Then she called in my form mistress and my best friend, and we all talked some more and I cried a lot. Finally we left her office and the form mistress travelled home with me. When we walked into our street, the first thing that I saw was a huge shiny car standing outside our house, and eventually it brought me here and away from my home forever.'

They had started walking again, and this was the moment when Conrad at last felt able to break his silence.

'Who was in the car, Tepee?'

'The family here in Singapore: Colonel Roger Mantel, his son Sebastien and Seb's wife Izzy, who has become my best friend. But Connie, let me explain all this. It won't take long.'

She tucked an arm into his and continued as they walked.

'My father's best friend in the Para's was Roger Mantel. Years ago, they served together in French Colonial Africa, but when my father was transferred to Indo China, Colonel Mantel remained in Cote d'Ivoire. They kept in touch of course, but weren't able to see much of each other. My parents met and married in this region, so although my mother knew all about the Colonel, she had never actually met him.

'After I was raped, I believe Mama was more traumatised than me. She had the support of our doctor, but she was a proud woman and she wanted help from her own. She would have shrunk from talking to our neighbours. She must have longed for my father, but without him, she turned to his best friend and set out to contact Colonel Mantel. He has told me since that Mama used her precious savings to go to the post office and make endless expensive calls to the necessary authorities in France, especially the Regimental Headquarters. She was told he had taken early retirement but she refused to give up. She got back on the phone to the Retired Officers Association and tracked down a number for the Colonel: at last, some luck for her. He was living here in Singapore with his son and daughter-in-law.'

Conrad put his arm around Tepee's waist and hugged her to him as they walked.

'Right,' he said, 'I can work it out from here. She called him, he came running to help, only to find the tragedy of her death just before he got here.'

'That's it exactly. He got in his big car and drove straight here.'

'It would've been quicker to fly.'

'Of course. But I guess he wanted a woman with him to win her trust and mine. That meant bringing Izzy and Seb wouldn't be left behind. So they drove, with enough space to take us home with them. In the event, it was just me.'

'So you've been living here with the Mantels for what ... five years?'

'A bit more, actually. It's seems like yesterday and a lifetime rolled into one. They're my new and true family and I owe them everything.'

'Have you ever been back?'

'Not yet,' she shook her head, 'but I want to. There are people I want to see again: the doctor, school people, my friends, our neighbours.

Most of all, I want to go back and talk to my Mama. We held her funeral and everyone came. The place was packed out and overflowing. The burial was private: just the four of us as they laid my Mama in her grave. I couldn't cry. I just stood there with Izzy by my side and Sebastien looming and brooding alongside us. And a little way off, Colonel Mantel, the tough old soldier at attention again, ram rod straight and the tears pouring down his face — weeping for his friend and for the lives which might have been.

Tepee stopped at this point. She stopped both physically and verbally. Conrad just put his arms around her and held her whilst she sobbed silently into his chest. After two or three minutes locked together, she broke off, blew her nose and smiled at him as she took his hand again while they turned to retrace their steps along the beach. She spoke again.

'Leave me here for this evening, Connie, and thank you for being such a good listener. I'm quite safe to walk home from here. I do so often when I have the chance for a little time to myself. But I'll be here tomorrow evening at five. I'll have the children with me, and I hope you'll come home and meet everyone. But you don't have to be here — not if you can't or if you don't want to be,' her voice trailed away. and Conrad was swift to reply.

'I'll certainly be here, looking forward to meeting the Colonel, Seb and Izzy too: and of course the children. What are they called?'

'They're twin boys, Connie. They're called Peter and Oscar. They're four years old, and they're mine.'

The silence stretched between them. Finally, Tepee said to him,

'If you can't handle that, Connie, I'll understand.'

'I'll see you here tomorrow at five. Don't be late.'

He leaned forward to kiss her gently on the lips, then turned away with a wave of his hand. When he reached the corner, he looked back. Tepee was moving off, and she was skipping.

The following evening was a success. They met as planned and went on all together, Tepee on her bike with the boys fidgeting and laughing in the trailer cart behind whilst Conrad ambled beside them. The Mantel house was a picture, an old colonial style building nestling between modern blocks. There was a wide veranda and from the look of the ground floor, Conrad guessed four or five bedrooms above. A large garden at the rear would have been overlooked but it was replete with trees and shrubs. There was a welcoming feel to the whole place.

Colonel (retired) Roger Mantel was exactly as he expected. A tall, slim military figure, almost Gaullist in profile. He was correct and formal to meet, with a hard handshake. He spoke excellent, fluent English with a Peter Sellers accent. Conrad didn't miss the twinkle in his gimlet eye. His son Sebastien was a giant, at least 6 feet 5 and wide to match with hair en brosse, sleeves above the huge biceps, a permanent six o'clock shadow split by a disarming grin. He insisted that he was delighted to meet an English soldier. Entente cordiale and all. Conrad was clear that humour and teasing was basic instinct to this family.

This was demonstrated by Seb's wife, Elizabeth, but only ever known as Izzy. You would really wonder, Conrad thought as he shook hands with her, how the two got it together. Izzy was over a foot shorter than her husband, short blonde hair, a tremendous bosom and running a little to plump. She brushed aside his hand and stood on tiptoe to kiss his cheek, taking the opportunity to whisper in his ear so that the Colonel could not hear.

'It does work, and pretty well too. But I have to be on top!'

Conrad blushed at being caught out, but Seb laughed with gusto and casually patted his wife's bottom with a giant paw. Tepee and Izzy went to put the boys to bed while the three men sat on the veranda over a pre-dinner drink. The Colonel asked about Conrad's career and lifted a discreet eyebrow as he detected the responding reluctance to go into detail.

'You need say no more. I understand enough, and I must say that I'm impressed.'

There was a growl of assent from Seb. He had followed his father into the army and the Paras but only for a short commission.

'You'd have been much too big for jumping,' Conrad remarked casually and thought he might have stepped out of line as his two hosts caught each other's eye. But no, they were again impressed.

'D'you know you're the first guy I've met who can appreciate that. Thank you,' said Seb and he leaned forward to clink lager bottles. The telephone rang for Seb and Conrad moved to change tack, asking about the Colonel's business.

'I'm still working,' he replied, 'I was widowed while soldiering in Africa. Sebastien has two older sisters living in France with five offspring between them. When I left the army, I came out here to start a new business and Seb joined me as soon as he could. We provide security arrangements for commercial organisations. We do both analysis and operational. It's been developing well and I predict that they'll be a large increase in demand over the next ten years or so. By then, I shall be completely retired leaving the business to Sebastien when I go back to France to spoil my grandchildren and drink a decent glass of Bordeaux.'

Soon after, they had dinner and spoke of other things for the rest of the evening. They talked in English to accommodate Conrad and also Izzy, who turned out to be New Zealand born. She had met Seb when he had holidayed there as a back packer.

Conrad left from the dinner table when the excellent meal was completed. He didn't want to overstay his first welcome. But over the following three weeks, he returned often to the Mantel residence and was conscious of being easily accepted there. For himself, he enjoyed the atmosphere and he loved the company. Most of all, he came to realise how much he loved

Tepee, how much she was laughing, how readily she came to anticipate him, and how much he was coming to yearn for her physically. That was reciprocated and their farewells at the end of an evening when the others departed tactfully inside became progressively more intense. One evening, they managed some conversation amongst the kissing and fumbling and Tepee guessed his thoughts.

'Darling Connie,' she said pushing him away and looking him the eye, 'you're wondering how I could choose to bear the children of men who raped me, and you don't know how to ask me the question. Am I right?'

He sighed deeply before saying, 'Yes, of course you're damn well right. But it's not for me to ask.'

She shook her head. 'No. It's right to ask. It's necessary. I just hope you'll understand.

After the rape, Mama and I didn't talk at all about what happened. I wasn't capable of conversation and she was an old fashioned lady. But she did talk to the doctor and he told her to take me to hospital to be properly examined. She didn't do that. I expect she was waiting. Waiting for me to get over the shock and for her to feel stronger. For the same reasons, probably, she didn't talk to the school or our neighbours. But of course, she didn't know what was coming.

When I arrived here in Singapore, I was very shy and withdrawn. They were all so kind to me in this house, and the Colonel was very insistent on giving me all the space and quiet I wanted. It took time for me to have the confidence to talk to Izzy, and by then I knew of course that things were not ... well not as normal with me.'

Conrad was touched that she was being so diffident but he said nothing to interrupt her.

'Finally, Izzy coaxed me into a full conversation with her and I relived the whole business. I got myself back into a real state, but she was a proper tigress for me. She refused to allow Seb, and not even the Colonel himself to speak to me. I went to the clinic with Izzy where they confirmed my pregnancy, but said that it would be possible for me to have a termination although they couldn't offer guarantees about all the consequences. Izzy and I went home then, and we sat out here on the veranda for a whole long afternoon, just talking things through. By the end of it, I knew what I wanted to do. I would have the babies, and I've never regretted that decision, never once.

'Why? Well, Connie, two reasons. The first is that as a woman, you separate in your mind the acts of conception and birth. For certain sure, there is cause and effect. In my own case, I had blood and pain and mess and trauma at both the beginning and the end of the whole process and I wouldn't wish that on anyone. But however beautiful the start, and however easy the conclusion, the part which really matters lies between them, when you have a new life waking up inside you, a person or persons who aren't concerned by their creation, but more by what they're going to do with the life which is offered to them. I love my sons and I'll do all I can for them, but my greatest gift to them will have been life itself.'

She was silent for so long that Conrad felt he must help her to conclude.

'You mentioned two reasons.'

'Yes. Sorry. The second is something very different. During our talk that day, Izzy told me that she can't herself have a child. She and Seb have tried everything and were desperate for a large family, but it's not to be. She can't conceive. She's marvellous about it, and so is he. She didn't tell me to apply any pressure; it just came out in our conversation. But the knowledge made itself a part of my decision.'

He knew she wouldn't say more after that, so he simply smiled at her.

'You're very brave. And you are wise. Thank you for telling me all this.'

'You needed to know. I've got no regrets, except one, and that is that I will honestly never be able to tell my sons who is their father.'

The following day at work was manic for Conrad and he

thought he was about to be called away, so he rang and asked Tepee to meet him on the beach that evening. They meandered in walk and talk. Connie rambled and Tepee stayed silent, occasionally squeezing his hand in what he decided was a sign of patient encouragement. He stopped abruptly and turned her to face him.

'I can't leave you like this,' he said simply, 'I love you completely and would like to ask you if I may become the father to your sons.'

Tepee's answer came without words as she clasped her arms around him and rested her head on his chest. He felt her tears soaking through his thin shirt but he was sure they were shed in acceptance of his proposal. Engulfed in their happiness together, they wandered for a further hour and it was well into drinking time before they walked up the veranda steps to join the others. Izzy fixed a beady eye on Tepee and immediately let go with a drum splitting screech of excited joy.

Very soon, the whole neighbourhood would have known from the whoops of joy and the popping of corks that something was up and a party in full swing. They had a very late and liquid dinner during which Conrad was worried that he had done nothing about a ring and Izzy was so amused that she fetched a rubber band from the kitchen which would have to do temporary service. With dishes, plates and glasses still littering the table, Seb announced that the Regimental tradition for welcoming a new member must now be enacted, and his father agreed with twinkling delight. Conrad wondered what sort of horror he was in for, especially when Tepee looked bemused and Izzy protested that this would be an unfair contest. But Seb would, just for once, have none of her objections and set about clearing one end of the long teak table, carefully placing chairs on either side and declaring that the honour lay in the conduct of the contest rather than in the result.

It turned out to be a simple boy's game — just an arm wrestle at which the new arrival was expected to give of his best. Connie was fairly flying by this stage and it hit him that they would have no idea of his particular strength to which this game played so well. He thought it was fair enough to show off a little on such an evening, so he settled himself at the table and stretched out his right arm, elbow flat, upper arm vertical, hand open.

Opposite, Seb regarded him with a friendly grin, flexed his gigantic arm muscles and advanced to grip Conrad's hand. The Colonel, glass of Armagnac in hand, pulled up a chair at the head of the table and the girls ranged themselves for best view, Izzy still protesting that 'you great ox' as she lovingly referred to her husband should not be taking advantage of her friend's fiancé.

The Colonel tapped the table lightly and the two contestants took up the slack and started to apply some pressure. Conrad was unsurprised to know immediately that he was going to win at a canter. The killer strength which had taken him straight through the opposition in Bahrain airport was now further honed and better directed. So now he allowed Seb to build up the pressure, putting his effort into bending Conrad's arm back from the vertical and into a reverse decline from which there could be no recovery. But the arm wouldn't move. Conrad was quite able to keep himself almost motionless, his arm wavering either side of the upright, and his eyes fixed on Seb's face, watching as the sweat built up on his brow and the bemused doubts grew in his eyes.

Suddenly Conrad felt it was enough. He'd made his point already. He picked up the pace and started his own pressure. Seb gave a groan of astonishment, trying to get back in the contest, but his huge arm went steadily backwards, gathering pace as it passed the fulcrum point to land with a mighty crash on the table top.

The Colonel looked thunderstruck. His glass wobbled and spilled his precious liqueur. Izzy whooped with the excitement, Tepee smiled smugly, Conrad looked embarrassed. But credit for the remark of the evening belonged to Sebastien. He smiled widely as he massaged his defeated arm and said.

'At last an English Para! I have found him, and he is my

brother-in-law.' With that he came around the table as Conrad rose to meet him and Seb swept him up into a bone crushing hug.

Conrad and Tepee were married the following month, and in the September, they went on a delayed honeymoon in Australia, timed to permit their attendance at the wedding of Alexa to Peter Bushell.

Conrad interrupted his reverie. He was back in England. It was four years on. He was travelling home on his first day of life as a civilian. It had been a serious decision. He had expected to go on until he was retired sometime in his fifties and then to look around for some little job to finish off with, but Tepee was worried he would end up bored and unfulfilled. Then Roger Mantel had come to stay for a weekend and he had come up with an offer. His business had prospered and now he and Seb wanted to expand by opening an office in London. They wanted Conrad to run the UK business.

Conrad's interest was stimulated but he did take his time. He talked to Tepee, to brother officers and friends. He wasn't surprised to find that the best advice came from David Heaven.

'Connie', David said, 'you must absolutely go for this! Your Colonel is dead right. Across Africa, there are squabbles and fire fights going on all the time, plus kidnaps and political shenanigans. Things aren't getting better and the trend's not going to change in my view. This is an opportunity tailor-made for you and you'll be brilliant at it. Also, there's a huge bonus. You know these guys. You respect them and like them. They are, in effect, Tepee's family. It really can't get much better for you than this.'

Conrad reflected, but not for long. With the enthusiastic support of Tepee, he accepted the Colonel's offer, and now he was about to embark on this new life. He slowed to pull into the narrow gravel drive He waved to his boys as they rushed towards his car, leaving their sister to stagger along in their wake. Tepee appeared through the front door, looking graceful and alluring, excited as she waved a celebratory bottle. He was home.

ALEXA BUSHELL — 1977

Peter Bushell died towards the end of February 1977, two months short of his fifty-seventh birthday. Alexa had settled him in his reclining chair on the balcony of their Double Bay apartment before she left for a short afternoon in her City office. She was worried that it would be too hot for him, but had been persuaded by his insistence and by the gentle breeze blowing in to ease the heat and humidity. Peter was lying there, content with the beauty of the constantly changing view over the Harbour and as the sun began to dip away, he reflected on his good fortune notwithstanding the depredations of the disease which had become too strong to resist. Presently, he closed his eyes sleepily and they did not reopen. He simply slipped away.

When Alexa returned later, she looked at him from inside the apartment and sensed his demise but couldn't accept it. He looked just as she had left him. She picked up the phone with tears in her eyes, and was still sitting there when Mark arrived at the run. He went to his brother's side and was back sitting beside her in a matter of seconds. He didn't have to speak to confirm her assumptions.

They say you are never prepared, that there is shock to absorb and a disbelief which will engulf you whatever your expectations. This held true for Alexa, but she found her equilibrium returning swiftly in the days after Peter's death. They had often talked, with black humour, of her 'afterdeath' and Peter had always said that as she would be easing him into death, so would he be helping her into a new life. Now he'd gone, she could fully appreciate just how right he had been. He would always be indescribably precious to her. He had saved her all that time ago in Bahrain, and he was still saving her now.

She went about the necessary arrangements. She devised a moving funeral service at the island church in which they had married. Deliberately, she didn't tell people in Europe of his death — not even her own parents — until it was too late for them to travel out to Sydney. She was clear that this was a departure both for and from Peter. This was his time and hers would come later.

Two days after the funeral, Mark stood beside her on the balcony in Double Bay as they watched the final farewell which Alexa had planned with Jeff Woods, a close friend of Peter's. They had enrolled together on a Qantas training programme years ago and Jeff was still flying 747's around the globe. Piloting was his passion and his hobby was performing aerobatics in a small display aircraft. He pulled in all sorts of favours with the authorities to honour his old friend in this style as he wove through the air over Sydney Harbour bringing whoops of joy from Mark, who watched spellbound as the tears cascaded down his face. And finally, suddenly, miraculously, the pilot brought the little plane to what seemed to the watchers on the balcony to be a complete halt in mid-air, right opposite them. The keener eyed amongst them could make out some movement of the cockpit canopy, followed by the release of a green flare which, as Alexa whispered to Mark, heralded the release of his brother's ashes out into the sky which he had so loved, to fall gently to the harbour's waters which had given him such pleasure. Then the plane described a wide circle and came past them for a final circuit, but much closer to their vantage point. They could see the pilot lift a hand in salute and he put the plane into a slow victory roll as he flew out to sea and reached the Heads, where he pulled back into an almost vertical climb and vanished into the setting sun.

Mark's face was still wet with tears as he turned to face her.

'I dunno how you managed that, Alexa love, but it was brilliant: just what he'd have wanted. You've done him proud. Thanks.' They were all the words he could manage.

Alexa didn't stop at that and she moved quickly. Peter's

collection of Russell Flint paintings went to Mark, and generous sums in trust for his nephew and niece. There were legacies to charity; some treasured photographs of pioneering flights went to the Qantas Museum in Longreach. The remaining majority of his estate, including the apartment in which they had lived together, was willed absolutely to her. Alexa completed all the formalities and consulted an agent in Rose Bay who specialised in prestigious harbour front property. In the middle of April she exchanged contracts of sale on the apartment in Double Bay. Then she went to speak to Mark.

They met one evening at the North Sydney Clinic and they sat alone together in his consulting room. She told him of the property sale and her decision to hand him the proceeds with the sole requirement that he should use them for his work and the Clinic.

Mark was horrified, saying, 'Alexa, you simply can't do this. That apartment is your home, it's where Peter wanted you to stay and be happy. And anyway, you need the money,' he finished lamely. Alexa smiled at his outburst, looking cool and elegant in her smart summer business suit which acknowledged the continuing fine weather.

'You're a lovely man, Mark Bushell, and you have often lectured me in this very room. But now it's my turn. That apartment isn't my home. Never was and never will be, but it has been a safe and precious haven in which I was lucky to spend a little time with a man whom I respected enormously. The truth is that I borrowed him from his first wife and I've been living in the home those two made together. I loved your brother, Mark, but that was the basis for our love and mutual regard. He saved me, and thanks to you and here,' she gestured with both arms around the room in which they sat, 'I was able to bring him some contentment. In every way.'

Mark looked up at her sharply.

'Yes, even physically, from time to time.'

Her eyes flirted with him as she spoke, and Mark let out a guffaw of delighted laughter.

'And I know,' said Alexa laughing with him, 'that you've been just longing to ask.'

They sat smiling at each other before Alexa resumed with a furrow of concentration on her brow.

'Now for your other point, the one about money. I really don't need it. Peter left me a great deal and anyway it's time for me to move on and start earning my living again. You know that I used to work in European banking and I've been getting my act back together. Now I've got the offer of a proper job which will get me back on track and I want to take it. I need the challenge. I'm still only thirty-three after all.' And looking five years younger, despite all she's been through, thought Mark, but he said nothing. He waited for Alexa to continue.

She said, 'I'm not going to make a speech, Mark, and I want to keep this short. But you see, I know just how much I owe to you personally. I was incredibly lucky to come into your care when I arrived as a broken shell of a girl in Sydney seven years ago. It's possible I might have survived physically, but I would never have emerged again from some form of institution without you. I can't ever repay that. Not really. I can say a pretty thank you and I hope I can convince you of what I know you accomplished, even though I can't start to explain how you did it. Actually, I'm not sure that you could answer that yourself.'

He nodded, 'Well Jeez,' he lapsed into his Ocker speak to cover his embarrassment, 'you were one shagged out Sheila, and a guinea pig to boot. There wasn't much left to lose when we started out together.'

'That's my point, Mark. There are plenty more shagged out sheilas crying out for your therapy, but most can't find you and more can't afford to stay. I want you to use this bonanza from Double Bay. Set up a Trust, form a Charity, take counsel but just do it. Use this money to do what you are uniquely qualified to achieve. I know that you can, and I want you to promise me here and now that you will. Please.'

The silence between them seemed to last for an eternity as Mark stared into her eyes, just as he had done during all the months of her therapy when he wanted to understand or to make his point of the hour. The difference now was that it was she in the driving seat. Finally, Mark, dropped his gaze and sat back heavily into his chair, folding his arms over his chest.

'Anything else,' he said simply, and then with a slight grin, 'any instructions or conditions?'

Alexa gave her special, warm smile in return.

'Only two. Call it 'the Peter Bushell Foundation', and put a little blue plaque in reception downstairs. I think he'd like that.'

'And will you come and do an opening speech?'

'I will,' and then a long pause before she finished with her news,'but you'll have to send me a bit of warning.You see, Mark, this new job. It's not here in Sydney. It's in Hong Kong, and I'm starting in a month or so. It's time to go.'

Mark smiled as he rose to his feet and opened his arms to her. Alexa moved into his embrace and he enfolded her in a great bear hug.

It was May Day 1977 when Alexa flew into Paris. She had left quietly, spending her final week in a hotel while she completed the arrangements which she referred to wryly as her 'premature change of life'. The night before she flew, she gave a relaxed supper party at The Works, a Woolahra restaurant which had been a favourite of Peter's. Her best friends in Sydney were there, the management provided champagne and Mark gave an impromptu little speech which had them laughing and crying. Alexa insisted on taking a cab to the airport the following day, and naturally, she flew Qantas. Someone wangled her an upgrade, and it was from a first class window seat that she looked her last on the Harbour. She knew she would be back, but never returning home.

Alexa was touched that her brother Bernard had come up especially from Toulouse to welcome her at Paris Charles de Gaulle airport, which had been opened recently. Alexa was duly impressed with its hub design, but she was glad to be guided away by Bernard to her parents' Paris apartment which overlooked the Bois de Boulogne. It was an emotional time, and also exhausting. There were many friends and relatives to see. Alexa tried to be vivacious and engaged, but she found the whole process of reintegration to be exacting and she was surprised by her difficulty in starting to think in French. She was happy to be in Paris again, especially in the magic month of May, nevertheless she was relieved when her mother proposed a move to the country and they drove down to the small chateau estate outside Limoges.

There had been time for relaxation with her parents and Alexa was able to lay some ghosts to rest. They talked long into some of those summer nights, not just of her experiences, but going further back to the time when Michel had been lost to them, and the effect which this tragedy had produced in Alexa herself. It was good and therapeutic conversation, as much for Joffrey and Elizabeth as herself. She felt the presence of Mark Bushell at her side, encouraging her to speak out about the isolation she had felt when they had been so obsessed with the fate of Michel as to have no time left for his younger siblings. When she spoke of this, her parents were wounded by the rebuke and squirmed before the account of her feelings. They still struggled to acknowledge the cause and effect which contributed to her leaving the tracks of family involvement.

By the end of May, there was little left unsaid and Alexa knew that further analysis of the past would likely result in resentments which could not be expunged. It was time to finish the chapter and close the book. She found herself looking for the opportunity to move forward into a new era. It was at just this point that providence provided the answer.

THE OXFORD FIVE — 1977

Alexa had a phone call from Tepee. She and Alexa kept in close touch and now she was ringing to say that by happy chance, four of the old Oxford team were going to be in London, and surely Alexa was close enough to make it five. David Heaven was taking a break from his travelling, Pente Broke-Smith was between ministries, Connie was of course with her and King Offenbach was anyway London based.

Still better, there was an obvious date around which to base plan a reunion. Tuesday the 7th June was the opening day for celebrations in London to mark the Silver Jubilee of The Queen, and David seized this opportunity to entertain his best friends, inviting them to inspect his firm's offices at 100 Piccadilly. From there, they could saunter across Green Park to mingle with the crowds outside Buckingham Palace. They might catch a glimpse of Her Majesty setting out for St Paul's Cathedral in the gold State Coach and afterwards, they would make their way back to a lunch in the Kirchoff & Son eyrie with its panoramic views over the Park.

Alexa was delighted with the prospect. It would be fun anyway, but it also gave a perfect reason for making a gentle break from her parents for ten days or so. She loved London, and would see other friends and do some shopping whilst over there. Then back to the peaceful countryside of France until early August when she had a flight booked to take her to Hong Kong where she would have plenty of time to make her contacts and settle in before she started her new job at the beginning of September.

At that late stage, it was not easy to get a plane ticket to Heathrow, and practically impossible to find a hotel room in London. She managed both, however, by persistence with the first and by spending a grotesque sum on the second. But it was worth it. Peter had been an ardent Royalist, and she salved her shame at spending so much in the sure knowledge that he would have loved to see her turning heads as she swept into the Dorchester to claim her reservation. That was on the Monday, and she spent a quiet evening revelling in the luxury and slept expensively well.

In the morning, Conrad and Tepee arrived to have breakfast with her in the smart restaurant. Afterwards, they left Connie reading the paper in the hotel's smoking room while they went up to Alexa's room, partly to get ready for the day before them, but mostly so that Tepee could get an eyeful of the luxuries with which the famous hotel pampered its guests.

'How are the children?' Alexa wanted to know.

'Very good. The boys are enjoying this bonus holiday and staying with their great mates who live just down the road from us.'

'So what have you done with my god daughter?'

'Oh, Camilla's happy, that's for sure. She's a bit further away, but loves to spend time with this little girl called Laura who's at school with her. The whole outing is a bit of a treat because that means Connie and I will be home alone tonight, and that doesn't happen any too often these days.' She arched an eyebrow at Alexa.

'Are you two going to try for any more?' Alexa switched into French to pose her question and Tepee paused to blow out her cheeks before replying.

'It so nearly happened — about two years ago. I had a miscarriage, at about six or seven weeks.' Her eyes clouded at the unhappy memory.

'Aaah. You poor, poor thing. How wretched for you both. Why didn't you tell me?'

'Honestly, Alexa, it's amazing the things you and I discuss over the phone but I thought I'd keep that to myself until we could see each other. I was wondering how to bring the subject up, and there ... you put your finger on it immediately!'

They smiled at each other and Tepee went on.

'If you're still OK to come and stay for a few days before you go back home, I'll tell you more, but for now, well I don't think it's likely we'll have another. Before, we weren't doing anything to stop one appearing, but it's different now. Connie wants the boys to go into boarding school in a year or so. That's a huge commitment and I know he's worried. The Bastion business is going well, but it's still early days.' She finished with a Gallic shrug.

'They really are his children, aren't they.' It was a statement.

'Yes they are. We never think of them as anything else.'

Tepee gave her trademark slanting smile, peeping from behind the cascade of jet black hair.

Alexa returned to English, saying 'Come on. Let's finish tarting ourselves up and we'll go out and take the place by storm. We'll have plenty more time to gossip.'

On their return to find Conrad still immersed in his Times, the girls looked like two million dollars on the hoof and set the Doorman, resplendent in his top hat, wondering what it was that this quiet looking Englishman had about him.

David Heaven's reunion party turned rapidly into a rollicking celebration.

They met on the pavement of Piccadilly and they lost each other from time to time as they meandered through the huge crowds enjoying the spectacle and the sunshine. They caught a glimpse of the procession in the Mall before returning to No. 100 where the true partying commenced.

David insisted on showing them the main working floor of Kirchoff & Son, empty on that special holiday. Then they trooped up the stairs to the meeting room under the eaves of the building, offering plenty of room for this gathering and blessed with its stunning view over the trees of Green Park, sporting their full canopies at this stage of the summer. Waiting there for them were Sol, Martin and Ruth.

It wasn't an occasion for introductions. Those who had not met before knew enough of each other to fall into instant conversation. Informality ruled. David and Ruth were responsible for the picnic lunch which defied its name. Spread out on the long table under the windows was a feast to tempt every palette. It was all self service with a huge smile.

They were interrupted by newcomers. It had been Connie's idea to introduce his business partner. Roger Mantel couldn't be there, but compensation came from the appearance of Sebastien and Izzy, who made a typical entrance with his physical presence matched by her fizzing personality.

Tepee gave a cry of surprised delight and rushed to greet them, admonishing her husband for keeping their arrival secret from her. Connie beamed from ear to ear.

David detached himself from conversation with Pente and went forward to meet the Mantels. They exchanged warm greetings: they had heard much about each other.

Pente stepped forward to add his welcome and his huge feet became entangled. His vast frame, swathed in its monk's habit crashed into Sebastien's similarly impressive bulk.

'Zut, I have caught a warring priest,' cried Seb in the heavily accented speech which he knew the English expected of a proper Frenchman.

'Hah!' retorted Pente as he recovered himself, 'you look like an established sinner. Come and have a few beers of repentance with me!'

The two giants, dwarfing all others in the room, ambled towards the serving table, talking as they went. No problem with those two getting on, David thought to himself as he prised Izzy from Tepee's grasp and established what she would have to drink.

And so the party partied. The company swirled, the talk unceasing, the laughter infectious. Plates were piled and glasses brimmed. They sat to eat at various pieces of incongruous furniture, pressed into service for the occasion. Seb and Connie made out well with a filing cabinet and two office chairs. Ruth and Tepee were dainty on a sofa until Pente plonked himself between them to risk a major upset. Sol flitted between groups like a hummingbird. Izzy, with her gift for easy talk and extracting information, cornered Martin into sitting on a low bookcase as they exchanged life stories. David was benign and busy with bottles. Alexa was happy to find herself next to

175

King Offenbach on a couple of huge wing chairs with a coffee table in front of them. He was just as she remembered him from their Oxford days, and briefly, at her wedding in Sydney. Slim, lounging, elegant: beautifully turned out, if a little formal in an immaculate double breasted dark suit.

'I want information, King,' she began and he gave his familiar, enigmatic smile as the fork stopped in mid-air. Alexa went on.

'You know a lot more about what I've been up to over the years than I know about you. Now's your chance, and I don't want to hear too much about the spy stuff,' she laughed as she waved a finger at him, 'but thank you anyway for all you did for me.'

King put down his plate as he turned to face her.

'There's nothing more to say about all that now, and sure, there's not much I should say about what I'm doing now. Hell, it's not too exciting anyway. But I'm real glad to see you again, Alexa, looking and sounding like you are. You've been through a whole lot, and you've done so well. And hey, congratulations on the new job. David brought me up to speed and it does sound great. Hong Kong too — what a place for a new start.'

Alexa drank some wine and looked at him with mock severity.

'You're not going to divert me as easily as that, Mr Offenbach! Now tell me about you. When are we going to see you settle down a bit and stop playing the field: and at your age too!'

He laughed with her, saying 'not that old yet and not quite over the hill although the view's getting a mite scary: forty this year.'

'Wow! Is that really right? Well take some comfort. You look a lot less and with everything to play for. But now tell me honestly, King, has there ever been anyone serious for you?'

'I don't generally speak of it, but hey, Alexa, no reason for you not to know I did get close once: was even engaged to get hitched, but it didn't work out. It was more my fault than hers.'

Alexa clunked down her glass in frustration. Getting information out of this man was like pulling hens' teeth, and she told him so.

King smiled wryly and pulled himself out of his lounging posture to continue.

'Look, Alexa, it happened this way. She was a fine girl from my Mom's home town and we courted for maybe a couple of years. I wanted to delay our wedding 'till I had things properly settled over here but that meant a whole lot of being apart. We got scratchy with each other over the phone, she resented still living with her folks, complaining it was all fine and dandy and playing around for me. You can imagine.' He flashed a question mark at Alexa.

'I certainly can. It's not a great way for a girl to plan her marriage and I bet her friends were saying she couldn't hold onto her guy.'

King looked amazed. 'You reckon that. Honest?'

Alexa couldn't help but laugh at him.

'Kingston Offenbach. I know you're one bright fellow, but on subjects like this, you're like any man. An emotional dullard.'

To take the sting out of her remark, she leant forward to kiss his cheek, smiling as she did so, and he responded,

'Yup. I guess you're right. Right about all of it.'

'And there's been no one since?'

He smiled at her, 'a few playmates maybe, but nothing serious. No. Not that. And you know, I don't think there ever will be. I guess I'm a very self-sufficient sort of guy. Plus, it doesn't help that I do a job which encourages me to stay ... well sort of private you might say.'

Alexa looked up to see Pente weaving an uncertain path towards them and knew that these two soul mates would want to spend some time together.

'You know, King,' she said rising gracefully to her feet, 'you may just be right and for myself, you strike a particular chord. I don't think that I'll be falling in love either,' and she smiled wistfully at him as she turned away, 'but now I must get to the loo which David tells me is downstairs. I'll leave you to Pente for a bit.'

Tepee climbed up out of the sofa to join her, and the two girls went downstairs together. Izzy was helping Ruth to conjure coffee for everyone from the percolator and David was circulating with a small choice of liqueurs. Sol had temporarily subsided and seemed to be taking a snooze in the corner.

The party mood was changing gear. David wanted to propose a loyal toast which seemed appropriate and was warmly supported.

'If there's one thing certain in this changing world,' he announced to the gathering at large, 'it's that she'll still be going strong for her Golden Jubilee.'

Martin chimed in, 'that'll mean a celebration in the next century. It'll be 2002 by then.'

It was an obvious cue for general conversation, although Sol continued in a noisy slumber. The remaining men drew their various seats closer together as David moved amongst them, topping up their glasses. Conrad commented that he was more interested in the next two or three years than the new century, and Pente came in to agree.

'We live in such turbulent times,' he said heavily, 'it makes me really fearful for humanity.'

'We've surely seen a lot worse,' said Martin with unspoken reference to his father's lifetime experiences, but Pente anticipated him.

'That's what troubles me most, Martin. The War is not so long behind us, just an eyeblink in history, and you'd think that lessons had been learnt. But since then we've had cold wars and standoffs. We've had assassinations and blackmails, we've got repressive regimes all over the shop and there's now more starvation in the Third World than ever recorded. That's to say nothing of urban terrorism. I wonder if the West Germans will ever be able to keep those Baader-Meinhoff people behind bars now they've caught and convicted them. I'm sure it's all enough to make the Almighty tear his beard out.'

King intervened. 'I'm pretty damn sure He'll be pleased by some developments, Pente. Just taking civil rights in the US as an example, we've made a helluva lot of progress there and I should know. I'm one of the beneficiaries.'

Pente waved his cigar in acknowledgement and it was

Sebastien who spoke next, but tentatively, not on account of language as his English was excellent, but rather to recognise that he was the newcomer amongst a long established group.

'I think that you are both right,' he said tactfully, 'but it is a favourite maxim of my father that we should all try to look at things through the eye of history, and to imagine what might have been the views of those who have gone before us on the challenges we face today.'

David was intrigued by this and asked, 'what do you mean precisely, Seb?'

'Oh I can tell you that,' put in Connie, 'I've often listened to the Colonel's musings. He was shattered by the French defeat in Indo China by the Vietminh: it turned his universe upside down and blew apart all his life assumptions. In a form of therapy he invented for himself, he found it helped to look at things through a reverse telescope. So, in this example, would Alexander the Great have ever got himself into Dien Bien Phu, and if not, why not?'

Seb took it up again, 'or the Berlin Wall for instance and the division of a country. How much sense does that make and how much misery has it caused? So how would Metternich have handled it? Or our very own Napoleon Bonaparte? Of course, we can only speculate my friends, but the mental exercise gives a new perspective on whatever crisis is tormenting you. It's something like an out of body experience.'

David liked the theory, but suspected that he was himself too obsessed with practicalities to embrace it. For now, he was keen to move the conversation.

'Seb, we have our expression here about an ill wind. I imagine that international jitters of any sort may be, in their own way, welcome to Bastion?'

'Ah, that's better,' said the big Frenchman with a grin spreading over his face, 'I like to hear the thoughts of a good English cynic. But David, I know you speak from experience of the places that you visit and here in London. But you're right of course. Sometimes I think that the world has as much conflict as ever, but just now we are in a period which is more subtle and selective in its enmities. Whatever, we are busier than we've ever been, and that goes also for Conrad's operation here. Connie has done marvels in the last two years but it's just the tip of an iceberg of opportunity.'

There was a moment's pause. Alexa and Tepee remained standing by the door as they chatted, but Ruth went to join Martin and Izzy stood behind Seb's chair, ruffling his hair playfully.

'This sounds like serious talk,' she said lightly.

'Serious reflection, more like, Izzy,' drawled King as he smiled at her, 'and like most heavy lunch time sessions, we'll struggle to draw much conclusion from it all. But just to put in my bit,' he went on addressing himself to the group as a whole, 'I've been bashing around black Africa for most of ten years now, so a fair part of the "winds of change" era, and I'll say that what gets most to me is that almost everywhere is going downhill. It's great to be post-colonial, but how much has that improved the lives of Mr and Mrs Average? Where's the democracy for them, and where's the future for all their kids?'

'Oh come on now, King,' Izzy shot back at him, 'the poor buggers running these places have been left with nothing and no place to go. Look what the Portuguese did: they simply abandoned both Angola and Mozambique, and that was only a few years ago.'

David was impressed by this firebrand girl, but he didn't want his party to descend into impassioned argument, so he spoke mildly.

'You're right there, Izzy, but the people in both places are battling on, and of course the crisis came from rebellion within Portugal. Even so, Lisbon was guilty of having no colonial policy rather than the wrong one ... or that's the way it seems to me.'

Before Izzy could respond, David could see her husband putting a ham hand of gentle restraint around her waist, and perhaps Pente, always alive to the sensitivities of a gathering, noticed the same as he chipped in quickly.

'I only know about the East Coast, but I do worry about the conditions of life where I'm living now. Tanzania's got a brave new political scene under Nyerere, but one heavy cost is in agriculture. Tanzania used to be a bread basket, but as things are now, she can no longer feed her own people.'

'But that's all part of development, isn't it', said Conrad, 'fledgling countries must be allowed, encouraged even, to go their own way, and we should stop foisting our standards and ideas on them. At the very least we should stop the exploitation by our First World corporations. I must say that I never had much time for Ted Heath, but I did admire him for bawling out Lonrho as the unacceptable face of capitalism.'

Martin surprised them all with his comment.

'Of course, I mostly keep the books back here and it's David who travels to all these places, but from what I see, you've got to wonder about many of them. Are the new rulers starting new countries, or are they more in the business of robbing the old? And that begs the question, does a dictator have the right to dispossess his people of their previous lifestyle? Can circumstances ever justify that?'

They had not noticed Sol waking from his siesta, but as he rose from his chair in the corner, it was obvious that he had been listening to the recent exchanges and David was fearful that the congregation might be in for a bit of a sermon, so he prepared himself to step in. But Sol spoke mildly.

'You know, Martin, many would argue that we did precisely that with the help of the British in order to create our own home. That's how Israel came into existence.'

A sudden light came on in David's head, sparked by this conversation amongst his greatest friends. By any measure, Black Africa is going backwards, but maybe there is a way to revive even a slice of this magic continent. It would take brains and balls and money — lots of it. It was a thought to conjure with and he savoured the fire of interest running through him.

But now it was approaching 6.30 pm in the summer evening

and there was the beginning of a natural move amongst the party to call it a day. The Kirchoffs went first, Ruth telling David she had made arrangements for a big clear up the following morning so he could abandon ship when he was ready. They were followed by the Avelings who left with Seb and Izzy. Pente and King departed together. With each contented farewell, there was the spontaneous commitment that this reunion must not be the last. The Oxford Five, together with honoured extras, must assemble again, and perhaps next time it could be in Singapore, Seb had invited with a booming laugh as his mighty feet clumped down the stairs.

Alexa and David were left alone to settle down amidst the wreckage and enjoy a post mortem conversation over a final Armagnac and a cigarette. They completed some jokey reminiscences of the day, who had said what to whom, and they flirted with when and where they might next be all together.

'Could well be Hong Kong,' David remarked, 'and what a great move in every way, Alexa. By God we're all proud of you! Especially that Connie, I might add. I saw him casting sheep's eyes at you.'

'That's absolute rubbish, David, and well you know it! These days, he looks only at Tepee, and he's right. What a fabulous girl, and how right they are for each other. It's a well deserved triumph for her after all she went through.'

'You're dead right. She's so good for him too — just about manages to lift him out of his bit of pomposity which I guess may get stronger as he gets older.'

'Yup. Well, we're all doing that. Although today, I've felt myself getting younger again. It's been a brilliant day, David, and now I'm the last to say a big thank you. I've had such fun.'

David demurred with a spread of his hands, and made to say something but Alexa cut him off to speak herself.

'Now, Mr Dark Horse, tell me a bit about what's been going on in your life. And I don't mean the blessed business. I can see all around me that Kirchoff's is fairly steaming ahead. But what about the rest and just try for once to avoid holding things back.

Tell me about the Heavenly love life.'

She winked at him, kicked off her shoes and settled on one of the sofas as David lounged back in his chair and gazed upwards for a moment. Then he sat up straight and looked her in the eye. He told her everything.

Alexa listened open mouthed as David talked about his love affair with Aischa, daughter of Jonas Savimbi, a liaison which had been making its uncertain way over the last seven years. He told her about his trip into southern Angola, his days spent with Savimbi, his evening in Mocamedes with Rafa and Benoit, with all their friends and of course with Aischa and Ouye. He told her about the night too and all the excitements, surprising himself by indulging in carefully phrased detail. Alexa's eyes widened considerably as she helped herself to more Armagnac and a cigarette stolen from his case.

Then he recounted how he and Aischa had met again in Lisbon, her marriage arrangement, her child whom David had yet to meet. He told her of Aischa's determination to remain with Alves Gomes as the best way of supporting her child and her warring father, now much more high profile internationally. Savimbi had a real chance to take power and Aischa would do all she could to help him. So it was that the lovers had to be content to meet as, where and when their strange circumstances would permit.

There was a logic in this which escaped Alexa and she deftly turned her doubt into a question.

'It sounds to me that you're not unhappy with this status?'

He looked at her sharply.

'By God, Alexa, you're as sharp as ever! The truth is I'm still terrified of emotional commitment. I love that girl, no question, but I hold back from trying to get her permanently by my side. There's her daughter, of course, there's this business which is a passion to me and then I've got my own grand plans. I know I'm bloody selfish but also, I think I'm kidding myself. The real problem lies in my weird childhood, all those memories which build a castle and keep around my independence. What is it they

183

say? "give me the boy till he's eight and I will give you the man".'

'Pretty apt for you, I'd say and I should know. I watched you growing your emotions from scratch and you certainly had to start later than most of us.'

'Too right,' he smiled, relaxed with the confessions off his chest, 'but what about you now? What do you think the future holds for you, and what do you want to find?'

'Do you mean now, or in the long term?'

'Both.'

'Well,' replied Alexa leaning forward to stub out her cigarette, 'I'm going to make a new life for myself. I have to get established in a new job and a new place. Those are big challenges, and as I push forward with them, I'm sure I'll meet someone along the way, perhaps more than one. I feel revitalised now, eternally grateful to both the brothers Bushell for all they've done for me. It's my fault, not theirs, that I have wasted time these years past but I'm determined to make up for that now.'

Alexa broke off and David was about to speak, but she cut him off.

'But as for now, David, I'm going to shock you. I am finishing a fantastic day with an attractive man who's an important part of my past but who's never been in quite the right place at the right time. Until now. So, I'm going to proposition him and by the sound of his true love, I think she'll forgive me for borrowing him — just for tonight.'

David could hardly believe his ears and thought he must be misunderstanding her.

Alexa laughed quietly at his confusion. Then she leant forward and kissed him full but gently on the lips.

'Darling David. What I'm feeling now at the end of this perfect day is happy, horny and available. I'm hoping you're going to do something about all that!'

'Wow,' was all David could manage right then, but a confident spring was back in his stride as they walked together into the Dorchester, and it was as well that a different Head Porter was on duty.

184

THIERRY CESTAC — 1980

Another August and Cestac had retreated to his bolthole in the Dordogne. Paris was dead and he wanted a period of peace and relaxation. He also wanted some time to gloat and there could be no better spot than this. The past few years had been particularly satisfying for Cestac. It was not a question of money. He had never been short of funds since the old roué who had befriended him expired under his exertions. Cestac enjoyed his luxuries, but he was never flamboyant so his outgoings could not keep pace with the inflow of assets and his portfolio kept rising. On the other hand, his thirst for power and influence was insatiable and his ambitions grew to exceed his success. He had found his true metier amongst the independent regimes emerging in French Africa from their former colonial status.

For nearly five years, Cestac had been devoting much of his energy to matters concerning the Republic of Chad, the huge but largely barren State which sprawls southward from Libya and is landlocked by its harsh terrain neighbours of Niger and the Sudan. In 1975, Chad's founding President Tombalbaye was assassinated by his own army in rebellion against his autocratic rule. This coup had failed to produce a new leader but had resulted in on-going insurgency, encouraging the existing fault line which divided North against South. Rival outlaw bands became entrenched in strife against each other and in 1979, an unholy alliance between two of them had succeeded in taking control of the capital, N'Djamena, disintegrating what little remained of any central authority and collapsing the influence of France as the former colonial power. A year or so later and little had changed. Sporadic heavy fighting continued against a background of permanent insecurity, aggressive theft and vigilante justice. No single group could muster sufficient firepower to take national control, and the varied interests continued a bloody struggle against each other.

Cestac was one of those who contrived to ensure that the stalemate continued. He had never visited Chad himself and had no intention of doing so: too dangerous and too uncomfortable. Anyway, he was better placed to influence events from Paris, where a number of the protagonists found their way to his door, each a supplicant for Cestac's ability to source weapons, mercenaries and equipment. On every deal, he extracted a huge commission payable in a mix of cash and kind in the form of a commitment to future power should the customer of the day rise to take undisputed control of the country. Behind his closed door, Cestac was simultaneously doing all he could to ensure that no one would emerge the winner. It suited him for bloody strife to continue rampant against the background of general anarchy and it helped that cause that he was not the only kingmaker. There were others at work, a Belgian of particular note, and then there was the government of France itself, humiliated at being kicked out of its former colony and determined on making its own brand of mischief. All in all, there was a fine old melting pot bubbling away to the benefit of Cestac's coffers and to satisfy his craving for personal power.

That day at his cottage, Cestac made himself a simple lunch of bread and paté and was washing it down with some palatable vin de compagne as he sat on the terrace and considered his next moves. Two matters were on his mind. First, it was amazing that the chaos in Chad had already endured for so long and Cestac's canny instincts told him that it could not continue for much longer. They must already be into some form of endgame, he told himself: he could feel it in his bones. And secondly, he felt physically vulnerable. There had been some wild men come calling over the years and the survivors amongst them were becoming increasingly desperate. It could be only a matter of time before one or another decided to take him out if only from jealousy and frustration. Their action would certainly be protracted, bloody and painful. Cestac knew he was defenceless against such an assault. He was supremely cunning and completely ruthless but his strength and his weapons lay in his brain and his psyche. He had no martial arts, did not know one end of a gun from the other and could wield a knife only to cut his paté.

He yawned as he drank down the last of his wine and stretched out in his wicker chair for a nap in the hot sunshine. He felt utterly secure here. He had owned this two-bedroomed cottage for over ten years and came to it only rarely. It was not far from the village in the valley, less than a kilometre, and approached by a narrow road which wound its way up the hill so that Cestac enjoyed a fine view over the surrounding country and had clear vision of any car or person making their way towards him. Behind his dwelling, the road petered out into a bridleway, seldom used. He never entertained a visitor here, he had no phone line. His small hire car stood in the yard, ready to take him shopping or to one of the local restaurants. He did not encourage conversation with the simple people of the community. He valued his loneliness. It was here in the Dordogne summer that he could pull up his drawbridge and truly relax. He closed his eyes and nodded off.

Cestac had no idea how long he slept, nor what disturbed him. He woke with the thought that the rustle had something to do with the half wild cat which earned her right to stay by keeping down the vermin in the little outhouse. He had arrived this year to find her with a litter of mangy looking kittens and maybe their antics had woken him. But he kept motionless with his eyes closed while his brain worked to identify the noise which he decided had been more of a slither than a rustle. Then he heard a human voice and could not prevent himself from sitting bolt upright as his eyes widened.

'Good afternoon, M'sieu,' the voice repeated and then, 'I apologise for interrupting your siesta.'

A short man of slender build stood before him in the dust of the yard beyond the small terrace. He appeared to have a drawn face and a sallow complexion, but it was hard to be sure as he was wearing both a wide brimmed hat and sunglasses. Tucked into his black jeans was a simple, dark blue shirt with long sleeves buttoned down to encase his arms. On his right wrist was a large watch with a larger strap, and against this he was stropping a knife held in his left hand. It was a constant, restless movement which produced that rustling, slithering noise.

Cestac felt threatened and his sanctuary violated, but he kept his voice steady as he replied.

'What do you want and how did you get here? Are you lost?'

'Not lost, M. Cestac, no. I came on my motorcycle, but the long way round and I left it way back up the track behind you. I don't do noise.'

'And what do you do?'

'I provide protection. I'm very good, very discreet. I attack also and I have been hired to assassinate you M. Cestac. But you are an interesting man. It seems that you are alone by choice. You have no friends and no colleagues. Nobody likes you, but all respect you. You move in the shadows and you are hard to find. All of that interests me. I could kill you now and collect on the contract I have agreed. But I believe it would be better for us to work together. I want a permanent position and a challenge for my skills. You are a wealthy and a powerful man but your only security is to hide yourself. That gives you no guarantee. I can. So now you have a choice. Die in pain, or hire me.'

Thierry Cestac was an evil man without standards or scruples. But he was a realist and he did not lack courage. He considered these alternatives and found them a fair statement of fact. But he did have a riposte.

'You are making assumptions. How do I know you're good enough for either?'

A thin smile appeared briefly on the gaunt face and the eyes behind the dark glasses must have flicked to the left to take in the writhing bundle of kittens playing together in the sunshine. He spoke as his left hand dropped down by his side and sunshine flashed on the bright blade of his knife as it flexed in his fingers.

'Black and white,' he said softly as the arm came up into a throw and the knife flew to bury itself with surgical accuracy in the throat of a kitten, which seemed to dance in its mid-air play before crumpling into a motionless form in the dust.

Cestac said, 'They're all black and white: but impressive even so.'

After a pause he added, 'What do I call you?'

'Toussaint.'

KINGSTON OFFENBACH — 1984

In November 1980, when Ronald Reagan won the White House, King was still active in Africa with the CIA. As Reagan started his first term in Office, he might hardly have heard of Liberia, but matters changed over the next four years, mostly at his own initiative, and there were reasons for his interest in this unsettled African State. By mid-year 1984, with King moving up in the Administration, and recognised as the CIA expert on Africa, the prospects of Reagan going on to a second term were looking starburst bright. He knew he wanted to concentrate on the world stage, building himself the reputation of a statesman. He was preoccupied with the Soviet Union and the so called Star Wars programme which might have been technically impossible but it did grab headlines. Ronald Reagan, ever the showman protruding from the costume of an actor slightly manqué, knew that you can't have too many first night triumphs even if they are in the boondocks rather than on Broadway and he had been pleased with his military success in Grenada.

He thought he would look for another opportunity to build his image and Liberia caught his attention. It is a country unique in Africa because it was founded for and by freed American slaves. Liberia owes nothing to the drive for colonisation by European powers in the 19th Century, but is a creation of the USA. What better springboard from which to launch a fresh era of benevolent American influence in Africa?

Liberia had suffered a life changing coup in April 1980 when President Tolbert and many colleagues in government had been assassinated in a particularly bloody rebellion orchestrated by a lowly soldier, Master Sergeant Samuel Doe who trailed guts and disorder in his wake. Reagan had been persuaded to permit an official visit to Washington by President Doe in 1982 and, in a disparaging private aside at the time had remarked that 'Doe is enough to convince anyone of the merits of slavery.' Two years later, he was scheming to cajole this semi-literate thug into being his footstool, at the same time sending a clear message to the Soviets that they should no longer expect the USA to stand aside while they spread communism throughout Africa. The added bonus was that haughty imperialism was a sure winner amongst hometown American voters who liked to see a proper degree of respect for America, right around the globe.

Flushed with overwhelming victory in the polls of November 1984, Reagan decided on immediate action and on Monday 3rd December, the State Department sent a delegation to Liberia. Its three members carried a brief for President Doe which amounted to a none too subtle bribe. America would provide an aid package to restore the economy, a US Military presence to 'guarantee regional security' and there would be 'advice on governance'. In straight language, we'll pay you to do as you're told.

Doe produced an interesting response, saying he had a better idea. The USA was to give him half the proposed aid, but in payment to his bank in Switzerland and he would then return the messengers who were now languishing in the high security jail outside Monrovia, Liberia's capital. This, of course, produced consternation in Washington. Reagan's well respected Secretary of State, George P Shultz, was furious that they had got themselves into this messy and unnecessary situation. The US Ambassador in Monrovia, William Lacy Swing, was obliged to report the abduction of the three Americans at midday local time on Friday 7th December, just when Washington was waking up to the commemoration of Pearl Harbour forty-three years previously. King Offenbach was put on immediate standby while the Administration figured out what to do next. King was CIA, he'd been knocking around Africa for years and hell, he was even the right colour. Surely he could come up with the ideas to get them out of this fix.

But King couldn't. His business had never taken him there, he knew no one in the country and had only been into Monrovia once, to change planes. Well whatever, they said, he had more knowledge than any other guy, so they hauled him back to Langley and Foggy Bottom to sit through some interminable crisis meetings, at the end of which the Administration decided that it had to pay up as a lousy alternative to welcoming home the three US citizens 'in small pieces' as the message from Doe had made clear — and he was believed.

So King was sent off as the bagman, armed only with his wits and a locked briefcase which was manacled to one wrist and contained two sheets of impressively heavy White House notepaper, both blank but clearly signed by the President of the United States of America, and two money orders from Treasury, the first for the full amount demanded and a second for a much lesser figure. He just had to do the best he could, and he was given this instruction personally by Shultz before he left for London and the Ivory Coast.

On 18th December, King took the Air Afrique flight from Abidjan to Monrovia, his insides churning at the challenge of getting back out again and his mission made no easier by the identity of the three captives, of whom none had been in black Africa before and one was a woman. Their leader was Robert E Macrum, a former Marine of sound reputation and grouchy personality due to the badly busted leg which had retired him early. He was accompanied by Ernest Wallinger, a nearly seventy Croatian born Jew who had never left the US since escaping there from Hitler's Germany: he was a prodigious statistician and a homosexual to boot. Thirdly, there was Melanie Stockton, a founding partner in Proudson and Partners, recognised as the preeminent public relations advisor to governments worldwide. Perhaps not so well known in Africa, King thought to himself, and presumably this soignée, elegant lady had been asked to publicise that America was returning to Africa with a Stetson hat and saddlebags stuffed with largesse.

What an almighty, goddamned mess. He was met at Robertsfield, the international airport fifty kilometres outside

Monrovia. An immense paramilitary escort accompanied him from the plane to a cavalcade of black Chevy Surburbans drawn up on the tarmac and they screamed off with motor cycle outriders and klaxons blaring. It was not a relaxed drive for forty minutes before they pulled into the courtyard of an imposing, colonial style building.

King was ushered straight through the hall and into a spacious office with full length windows overlooking gardens. A long desk stood centrally and a man rose from behind it to greet him.

'I am Major Andrade, Head of State Security. I believe you are Mr Kingston Offenbach, representing the President of the United States of America in this matter. Please take a seat', and he gestured to chairs set around a coffee table.

King was content to overlook this grandiose, self-serving introduction as he made an assessment of the Major, of whom he had heard much from Ambassador Swing over guarded phone links. Andrade was a neat man, slight in build, a little below average height, sallow in colour with a head of very black hair and a pencil line moustache. He was ominously quiet and controlled. There was the threat of evil in his looks and mannerisms.

Andrade broke the silence. 'You have brought with you all that is necessary to complete our business?'

King lifted the briefcase chained to his wrist in unspoken answer. Then he posed his own question in the form of a statement.

'I will need to see my colleagues, however, before we can proceed with the arrangement concluded between our Heads of State.'

'Very well, Mr Offenbach, I can accommodate you in that request, but there will be some delay. Macrum, Stockton and Wallinger are being held at our detention compound for high risk detainees. It is some way from here. Their transfer will take over an hour from when I issue the instruction.'

King was not going to rise to this self-importance. He sat and waited. Andrade continued,

'This building is my Headquarters for State Security. Suspects come before me here for questioning before they are ... moved on'. There was meaning in that slight delay as he continued, 'but you will not wish to be delayed. Let us proceed to study what you have brought with you. I am empowered by our President Doe to approve the detail.'

I'll just bet you are, you little bastard, King thought to himself as he kept his demeanour and gazed back. He had suspected and was now certain that Andrade was the brains and the prime mover behind this whole deal. It was rumoured and had been confirmed by Ambassador Swing that Doe was now a hophead and close to incapable of thought for himself. King placed his case on the table between them and busied himself with the tumbler locks. He left no possibility for Andrade to read the numbers as he rotated them, and he caused further distraction by asking a question.

'You are evidently in a position of great authority, Major, and yet you are not a national, I believe. I understand you are Cuban by nationality?'

'You are well informed, Mr Offenbach, and you are correct although it is some years since I was in Havana. I am here because I gained the confidence of our illustrious President and now I am indispensable to him. They have plenty of brawn in this country, you understand, but not so much brain, and no understanding at all of the finesse required for international relations. But before you open your case, do you wish me to summon your Ambassador. I anticipated that Mr Swing would be present to witness the matter.'

King was not displeased to note the smug confidence in this toad. He replied easily.

'No thank you, Major Andrade. It is better for our Ambassador to remain uninvolved and more fruitful for him to concentrate on the development of the relationship between the peoples of Liberia and the United States.'

Andrade looked momentarily disconcerted but he smirked knowingly. 'Very well.'

King maintained his advantage. He removed the money

order for the full sum demanded from his case and passed it to Andrade for inspection.

'You will note that it is in three copies, Major. One for President Doe, one for me to retain, the third for your approval and signature please. When you are satisfied, I will replace all three in my case until my colleagues are returned to me.'

There was a long pause as Andrade scrutinized the document in detail and King surmised that the Cuban was using the time also to commit his confidence to the handover arrangement as proposed. Finally, he spoke.

'That is satisfactory, Mr Offenbach,' he said rising and moving behind his desk where he picked up the telephone and gave an instruction in hectoring tones.

'And now,' he said returning to stand in front of King, 'now we have about an hour to wait. Come with me and I will show you around here. I believe you will find it instructive. You may leave your case if you wish. It will not be moved.'

King gave a wintry smile as he rose, 'that will not be possible' he said indicating the chain which bound the handle to his wrist. Andrade shrugged and led the way from the room.

The tour which followed was all too familiar to King. They visited a series of rooms on all three floors of the building in which the occupants — almost all men and all in uniform — were seated at battered desks or peering into decrepit filing cabinets. All of African state bureaucracy was there, the normal smell, the dust and decay and grubbiness: all the piles of files which he would find from Benghazi to Brazzaville. The Major maintained a monologue of explanations, but there were no introductions. There was much springing to attention and flamboyant saluting but the coal black faces remained closed and unwelcoming.

They returned at last to the hall and Andrade stopped by the one door through which they had not yet passed.

'This is our waiting room for those being held for interview', he remarked with a gleam of anticipation in the dark eyes. For King, the first sensation was the smell which hit him in a blast. It was pure Africa, the combination of heat and sweat and dust and dirt. It was overlaid with a greater pungency, a rancid, penetrating mixture of urine, blood and excrement: sharper still was the stench of human terror. He stood motionless in the doorway and let his eyes wander.

The room was oblong in shape and measured maybe five metres by three. The walls on three sides were of plain concrete, roughly finished. The ceiling was crudely plastered with holes through which could be seen the steel floor formed in the room above. The fourth wall was made up of windows, sealed into their concrete surrounds. These had a few cracks which spoke of poor workmanship but which provided the single source of ventilation. There were no blinds or curtains and the blazing midday sun made a furnace of the room.

There were six occupants of this hell hole, three men in rags and a fourth, completely naked and stretched out on the floor. Two bulky guards stood roughly at attention as they saw the Major: each held a heavy rubber truncheon dangling from his hand.

Andrade flashed a quizzical expression but King refused to comment, knowing how much the Major was relishing the effects on him of this little peep show. They withdrew to return to the office and King noticed that one of the guards followed them. He glanced at his watch. The hour had almost passed.

Andrade turned to say, 'make yourself comfortable, Mr Offenbach and I will go to supervise the arrival of the prisoners. They were foolish to come and will be fortunate to leave, but they did not have suffer our waiting room for too long — no more than twenty-four hours as I remember and there were some fringe benefits.'

King forced a neutral expression onto his face, refusing to ask the questions and knowing that Andrade could not resist continuing. What an opportunity to taunt the CIA and the whole American ideal. The Major spoke again.

'Poor Mr Wallinger is elderly and became distressed quite quickly. He tried to run for the door, but was of course prevented by my guards. They're big fellows as you see,' he waved a hand at the uniform which had followed them in, 'and perhaps he quite enjoyed a little of their black muscle. Your retired Colonel Macrum also became agitated because he can neither sit nor stand for long. His language was offensive and he must have been quite a fighter in his glory days although he was no match for my people when they had to subdue him. I expect the new pains of a broken head and a few smashed teeth took his mind of that bad leg of his.

But it was Ms Stockton who surprised me most. A most attractive and spirited lady so I had her removed to my office here where I could entertain her properly.'

Andrade was smirking as he finished and King had to hold onto his fury as the nausea rose in his throat. He forced himself to speak calmly.

'Just get on with it, Major, and I'll be waiting.'

'So you will, and my man there will be waiting with you, just to make sure you have all you require.'

Andrade made a soft, unhurried exit, carrying an aura of superiority with the promise of the best prize yet to be enjoyed. King sat down at the table and turned his attaché case around to face him, the retaining chain hanging down almost to the floor. He pretended to fiddle with the locks: he knew what would happen next and it duly did. King sensed the big guard move across the room behind him, could hear the heavy footfall as he came close, smelt the bad breath, felt the massive arms clamp down around his chest. He knew what this was about. Andrade was titillated by violence. He'd had his fun with the other three, more amusing than the pain he wreaked on his regular 'visitors' and why not finish up with a number on this gangling black Yankee who had the answers and talked pretty but looked like a puff of wind would blow him over. There was no risk to the deal after all: none of them would be leaving without that money order which he had already inspected being safely in his pocket and ready for Doe when he woke up from his latest excess. The Major was already looking forward to the bonus of seeing a bowed and broken Offenbach as he strode out to collect the prisoners off their transport bus.

Back in the office, things were not going to his plan. King waited for the big guy to tighten his grip before he stood abruptly, kicking back his chair and grunting with the effort of picking up eighteen stone of flab and muscle. Without an instant's pause, he bent forward and tipped the guard clean over his head to land on his back across Andrade's polished desk which, satisfyingly, lurched on broken legs under the impact. King was on the big man in a flash, beating the stolid black face with a flurry of blows and finishing with a crashing blow to his forehead from the heavy glass ashtray which had been sitting on the table. The guard lay senseless on the Major's smashed desk and King calmly went to work.

He opened his case, withdrew the money order and one sheet of notepaper signed by Ronald Reagan. Above the signature, he wrote a polite message to Samuel Doe, placed it with the order in an envelope which he closed with the Seal of the President of the United States of America, using equipment carried for the purpose in his case. This he locked again, adjusted the chain around his wrist and sat back to wait.

Fifteen minutes later, he heard Andrade enter the room. King spoke without turning round.

'Here's what due to Mr Doe', he said. 'with a copy for you as I promised. One thing, though Major, you need more than one of these goons to damage me. And now, I hope my people are here as we have a plane to catch'.

The four of them were back in Abidjan that evening, three abused and shocked citizens of the USA who would never again visit Africa. King Offenbach was relieved, but he allowed himself more satisfaction some weeks later when Ambassador William Lacy Swing was on leave in Europe and they met at the American Embassy in London.

'A week after you left,' he reported, 'we had a public execution in town. The President himself used the sword to take off old Andrade's head, and he had to have a few swings at it. It may be scuttlebutt, but the word is that he got only half the payment and that he was upset by a personal letter from the big Cowboy, explaining that he'd given the other half to the Major. Now, how can all that have happened?

DAVID HEAVEN & MARTIN KIRCHOFF — 1985

One Monday morning in June, Martin failed to arrive at the office after the weekend and David was becoming worried by late afternoon when Ruth finally rang with the news which he had guessed would be the explanation. Sol had been rushed into hospital on Sunday evening and they thought they would lose him during the night. It was not a new problem. Sol habitually caught chills which went to his chest and knocked him out for a couple of days, but this one was much more serious and had quickly developed into a life threatening pneumonia.

Sol was, however, never a quitter and by the end of the week, Martin was back to report that his old Dad looked to have turned the corner. David was delighted and relieved, but he also saw an opportunity.

'As soon as he has enough strength, Martin, we must tackle him about the rent question.' Martin knew he was right.

Kirchoff and Son occupied 100 Piccadilly under a smoke and mirrors sublet contract of a type beloved by old Sol, but Martin fretted constantly about the arrangement. Their landlord was a shadowy individual with a vaguely described business which took up most of the building. As Martin and David agreed in the pub one evening, the two of them had no idea what sort of deal Sol had struck. They knew they were paying much less than prevailing market rates, but they didn't know why and Sol had remained determined not to discuss the matter.

'It's my little gift to the business,' he would say to deflect them, 'just enjoy the benefits and stop fussing about it.'

But now they had to fuss. They went to see him at home shortly after his release from hospital and sat down to talk under the eagle eye of Naomi who warned them not to tax him for too long. Knowing him as they did, they were not surprised when he forestalled their questions.

'Yes, yes, boys. I know you're both right. We can't risk me pegging out without you knowing how to keep the roof over our heads,' and he continued, looking frail but still as smug as only Sol knew how, 'but I'm still not going to tell you the deal I had these years past because you don't need to know now.'

'Please don't string us along any more Dad,' put in Martin and his father turned on him with a flash of the old spirit in his eye.

'Just listen to me, Martin. Our landlord in Piccadilly is that old rogue Gluchamheig.'

He ignored their astonished faces as he continued, 'I won't have to tell you how I got such preferential rates for us. He owed me big time for sending you, David, off on that wild goose chase to Windhoek and beyond — promising us diamonds when he meant arms, and knowing full well that I would never deal in weapons. You boys know where I met Gluchy and I always thought there was honour amongst us victims of that era, but apparently he thought differently. Well at least he's paid for it now — paid by giving us a smart address over the past twelve years for a fraction of its value.'

Sol stopped to recover his asthmatic breath and give himself a sip of water. When he went on, it was in a calmer, quieter voice.

'Well anyway, what's past is gone, but there is very recent news. Old Gluchy is even older than me and his business has been going bad on him: his health also. What a pair we are!' he said as he shook his shaggy head mournfully.

'Now he wants out — to give up as soon as he can. He's been on the lower two floors, the good ones, for years now and I suspect he hasn't looked after them any too well. He's paid up until the end of next quarter, so he'll be gone by autumn. What you two must do now is to get your backsides into a meeting with the very smart gentleman who owns the freehold. My advice is to put our cards on the table. We've never been part of Gluchy's outfit so probably we should never have been there, but we've paid our way and never been any trouble. You two weren't responsible for the arrangement and you can truthfully say that you knew nothing about it. It was all down to your doddering old dad who is fast losing his brains and perhaps his breath before much longer. But as for the future, well how different could it be? Here are a couple of bright sparks, already established in the building and with a great business which wants for nothing except a bit more space. You should propose to take on the whole place when Gluchamheig moves out. You offer full market price on a repairing lease, plus we'll fund a renovation to owner's approval of those two lower floors. I'm pretty sure he'll go for that!'

Sol sat back looking pleased with himself. The reactions from Martin and David were predictable. Martin gibbered with doubts and concerns, David was gung ho but they were together in doubting that the owner would be interested in the proposition. In that, they were both happy to be proved wrong.

There was little to be done before the end of September because the reclusive Gluchamheig remained in silent situ behind closed doors, but they were able to calculate the financial impact for this new responsibility. The figures turned out to be less demanding than expected, partly because they would be saving on the two overflow offices which they could now close, but also thanks to Martin's cautious foresight. It transpired he had worried about his father's handshake deal and had been siphoning off profits into a 'rainy day' account which could now help with the costs of refurbishment and a larger rent. It became Martin's turn to look smug, and both Sol and David assured him that he deserved to.

Sol had another surprise for them. Three weeks later, he took them to lunch in a favoured restaurant in Shepherd Market and there explained his proposal.

'Boys, we all know that I'm supercargo in the business these days, and there's no regret or shame in that for me. It's made me one happy old Jew to see how you work so well together and what you've done with Kirchoff and Son. And that's my point. The business has changed and moved on a long way —

so far indeed that it now has the wrong name. Kirchoff must go out with me. It's high time for a new brand. Isn't that what you smart crowd talk of these days David? That's what we need now, a new house with a new name on the door. You must choose one that the business can grow into.'

Martin and David looked at each other and knew immediately that they agreed with him. Kirchoff and Son had never been technically correct, although practically no one alive would know that. With Sol's almost complete retirement, it now sounded wrong and Martin was even more anxious than David that their title should be international rather than overtly Jewish. Sol was right. They should find a name which offered room for growth.

The problem, of course, was what? The three of them went for days scribbling lists of possibilities and they were still undecided come October when they had the keys of the entire building and were swarming with builders and decorators. At the first opportunity, Ruth came in to take a look around. She was startled by the size of the place. It somehow seemed to be coming together as more than two extra floors, plus of course the basement which had been quite overlooked in the past. And there was more. Restoring it into one was putting the very soul back into this splendid building with so much history trailing in its wake.

As she finished her wandering, Ruth happened to find Martin and David on the ground floor in the entrance hall, comparing notes and costings. Ruth was a very literary lady and despite her upbringing and her faith, she liked to quote the Bible, 'for the love of its language' as she used to say. And now she approached her husband with a typically discreet nod of approval, further emphasised by the sparkle in her eye.

She teased him. 'St John. Chapter 14. Verse 2.'

Martin raised his eyes to heaven and smiled lovingly as he spoke.

'Go on then, Ruthie. You know I won't get the quotation. Just tell us.'

'In my Father's house are many mansions.'

That was the new name for their business. The Mansion House.

THIERRY CESTAC — 1986

Cestac heard the news on the radio late in the evening as he was sitting over a cognac at his house in the Latin Quarter. It was as he expected, but he was nonetheless pleased to receive confirmation from the BBC World Service.

Earlier that day, a Soviet owned and operated Tupolev airliner had crashed in the Lebombo Mountains of South Africa whilst on a flight from Lusaka to Maputo. The aircraft was carrying a delegation of the government of Mozambique, coming home from an international conference which had been hosted in Zambia. It was reported that there was a handful of survivors, but over thirty passengers and crew had died and these included the pilots and the most significant traveller, the First President of Mozambique Samora Machel.

Cestac would have been yet more gratified if he could then have known the extent and longevity of investigation which this event was to set in motion. To confuse had been his role and motivation from the first. Machel had been a determined and ruthless leader who fought his way with gun and word to assume control of a fledgling nation which had finally battled itself clear of Portuguese colonialism and internal strife. Over years past, he had been forced to accept material help where he could find it. His sources had included the Soviet Union, still smitten by its vision of neo-colonialist grandeur throughout Africa, and the extreme right wing politics of apartheid South Africa, anxious to keep its resource-rich neighbour quiescent and available for exploitation.

The shadowy figure who approached Cestac in 1985 worked for the USSR. He was a diplomat attached to the Soviet Embassy in Paris and had plenty of opportunity to move cautiously in developing his relationship with Cestac. Over time, his confidence in the discretion of the Frenchman increased to the point when he was prepared to start talking about specific objectives. Cestac kept his views to himself, but he found this Russian to be a self-important prick, forever rolling his eyes and speaking darkly of State secrets which he could not impart while the whole damn strategy would have been obvious to many a lesser brain. Cestac hung on, feigning admiration for his contact's intelligence assessments and expressing support for the Soviet Pan African cause. Money was no longer a subject of interest to him. It kept rolling in but it was important to his reputation that he continued to charge ever more eye watering fees for his services. In addition, he would still provide satisfaction for some aberrant taste, particularly if in doing so he could position himself to acquire influence over those with whom he was working.

Satisfyingly, that had been exactly the situation with this Russian, a jumped up toad for all that he was a full Colonel in the KGB. The man was heterosexual, but unwisely let slip to Cestac one day that he enjoyed the attentions of an energetic dominatrix. It had taken Cestac one phone call to bring Madame Louche into the picture and she made an excellent film record of the attentions which she wreaked on the Russian's miserable body in the secure cellar beneath her luxurious apartment, within screaming distance of the Avenue de l'Opera. When Cestac had started to play the video to his guest two nights later, he had been careful to be accompanied by Toussaint who sat silent, stropping his wicked knife on his right wrist and gazing malevolently at the Russian who expostulated with rage and panic. Toussaint did not need to be told that this was all about Cestac's ceaseless play for power. The KGB officer was well and truly caught between two extremes, each as uncomfortable as the other. If he stormed out to reveal to his masters that he had fallen rash victim to a scam, he would be disgraced, demoted, likely eliminated. If he tried to dispose of Cestac himself, he would have to face Toussaint first and one look told him that would be infinitely more painful than his session with la Louche.

So he took the third course as proposed by Cestac in reasonable terms. He capitulated to the request and introduced Cestac as the prime expert who must speak directly to his seniors running this operation. The Russian's escape seemed to be as simple as that. A week later, Cestac was introduced into a council of extremely senior people at the Soviet Embassy and quickly won respect for his intimate knowledge of the shadows of Africa. It was what Cestac craved: the audience which made him a kingmaker. And he was good. He had the history, knew the people, understood the aims and ambitions. In this case, the big picture was not hard to grasp. The Soviets had not lost their appetite for Africa, but they had experienced their frustrations — on the West Coast, in Angola and Zaire. In the East, they were active in the Horn of Africa, but their star asset lay in Mozambique where they had fermented revolution and cultivated relationships over many years. They believed they had Samora Machel in their pocket and that they could control a puppet regime right by the back yard of Western civilization as represented by South Africa. But now there was trouble to confront. The recently established President Machel was starting to demonstrate his own agenda. At best, this was going to see him riding two horses and permitting some slippage towards the West. At worst, he might move to abandon completely the Soviet hand which had been feeding him.

Moscow could not allow this to happen. So the conversation in Paris had turned towards the means of engineering a replacement for this popular President. How? After two fruitless discussions at the Embassy which struck Cestac as being flabby in content and ill directed in tactics, it was he himself who tabled a suggestion on the third occasion. He identified the opportunity, set the date and proposed the means.

'A staged air accident,' mused the Chairman. 'Neat. But how do you guarantee the right people die? And what about our aircraft and crew?'

Cestac was ready for that.

'Monsieur,' he replied, 'You will have a team on the ground to move in if the wrong people survive. As for the rest, the USSR can surely lose one plane from such a mighty national fleet and there must be many more pilots available.'

It was a moment of glory for Cestac, exactly the drug of adulation which was the imperative for his existence. He basked in the ensuing praise and admiration, whilst remaining privately sceptical as to how well the plan would work out at any level. Not that it mattered. The poor boy from Pau was becoming known in the world.

Typically, Cestac did not allow himself to overlook the important details of clearing up. A month later, the decomposing remains of his first contact, the much junior Colonel with unusual preferences, were discovered seeping from a large bin liner by urchins playing on a rubbish tip south of the city. It would have been better if the body had rotted in peace, but it really didn't matter much. There was no ID on the corpse, but it bore the hallmarks of gangland. The marks of a heavy whip to the torso, and the entry point of a slim knife behind the right ear.

ALEXA BUSHELL — 1987

It was early evening on Friday 4th September, the start of another weekend and it was ten years to the day since she had arrived in Hong Kong to start a new phase in her life. A long time, but looking back over all that had happened, it seemed longer. The first job had been OK. Alexa knew from day one that it was not going to be her heart's desire, but it was an entree. It kept her fed and clothed and housed in pretty considerable comfort, and since it was with Barings Bank, it gave her some social introductions.

After nine months of this existence, she took ten days holiday and flew back down to Sydney. She saw her friends, spent much time with Mark and inspected developments at the Clinic. The Peter Bushell Foundation was up and running, and there was a blue plaque on the door to say so. Alexa fulfilled her promise and made a speech at a ceremony. She stood outside the apartment block in Double Bay and thought of him. She returned to Hong Kong, conscious that she had turned a corner and should now be accelerating her progress. She started the search for a new job and a more satisfying apartment which she could make into a home.

Alexa had met a few people despite leading a pretty quiet life. There were some girl friends from work and other contacts. She played regular tennis, went out for early evening suppers, did some sailing and picnicking. She became close to an American girl, Tina Fullerton, married to a British husband Bill, who was a currency trader. Tina was gregarious and well connected. She moved quickly to introduce Alexa to a head hunter who was recruiting for some corporate lawyers from London. They were getting established in Asia and they hired her at once.

Alexa relished her new job with Ince and Co. They were

nice people with no doubt brilliant legal brains, but not always great at organising themselves. As the company expanded, the Partners came to value Alexa's ability to administer things with grace and style. In the same timescale, she established herself in a far bigger and better apartment, widened her circle of friends, did a lot of partying. She rediscovered her joie de vivre and enjoyed a brief affair with a wild but entertaining Irishman.

Alexa was composed and happy with her life when she met Hugh Dundas for the first time in May 1981. Hugh was buying a small shipping company owned by a client of Ince and Co and Alexa had been present at a meeting of all parties involved. She was there to ensure that people and arrangements were in the right place at the right time. Hugh Dundas took notice of her, more in fact than she noticed him. She knew his name, of course. There were few in the Colony who did not. He had, it was said, a computer brain linked to a Midas touch. What he did not have, as Alexa observed when they were introduced, was much in the way of style.

Dundas was a gaunt, thin streak of a man. He was then forty years old, stood almost six foot six, but was prematurely stooped with iron grey hair cut too short. He wore heavy, granny spectacles and dressed in clothes which would have better suited his grandfather. The wags claimed that he wore black brogues on his huge feet even with shorts. But he disarmed with charm and his sombre face could light up with a mischievous grin which gave the lie to those jealous souls who sought to dub him as a brilliant, geeky bore.

The shipping company was no big deal for Hugh Dundas. It was neither large, nor especially expensive. Alexa had no idea of its purpose within his grand design but she did take note of the exemplary manner in which he handled the final arrangements. He seemed always to have time. Hugh was never in a rush, always moving calmly on those great feet, always ready with a gracious comment to those around him. But in a way, it was not quite fair. He could better afford the time for polite asides than most of us because he needed less for the essentials. His memory was prodigious, his grasp of detail fearsome, his choice of word and expression unfailingly well-judged and his vision for the total big picture apparently crystal clear with a decision, once taken, never being revised. In an age before the concept of multi tasking, Hugh Dundas was already a master of the craft.

It happened that Hugh was back in the Ince office only a week later, to have lunch with Roland Carpenter, one of the founding partners who was a friend from schooldays. He was sitting in their comfortable visitors' area waiting for Roland when Alexa was passing through. She thought he should be better received, but he was entirely relaxed and happy to chat to her for a few minutes. She was impressed that he remembered her name and role in the organisation.

'It's good to find a bit of organising flair here,' he confided with an attractive, lopsided grin, 'Lawyers are all very necessary in life, but they're not so good at taking decisions.'

Alexa was all too conscious that she was simpering like at a schoolgirl at his compliment. Rather more alarming, she felt a surge of energy pass between them. Dangerous ground, she thought and felt both relief and frustration when Roland appeared in a rush to claim his guest. There was no further contact between them for a couple of months, but then Alexa was helping Roland with an art exhibition in which the company had a legal interest and Hugh slipped in on the final evening. He advanced towards her desk and she rose to greet him.

'How nice of you to come,' she said, 'and only just in time. Do you admire what you see?'

'How are you Alexa,' he replied bending from the waist like a courtly, old fashioned hussar to kiss her cheek, 'and actually No is the answer. I really don't care at all for this sort of stuff. I prefer a painting to be of something I can recognise.'

Alexa relaxed. 'Yup. I must say I agree and I've been having to look at it for days on end so you're getting off lightly.'

'Well,' he said, 'we mustn't be that honest with poor Roland. He would be disappointed in our inadequate taste.'

He paused for what seemed an age before resuming with a question.

'Since you've had enough of all this, what about a drink somewhere?'

In that moment, Alexa knew that the electricity between them was not going in one direction only. There was chemistry at work, and all this was leading somewhere. It was going to happen, but she knew this was not the time. So she shook her head and fixed him in the eye.

'I'd love to, Hugh, but not this evening. I really must finish this job properly and make sure we're all ready to move out first thing in the morning. But thank you.'

Hugh inclined his head.

'Of course. I respect your dedication. Roland evidently doesn't know how lucky he is to have you around him.'

Alexa was trying to decide if there was a further meaning in his words when he continued.

'And when you finally do get away, how do you wind down from all of this?' and he asked the question as one long arm wandered around the room.

Alexa knew she must stay firm.

'By going home to put my feet up, have more than one glass of wine and finish my excellent book.'

He nodded his understanding, but was not yet to be put off.

'How very laudable,' he smiled, 'and somehow I guess that you're not reading either War and Peace or a bit of Jane Austen?'

'You're right. But the first is close. Actually it's War and Remembrance.'

His eyebrows rose. 'An excellent choice. Such an epic novel and worth the long wait since The Winds of War. What led you to Herman Wouk as an author? The Caine Mutiny?'

'Actually not, although I've read it and seen the film of course. No, my first Wouk work was Youngblood Hawke which I loved. I like the way he tells a story and I was under the spell from page one. The idea of a hillbilly who's a brilliant writer but looks like a truck driver captures my imagination. But then I've often been attracted to people who are not what they seem.'

Alexa turned away, suddenly embarrassed by her own

candour, but Hugh just stood there with his long arms folded about him and grinning with unrestrained pleasure. Finally, he said.

'Well message taken. Oh, and I do hope to see you again soon.' And with that he left her.

As things turned out, it was not that soon. July turned into August, a month which Alexa had come to regard as her least favourite of the year, when it was hot, humid and brazenly sunny. She was reminiscing over her last trip to Sydney and starting to anticipate her mother's visit in September. She was conscious of being irked by some of the demands of working at Ince. She loved her apartment and tried some redecorating but decided the results were disappointing. She was unsettled, distracted and frustrated when Tina Fullerton precipitated a crisis.

'Bill and I are throwing a bit of a party,' she phoned to say, 'it's at the Club and it's to celebrate being here ten goddam years. Would ya believe that, Doll!'

Garden lights were twinkling prettily as Alexa got out of her taxi and a buzz of lively conversation stirred the languid air in the spacious area between the Club's main pool and the tennis courts. There must be a hundred or more here already, Alexa thought to herself as she collected a glass, waved to a couple she knew and went to find her hosts. Bill was busy talking but Tina peeled off from somewhere to give her a hug of welcome. They had no time to natter before the restless swirl of gossiping guests moved to reveal a familiar figure standing a few feet away with his back to them. Tina muttered something like 'great timing' and moved across to tap him on the elbow before a horrified Alexa could stop her, then Hugh Dundas turned around and his smile of pleasure embraced them both.

'What a great party, Tina,' he said, 'how did we get on for entertainment here before you and Bill arrived? Alexa, how lovely to see you after much too long. Have you brought Herman Wouk with you?'

Hugh laughed as he bent forward to kiss her cheek and at that moment she heard Tina say, 'And hey, Alexa, have you met

Hugh's wife Janey?'

Alexa was never to forget that introduction. Janey Dundas gave the sweetest smile and held out her hand which carried a warmth of greeting.

'No, we haven't met before and I'm so pleased to do so now. Hugh has often spoken of you.' Janey spoke with the voice of a genuine English rose, and she had the complexion to match. She had a sweet face with gentle laughter lines and the slightest suggestion of a dimple in each cheek. Even in this light, Alexa could make out the compelling violet colour of her eyes which sparkled with her vivacious spirit. She wore her enviably thick auburn hair to her shoulders and the lights from the pool caught the double row of diamonds about her neck where they rested on her fine bosom encased in a white silk top which was set off by slight and delicate embroidery.

A proper English lady, Alexa had time to think to herself as she took the proffered hand and smiled her own greeting. She had to bend down. Janey Dundas was in a wheel chair, and she could never rise from it.

In sharp contrast to that moment, Alexa could never remember quite what happened next. She had vague memories that they chatted in a group for a few minutes before Hugh found the right moment to push his wife on to speak to other friends. As they stood alone, Alexa turned to Tina and said,

'Be my friend. I'm going home now, but call me.'

Tina Fullerton didn't ring her the following day, but went one better. She was waiting on the door step as she returned from work, and they went for a pasta supper together before returning to Alexa's apartment for a talk on the balcony which lasted most of the night. Bill had been warned that he would likely be on his own.

After Alexa had apologised for ducking out of her party, Tina told her about Hugh and Janey Dundas. Alexa had not appreciated that the couples went back a long way. The men had been childhood friends and had gone through school and university together. There was a considerable difference in their brain power and a greater contrast in their wealth. But Tina reported that in her typical, straight talking style.

'Hugh's an absolute fuckin' brainbox. He's a bloody genius. And yet with all of that, the bastard's just a nice guy. He's gentle, thoughtful, never pushy. And as a friend, well let me tell ya Alexa that he's just the best. Ah, Jesus, just the very fuckin' best.'

Tina's language was inclined to deteriorate as her alcohol intake increased and Alexa was content to wait while she filled both their glasses and lit up another of her favourite cigarettes. She curled her legs under her on the sofa and continued.

'Hugh's got my Bill into jobs and out of scrapes over the years more times than I care to recall, and to be honest with you, the two guys are really not in the same league at all. Bill would be the first to agree. He couldn't live with Hugh in any sort of a race. And you might expect Hugh to lord it a bit. But he never does: never has done and never will I reckon. He doesn't do patronising, he's just there for you when you're in the shit, and he somehow manages to pick up whatever sort of tab it is without you even noticing. I know he's razor sharp and he sure can be fuckin' ruthless. I've seen it. But if you're his friend, waal, you're lucky ... and you're goddamed guaranteed.'

All of which was good to hear, but it wasn't the background history which Alexa craved, so she broke in gently to steer her friend with a question.

'How long has she .... I mean how long have they been living here now?'

Tina didn't answer immediately. She lay back on the sofa and stretched her long legs out to rest on the coffee table. She took a long drag at her Camel and pushed aside the long black hair. Then she sat up suddenly and wagged a slim finger.

'Ok, Alexa. Now listen up. First, I'll give you the short history. Then I'll tell you where you're at and what you've gotta do about it. OK?' Without pausing, Tina went on, 'and here's where we are gal. No interruptions. No questions. Nothing I say gets repeated. To nobody. Not ever. Not even your goddam mother. Is that a deal?' And she looked pretty fierce.

Alexa nodded, 'I promise.'

Tina nodded with her and reached for her glass. She took a swig and started in.

'The short version, heh! I was born in Small town Dakota, US of A. Bright kid, did well at school, graduated near top, heading for Wall Street, took six months out to travel Europe. Did France and Italy. Saw the museums, test drove the boys. Finished up in London. Went drinking. Got picked up in a club in Belgravia. Some fancy speaking Limey schmuck. Fell for him and married him. So. Tina Goranko becomes Mrs Bill Fullerton. Leaves behind her Polack past and joins the British upper class.' She threw a face and mimicked a regal dowager look which gave Alexa the giggles.

'OK so far?'

'Gottcha!' and they both laughed together.

Tina continued, 'Bill Fullerton. Second son and third child of well connected, so so financed English for ever family. Farming in Cheshire since the Romans. Schooled at Rugby, known for cold showers and bared bums' — this in a grossly parodied true blue accent which had Alexa smiling —'there met Hugh Dundas, only child, orphaned through a car smash, lives with uncle, aunt and cousins in wild Northumberland. The two become inseparable, asshole buddies as we say. Hugh gets Bill through exams and into university. They room together, drink together, chase women together. Hugh has more brains than blood. Bill is the sportsman: really good at cricket and a shit hot golfer. Hugh is a mug at any sport and he's not so strong as Bill at pulling down the girls. So they balance a bit. Still get the picture?'

Just a nod from Alexandra.

'The guys graduate and move to London. Set up house, get work. Both in the City. Hugh is snapped up with his double first, Bill is hired and in those days, a name was as good as a brain. For a couple of years, they have a ball. Work a bit, party a lot, holiday as and when they can, visit each other's family etc. All that good stuff. And can you guess what happens next?'

Tina poured more wine and reached for her packet of Camels.

Alexa replied tentatively.

"Ah ... you met Bill?'

Tina shook her head, 'Not yet. First up, it's Hugh who falls in love. He goes in a party to some concert — the Stones I think — and he's introduced to Janey. The Honourable Jane Williams-Blake, third of five daughters who hail from some goddam great pile in Wales. Janey and Hugh are smitten and get engaged in the fall of 1966. They're pretty young, but everyone agrees it's a terrific match. Just the best and set for life.'

Tina paused to swig at her wine before she continued.

'This next bit's tough and I wasn't on the scene to see it myself. It all comes from Bill. Like I said, Hugh was never into sports. But he did love cars and Bill says he used to drive them pretty well and goddam quickly. He had a little old British sports car, an MGB race prepared. Hugh takes Janey out to show her the works. Hugh is trying hard and showing off. He overcooks it, spins, clumps the bank, turns over twice, ends upside down. He's fine, belted in. Janey isn't. She's thrown out: onto tarmac: damages lots. She can't walk, hasn't walked since, will never walk again. Plus a few things more, like no control, no sex, no children. Not ever.'

Alexa was chilled by Tina's account but kept her promise not to interrupt.

Tina contiued, 'I didn't come on the scene until '68. Bill and I zipped home in the October, marrying before the worst of the Dakota winter started to hit. We were back in London before Christmas, when I first met Hugh and Janey. By then, they'd been married about six months I guess, so a long time after the planned date, but on lots of levels incredible to go through with it at all.

'I can hear all the questions in your mind, Alexa, and I have to say, well shit, I don't have too many of the answers myself. Bill says that after the accident, Hugh was calm, but both grief and conscious stricken. He wouldn't talk much about it, not even to Bill. He wouldn't hear about getting out of the marriage or even postponing it beyond Janeys's critical recovery time. He was —

what was Bill's word? Obdurate. Yup, that was it. Obdurate. This is the girl I love, he seemed to say, and I'm sticking with her. For better or for a great deal fuckin' worse, and he hadn't even signed up to the goddam vows by then.'

Tina waved a languid hand that suggested Alexa was now permitted to speak. She picked up her own glass and a cigarette before she replied.

'Golly Tina. What you've told me is such a desperately sad story. Thank you though, thank you so much for telling me. I feel a whole lot better for knowing but I haven't a clue what to do next. The thing is that although there's been absolutely zero involvement between Hugh and me, the chemistry is there and we're already some sort of soul mates. I know it sounds crazy to say that,' she finished limply.

'No it doesn't. Why d'ya think I've opened up like this? You and Hugh have got neon signs all over you. The worry for me and Bill is that this has never happened for Hugh before. Christ knows why not but I guess he just hasn't met the right broad. Oh sure, he takes himself off now and again for a bit of mischief, and even Janey knows that and of course she knows why. But I reckon she thinks it's a bit like a guy who just has to go gambling once in a while. And anyway Alexa, I never had the chance to know Janey before the accident, but I have to say I doubt we'd have become that close whatever. I think I'm a bit uncouth for her. We don't get a laugh out of the same things and I do declare I would've always found her a mite stuffy. The English rose with the upturned nose. I'm not so sure they were ever that passionately in love. Bill says I'm wrong, but Bill's a man and what do fuckin' men know about these things, huh?"

Alexa had to laugh again, but inside she felt her spirits drooping. Tina sat bolt upright as she noticed the sudden change in Alexa.

'Tell me, honey. Say what's griping. Better yet, tell me about you and yours and the past.'

Alexa surprised herself by doing just that: going right back to the loss of her brother Michel, to Oxford and the Five, to

Thierry Cestac and Bahrain: to Connie's intervention and Peter Bushell's action, to her collapse and eventual restoration thanks to Mark: to all the time at the Clinic: to her marriage to Peter and his death.

It took a further couple of hours, her monologue interrupted only by the regular rasp of Tina's lighter and her astonished profanities as the life history unfolded. When Alexa was finally finished and the tears pouring through her ruined makeup, Tina just said.

'It's dawn doll, or goddam near it. Let's you and I get at least some rest. By and by, I'll tell Bill your story, and tell him to tell Hugh. That'll be for the best, you'll see.'

Alexa was too tired and drained to protest. For the first time ever, she rang in sick early in the morning and then went back to bed to sleep through until after lunch time. She snoozed again and woke for long enough to have a bath and a boiled egg, followed by a further, dreamless sleep. She woke early the following day and made her customary journey to the Ince offices, hoping that she would hear again from Tina. It was a Friday and Alexa was starting to fear a long weekend of recriminations and self doubt.

She returned to her apartment in the early evening. There had been no word from Tina, but she found Hugh Dundas standing on the pavement waiting for her. He spoke no word as she walked up to him, but simply opened his arms to her and enfolded her in an embrace that seemed to last a lifetime. Finally, he whispered softly in her ear.

'I have to go to Manila this evening for the weekend. You're coming with me and our car arrives in fifteen minutes. Go and pack. You won't want much. I doubt you'll get out of bed.'

They arrived late and were driven to a hotel of great style and grandeur. Ushered into a suite the size of a ballroom, it was Alexa who took control.

'This is not our time,' she said, 'not quite yet. You go and sleep. Tomorrow is for us.'

She heard him leave in the early morning, but didn't get up herself. She spent much of the day snoozing and snacking on room service. She knew exactly what she was doing, reaching for relaxation as she had practised under Mark's care in Sydney.

She was showered and ready when Hugh returned in the late afternoon. He was uncharacteristically uncertain, letting himself quietly into their room and looking around as if expecting to find that her presence was only in his imagination. She sent him off to the shower, and whilst he was there, she undressed and put on the silk dressing gown which she had brought. When Hugh emerged, she smiled at the huge feet sticking out from the towelling robe. She stood on tiptoe to smooth down the few spikes of unruly hair and she removed the specs from his nose. Hugh did not protest, nor when she took him by the hand and led him into the master bedroom.

She pushed him down gently to lie on his back in the middle of the huge bed. Then she slipped out of her dressing gown and came to lie on top of him. Her feet seemed to get scarcely past his knees, but their faces were together and she kissed him gently on the lips. Hugh's eyes were almost shut in his face upturned to the ceiling, but his hands were caressing her back and buttocks, and she could feel him coming alive beneath her.

Alexa lifted herself and placed her hands on Hugh's shoulders with her arms straight. She looked down on him and he opened his eyes in response and smiled up at her. She spoke.

'At last, my darling Hugh. And now I want to ask something of you.'

He said nothing, but his eyes flickered with enquiry as she continued, 'try your best not to hurry and to wait for me.'

'Of course,' he said with his warm smile as he brought one arm up to stroke her breasts, 'but tell me, do you always dish out instructions in advance?'

She shook her head slightly and her hair cascaded about her so that he had to strain to hear her words.

'No. And it's not what you think. It's just that I've never been in love before.'

That first, stolen weekend in the Philippines had stared the era of AD in Alexa's calendar: After Dundas. Hugh had been right.

They hardly got out of bed for the following twenty-four hours, spending the time in gentle exploration of each other's body, mind and memory. There was passion, laughter and tears. There were explanations to share, regrets to offer, secrets to reveal.

From this beginning, a pattern of life became established, one which Alexa would never have believed herself capable of accepting. She was astonished to find fulfilment in being a part time lover and partner, even almost a wife to Hugh at times. She was pleased that he was so stimulated by her body, happy that he rejoiced in her spirit, but delighted that he became captivated by her thoughts and the nuance of her opinions.

There was never a ménage à trois, and Alexa and Janey scarcely met again. From the outset, Alexa knew that she would not and could not influence Hugh to leave his wife. He had made a commitment from which only death could release him and he would lose Alexa before reneging on it. In her private thoughts which she shared with no one, Alexa sensed that there was a bit more to this than old fashioned honour. Janey was some sort of talisman to Hugh: it was as if standing by her brought him compensation in the success of his career, which was not just about money and the inexorable expansion of his business. He was also absorbed by the great range of people to whom his influence gave him access.

As time passed, Alexa came to appreciate that his relationship with Janey was changing. The girl whom he had loved, irreparably damaged and then made his wife was herself changing and becoming, it seemed, ever more a dependent child rather than a companion. To do credit to Janey, she never complained about her condition, but sympathy suffers without the oxygen of effort, and it frustrated Hugh that Janey found it enough to exist rather than to look for stimulation in any of the interests which she could have pursued in spite of her condition.

Alexa had her first chance to introduce her mother to Hugh in September 1982. She had been confident in advance of how well they would get on, and she was not disappointed. Elizabeth mentioned Joffrey's interest in Hugh's business. He had been impressed to read that Hugh's primary holding company — Head Investments — was estimated to be worth some $250 million. Is that really true, Elizabeth wanted to know, and was that US dollars or Hong Kong?

Alexa recognised the tongue in cheek but didn't resent the question. Hugh had told her often enough that it was no secret, and that he wanted her parents to know about him. So she replied.

'Actually, Mumsie, I believe it's a little more than that now. It seems to keep growing like Topsy, and the currency is neither of those. Hugh being true blue will only measure his assets in good old pounds sterling.'

Her mother's elegant eyebrows had shot up at this revelation, and she struggled for a further comment, finally settling on another question.

'And what does the name signify? Being that successful, why doesn't he call it Dundas something?'

'Well, actually he has. He was saddled at birth with a lot of names – Hugh Edward Arthur Dundas. That's what gives the name.'

There was a pause before Elizabeth resumed on a tack which Alexa had anticipated.

'Tell me to stop if you must, Darling, but you can't be surprised at your old mother thinking of this. I do understand that this man is your true love and I am thrilled for you. You know that. I can see that you have to lead the life that you have now, and that there's no chance to be married to him, but what about a child? Wouldn't Hugh himself like to have an heir?'

'Mumsie, I'm happy for you to ask, and glad to tell you, but I'm afraid there's absolutely no chance of that. The complications would be immense but there's something more basic than that. I think probably that my past is finding me out, but I've taken a whole lot of professional advice, and it seems that I definitely can't conceive. I'm not sorry for myself, but I do regret it for you and for Papa of course. At least you have Bernard and Els with their two.'

They left it there, both glad to have the conversation behind them, both conscious that whatever was denied to Alexa, she did have the love of her life.

AISCHA GOMES — 1989

The month was June. David Heaven sat in the aircraft, relaxed in anticipation as he always felt when en route to see Aischa. They were meeting in Lisbon again. Aischa had been living there for the past twelve years, sometimes accompanying Alves to Luanda and from there making rare visits with discretion to see her father, Jonas Savimbi, surviving on his passions somewhere in the deep bush of southern Angola. Aischa was better placed in Portugal, living comfortably in the stylish house which she and Alves had bought, working more for amusement than need in an art gallery, developing her own painting with growing confidence. Occasionally, she travelled to California where Rafa was now living with his family.

Mostly, she was in Lisbon for her daughter Anna who had been brought up there and was now rising eighteen and about to move into university life. David had never met Anna, but he was introduced to her briefly that afternoon as she had been shopping with her mother and was going on out to meet up with a crowd of her friends. She was very sweet, lively and pretty with a superb figure like her mother. She was friendly and charming, but of course David was of no account to her. A mob of them for dinner and dancing somewhere was her priority and quite right too. David had a glimpse in his memory of that other evening by the sea in Mocamedes, all those years ago.

Anna went off with a smile and a little wave to David, a big hug for her mother. They were obviously close and David noted the whispered exchange between them. It sounded like some motherly advice and probably admonition not to be too late home. He reckoned that he and Aischa would have a lovely long evening together, but not the whole night.

Aischa confirmed this as they moved away themselves, her arm tucked lightly in his.

'I'm sorry, my Darling, but I must go home at some stage and not too late, and without you I'm afraid, but tomorrow's different of course. Anna is staying over with her girlfriend for a couple of nights. But look, David, let's start our evening with a stroll for a while. The city is looking its best in this lovely weather.'

And so it was. Aischa was a competent guide and enjoyed her love for this ancient city with so many past tales to tell. She chose a route which brought them to the river bank and they wandered for an hour beside the Tagus, drinking in the scenery, relaxed in the evening warmth, holding hands from time to time and chatting like the long established lovers which they were.

David had just moved into his apartment on the top of 100 Piccadilly and Aischa wanted to hear the detail. About a year previously, Martin had started fussing about the wasted space on the top floor and this had given David the idea of living over the shop. Aischa helped him with the design and in reality, she'd done most of it, teasing him that there was only space up there for a decent bachelor pad, quite inadequate for a man with a wife and maybe some children. All too typically, David smiled graciously and held his peace.

Now she wanted to know if the pictures they had chosen together were looking good and were properly lit. What about that lamp on the table in the hall, and where .....'

'You'd better come over again,' he said laughing at her.

'Oh I will. And you'll be in trouble if I find you haven't made a proper job of things.'

Eventually, they caught a cab and returned to the city centre, then walking on into Bairro-Alto and to the restaurant which was always their choice for the first night of his visits to Lisbon. Giacomo Mori, the proprietor, seemed to defy the passing years as he greeted them with his normal warmth and took them through to what had become 'their' table by the little gossiping fountain.

'You are looking well, Signor Heaven, and still so young,' he remarked as he moved behind Aischa to adjust her chair.

'You're flattering me, Mr Mori. And you know it,' David smiled up at him, 'and you yourself, still as ever?'

'Ah no, I am feeling older and more tired. But I do not wish to leave Lisbon. This is my home now and I hope that one day my son will come to join me in the restaurant. We shall see.'

He flitted off with their order, perhaps embarrassed to have lifted a corner of the veil over his life. Much later, after they had finished eating and were sitting quietly in the warmth of the night with a cappuccino and a cognac before them, David lifted his glass and said,

'Well. Here's Happy Birthday to Anna. Eighteen is a big landmark, isn't it? I'm sorry, my love, but you'll have to remind me of the actual date. I must get her something for it.'

Aischa put down her coffee cup and moved to clink their liqueur glasses gently together. She said. 'It's next week on Friday. Her birthday is the thirtieth of June.'

He nodded, 'She's a delight to meet, I must say, and a picture to look at too, just like her mother of course! I can see how close you are, you two. Real friends, I'm sure, as well as mother and daughter. Her birthday must be as important to you as it is to her.'

Aischa gave a wan smile and turned her head away to light her cigarette. It was something that he did for her when they were alone together and there was a suggestion of independence here which made him feel excluded. David sat still and quiet, knowing that she would speak when she was ready. He took a sip of his cognac and was still replacing his glass on the table when Aischa sat forward to reply.

'Yes. June 30th is a very important date in my calendar, just as it is for Anna also. It's the day on which she was born, and also the day on which her mother died.'

David stayed motionless while his mind raced, but it didn't have far to go. Aischa's eyes remained fixed on him whilst he settled his glass, took a cigarette for himself, lit and drew deeply on it. Then he spoke one word, as a statement and not a question.

'Ouye.'

Aischa looked at him as the tears welled in her eyes. She gave a long, slow nod.

'Yes Ouye. My twin sister Ouye, who died almost eighteen years ago while giving birth to the baby girl who is now Anna: my special friend Anna, who is my daughter even though I'm not her mother. She has grown to be so like Ouye that I sometimes feel she is my sister recreated.'

David picked up his glass again, swirling the brandy around as he phrased his next question.

'Aischa, why didn't you tell me this before? Do you remember we were in this very place, the first time we came here, I asked about Ouye and you told me she had died of some female difficulty was your word I think?'

Aischa cheered herself and even smiled a little.

'I believe I said 'a feminine problem with much blood and pain' and I knew that you, a man of men if ever I saw one, would not dare to ask more. And you haven't. But really, darling, I think I gave a fair description of childbirth.'

'So you took on her baby.'

'What else? I never gave it a second thought.'

'And you were never challenged? Not by your father, or by Rafa? What about Anna's father?'

'My father and brother were content with the arrangement: they found it natural. They'd accepted Ouye's pregnancy, they were both made miserable by her death. They wanted all that could be done for the baby she left behind. But as for Anna's father, well that's different. He's never known and never asked. But to answer your next question, David, yes I do know his identity. I know him very well indeed. And I love him. So you should not buy Anna a birthday present. You have already given her life itself.'

David slumped back in his chair as the breath whistled out between his teeth. He had seen the blow of surprise coming at the very last second. But he knew that the revelation was true. No doubt at all. He knew when, and the memories came so clearly to him. The droning fan, the barking dog, the opening door and the giggled whisper 'you can't tell us apart if we're not dressed at all'.

They sat for a long time in silence which was broken only as Mr Mori appeared unbidden to refill their brandy balloons and to place fresh coffee on the table between them. When he had left them, David hunched forward to spoon some sugar into his cup and to ask,

'Why didn't you tell me Aischa?'

'You didn't ask me, did you, my darling. But you see before that, after Anna was born and Ouye taken from us, well I knew what and when, but what did I know of you? That night in Mocamedes was just a bit of naughty fun and with a result that's been happening down the centuries. I didn't know anything about you, did I? I knew your name, but nothing else much. Not really what you did, where you lived. And I certainly had no idea that I would ever see you again, still less that I would fall into a love for you that I simply can't shake off. And don't forget, David, that Anna was almost three years old before you and I met again by sheer chance. And since then? Well, perhaps I should have said something, and if so, then years ago. I held back because I made a life with Anna as my daughter which works. It works well. And while my time with you is so precious and vital, it's still just that. It's time, but it isn't a life. I think I was always scared that in telling you about Anna, I might also lose you for myself. Can you understand that?'

'Yes I can,' was his immediate response, 'and to be boring and factual, I can see also that there was no real need. Not in the usual way which affects things like this. I mean, there was no problem with money and so forth.'

He hadn't put it as a question, but she answered him anyway.

'No. None whatever. And it's strange, you know, but marrying Alves has helped in other ways also. He's an absolute model in the father role. He's very proud of Anna, always there but never interfering. You know, we've settled into Lisbon very nicely thank you, accepted as a family and as a one child couple when we're nothing of the kind. Three of us unrelated, more or less, but just good friends. Funny really.'

Aischa was musing as she noticed David grabbing at his table napkin to brush away the tears which rushed suddenly to his eyes.

'I'm sorry,' he was embarrassed, 'I should be true blue Brit. No nonsense and no blubbing.'

Aischa reached over and put her hand over his.

'Don't stop. You should be proud of your reaction, not ashamed of it,' and she sat back smiling, pleased with him as she asked, 'what brought that on with a rush?'

He smiled with her, and chucked the napkin back on the table.

'Those lines from Rogers and Hammerstein came into my mind. From Carousel wasn't it? —"you can have fun with a son, but you've got to be a father to a girl". Instead of which, Aischa, I have gone blithely and blindly about my own life. Driven to succeed, whatever that may be, and always too obsessed with my distant past to either make or to meet my emotional commitments. I am ashamed. Instead of doing some giving, I've done way too much taking. I could've been more there for you over all these years. And for Anna. Well for Anna, I have done absolutely nothing. For my only child and daughter, I have done completely ... fuck all.'

Aischa's sparkling smile seemed to light the night around her. She arched one eyebrow and remarked in her most mischievous tone,

'If I recall correctly, that's exactly what you did do!'

David shook his head and laughed with her. She wouldn't permit him to lather himself in a bath of righteous self recrimination, and she was so right. He pulled himself sharply together and said,

'OK, and thank you. Unspoken rebuke accepted. But tell me, Aischa, what do we do now? Do we have the full and frank discussion?'

Aischa shook her head as she sipped some cognac.

'No, we absolutely do not. Look, David, you're not quite through with surprises for this evening. So sit back and listen.'

David did as he was told and she resumed.

'You know, God really does move in some mysterious ways. I know Anna is still only seventeen — well just — but she's a pretty mature young lady and she already knows a fair bit about life. Probably more than you would care to know actually.'

David refused to be drawn, and Aischa went on,

'I've said that she's mature for her age. She's fun but she's not madcap. She's realistic, but determined. I've known for a while that there's one man in her life. He's young, of course, but he is nearly five years older than her and like her in character. He's very focussed, very sure of his own ground, quite certain of where he wants to go and with whom he wants to spend his life. And that's Anna. And she wants him too. They're set on getting married sometime next year and moving to England where he has a career — something to do with land in the wilds of the country. I've tried to slow things down a bit, but what can you say? A hundred years ago, she would have been on the shelf at sixteen, so who's to say they're wrong? Even so, I really couldn't form a judgement until I met him and Anna understood that, so she arranged a get together for the three of us just last week. He had a bit of holiday due and flew over specially. We had fun together and I like him. I really do. I think the two of them are going to be good together. Exceptionally good and I was happy to give them my blessing.'

David had to interrupt. 'I trust you. I'm sure you're right. But this is good news, isn't it? Where's the problem?"

'There isn't a problem, but there is a bearing on your question about talking through everything, and that's because of his identity. You see, Darling, Anna has fallen in love with the son of one of your greatest friends. She wants to marry Oscar Aveling.'

David was stunned, 'Good God! That's incredible,' he shook his head, 'what an extraordinary thing. But how did it happen — I mean who introduced them?'

'A bus conductor it seems! No, actually that's the pure chance part. Oscar was over here on some friend's stag party for a weekend. He went out on his own for a couple of hours to see the sights and he got lost. He can't speak any Portuguese and he asked directions from a bus conductor who can't speak English. Anna happened to be at the bus stop: boy meets girl and there you are!'

'Well I'll be damned. It sounds like a film script but I guess it is the sort of thing that happens: and what a great story.'

He paused to light a cigarette and looked serious as he took her hand.

'You know, Aischa, you don't have to spell out the rest. I've known the background for a long time and I imagine Anna has told you. Oscar is one of twins — and incidentally, how different from his brother Peter who is a scallywag if ever I met one. They're the sons of Tepee Aveling, but my old chum Conrad is not their father. Indeed they may have different fathers because Tepee was gang raped and they are the result. That was years before she met Connie and he loved her more than enough to take them on. But what this means is that Oscar and Anna both are children of an unknown father, and that is one of the things which binds them together. So why say more? That's your thought isn't it?'

'Precisely. But can you accept that?'

'Oh yes, my love. Quite definitely I can and I agree with you one hundred per cent. But with just one condition.'

'Which is?'

'We leave the status quo as is, but if at any time in the future Anna should ask you about her father, then you must tell her. It's one thing to keep silent, but something else to lie about it.'

Aischa considered for a moment, but she knew he was right and she nodded her acknowledgement as he went on speaking.

'Does Alves know?'

She nodded again, adding, 'Yes, of course. We've never kept anything from each other, but there's no one else. I've never told my father, nor Rafa either.'

David sat forward again and reached across the table for her hand, saying,

'In which case, I've got a request, a favour which I'd like to ask of you both.'

This had Aischa rolling her eyes but she squeezed his hand to encourage him.

'It's just that I want to pay for their wedding, and they must have whatever they want. Big, small, grand, discreet — absolutely whatever. You and Alves handle this anyway you want, but whatever it is, I just want to cover it.'

'How very male. Many things you may be, David Heaven, but subtle you aren't. We'll see, but I expect we can work that one out, and I love the thought behind it.'

David hesitated before he put another question to her.

'Does Anna...does she know about us?'

'What a question, darling! Anna's a girl and we women give far more thought to these things than you giant killing, hunter gatherer guys. But look, you better have more of an answer'.

She paused to take another cigarette and let David hold a light for her before she resumed.

'I should say first that Anna knows all about Alves and our marriage: she's known for years and she has no problem with any of that. She likes Alves — loves him even, and she values very highly the time and guidance and support which he has given her during all her years of growing up. He has been a constant for her.'

David flinched as her words nipped at him, but he kept silent as she continued.

'She knows about you, too: not that you're her natural father, but that you are my lover and companion. She cares about me, about my happiness and fulfilment, and now she is wondering about my future and what will happen after she has married and gone off to start her new life in England. I tell her that I'm content with Alves and I'm in love with you, except that I can only have you on high days and holidays.'

'But that's not fair, Aischa, you couldn't just abandon poor Alves ...'

She interrupted him, leaning over and pressing her forefinger to his lips.

'No, David my darling. It is fair. This has nothing to do with Alves: it's all to do with you. There are times when I wish I could stop loving you, and God knows I've tried. There's been no one else for me since you came back into my life, right here by this same fountain, and what was it, fifteen odd years ago? But you're part time, aren't you? There's not room for me permanently, not even in that apartment of yours in London. I'm not saying you're married to your job. It's not that. You're just like my father — married to an ideal, a dream, a vision. You don't want to conceive a child, you want a whole new civilization and a country to put it in!'

Aischa paused to pull on her cigarette and then to stub it out before she continued,

'Mind you, David Heaven, I'm pretty determined myself. You don't get rid of me easily either.'

There was a warm pause between them, a look of love and a conspiratorial smile. Then she said,

'And now, before I go home to our daughter, would you please take me somewhere where I can make love to you.'

HUGH DUNDAS —1990

It was late in January when Hugh met David Heaven for the first time. David had been travelling in Asia for two weeks and he called into Hong Kong on his way home to London. They found an instant empathy and acknowledged Alexa as the catalyst. At dinner on their first evening together, she chided David for not bringing Aischa with him and pointed out that the two couples had much in common: both so much together and yet still apart. This candour made for some intimate conversation and set the style for a business discussion in Hugh's office the following day.

David was already well briefed on the size and scope of Head Investments. He had some idea of the wealth of Hugh Dundas and he could certainly appreciate his influence. The man was now regarded as another Warren Buffett and his global activities formed a staple diet for leading financial commentators. But no amount of research could have prepared David to meet the Hugh who had been memorably described to Alexa by Tina Fullerton as an 'absolute fuckin' brainbox, yet the bastard's just a nice guy'.

As they sat talking that morning, David was alarmed to find himself struggling to keep up. It was one thing to have the background, the reputation, the knowledge and the prescience, but Hugh was further blessed with the calm confidence which rounded his ability. He'd had his setbacks and disappointments of course, and he told David about some of them, but in such a way as to illustrate how they had all become experiences which had brought ultimate benefit. There was more to Hugh than all of that: much more. As time passed, David was stimulated by the growing conviction that he was talking to a fellow traveller, a man with a lifetime mission on which he was not yet properly embarked. There was one big difference between them. David knew exactly what he wanted, whereas Hugh Dundas had yet to identify his lifetime goal.

This became clear to David while Hugh was talking about his work for charity. In behind it all, David felt he could see some more payback for Janey and he knew about the background from Alexa, plus there was more of course. Hugh was vastly rich and successful. His genuine desire was to contribute, to make a difference and there were examples which he admired like the Gates Foundation, but it was obvious to David that here was a subject of rare indecision for Hugh: he was not yet convinced of the area in which to make his commitment.

Lunchtime interrupted them before David could enquire more as they were going out to join Alexa. The three of them reminisced over a light snack, during which David was amused to find that Hugh's outstanding double first had been won at Cambridge, but there were still places, people and experiences which they could share: they were of much the same age. David could see clearly that Alexa and Hugh had an incomplete, but very fulfilling relationship. They really were a matched and balanced couple from whom the happiness simply radiated. He had understood this before, but it made a difference to witness it for himself. He admired how Alexa had reconciled herself to the circumstances — to make the most of her time with Hugh and not to suffer from what was lacking. She had told him privately that she had been much influenced by advice from Tepee who had said 'in my experience, if what you've got is good, hang on even if it's not enough.' She might, thought David to himself, be speaking for Aischa as well.

That afternoon, Alexa left them and the men returned to Hugh's office which was understated in its comfort, the only ostentation being in the awesome view over the harbour. The relaxed ambience spoke volumes to David: despite the pressures of success, Hugh's priority was to organise his life — not the other way around. Then came a further revelation. At Hugh's request, David put some flesh on the bones of The

Mansion House, of which his host already had a comprehensive understanding. David told him about early days, of dodgy deals and difficult people, tortured communications and testing travel. Hugh was fascinated and pressed him for more stories of journeys in Africa, reminding David of Ruth Kirchoff and how she would drag from him over those homely suppers in Highgate the details of faraway places. David spoke about their current position, why he and Martin were determined to stay with the formula which worked for them and in areas where they had proven expertise. Africa was their ballpark and in specific business groups. Mining, transport — but by land only: they didn't venture into shipping and stayed away from airlines and cargo. Building, not houses or office blocks, but civil engineering, especially dams and bridges. Food production, but not agriculture, and finally, finance. This last and transport were their links to the past.

He finished by saying, 'but the world moves on, doesn't it Hugh. The Mansion House used to be all about trade from Europe into Africa with a bit of supply from the States, but nowadays our supply sources are increasingly from Asia and that's why I've been spending time in this region. We need the knowledge and the contacts.'

'Oh I do agree with you. I'm sure you're right about your own business, David, and after all, the results speak for themselves. As to the principle, the same applies to us here. I'm myself preoccupied with how things will change when the Colony reverts to China, and that's not far in the future. Actually, I'm using it as an opportunity to think things through to a completely different level and for exactly the reason you have expressed. The world will change, like it or not, and for me, the thrill of that lies in the challenge of what we can make of it. I confess to being a bit fixated by this part of the globe, but this is where I have most knowledge, and I do have a grand plan.'

'Is it something you can speak about?'

Hugh removed his large spectacles and rubbed the sides of his nose.

'Actually, yes, I think I can. After all,' he smiled his lopsided grin, 'you're sort of family! More than that, I have a good instinct for whom I can trust and anyway, this is just stargazing for now. But I have started work on the project. You see, David, I think that there's room for another sort of Singapore, especially if we assume that Hong Kong as we have known it will disappear under direct rule from China. So I have been wondering if I could talk the Australians into selling a chunk of the Northern Territory, not a huge acreage in view of how much they have there, but enough land and coastline in which to establish a brand new sovereign state. It would be principally a financial centre of course, but with a population drawn from around the globe and nurtured by a constitution which would give humanity a bit of a fresh start. As you say, we all need to move up a gear from time to time. But it's grandiose notion, arrogant even, and I expect you to say it sounds barmy to you.'

'I think it's remarkable, Hugh, extraordinary.'

'Polite words for mad is what you mean.'

'I don't. I meant exactly what I said. I've got my own wild vision, you see, and I've been thinking about it over the last twenty years. I want to take over a country in Africa. I want to win power, and then start doing things differently. I guess that makes us both mad megalomaniacs.'

Hugh sat up straight and gazed at him.

'Really. Please go on.'

'I'll explain, but in essence I believe I've got the what and the why and the where. I don't yet have the answer to how, and in particular, I don't have the finance.'

'Ah well,' Hugh replied, 'that is of course my strong suit. Would you like to tell me more?'

David delayed his departure from Hong Kong by twenty-four hours and Hugh cleared his diary. They passed another day and a good deal of the night in lively conversation which included Alexa for much of the time. He was surprised to sleep well on his flight, but his mind was buzzing again as his car bore him from Heathrow into Piccadilly. He entered The Mansion House and took the lift to his private staircase and on up the short flight to his apartment.

He had returned here so often from his forays overseas that he had fallen into a routine which had become a ritual. He dropped his elephant skin luggage in the small hallway and went into the sitting room which seemed to smile at him in welcome. He breathed in its pleasing features: the generous, rectangular shape of the room: the masculine, rather clubby furniture whose effect was redeemed by the greens and pale yellows of the decoration. He scented the fresh flowers in their squat, wide mouthed vase placed on the refectory table which he passed to take in the lofty view of Green Park from the two windows. He grunted in appreciation and turned to retrace his steps, this time ignoring the lift and walking down the broad staircase.

David passed the next level of the building which was home to finance, marketing and personnel. He descended to the first floor and entered the Communications room. It looked more like a news base in a national paper, a large area with desks and work stations organised like the spokes of a wheel. Each spoke was dedicated to servicing a number of countries on the continent of Africa, allocated according to a mix of country size, location and language. Information from and to each destination was controlled at the spoke and fed on from there towards the hub, the central control point which was the domain of the Belgian born Felix Maas, the most completely competent man whom David had ever encountered. Felix was multi lingual, multi tasking, multi capable and all in a calm and measured personality with an abundance of good humour. Under his control, they were ever evolving, always seeking the latest technology which could give them the edge in guiding their decisions, investments and means of influence clear across the continent. But to use information, you must first acquire it. In addition to published detail, informed comment and arbitrary gossip, there needed to be a permanent drip feed from reliable, well placed sources in each country of interest, and for The Mansion House, that meant any sovereign state between the Mediterranean and the Cape of Good Hope. David had collected his contacts over many years of crisscrossing the continent. They were people of both genders, varied age, any colour, creed, nationality or provenance. Over time, he had slimmed this Babel house of communication, choosing just a few correspondents in each destination. People came and went but it was often just word of mouth which found a replacement. In the early days at Westbourne Grove, communicating was such a challenge with dodgy telephone links and the marathon process of the telex message. Then it seemed that technology would make his people network redundant but nothing replaces local knowledge and gems of information still flowed from these sources on the ground. They called them the 'Scribes'.

David didn't dawdle. He turned on his heel and went back to the staircase, trotting down the final flight to the ground floor. He crossed the reception area and walked down the corridor to his office in the corner of the building. This personal sanctum was simply decorated to provide a restful environment. It was never locked, and David would nip down here from his apartment at odd times of night or early morning. The building as a whole never slept. Only on Christmas Day and New Year was there no one at work, and even then there was at least one of the security staff on silent patrol. Otherwise, there were people here day and night engaged in their myriad computer operations, the vital organs of the constant communications ability upon which so much of their business depended. Sharing the ground floor with him with a similar office next door was Martin Kirchoff and across the corridor lay two reception rooms in which visitors to The Mansion House could be comfortably accommodated. There was also a dining room which could seat twelve at a pinch and was serviced via a lift system from the kitchen in the basement.

He checked his desk briefly, then turned again. He had done his rounds now. It was still early and he would go back up to his apartment to shower and change, then to tackle a pivotal conversation with Martin. As he returned to reception, David hovered as his eye fell fondly on the copper, head and shoulders bust which stood on a side table in silent welcome to all who entered The Mansion House. It carried the simple inscription which read 'Solomon Kirchoff'.

Dear Sol had died in 1987, almost exactly two years after they had taken over the whole building. He was seventy-five years old: not a great age, but quite an achievement given the circumstances of his war years. The end had come through another of his chest infections. It had been quite swift in the final stages, with little drama and no pain. David had dropped in to see him the evening before he died and they both knew that the purpose of his visit was to say goodbye. Sol had been determined to stay at home with Naomi content to be beside him. He and David had a few words together and a bit of a chuckle, two old fashioned men of different generations but similar disposition. They both recognised that the time had come and their farewells were muted, a warm grasp of hands and a parting look of appreciation. David didn't go to the funeral and his reason was clear to Martin. Both remembered Sol's instruction from years before: 'don't come up our way, Davy. We love you, but you're not a Jewish boy and you wouldn't fit in.'

This morning, David paused to wonder what Sol would think of his intention, the commitment to himself which had sprung from his conversation with Hugh Dundas. He fancied he could see the beard quiver with excitement.

THIERRY CESTAC — 1991

Paris. Christmas Week with short days, a cold and sleeting rain. Cestac walked to his house in the Latin Quarter following a long lunch at a local brasserie. He was accompanied by Toussaint, keeping his eye on the hordes of shoppers. Both men had turned up the collar on their coat and were walking briskly.

It had been a most interesting conversation. Cestac had been surprised to hear again from the Russian who chaired those meetings at the Embassy about the Mozambique business. That had been what, five years ago, maybe going on six. At the restaurant, he seemed much as Cestac remembered him, still a sleek looking fat cat and now confident enough of himself to come alone. Cestac would not have done the same and Toussaint was now his permanent shadow.

As soon as he got home and into his study, Cestac dragged out his comprehensive world atlas. He settled down to study it along with the notes which he had taken during the lunchtime conversation. He was not surprised to be so ignorant of the lands which made up the USSR. Geography had held little interest for him during his school days and in those times anyway, all that vast part of the world was closed, covered in red and decorated with hammers and sickle. Cestac was a well read man and kept himself properly aware of world affairs so he was perfectly conscious of the implosion of the Soviet Union, its official confirmation now just days away. What he had not appreciated until today's session were the possible benefits to him personally.

His host at lunch had explained that he was himself not Russian born, but a native of Kazakhstan which was about to become independent, the largest and wealthiest of all those former Soviet Republics which were on the point of being turned loose. Yari, as he now called himself, had covered some of the big picture facts and statistics before moving on to explain a particular injustice of fate which was now threatening him and many of his circle. Yari spoke good French and laid it out for Cestac.

'In the old days, the command structure of the USSR was overwhelmingly centralised: top down management as they would say in today's business schools. That meant that if you were born in what you could call the Provinces, so in my case anywhere in Kazakhstan including Alma Ata, you struggled to get out. You strived to get to Moscow, through university there and on to a career ladder, probably in the military or better still, the KGB which is what I managed to do. That achievement got you status and a real future, unless you lacked self discipline like that idiot you put out on the rubbish tip.

The whole system meant that we high flyers left home young and stayed away, only going home for a family visit maybe once a year or even less. The contemporaries of your age who didn't make the first grade were out of your life and anyway you didn't want to know them: they were losers.'

He wagged his finger at Cestac, 'Now, the cruel irony is coming home to roost. Because you see, the second and third division guys who stayed behind have had all these years to consolidate their positions, to scratch their way along in what used to be regional, back water government, the best of them getting to run the local waterworks, power supply and so forth — even the rubbish disposal.'

Yari allowed himself a chuckle before he went on, 'The worst of it, M.Cestac, is that these undeserving and inadequate people are now set to make themselves very rich indeed.'

'How come?' Cestac asked.

'Because they're there. They're on site, in position, fingers on the buttons. And believe you me, my friend, independence in a dump like Dushambe is going to make huge opportunities for graft and power in the pocket. It won't last forever, but there's

239

surely going to be time and chance to fill your boots if you've got the balls for a few risks.'

'OK. I follow the argument and I'm sure you want to get into the action. But where do I come into this and what's in it for me?'

'Like this,' Yari replied, 'You see, I need people, the sort you can identify. I need them very fast indeed and I don't have the time or the contacts to find them. I will pay you top dollar to recruit them for me.'

'Is this for protection? Are you expecting to get taken down when you go home?'

'I wouldn't be surprised. I won't be popular turning up to push to the top of the queue. But it's more than that. What I really need is a small, private army. I need guys with me to help in some ruthless persuasion. I'm going to have to fight my way to the top of a pile, and then fight some more to stay there. But I'll pay big time. It's worth it for me. This is the chance of my lifetime.'

'Could be,' said Cestac, 'and yes you're right. I have the names and contacts. But for myself, I'm not so much interested in money.'

'I know that. That's why I asked to meet again. What holds your interest, M.Cestac, is power. Power and influence. And that's what I'm offering for your participation.'

There was a pause in their exchange before Cestac called for more wine over which they had settled to talk facts and figures. This was the detail which Cestac was now mulling over in the calm privacy of his study. He was going to do it, for sure. The opportunity was irresistible and he could see that there would be only one chance. But it needed some careful planning, both to succeed and to ensure that he was not himself sacrificed in the process. Cestac trusted no one, especially not a former KGB supremo now on the make for himself.

AISCHA GOMES — 1994

The year had started well for Aischa. During the first week of February, David and she managed a lunch at The Mansion House for the Oxford Five which meant that there were ten of them round the table. Aischa was pleased to be hostess for David, his other half rather than another guest. Alexa flew over from Paris with Hugh. They stayed one night and returned to her parents the following day. Hugh was off to Japan, but Alexa would remain in France for as long as she was needed. Her father Joffrey had gone downhill during the last twelve months and was thought to be fading fast.

Conrad and Tepee Aveling came to London for a couple of nights so they could be at the party and give themselves a rare break. King and Pente arrived together but by chance and from different directions. King was urbane as ever, but Aischa thought Pente was looking weary although the noise level was increased by his presence: also the smoke cloud. She wondered how he kept going but he seemed irrepressible.

Martin and Ruth Kirchoff were there of course. They both loved these occasions which invigorated Martin and Ruth sparkled with her wit and welcome. The lunch was a huge success. They were still sitting there at nearly 6 pm, moving round the table to usurp each other's chairs and to ring changes to their company and conversation. Aischa noted a warm gossip between Tepee and Alexa who were such good friends, and as normal, Pente got into a huddle with King Offenbach.

Aischa's concern was to see Martin looking a little nervous — or was it wounded? — that David spent so much time with Hugh Dundas. She had a word in David's ear and was gratified that he responded at once, including Conrad and Martin in their conversation. It was a happy interlude, a recognition of over thirty years friendship amongst the original Oxford Five.

After that, Aischa spent the remainder of the European winter in the mild climate of Lisbon and David flew down to join her for a couple of weekends. They walked and talked. He gave her news of his steady progress on his grand plan and from all of this, she could understand the significance of Hugh Dundas. Her David had the vision while Hugh had the means. They made a formidable pair but she feared for other relationships along the way, and that included her own with the man whom a part of her wished that she did not love so completely. By his own acknowledgment, David Heaven was both driven and selfish, almost paranoid about personal commitment and prepared to sacrifice human contentment before the altar of his dream. She tackled him again when he was with her as spring was starting to break out on the banks of the Tagus.

Aischa opened the conversation in their apartment when they were having a drink before dinner. The apartment was a story in itself. On a visit two years ago, they dined as always at their special restaurant, chez Giacomo where he revealed that he was going to sell the restaurant. He had grown too tired to go on, and his son in Perugia lacked the funds to join him. On a whim, David stepped in with financial help. Within a month, son Mario and his Isabella arrived with their brood of five to breathe new life into the restaurant and insisted on taking his father into a family house which they rented down by the beach. This left vacant the apartment above the business which had been home to Giacomo for many years, so David had entered into a long lease on the property. Aischa refurbished and redecorated it and when the work was finished, she and David had the first home of their own. She made it into an entrancing oasis, rich in character and priceless for them in its quiet and calm. They continued their habit of always eating in the restaurant on the first night of a stay together, and on these occasions Giacomo turned out from his semi retirement to lead them to 'their' table and to wait on them for their meal. The food improved under the influence of the younger Mori's, but the high quality service continued as it had always been.

So in their home, their love nest, their retreat from a busy world, Aischa could speak frankly to him. She started to talk to David by repeating her respect, her regard and her love for him. He was her man, and she wanted no other. But as she said, she had him only part time. She reminded him that they had been lovers for over twenty years and in all that time, they had never been together for longer than a week, never apart for more than three months. She had only once lost her patience and her temper. She had stalked out of their hotel in Rome — the only time either of them had visited that beautiful city — vowing that she would never see him again. But she had been in Lisbon again a year later when he went to see Alves, and Aischa had known of it, had tracked him down at his hotel, said not a single word to him until she had removed the clothes from both of them and got him inside her. And then. 'Don't ever leave me again'.

But they were older now and should be wiser. What was she to expect for the future? David heard her out in silence, his eyes following her face as she moved gracefully around their sitting room with occasional gestures to emphasise a point. When she finished, with her question hanging over them, she came to sit next to him in the window seat and he took both her hands between his as he continued his gaze. He leant forward to give her a chaste kiss on the cheek and then he sat back to make his reply.

'Well said, Aischa. Well and bravely spoken, quite right in every detail. You know, my Darling, I keep going over the same thing myself — to myself, and every single time I'm flying to join you. I confess I sometimes take comfort from thinking that Hugh and Alexa are in the same boat, but then I reproach myself. It's not at all the same and Alves is no barrier to be compared with their Janey. The problem is with me: it's my fault and my responsibility.' He smiled at her, but Aischa was not to be put off.

'David Heaven. You're very good at this mea culpa stuff, but it won't do and you know it. It's not I want to hear.'

'Yes, yes. I know that,' David rose and started his own circuit of the room as he spoke.

'OK. Well here goes with a full answer. I'll start with a declaration.'

He stopped for a moment to fix his eyes on her face and then continued speaking as he walked.

'I love you Aischa. I've been in love and in thrall since that evening when you walked into my hotel with Rafa, and I've never lost that feeling since. Not for a moment. But I wonder if you really understand the extent of that love, and all the forms it takes. Aischa, God knows how often we've talked about my background, my childhood and all that and I'm not going over it all again now. But you see, you're the love of a mother to me, you're the love of a family, you're the love of friends. You're companion and confidante and counsellor and kick-me-in-the-arse all rolled into one. And most important by far, you're my lover: passionate, thrilling, sensual, sexy. Completely knock out every single time.

'Put all that together and what d'you get? Or rather, what have I got? How do I describe it? There's no name for the feeling. I could stand here all evening and not find a proper summary. I could talk of satisfaction, completeness, fulfilment maybe. But there's no language available to sum it up. There's no poetry to capture the sense of it. Aischa, the best I can say is that when we're making love and you invite me inside you, my excitement is mingled with the sensation of coming home.'

He shrugged helplessly as he finished and Aischa couldn't stop herself. A tear welled in her eye as she moved forward on the window seat and stretched out her hand towards him.

David smiled and said, 'Now don't you dare start now! I haven't finished yet and if you touch me now, I'll only disgrace myself and start blubbering again'

So Aischa sat back again as he continued.

'That's what I feel. What I want for our future is for us to be together. Not as we are now. Not on this — this sort of timeshare arrangement, but permanently. All day and every day. But there's a roadblock, Aischa, a barrier. The barrier is self imposed and only by me. You know about my pinnacle plan. It's getting close now, I can't say quite how close because I don't know, but close anyway. Win or lose, what I want is for us to be permanently together. But I just can't start yet. There's no explanation for that in logic. Not really. It's much more a thing of the heart for me. Maybe it's a primeval urge. Stake out your territory first, then put down your foundations. Whatever, I've searched my soul often enough and I know I'm stuck with it. I can't change it, or perhaps better to say that I know I won't change it. That's me.'

He broke off for a pause which seemed eternal to them both. Finally, and in a voice that sounded unusually shaky,

'Aischa, please wait for me. Please. But if you can't or won't, you'll still be my only and my complete love.'

She stood then and walked over to him, putting her arms around his neck and pulling his face down to hers.

'You're a very demanding guy, David my Darling, but I love you too and it sounds as if you should come home. Right now and right here.'

Midsummer brought an especially happy occasion for Aischa. During the heat of July, Anna and Oscar Aveling came to Lisbon for a holiday week, bringing their two children with them. Oliver had been born on New Year's Day 1991 and his brother Edward followed in August of the following year.

It was therefore quite a family unit which Aischa collected from the airport and she drove them home while chattering to Anna about all the child bag and baggage which she had got in, and all the things which they might do together. Anna was very aware that Alves had been diagnosed with prostate cancer and although he was holding his own, the prognosis did not sound bright. Aischa had planned a few outings with her grandchildren so that Anna could spend time with him.

It amused Aischa that Anna and Oscar appeared as a couple

acting rather older than their years, and traditional too. She half expected Oscar to arrive into the heat of Portuguese summer in his cords and tweed jacket and she smiled when she saw his blazer and tie. But he was good fun and good company. Her daughter was looking brilliant. Anna was a stunning girl with an inherited sense of style and presentation. Aischa was proud of her.

They seemed to be naturally marvellous parents, seldom fussed, always in gentle control and seamlessly sharing in the constant work and guidance. This made for ease of existence in a household unused to small children and they had happy days and varied outings together, a few of them including Alves.

David arrived in Lisbon at the end of the week and joined them at the Mori's restaurant for a tea time party which Aischa had planned with Isabella, who produced a feast topped off by her legendary ice cream. David had a comforting conversation with Alves who sounded much stronger than he looked, and they were both impressed to hear how Oscar's career was advancing. He's calm, confident and bright is that one, thought David to himself. Not as much mischievous fun as his brother Peter, but more set for stardom. And young Oliver was a treat. The little chap was sent by his father to say hello to David, who squatted on his haunches to exchange a few words.

'I admire your outfit, Oliver,' he said to him, 'very smart,' and he waved a hand at the military fatigue jacket and trousers. There was a bit of a wriggle of self consciousness before the boy replied.

'Thank you. But sorry I can't talk now. I'm a soldier you see.' As David nodded in sober understanding, the child added as if in secret aside, 'my friends call me Olty.'

Shortly afterwards they were all gone, leaving a lonely table for David to occupy by himself. After lunch the following day, Aischa came to him. She had left a nurse with Alves and driven the young Aveling family to the airport. They would now be in the air on their way home to Hereford.

David thought she looked tired and sounded subdued,

understandably so after a week of visitors and children. Whilst he read, she went into their bedroom in the apartment and slept for a while. Later, he heard her from his chair in the sitting room as she ran a bath, and some time afterwards, she appeared looking her best and normal self, radiant and happy.

They talked for a while as she told him more of what they'd been doing over the last few days, dwelling on the antics of the children and the pleasure which she took from their outings together. 'But golly,' she finished, 'it does wear you out.'

They moved on with their conversation ranging over other things, including dates and what were to be their next plans. David had a note of his travel commitments for the following couple of months, and Aischa used this as a prompt.

'Darling one, I'm going to travel myself next month, assuming no crisis with Alves.'

David looked up at her. This was unusual, and the question was in his eyes.

'I'm going down to Angola. I want to say Harisha to my father.'

'Well,' remarked David without thinking, 'Say so from me too.'

He knew it was a flippant comment, but he was surprised at her forceful response.

'Don't be stupid David. I can't do that.'

After a pause, she came to sit on the sofa which was placed near to his chair. She tucked her legs under her and looked at him.

'I'm sorry to snap like that. It's not your fault that you wouldn't understand.'

'That's OK,' he smiled, mollified, 'but what does it mean, this word you used?'

'Harisha. It's one word which encapsulates a custom and a practice which for us goes back as far as time itself. Harisha means literally 'I see you'. It's a salutation and a greeting, but also a form of farewell. I believe there are other words and phrases in the tongues of Africa which carry the equivalent message, but for our people, the Ovimbundu, it's Harisha.

Harisha is a word used only by a woman in speaking to a

man. Harisha is employed as an expression of farewell with honour and affection. And so it may be said by wife to husband, by daughter to father, by mother to son and so on.

She will use it only once, although she may say Harisha to more than one man. I don't know all the details of provenance, I don't believe anyone does know except that it stems from long ago days when women stayed at home to watch over children and to keep the fires burning while their men were off hunting and fighting. That's why it may also be used when a woman greets her man with 'Harisha' if he is returning from a tribal fight or such an extreme hunt that it may be recognised as his pinnacle achievement — as good as it can get, you might say. That's Harisha.'

Aischa stopped abruptly and looked at him, much more relaxed now and a smile playing around her lips.

'Thank you,' said David, 'that's interesting and strangely moving. We have no equivalent really, do we?'

She shook her head, 'No. We don't.'

Then he continued with a question, posed gently, 'and why now, my love, if I may ask you that? Why must you go now?'

'Of course: I suppose it's now for a combination of reasons. First, I think my father is going to get more and more difficult to find — in his mind I mean as much as in location. Even with the Accord signed last year, I don't think he can accept that it means a future which merits his support. I don't say he's right and I don't think he is right. I'm just saying that I'm sure he will never stop trying to fulfil his own obsession. That means he will become more and more driven and increasingly desperate. I'm afraid that he'll lose support. More and more Angolans want to lay down the hatchet and start working in cooperation to build a new life. I honestly think he's being left behind and I know he'll never understand that. I'm fearful that he'll never come in from the bush. I think we'll lose him there and I believe that he will almost certainly die a violent death. But I still love him and I respect him. And so I need to go and find him one more time, to say Harisha.'

DAVID HEAVEN — 1995

Nigeria loomed large in the business plan of The Mansion House. Africa's most populous and energetic nation could never be ignored and David had loved his frequent visits over many years. He cherished days spent in the north — anywhere from Jos to Kano and west into Sokoto State, but business demanded him in Lagos and later in Abuja. Then there was Port Harcourt where they had interests in oil extraction and drilling equipment.

Towards the end of the year, the world's media was fixed on the fate of Ken Saro-Wiwa, musician, author and the coherent voice of MOSOP — the Movement for the Survival of the Ogoni People, a small tribe in the Niger Delta whose existence was under threat from the Federal government. Ken and his eight colleagues were tried by a military tribunal, convened for the purpose by Nigeria's de facto President, General Sani Abacha. The general had assumed power in mid 1993 and was soon recognised as a villainous dictator, repressing opposition and extorting vast bribes from the international community. He was particularly vindictive towards the Ogoni Nine and saw to it that the Tribunal found them guilty with a sentence of death by hanging.

David was distressed. He had met Ken only once, but he knew well another member of the group who had acted as a Mansion House Scribe for many years. David had been negotiating behind the scenes and believed he had a deal for their pardon and release. It was simple enough — alms for Abacha and plenty of them. He was familiar with the General's scheming and he had the measure of his bagman, Colonel Peter Hamza Tahawa-Hamadou who was based as Military Attaché at the Nigerian High Commission in London.

Hamadou was tall, lean and good looking. He was dedicated to Abacha and acceptable because he was a Muslim from somewhere near Kano, which was the General's birthplace. He was as unprincipled as his boss and since he loved all the good things of life, he needed the money to make the most of his chances. David had made contact much earlier in the year, wining and dining the Attaché, pushing some extra money his way while using him to settle a deal with Abacha. A fifty per cent down payment on the figure finally agreed had been paid, the balance to follow by transfer to a Swiss bank as soon as the plane carrying the Ogoni Nine had left Nigerian airspace.

But then they hanged them anyway, all Nine and one by one, with Ken the last after multiple botched attempts. David got the news by telephone that November Friday evening and he sat at his desk at 100 Piccadilly late into the night, chilled to the core, furious, thinking and finally planning. He started with an obsessive fear that he was losing his touch, convinced that he had misread the signs and had bungled his handling of things. But then he brought his icy logic into play, backed by his experience of the passions and power play of Africa. He just knew he'd done all he could. He had used the right contact in Hamadou and he had made the right offer. He had lost, and Abacha, well documented as a corrupt kleptomaniac, had been better bribed by someone with a different agenda. The bonus to the General was that he could now make off with the down payment while thumbing his nose at the world-striding white man of big business. Probably, it had not mattered a toss to him whether the Ogoni Nine had lived or died. David went to see Martin at home the following day, Saturday morning. He set out his thoughts and his plan. He both needed and wanted his partner's agreement which was not withheld.

'I'll go along with that, David,' Martin told him, 'of course I will. The bastard deserves what's coming to him and the cash is something of nothing in the scheme of things. Do it, but do it quickly.'

David nodded his thanks and left to return to The Mansion

House. At the door, he met Bill Evans, their Head of Security who had come in at his special request. Evans was a proper Cockney, having hardly been out of London in his life. He had been a high-flying police officer, but was retired early following a car accident whilst in hot pursuit of a stolen car. The Mansion House had been lucky to find Bill and now he sat quietly, waiting for his brief from David. When he had finished, Bill ran a hand over his close cropped hair as he responded.

'Right then Guv. I get the picture and I suppose you want this done quickly. Happens I know something of this man Hamadou, like where he lives and how he likes to spend his Saturday nights.'

'Good God, Bill, how the hell d'you know that? Any of it?'

Evans was unmoved. 'It's what you pay me for, Guv. I just keep an eye on regular visitors. Most often it comes to nothing and no threat to the Mansion, but sometimes it's paid off and this looks like one such. Now this Hamadou lives in a plush pad off Eaton Mews. On his own but he pays big money for his company. He uses an escort agency run by a woman I had police business with, so she keeps me in the picture. He likes to drink in Soho — only the straight pubs mind — and he gambles in Belgravia. I can set up a party for him this evening, only I'll need the dosh obviously.'

They agreed on a plan and the timing. Bill Evans left. At 7.30pm that evening, Peter Hamadou was halfway through a bottle of champagne at Crockfords Club in Mayfair. He received the message that he had a visitor and went down to find two young women waiting for him. Peter knew one of them under her working name of Kayla. She introduced her friend as Portia who was tall and lissom with honey blonde hair and a knowing look. Kayla announced that the two of them were going to the Blue Lagoon for a bit of dancing. They needed a 'big dark handsome guy who can manage two'.

What the hell, thought Hamadou. I deserve a celebration what with those Ogoni vermin killed off and some extra for me from the General thanks to the scam over that silly old sod,

Heaven. So he agreed happily and didn't spare a glance for the driver of the cab waiting for them. He didn't notice Bill Evans activate the door locks but it did seem to be a long drive, even with the distraction of Portia's hands playing lightly over his crotch. Kayla reassured him that although Lewisham wasn't quite the West End, this club was something special. She was right: so special it didn't exist, but Peter was still unconcerned as the girls led him playfully through the garish front of a pub called The Tiger's Head and straight through a packed bar to a solid looking door at the back. This was the point at which the girls vanished, the door opened and strong arms pulled him inside. There were two guys to handle him, one black and one white: both were large, solid and silent.

They ran Hamadou across a large, unfurnished room. What appeared to be a ballet barre was fixed to the length of the back wall and his assailants wrapped a pair of handcuffs around it and back to clip over his wrists. Then they walked off without a word. Hamadou could walk up and down but he couldn't escape the barre. What the hell was going on here?

At 0100 on the Sunday morning, he was slumped on his knees, his wrists still captive, his suit dishevelled and stained where the champagne had caught up with him. He stirred as a draught of air reached him. He looked up to see that two more women had entered and were advancing on him. He felt encouraged. They looked to be a couple of good sorts with long legs beneath short and twitching skirts and again, one was black and one white. He struggled to his feet, hardly noticing their companion who was a short, scruffy man with a beer belly and a mass of camera equipment around his neck.

The girls came on without a word or a smile or a threat. It was the absolute absence of expression which was the most unnerving. The Black produced a knife which had Hamadou quaking, but she used it simply to cut away his suit jacket and shirt. Simultaneously, White squatted beside him, lifting one foot to remove the shoe: then the other. She undid his belt, pulled down his trousers and underwear and kicked the pile of clothing away.

Peter Hamadou stood naked in his socks, his hands still manacled around the barre, still expecting some bizarre but titillating experience to follow. The girls started to undress themselves, a pink blouse from White and a flowing hairpiece from Black to reveal a crew cut, bullet head. They moved together in front of him to peel off their skirts and reveal that they weren't women ... but men. He recoiled as they crowded in on either side in a provocative pose as the fat little photographer snapped and sniggered, scuttling round for the best angles of this unseemly threesome.

This first photo shoot did not take long and he was to wish it had taken longer. White broke off to rummage in her handbag and came up with a second pair of handcuffs and keys to the first. The two of them grabbed and held him with dominant strength. They bent him over the barre and secured the cuffs wrist to ankle. Hamadou was entirely captive and yowled his protest as Black and White took up the short, whippy quirts they had brought with them and went to work on him in earnest. They were fit and strong: pretty soon, Hamadou forgot his lack of dignity and concentrated only on the pain. The plump photographer kept working with a lascivious grin, wreathed by the smoke rising from the cigarette clamped between his teeth.

At midday precisely, the same cab arrived at Heathrow Airport and Bill Evans emerged to help Peter Hamadou who was unwashed and unshaved, his back and buttocks still bloodied beneath his jeans and shirt. Despite his appearance, he had a first class ticket for the Nigeria Airways direct flight to Port Harcourt. Evans had the connections to let him accompany the passenger right though to the gate, even to see him to his seat on the aircraft. At the same time, David Heaven was in The Mansion House, overseeing the despatch of details and photographs. Hamadou was collected in Port Harcourt and escorted to a personal interview by General Abacha who was known to abhor homosexuality and who required an explanation for the $25,000 in cash found in Peter's luggage. But perhaps the General should have given more credence to his account.

Abacha himself died three years later from poison administered by Egyptian prostitutes. It was never clear who had hired them.

That Sunday evening in London, David Heaven sat alone in his apartment above 100 Piccadilly and reflected. He had wreaked some vengeance and started the plan for more. But that was not enough and he knew it. He was resolved. He had reached his point of decision. He was sick and tired of balancing the books of influence, of blustering and bribing, of bobbing and bowing and hoping for the best. It had taken the fate of the Ogoni Nine to fire his starting gun.

THE OXFORD FIVE — 1996

They had gathered at The Mansion House on a blustery day in late March. There were nine of them. Aischa was with David, Alexa and Hugh had flown in from Hong Kong, Conrad alone, Pente from Northumberland and King from Grosvenor Square. Martin was there, and finally Ursula Hampton, David's PA and close friend.

David had assembled them for a business meeting, saying there would be a sandwich lunch with tea and drinks later. He wasted no time in getting started.

'It's good to see you all. I expect you're wondering why you're here and at least that's easy to answer. You're important people to me: my best friends, with whom I've shared a lot of years. What's more, you've each got experience and expertise which I need. I have a Grand Plan, you see, which I want to share with you. Afterwards, I want your reactions.

'Now I just have to set the scene. I want to talk to you about Africa which has been my business, my heart and soul for the last thirty years. I love Africa, you all know that, but the fact is that the continent has been going backwards for all the years I've been travelling there. Let me give you a tour around as we sit here.

'There are some bright spots. South Africa may be one of them and what a bonus to win the Rugby World Cup last year. But Nelson Mandela is only one man, even if a saint with wisdom. He can't do it all himself. I worry about what comes next.

'Developments are pretty good in Ghana and I think the pace will be sustained under Rawlings. The world view of Museveni in Uganda is positive: he can't do worse than Idi Amin. Stable times continue in Cameroun, and there's good growth in

Senegal. Chissano has ended the civil war in Mozambique and the refugees are coming home. There is great potential in Angola. Kenya is ... well OK, but Tanzania is nothing like what it should be. Nigeria is the curate's egg — good in parts.

'So there are nuggets of encouragement, but taken overall, it's not a terrific record since Macmillan started us talking about the Wind of Change thirty-five years ago. And that's before you start looking at the other side of the ledger.

'In the north, Chad and the Central African Republic are landlocked, remote and desperately poor. Nigeria is under a despot, so is Zaire which should be the richest state on the continent. Mobutu is a sick man who can't last long and there'll be a bloodbath to follow. There's the wretched history of the Rwanda genocide which the world stood by to watch. Zimbabwe is on the road to ruin. Sudan is divided in itself and ruthless in its squabbles with worse to come. On the East and West coasts you have Somalia and Equatorial Guinea, two regimes which are a byword for basket case.

'I could go on, but this isn't a lecture and you get my point. Fifty years of transition from colonial rule to Independence and we don't have one single success story to show for it. Not one. So what do we have? I put it this way. If the whole continent was a company, then the directors would be due for the chop. The results speak for themselves. Sales down, profits down, assets devalued, infrastructure crumbled. People numbers way up, their welfare and skills down through the floor. Morale? Don't even ask.

'There's more too, but outside the commercial analogy. Clear across the continent there's torture, graft, corruption of every kind, wilful incompetence on a scale to beggar belief.

'So what's the rest of the world doing about this desecration? Well, we're just about past propping up puppet regimes. We wring our hands and chuck more money at the extreme problems. We update our language and call Africa "developing" rather than "third world". Otherwise we shrug it off, expect nothing and hope for better. And that works in a way. Look at us around this table. Connie's Bastion business is flourishing, The Mansion House is going great guns, Pente isn't running out of souls to save … etc.'

David paused for a minute while his eyes drifted slowly round his audience. Then he resumed.

'I'm fifty-three now. I can go on for another ten, maybe fifteen years and I'm sure there will be another business lifetime for those coming after me. But I've decided that's just not good enough. Not for me. I'm sick of picking the good bits out of a decaying carcass. I've had enough of loitering on the sidelines, watching all the castles crumble and listening to the statesmen prosing. I want to spend the rest of my time in regeneration.

'There's simply got to be a better way forward for Africa: a clean sheet and a fresh start somewhere. But how do you manage that? There's no part left unexplored, no unclaimed territory to settle. You can try to influence events and you can buy people and politicians. But you can't buy sovereignty.

'The remaining option is acquisition: a takeover. That's what I propose to do.'

He sat back in his chair and picked up his cup of coffee.

There was a stunned silence which overlaid the background noises of Martin fiddling with a spoon and the rasp of Pente's lighter. King Offenbach was first to react.

'Say, David, this is kinda momentous stuff isn't it?'

'Yes it is. It's tough to spring it on you like this King, and that goes for Connie and Pente too. For different reasons, I've spoken to the others already but the basic concept has been revolving in my mind for years now.'

Pente puffed a cloud of cigar smoke and tugged at his beard.

'David', he said frowning, 'I'm really not understanding this. I've known you most of my life, and you're not one for the grand announcement. Normally it's quite a job to dig things out of you, and yet here you are sounding like a politician at the hustings, setting out your stall. And what a proposition! Are you honestly serious? You're planning a coup d'état?'

'Pente, you've been yourself where I am now. It's all about

when you recognise that here comes your opportunity and then you have a choice: walk away forever, or stand up to be counted. So yes, I am planning a coup d'état, but aiming for a coup de maître. That's not to split hairs. I want a master stroke — swift, sure and with minimum casualties'.

'But still some?'

'Inevitably, I'm afraid.'

There was a heavy silence in the room.

David felt the tension around him. There was surprise, a sense of disbelief, but also unhappiness, animosity. He was helped by an intervention from Aischa.

'I am the only one amongst you to have been born a child of Africa. I should therefore care the most but probably I worry the least over the principle at stake. In Africa, every country was colonised and most gained independence leading to internal strife. So history makes us accustomed to change and tolerant of some new chief coming in. It doesn't bother us greatly unless we're placed in extreme danger or great discomfort, and those two often go together. We're cynical, you see, we've heard all the great promises before. But we're patient and resilient as well. We get by. If someone like David wants to bring in change, Mr Average is likely to say "Oh yeah? I'll believe that when I can feel it, but bring it on anyway and let's have a look."

'There's something else. The two most important men in my life are my father and my David. They're both fixated with the need for something new. My father's day is almost done but I think his spirit is carrying on with David. That gives me a very personal reason to support this, but speaking just as another African, I think I'd be willing to give it a try.'

King Offenbach came back at her, sounding less than convinced.

'You sure about that last bit, Aischa? It sounds a mite casual to me, and when all's said and done, you're not just another African even if you were born there.'

Before Aischa could reply, Alexa had an answer for him.

'King, you've told me about your childhood. Would your

mother have cared who was in the White House when she was struggling with kids and bills?'

'It's a fair point,' said Hugh supporting her, 'and Aischa's right too. None of us here live on the breadline. We don't have to think before popping into the supermarket or putting petrol in the car. So we don't have the same priorities as a destitute family in Africa, — or one in Manila or Jakarta or Vietnam let me tell you. Wherever in the world, if wondering where the next drink is coming from means simply finding fresh water, then you're struggling through a life which none of us have experienced.'

David wanted to hear what Connie had to say, but it was Martin who chipped in first.

'I've had more warning of this,' he said, 'because David had to think of the implications to our business. If he goes ahead, he'll have to sever all connections with The Mansion House and that has consequences for me as much as for him. I can't say I'm delighted at the prospect. The company is doing very well and of course, it's a large part of our lives. My role is to keep the books here and I've never crossed the coastline of Africa in my life. So my first reaction was, why give up so much for such an uncertain future? Why take such an enormous risk which is certain to cost your reputation, probably your health and perhaps your life? Why?

'I talked it over with Ruth and she had good advice: she generally does. Think of how your father would have reacted, she said, so I've done that and come to a reluctant conclusion that he would have supported David. He was a great one for tilting at windmills, was my Dad, and he had enough horrors in his own life to know you must sometimes think the unthinkable.'

King came back to ask, 'Why have you got us together, David? Is it just for support? For approval? And why now?'

Pente nodded in agreement. Conrad was unmoving.

David replied, 'You're my friends, King, and you're my family: of course I'd like your support, but I want advice as well and each of you is a vital asset. As to timing, let me tell you more.'

He was interrupted by Conrad pushing back his chair. He

259

rose and stood looking at David.

'No,' he said firmly, 'don't do that. I don't want to know more and I wish I hadn't heard this much. I'm entirely opposed to this wholly madcap scheme. You've been too long in the African sun, David and it's taken your mind and your morals. I'm pretty sure your plan is impossible in execution, but anyway it's indefensible in concept. How can you have the arrogance to assume that you know best? How dare you think that you should reorder the lives of an entire population? What gives you the right? What's the difference between this and Saddam's move into Kuwait? You've made no mention of rights and respect; apparently you have no concerns for international law or democratic values. Are you really expecting the rest of the world to stand aside and welcome in some sort of latter day buccaneer? And after your example, who next? I suppose we should expect some Mafioso or maybe a Columbian drug baron to start helping themselves to their own patch somewhere and bugger the locals.

'It's appalling, the very idea of it. I'm surprised, Pente, that you don't seem as outraged as I am. I've really got the same comment for you also, King. And as for you, Hugh, I may admire your achievements, but you really can't go zooming round the world just buying up what you fancy. I think you and David should both recognise that you live in this world, warts and all, but not above it.'

Across the table, Alexa jumped as if she had been stung. Three men of monumental importance to her and it looked like war was breaking out.

'Connie....' she began, but he cut her off with a sweep of his hand.

'I'm sorry,' he said, 'it's not me provoking this rift, but as far as I'm concerned there's no more to be said. Not now or ever for me. I'll keep my peace because of our past together, but I want nothing more to do with this. It's just so wrong.'

He walked swiftly from the room and did not look back.

Mute silence followed his exit.

Hugh sat back in his chair and reached for a glass of water.

Pente's hand hovered over his cigar box. King studied his fingernails. David waited. Finally, he stretched both hands out in front of him to grip the table top and he spoke more mildly than he felt.

'Well. That was certainly not what I expected. Not what I wanted either,' and then to the world at large he added, 'I wonder where the hell I go from here.'

Before anyone could respond, Alexa rose and slipped away.

Hugh commented immediately, 'I expect she's gone to ring Tepee. She could do with some warning and perhaps she'll calm him down. I'm sorry about this David.'

Aischa signalled to Ursula and they got up together to organise some tea. Martin excused himself to check on things in his office, a shorthand for getting out of the atmosphere for a break. Hugh sat quietly to reflect. He had no doubt that Conrad's feelings were genuine, but he suspected an additional agenda. He had felt a bit of animosity from Connie, a resentment that his long established relationship with David was under threat from him.

Pente lit one of his cigars and climbed out of his seat to stalk around the room. As he walked, he prayed. They could use some help here. King was motionless as he watched David. The guy could use a little space.

The three men remaining at the table sat on in silence, each immersed in his own thoughts. There was no self doubt in David. He was shocked by Connie's outburst, but still as sure as ever. He was right. This was his crusade and he was committed to it.

The tableau was preserved for a further five minutes until tea and drinks arrived. They served themselves and were seated again, Connie's chair eloquently empty, as Alexa reappeared to flash a worried smile as she took her place beside Hugh. She was followed into the room by Martin, who remained standing.

David said, 'Look all of you, that was bad. I asked for reaction and I didn't expect Connie's, so now I feel like he's been banished. Why don't we wind things up now and I'll call you.'

'Just hold on there, David,' the interruption came from King, gesticulating with his elegant forefinger, 'I do believe you're reading this wrong. Credit to Conrad, he's come straight out and said he thinks the whole deal is a crock of shit. Maybe so, maybe not. But what about the rest of us? We've not said and you haven't asked. Right?'

David just nodded.

'OK then. Here's my contribution. I don't have a problem with the principle. I find it has style and potential. But you've not given us anything more: nothing on where or when or how. And all that's goin' to be real tough, perhaps not possible. Still, if you can work it through, I'll be listening. On that basis, I'm in.'

David could see Pente stirring and turned to him.

'I agree with King. I'd like to hear more. There are other issues for me, matters of conscience and faith. I need time for them and I need seclusion, but I know now that I don't share Connie's outright rejection. I'll be waiting David.'

David blew out a deep breath.

'Thank you both. Now I know where you all stand. It's up to me to take things forward. I have to put flesh on the bones. I'll do that and then get us together again. Meanwhile, I'll leave you with a code name which is also a clue. I call it Project Zero.'

CONRAD AVELING — 1996

Connie's anger was intense as he left The Mansion House, further fuelled by the memory of that day of savagery in Zambia, but his remedy was the polar opposite to David Heaven's. To raise the bar of standards, you have to work with what you've got. You have to involve, to research, to improve and to train: but evolve, not replace. Not for him David's chuck out the old and start again. That way lay anarchy. That meant mounting chaos as succeeding pirates imposed their own, self serving rules on a community. Connie thought of some unsavoury Bastion clients and shuddered at the idea of them mounting a takeover. David must be losing his marbles: that or carried away by his own power complex and by the influence of Hugh Dundas. Connie would never have believed it. This was a bloody dreadful day.

He took the train to Basingstoke, found a seat, tried to relax and failing, looked out on the suburbs and saw himself standing in the dust outside the small airport at Ndola, Zambia. He was tired, hot and irritated that Rory Trollope was late. It was April 1992.

Rory Trollope had been with Bastion for only a short time. Conrad interviewed him in South Africa and he joined the company the following day, flying to Ndola where he took over the small team on assignment to ZCCM, the Zambian Government owned conglomerate which controlled the country's vital mining interests here in the copper belt. They needed the copper to sustain the lurching economy, they needed expatriate expertise to produce the copper, and they needed Bastion to keep the expats feeling secure enough to work and to keep their families here.

Finding the right recruits for Bastion was a permanent

challenge and Conrad insisted on talking to applicants himself. One of those he rejected was Rory Trollope. Conrad's gut feel said that the guy was overconfident and gung-ho, but that evening brought a knock on his hotel door. He opened it to see a man who looked to be in his late sixties, average height, trim figure, remaining head hair grey and trimmed, upright bearing, immaculate in grey flannels, highly polished shoes, smart blazer and a regimental tie which signalled a loud message to Aveling.

'Good evening, Sir,' he spoke soft but firm, 'Might I have a word please, Sir. I'm Rory Trollope's father, Josh. Formerly of the Grenadier Guards, Sir.'

He would have snapped off a salute had that been in order, and Conrad replied 'Come on in, Mr Trollope, and tell me what's on your mind.'

With some difficulty, Josh Trollope was persuaded to accept a beer from the minibar and to take a seat. But he was not reluctant to speak.

'Mr Aveling,' he said, 'you and I are from the same background, Sir, long term service in the best professional army in the world. I came out in '64, just married to my Moira who comes from these parts. Her father, long gone now rest his soul, had a farm outside Nelspruit and we took it on. It was a new life for me since I joined the Colours as a boy soldier. It was tough going, but we made a fair go of it. Our son Rory is our only child, Moira couldn't have more. She and I have decided to move back to UK. We've just sold the farm and will be on our way by Christmas. We have just enough saved to get us by and I'm afraid I shan't be sorry to go. There are big changes coming and they may be right and proper, but I reckon that things here will get a lot worse before they get better, and that won't be in our lifetime. For Rory, well it's different of course. He was born, bred and educated here: never lived anywhere else. He's got to make his own way, but he's all we've got and I'd like him to have the chance to widen his horizons a bit. Your firm straddles two worlds and he has two passports. Your job seemed like the perfect chance for him and that matters to me. And so begging your pardon, Sir, but that's what made me drive in this evening to ask what you see wrong in him, see if there is anything I can explain.'

Conrad was careful to keep any suggestion of a smile from his face, but he rejoiced to hear the military discipline of a short, sharp précis and it came from his sort of man. Salt of the earth and a fighting soldier from way back, the very type to have beside you and behind you.

He said, 'Tell me why I should change my mind and take him on.'

Josh Trollope put down his glass on the table beside him and screwed up his weather beaten face in concentration before he replied.

'My Rory is a tough nut for sure: fit, confident, well trained. He's officer material, I'll be bound Sir, and I've seen enough to know. Rory started with National Service and then stayed in. He went through the full training and did well. Then he spent time in the Recces — that's what they call the Special Forces here — and was noticed for his ability in covert ops. He had good career prospects but he got restless. You know what the young ones are like these days, Sir. Sum it up, Mr Aveling, it's hard to judge as a parent, but my own feeling is that he's weak in strategic appreciation. Tell him to kill or destroy ... and it's job done. Ask him to consider why, and he's lost. But he's bright and he can learn. He just needs a firm hand and the right leadership.'

Conrad was impressed. In his terse summary, Josh had put his finger on the very point. He decided to take a chance.

'Alright, Josh, you've persuaded me. Tell Rory I've reconsidered and he can have an immediate start with Bastion. At 1000 hours tomorrow, reporting to me here. I want him up in Zambia. Tell him also that he has the job against my own first judgement and only because of what his father had to say to me. And thank you.'

The episode was in his mind as Rory pulled up in a dust cloud, springing out with a welcome and apologies. They drove off towards town, Conrad sitting quietly as he listened to Rory's account of the state of play for the small Bastion team operating here. He seemed on edge and was looking tired. Presently, Rory turned off the road into the shade of a large baobab tree. He switched off and turned in his seat.

'Boss,' he said, 'I need to tell you some history.' Conrad kept silent as he listened.

Rory's undoing had been his eye for the girls. If it hadn't been for Dolly, he would never have been there that evening, as theatre had no appeal for him and certainly not a production of the Mikado by the Ndola Amateur Dramatic Society. But Dolly Arkwright was another matter and she was a stalwart of the Society as a committed member of the costume and props team. She'd flashed her eyes at him when saying that he must be there for the rehearsal evening. Dolly had put a wealth of meaning into this invitation, leaving Rory in no doubt as to what further was on her agenda.

He wouldn't be the first. Dolly had put herself around the expat community during the two years that she'd been living there, but she was reasonably discreet, extremely pretty in a vapid style and she had the burden of being married to the enormously worthy but equally dull Desmond Arkwright, who was a diligent accountant on his second contract with ZCCM.

The Drama Group couldn't manage a venue of its own in Ndola, but borrowed the local rugby club which had a fine ground and club house on the outskirts of town. Dramatic productions took place every six months, and a prefabricated stage was hauled out and erected with sweating volunteer labour. Rehearsal meant a busy time for Dolly, seeing that curtains were hanging straight and costumes were in the right place. She was in high spirits, and to add to them was the prospect of a little mischief with that Rory Trollope who had caught her wandering eye.

She was pleased to see him turn up in good time and he busied himself in humping scenery around while the normal mayhem of activity chattered through the Club House. Soon after 10 pm, the Director reckoned they'd done enough so the cast and crew started to collect themselves and move out to their cars. Dolly made sure she had some final jobs to finish and at this point, the saintly Desmond made things easy for her by saying that the box office was ready but he had some ZCCM work to finish off before bed, so perhaps she could get a lift back with one of the others. She could hardly believe it: he went so far as to suggest that Rory, who lived not far from their house, might oblige?

By 10.30 pm, the Club House was deserted, dimly lit by a couple of generator powered security lights outside and with Rory's Land Rover the only vehicle remaining in the car park. Standing watch over it was the 'nightwatch', an agency guard recruited for the Mikado season and he would remain there only until this final owner had left, after which he would seek a comfortable spot under the surrounding trees to snooze away the dark hours.

Meanwhile, towards the back of the stage in a pile of loose props and costume material, Rory and Dolly were wasting no time. Dolly was fond of her dull Desmond but he was a bit unfulfilling in the bed department. As she conveniently judged matters, a bit on the side was of help to them both. She took seconds to let down her long blonde hair, slip out of her jeans and release the splendid breasts in which she took such pride. Rory was hardly slower, but still pulling off his shirt as she dived both hands down his shorts and shivered in anticipation as she felt him coming up like a lift. He delighted her as he took control. He didn't trouble to remove his desert boots, simply pushed her roughly onto their make shift bed and used her hair to pull back her head as he fixed his eyes on hers and pounded into her. Dolly responded by raking his back and buttocks, urging him to greater and rougher efforts. It didn't take either of them long, but that was just the first round, and afterwards they lay with straying hands probing and fondling in preparation for more.

Rory wasn't sure whether it had been the noise or the movement which disturbed his concentration from Dolly's absorbing body. There was the sound of a soft thump and the sensation of a mild puff of breeze blowing briefly over their almost naked bodies. Instinctively, he moved his left hand from her breast to her mouth whilst simultaneously putting his right index finger to his own lips. Then he twisted his head, but didn't raise it as he gave himself the best of a poor view back down the auditorium of chairs, part arranged in stacks and clusters, towards the main entrance to the hallway and the dim light outside it. Rory was in no doubt that somebody other than the guard had entered the building, and he was expecting to see a member of the Company returned to collect something forgotten. The reality was worse.

Two columns of men, all Africans, had entered the Club House and were now advancing silently towards the stage, walking in two single files. As they reached an area in the middle of the room which was unencumbered by chairs, they turned inward to face each other. There were twelve in all. They slipped gracefully to the floor to sit cross legged, shifting slightly to form two half moons of six men each. Rory was not too familiar with Zambia but he did know his Africa. He recognised the traditional format for a business meeting, the gathering for a discussion between tribes. He also understood that thump: a pound to a penny it had been the body of their guard, the nightwatch being taken out. Rory pressed his mouth to Dolly's ear and whispered slowly into it.

'You must keep completely still. Don't move a muscle. We have some Afs in here. They don't know we're here and they don't want us. But they mustn't find us. Nod if you understand.'

A look of stark terror came into Dolly's eyes, but she nodded and squeezed his hand.

'Good girl,' he breathed as he squeezed back and laid his head beside her, straining to gain more information. But this was not easy. He and Dolly were covered by folds of costume material but Rory knew he mustn't raise his head. Movement attracts peripheral vision and these people would be alert. They had truly caught him with his trousers round his ankles. Left to himself, Rory would be a difficult target to identify, much less to attack. He was practised at blending into the background and could keep silent and unmoving for hours at a stretch. But he wasn't alone, and he knew that he couldn't expect the same of Dolly. If she revealed herself, she would reveal him into the bargain.

It was obvious to Rory that this was some sort of war party, a meeting to agree their next move in an uneasy alliance. He guessed that one group was local, while the other had slipped across the border from Zaire during the early part of the evening. The crossing was hardly more than five miles distant: they would be over and back again during the hours of darkness and it was common knowledge that the provincial capital of Lubumbashi, so close to the Zambian Copper Belt, provided any number of brigand bands who were adept at making swift, pillaging expeditions over the border. It made sense that some would have links with villains in Zambia, people with local knowledge and English rather than French as a second language. Rory had picked up from some bar chat that there had been recent problems with joint nationality gangs operating around Kitwe, second city in the Copper Belt.

He had to keep Dolly quiet until the guys had finished their pow wow and moved on out. Their conversation droned on. He guessed their common tongue was an African dialect which he couldn't understand, but all he could hear was a background lilt of just two voices. This would make sense, with the two leaders in debate. The other five on each team would be the muscle in support.

Rory was a good judge of time and reckoned they had been lying there for a full hour. Allowing for the quick bonk, it would now be approaching midnight and fresh worry which had been brewing in his mind blossomed further. Three minutes later, the sounds of an engine and then wheels on dirt road as a car turned off the tarmac and ran through the dust of the approach road to the Club House. Its door slammed shut and a voice called out for the guard. Rory recognised that it was Desmond, returned to look for his wife. He heard the door of the Club House creak

269

slightly as it swung it open. He guessed the war parties would remain seated like statues in their semi circles, confident that the intruder wouldn't notice them until he had acquired some night vision. They probably hoped he would decide he was alone and depart. They would be entirely certain that they could deal with him if he did otherwise. They wouldn't bother themselves unnecessarily with one white man of slender build, blathering to keep his spirits up in this suddenly sepulchral hall.

Desmond surprised them all.

'Dolly, are you here somewhere? Dolly!' Simultaneously, he stretched out a hand and flicked on the main lights in the Club House. The generator was already running, therefore the illumination was immediate. All the occupants of the large hall were temporarily blinded by the light except for Rory, whose innate instinct made him thrust his head into the neighbouring fold of material which gave him a filter.

The twelve men on the floor sprang to their feet, each taking up the weapon which he had laid before him as he sat, a mark of good faith whilst he was in counsel. In an instant, therefore, two who had been speaking plus ten in silent support became twelve armed, threatened and dangerous. Desmond was understandably aghast at this apparition, but terror turned to desperate relief as he recognised one of them.

'Alfred,' he cried to the black man whom he knew only as his own house steward, 'Alfred. It is you, isn't it? What's going on? Where's Mrs Arkwright?'

The man called Alfred stepped forward. He was one of the support members from the home team. At Desmond's standard but comfortable house, he was accommodating, almost insignificant as he padded around the dwelling performing his duties of washing, cleaning, some doubtful cooking, appearing when bidden from his basic quarters at the bottom of their garden. He seemed very different here in these unfamiliar surroundings and shadowy light. He was stripped to the waist, still the familiar short figure but with his barrel chest now oiled to show off the rippling muscles. A panga knife dangling from his right hand and the overhead light gleaming off his wide, bald head.

There was a furtive smile on his broad face as he walked up to his boss.

'Good evenin' Sah', said Alfred as he swept Desmond's legs from under him. A single stroke of the panga, sharp, heavy and wielded with all the force available from Alfred's powerful body, was enough to nearly sever both limbs between thigh and knee. The blood loss was a torrent, and the shock catastrophic. Desmond sprawled on the floor, screaming out the last of his life. Poor Dolly was quick to join him. She moved like lightening, wrenching herself from Rory's hand and springing up to run from the cover of the stage into the lighted arena of carnage, gasping out her anguish and unconscious of her state. If the twelve Africans were startled to see the appearance of a naked white woman, they were equally quick and deadly in their reaction.

Before she could reach her husband in the pool of his blood, Alfred grabbed her. He dropped onto one ham knee, forced her backwards over it and sank his teeth into one lily white breast as he reversed his panga and swept it up between her legs to rape her with its broad handle. He held her easily whilst she added to the screams before one of the Zaire gang stepped forward and used his knife to slit her throat from ear to ear.

Rory was accustomed to the bestiality of his native continent, but he had never witnessed the like of this. He was in profound shock. He took a millisecond to curse himself for failing to anticipate before his training kicked in and he became a fighting machine. Assessment: heavily outnumbered and zero help or weapon to hand. Only action possible: go to ground and wait for revenge. These people are cruel and deadly. There is no evidence that they are stupid. They know there is only one car outside, only one guard already despatched. For certain sure there's a man here with this naked blonde carcass which was recently a woman.

Rory gave himself some cautious visibility. The group of men was filtering apart and padding noiselessly towards the stage, in skirmishing order, intent to find and destroy. Rory was hopelessly outnumbered. He managed to squirm his shorts back up over his hips, attaching a button without attempting the belt. He lay quietly on his back, loosely covered by the curtain material and waiting for the signal which he knew would come. Smell.

Black men and white smell differently, especially in times of fight or flight. Rory couldn't see the enemy, nor hear it. But he could smell it, and that gave him all the advantage he needed. Given the choice, he would have liked Alfred to pass by, but it was another, much taller and lighter man who placed a naked foot by his head and paused. Rory knew what he was doing, peering into the increasing gloom towards the back of the stage, just the spot into which a single adversary would have retreated. Wrong.

The man advanced his other leg over Rory's recumbent body. He smelt the rancid odour of the man's crutch and caught a subdued glint from the panga which hung from one wrist. Rory struck with expertise in his hands and vengeance in his heart. His left hand shot up through the open loin cloth and grabbed the testicles whilst his right took the wrist which held the weapon and shook it violently. The man collapsed with a shrill yowl on top of where Rory's head had been lying, but that had moved in the same split instant, twisting smoothly with his body as he caught up the panga, slashing it into the body as he slammed the head into the stage with crushing force. One down, whether dead or incapacitated made no difference. The nearest two companions were a bare metre away on either side of him and turning like quicksilver. They had only now to destroy the enemy. But that was not to be so easy.

Rory Trollope, blood zinging and impelled by fury, had his way clear and he took it. He feinted in one direction, turning his back on the other assailant in deliberate invitation but then he kept swinging in a vicious 180 degree arc with his weapon extended, held in both hands and in perfect timing to meet the neck of the guy moving in behind him. The kick to his arms felt as if he had taken the head off but he didn't wait to verify. With two large strides and a jump, he was off the stage and running for the door. Ten against one remained poor odds and he could hear the frenzied pursuit: more telling, he could smell it. The divided glass door remained ajar as Desmond had left it. Rory deliberately chose the closed half and simply ran through it, bursting the frame and scattering shards of broken glass as he did similar damage with the panga to the other half. Broken glass would not delay these guys for long, not with their feet rock hard from walking, but a very little was enough, just enough to let him reach his car.

The Land Rover was never locked and he could feel the keys in one pocket of his shorts. Only time for one shot at this. He forced himself to stay focussed as he flung open the door and fed the key into ignition. Engine fired, door slammed shut and the mob was on him, grabbing for the door handles, slashing at the windscreen. But they were unprepared and disorganised. Once on the move, he was unstoppable. He picked up two of them on the bonnet and one was still there as he ran him into an upright of the Club House building. He found reverse gear and felt himself crunch over at least one more. Then he was away and accelerating with a man still hanging onto the driver's door handle until Rory wiped him off on the gatepost. He still had the panga on the seat beside him. He was doing sixty and hitting fifth gear when he joined the highway for town.

By Rory's watch, it was a little after 12.30 am by the time he made it back to the house which he shared with the Belgian communications man. He wondered if Alfred had been among the casualties of his escape. He hoped not: he had other plans for Alfred. Rory reckoned the African would walk back to the house of his employers whom he had just murdered savagely. Alfred would have hardly seen him in the chaos at the Club, but this vehicle, that was something different. He would have seen that clear enough and might recognise it again. Rory would not risk that. He had a score to settle. So he manoeuvred the Land Rover as far into the car port as it would go and chucked an old tarpaulin over the back of it. Then he went into the house and changed into a pair of drill trousers. He put on a clean shirt and a light sweater before returning to the shady recess of the deep veranda, settling in an easy chair with a very long, strong whisky and a packet of smokes. Rory didn't doze. He stayed silent but alert, stoked up by fury and regret. His vigilance was rewarded at 3 am when he saw the squat figure of Alfred trudge past in the still of the warm night. Rory closed his eyes and gave himself a couple of hours sleep in his arm chair.

He awoke before 6 am and made himself a cup of coffee. The Belgian slept on. The house was silent. He walked into the living room and took a reel of fishing line from the drawer of the dresser. In the kitchen, he found a pair of pliers and one of the heavy plastic straps which their gardener used to secure the jacaranda trees. He walked out to the Land Rover and removed the tarp from its rear before climbing in and backing out onto the road. He moved slowly and without much noise. In less than five minutes, he was outside what had been the Arkwright dwelling which was a mirror image of his own.

He reversed the Land Rover into the yard, stopping level with the veranda, climbed out and went to knock loudly at the front door: surprise, surprise, no reply. Rory pulled open the fly screen and turned the handle of the main door. As he expected, it opened to his touch. If ever they had locked up, it would not have occurred to Desmond to do so before leaving in search of Dolly. Rory continued his charade, walking into the living room and calling their names. The answering silence mocked him. Finally, he heard a soft shuffling coming up the path from the garden and the familiar figure of Alfred came into view, his shirt and shorts rumpled as if from sleeping in them. He could hold his nerve, this one. He walked into the kitchen and stood respectfully in front of Rory.

'Mornin' Sah. No one done up yet Sah. Can I get you coffee please?'

Rory gave him the wide open smile that had so attracted Dolly before making his sudden move. He reached down from

274

his greater height, interlocked his fingers and used both hands to grab the bullet head and pull it sharply down onto his right knee, duly poised to meet it. Alfred grunted with the pain of an instantly broken nose. He was groggy, caught off guard: he had no time to react. Rory seized him by the shoulders, whirled him around and ran him into the outside wall of the kitchen.

'No coffee, but the day of reckoning for you, you evil bugger.'

He said this quite softly but with infinite menace and as Alfred groaned with the pain of a nose twice afflicted which made him battle for breath, Rory whipped his arms behind his back and used the tree strap to bind them together with a force which had Alfred whistling through his teeth. Alfred might have been short in stature, but he was heavy in bulk. He could have been a modest sack of flour, however, as Rory caught him up over his shoulder and walked out to his vehicle. He steadied the struggling burden over his shoulder with one hand as he used the other to open the rear door of his Land Rover. He threw Alfred onto the floor inside and slammed the door. He walked around and climbed behind the wheel.

Rory drove out of town to a road which had been carved out for the disposal of mine tailings. It was little used these days, but Rory had located it for an earlier amorous adventure. It was steep and rough and lonely. Two miles up it, he stopped and went around to the back of the Land Rover. He reached in, pulled out his captive and dumped him in the dirt and the dust. He left him lying there while he rummaged for a long length of tow rope. He looped the rope around Alfred's feet and tied the two ends, one to each of the brackets which protruded from the rear wings of his vehicle. Spread eagled with arms still secured behind his back, Alfred could only glare balefully while Rory made the remainder of his preparations. First, he fetched a Stanley knife from the parcel shelf and used it to cut off all of the black man's clothes. Then he used the pliers to cut a length of the gut shorter than the towrope. He fashioned a loop in the centre of this and bending down, he passed it around Alfred's genitals and pulled it up tight. He fed both ends around the tow ball of the Land Rover, using the pliers to whip these into a firm knot. He went back to Alfred, pulled him upright by main strength, and undid the gardening strap which pinioned his arms together.

Alfred's stood there naked, pawing at the fishing line which encircled his manhood. Rory climbed back into the driver's seat. He moved the transmission into low range, selected third gear and moved off at a sure but gentle pace. Alfred lost his footing immediately, flopped on his back and was pulled by the fishing line and his balls in screaming agony until they gave up the struggle and were wrenched from his scrotum. Thereafter, he bawled some more as the towrope took over and bounced his head over the rocky ground until it split and his life left him in a bloody, messy pool. Rory didn't stop for half a mile. Then he paused for long enough to cut loose the cadaver and kick it over the bank of the track and into a shallow ravine. He turned the Land Rover and drove back down the track. It was eight o'clock before he was able to negotiate the peak traffic in town and to get to the airport to meet his boss.

Conrad listened to the full story with mounting nausea. God knows, he was no stranger to violence and was familiar with the horrors of Africa. But this account of attack and revenge truly horrified him. This sort of action was worse than some of the tales bandied about of the earliest exploring and colonial days, worse even than the treatment meted out by slavers of days long gone. This was wild frontier behaviour perpetrated by a young man of the vintage of his own sons who had themselves come into the world as result of cruel and humiliating use of woman by man. By Jesus Christ, would we never learn?

Conrad was still reliving that dreadful day as his train arrived in Basingstoke. He collected his car and drove home to Tepee. She had been helped by that bit of warning through Alexa's quick phone call, so she was ready for him. Connie had opened up immediately which was unusual for him. More extraordinary, he had cancelled appointments and stayed away from Bastion for two whole days whilst he went on a repetitive rant which meant that Tepee had to juggle her own schedule around so she could settle back and listen. After that, she got tough and drove him out of the house, saying that he was overreacting and that they had to get their own life back. Connie took this calmly enough, but he became withdrawn and moody. It was obvious to her that was shocked to the core by David's intention, but there was more to his condition. Conrad was a tired man. He had built a great business at Bastion, but he carried too much of it by himself and he couldn't stop yet. Worse, Tepee noted, was the jealousy. Connie would never articulate it, but it was clear to her that part of him resented how close she had become to Alexa down the years and this had become emphasised by Hugh's arrival on the scene. Connie, by his own admission was a plodder. He achieved much, but by laborious effort while Hugh was forever soaring. It bugged him that the girl he had saved in Bahrain was now enraptured by this financial wizard and a soul mate to his own wife, for God's sake. All this was absurd, of course, and it was nonsense. But she knew that he was plagued by such thoughts: he was becoming morose and withdrawn and she worried. But her own love for Connie remained undimmed and she was sure and determined that she would pull him through it eventually. It would just take time. It would have helped her to help him if he had told her about Rory Trollope in Ndola, but he never did so.

DAVID HEAVEN — 1997

A great emotional burden fell on Alexa and Tepee. They were such close friends and their relationship was inevitably touched by the schism between Conrad and David. Tepee had to admit that it was more of Connie's making. Meanwhile, there were tough times for Alexa also. She had grown accustomed to frequent contact with Tepee, meeting as often as they could. Alexa was all too aware of the problems Tepee was having and was upset that the best help she could provide was to keep her distance. That was the last thing the two girls wanted, but it was how matters developed during the remainder of 1996 and into the following year.

At the beginning of March, Alexa and Tepee managed to scheme a get together to include their men plus David and Aischa. The six of them met for a long lunch in Knightsbridge and it was a good party, distinguished by Aischa and Connie chatting about their shared grandchildren, the family of Oscar and Anna which now included Olty, Edward and Christina, with probably more to come, as they agreed. Then David spoilt the mood. Flushed with fine claret and bonhomie, he tried to draw his old friend into providing some military advice for his mission. Connie froze and there was almost a repeat of that wretched stand-off at The Mansion House. Aischa was furious with David, but too late. Old wounds had reopened.

By this time David was fully engaged in his Project Zero. He started with Martin. Their priority was quietly to extricate David from ongoing Mansion House business. There were some promising younger people who could now move up and they reasoned that since David was nearly fifty-four, it would indicate good governance to observers that he was preparing his retirement. They started with two key appointments.

Felix Maas was already established as a key new member of the team, who was now to work full time with David. That meant that Felix needed to know everything but David saw no risk in this. Felix was a friend and a long time colleague, but he was also a vital asset. They couldn't manage this without him and Felix was fascinated by the planning exercise of a lifetime. But he would have to replace himself in the role of moving The Mansion House communications from catch up to new frontiers. He might just be able to keep a watchful eye on it, but he would need someone to run it for him and he knew just the man.

Robert 'Ginger' McCabe was a flamboyant character with flame coloured hair and a wardrobe of brightly patterned waistcoats which he wore with jeans. He was football mad and a passionate supporter of Everton. He was rampantly homosexual and moved like a hummingbird from one brief liaison to the next. What mattered to Felix was Ginger's brilliance with computer technology.

'Better than me, I have to say,' he told David, 'and perfect for The Mansion House right now. He won't stay long, but he'll deliver for us.'

'What about his discretion?'

'Absolutely nil,' replied Felix, 'that's not a problem on The Mansion House technical stuff but we'll need to keep him well away from Zero.'

The Mansion House settled well under the younger management. Martin, more the sole captain on the bridge, found himself perversely more relaxed. Business was good, the prospects bright and the general mood at 100 Piccadilly spoke of vitality and expectation.

Meanwhile, David started to turn the vision of Zero into reality. Cloistered for long days with Felix Maas, his first objective was to identify the six states on the continent of Africa from which he would choose his final target. He was honest in recognising that his own judgement, whilst well informed, was inevitably subjective. He needed the incisive objectivity which

Felix brought to bear and their lengthy sessions forged a strong working bond between the two men despite their disparities of age, skills and experience. They based themselves in David Heaven's ground floor office and occasionally adjourned to talk into the night in the comfort of David's apartment. David spent much time trawling through his stack of old fashioned travel notebooks, maps and memorabilia reminding himself of people, places and visits over the years. Simultaneously, Felix would be working on his ever expanding database, a cornucopia of facts, figures, trends and expectations. His fingers would whirl over his keyboard as he assembled the bones over which David's rich memories could be most effectively draped.

David kept spasmodic contact with both King and Pente. The American seemed to be doing a lot of travelling, much of it between London and Washington, but he sounded positive and keen to get a full update on progress which David took as a promising sign. He said that he had some good news of his own coming up, but refused to elaborate until they could get together. Pente went completely out of touch for a couple of months which worried David and he rang the Order in Hexham. They were cagey there and took some persuasion to tell him that the Pente had gone down with a severe attack of malaria in Tanzania. He had recovered, but was taking time in recuperation and he certainly sounded as boisterous as ever when he finally telephoned.

David and Hugh spoke frequently, mostly on the phone although they did manage some infrequent meetings when Hugh dropped into London for appointments in the City. They would often speak about the situation with Conrad. This was partly because Hugh was sensitive to the whole matter, but increasingly they were concerned about the military aspect of Zero. David had always assumed that he would rely on Connie in this key area and now he felt bereft of guidance. Hugh could be of no help either, but he was putting pressure on David to come up with an alternative.

'I have to know the cost of what and who we're going to buy,

David, and my own best guess is really not good enough.'

David was cudgelling his brains over this one when a fresh and unconnected crisis came up. Felix asked to come up one evening and appeared with a laptop under his arm.

'I may not need this,' he said, 'and I promise not to be a geek and dazzle you.'

David merely grunted as he poured them both a drink.

'What's bothering you Felix.'

'Security, in a word. You see, all my files, all my notes, just the complete databank on Zero, I keep it all quite separately, heavily protected and only accessible by me. I've got the lap top so I can give you a demo of the whole process I go through every time I open up or shut down.'

'No need to do that. Coming from you, Felix, I'll take it as read.'

'OK. The point is that I'm picking up signs of someone trying to hack into it. I'm sure they've had no success so far but I can't guarantee that they won't keep at it and the further we go with Zero, the more dangerous and incriminating this would become.'

'I agree. That would be bloody serious now and it'll get worse as you say. I think you're going to tell me that you suspect Ginger's hand behind this?'

'I am, David. That's exactly what worries me. I can't believe that anyone else would have got this far, and if it is him, then he'll crack it eventually. Ginger is that good.'

'And I guess it wouldn't help us to kick him out?'

'The reverse. That would send the message that I'm on to him and he doesn't need to be within a thousand miles of this building to keep sniffing around. He could be anywhere.'

They looked at each other. 'Do you have a proposal then?'

'Yes, two in fact. First, I'll start a whole new suite of programs for the work we're doing and then a second one to let them speak to each other. That way, I can more easily disguise things to look like commercial market research.'

David nodded his agreement and Felix went on, 'but secondly, let's keep him inside the tent and pissing out. I suggest we put a tail on Ginger. Trouble is, David, McCabe is basically a lovely guy but he's just so promiscuous and not just with his body. He loves showing off his brilliance and for a couple of bob, he's anybody's.'

David had to smile at the Dutchman's extraordinary grasp of idiom. Talk about international. And then he smiled some more. This whole, unwanted problem might be the means of resolving another. He promised to take action immediately, and when Felix had left him, he telephoned Conrad at home. Tepee answered: she was welcoming as if he rang every week and not after months of silence. Connie was calm if not ecstatic, but that was anyway his style. He agreed that industrial espionage was covered in Bastion's portfolio and that he would accept a brief from The Mansion House if David would send him more details tomorrow. He was helpful but still reserved.

David felt happier as he prepared for bed. The whole episode had given him a further idea. In the morning, he made a further call and that evening he took a plane to Singapore. The giant Sebastien Mantel, whose father had saved Tepee, was there at Changi and they went straight to a hotel. Seb knew of David's estrangement from Conrad and he knew the original cause. He understood that David wanted a conversation about Zero and not about anything else. He could accept these terms although he was saddened by the background. It was Seb who started the conversation.

'Over the phone, David, you told me enough to start me thinking and I've been concentrating on one individual. This is a guy who approached me, actually. That was about six months ago but I have checked that he is still available. I have a file here if you wish?'

'Thanks Seb, but I'd rather hear it from you first.'

'OK.' Seb settled back in his chair and began to speak. It was entertaining to hear such a true blue character described in Seb's competent, but heavily accented English.

'His name is Fergus Carradine: you pronounce the 'dine'

as in 'wine'. He's about forty-five. Born in Dublin. Educated at Charterhouse and Bristol University. Commissioned into the Royal Irish Rangers, served with the SAS, returned to his Regiment, resigned just before it was disbanded in 1992. Emigrated to Australia to join their army and SAS Force. Saw service in East Timor. Much respected as planner for covert ops. Olympic archer, fine pistol shot, five handicap golfer. Military historian recognised for his specialist knowledge of the Peninsular War. Has been twice married and twice widowed. No children, no surviving family. He's retiring from the Australian army and wants a job. But he also wants to return to live in Europe and revive his Irish roots. I think Carradine could be your man, David.'

'I hope you're right Seb. When can I meet him?'

'Right away. He's waiting for us in the lobby. I'll ask him to come and join us here.'

FERGUS CARRADINE — 1997

Fergus Carradine had brains, poise and style: with them came perception and sensitivity. He was not a big man, a little shorter than David. He looked lean and fit. He was soberly dressed in a dark lightweight suit, blue shirt and a plain tie. He retained a full head of hair, neatly cut and revealing the first tinges of grey. He wore a small moustache which did not look affected beneath his long nose which he stroked gently from time to time as he listened to David. In his speech, he had picked up an Australian twang which went with some of his colloquial expressions. He had a habit of pausing before he posed a question, and he chose his words carefully. He had humour and carried an aura of command. David liked him immediately and felt that Seb could be right.

They covered Carradine's military career first, with Seb going through it and asking most of the questions. David felt that this was all easy going for Fergus, who knew that he had the track record. He certainly made a strong impression. They moved onto personal matters. David was good in interview. He could find his way into the burrows where secrets might lurk. He was never reluctant to ask and so he grilled. Fergus was open to most points for discussion, but he had his limits. David enquired about the two marriages and Fergus explained that his first wife had died in a car accident, while his second, an Australian, had been lost to cervical cancer. David asked if he would try again, to be told politely that the subject was off limits. Fair enough, David thought to himself and picked up a faint nod of agreement from Seb.

Then it was Carradine's turn, but David wanted him to have fair run at it so he first told him the principles and objective of

Zero, plus the status as at that date. He was completely candid: he was taking a risk but it would have been an unproductive conversation on any other basis. Fergus heard him out without raising an eyebrow, but when this introduction was finished, he embarked on his own interview and some of the questions which he asked of David and Seb were very testing.

After a couple of hours, they decided to call it a day. David was tired from overnight travel and he wanted time for reflection on his own. They agreed to meet in his hotel suite the following morning. Carradine took the initiative and his comments carried the supposition that he would be offered the job and that he would accept it. First, he was concerned about the timing. If it was unacceptable to delay the invasion date, then they would have to move fast.

'To carry this off,' said Fergus, 'we'll need to be at battalion strength, with five hundred in the front line and a hundred and fifty in support and administration. That's an estimate because I don't yet know the target, but from what you've told me, I won't be far out. However, that's a large number to recruit, as Seb knows. It's never straightforward to find the right calibre of people. Then they have to be trained and worked into a coordinated team, but we are well served for a location. My choice would be Papua New Guinea. I know a bit about PNG. I can establish a camp in the Highlands which will be entirely discreet. The terrain is demanding and the climate taxing. You don't ask questions in that country and expect to get polite replies. The total environment is not unlike Africa, and yet it's more or less on the other side of the world. It will suit our purpose very well.'

'You'll want a few people immediately?' asked David.

'Correct. I can nominate the half dozen I'd like with me to get started, but there isn't one amongst them who knows Africa. I'll need your help there.'

Seb put in that he had Rory Trollope in his office on secondment from Bastion in the UK and he gave Fergus a quick brief on Rory's African background and military record.

'He sounds good and it's useful that he was in the Reccies. I'd like to meet him but I assume he knows nothing of Zero yet, and that I will tell him as and when I judge it's time?'

'Agreed,' said David and Sebastien in unison. Carradine nodded and moved to his next main point which was money. David had anticipated this and was able to answer that all the funding which they would require was already planned and would be available as and when needed.

Fergus raised his eyes.

'The cost of materiel and people will be enormous, David. You don't have the figures yet, but you sound very confident.'

'So will you be when you meet Hugh Dundas. It's good that you live in the same part of the world. I take it you'll be staying here for the present?'

'Yes I will. I have an apartment here in Singapore.'

'There are people in London who you should meet: my business partner, my collaborators in this venture, Felix Maas who handles research and planning. When could you come over?'

'I could come at any time, but I recommend that I should not do so until late next year. The best basis for covert action is always "need to know", and they don't need to know me yet.'

David said 'I understand,' and after a pause he went on, 'Fergus, all three of us have been talking in language which says that you're already on board. I'm very happy with that and I'd like to shake hands on it. We need, of course, to cover the detail of your remuneration and how it's paid. How we communicate. But first, may I assume your acceptance in principle or have you anything else to ask first?'

'Just one point. I'm surprised, Seb, that your UK partner Conrad Aveling isn't here. I've never met him, but he enjoys a good reputation and had a relevant military career himself.'

David took the lead. 'I'm surprised too, Fergus. Conrad is my oldest friend and his experience would be invaluable to us. But he doesn't share my ambitions, is actually very opposed to them and as a result, he has voted himself out. I much regret his decision.'

Fergus nodded slowly.

'Thank you for telling me. I'd still advise you to try and get him more onside. He knows conditions in Africa very well indeed and I would really like the chance to pick his brains. And now, you'll want contact coordinates for me,' and he handed over a business card. David saw that his email address began 'cogs@'. He queried this.

Fergus said, 'Oh yes, that. Cogs Carradine. It came out of typical Aussie humour. In the Mess, they thought I did the crossword too easily and pulled my leg about having a whirling brain. It's a good alliteration and speaks of a hearty sort of image which can makes for useful disguise.'

'And it's not a challenge to your authority?'

'Oh no, David,' said Fergus softly, 'I don't make the policy, but when I give the orders, my people listen. And they don't argue.'

THE OXFORD FIVE — 1997

Stimulated and relieved by his recruitment of Fergus Carradine, David flew back to London where he found the contract from Bastion waiting for him. This covered the action they would commence to provide data security for The Mansion House and their watching brief over Ginger McCabe. There was a hefty deposit to be paid and David cheerfully signed it off, explaining all the circumstances to Martin. They agreed that it was necessary and were delighted to recognise the contract as a sign of Conrad returning to the fold.

Then, towards the middle of May, they had a visit to Piccadilly from Pente Broke Smith. He arrived unannounced late in the afternoon and David cleared his desk immediately. They went for a walk together around the Park. Pente was very unhappy about the rift with Connie and David was pleased to be able to give him the latest and better news. The big man looked happier, but less than convinced. They went to eat in a small bistro in Shepherd Market, nothing fancy but perfect for a quiet conversation. They ordered, and David started straight in to ask about Pente's deliberations over Zero.

'I think you'd better hear about me first. I'm being moved out of Africa and back home to Hexham. The Abbot wants me to take over the Instruction of our novices and I'm due to start in October. I'm on some extended leave until then, but I'll be based in Northumberland. I've already left Africa for the last time. Or maybe not?' Pente beamed his big smile and it was good to see it back on his face.

'Is this something to do with health?'

'Yes, part of it. The new job's genuine enough, but the last bout of malaria really did knock me out and I've been very slow to recover. Can't seem to get my energy back and you get even more tired in the climate down there. They think I'm due a big change and a long rest: I didn't argue.'

'You've certainly earned both.'

'That's as may be, David and it's a done deed now anyway. But it's not been the main reason why I've been looking forward to seeing you.'

'No?'

'No. You see, I finished off with a few weeks convalescence at our Home in Dar. It's a fine place which our Order of the Saints has there with a particularly attractive garden which is rich in peace and calm. I had day after day to sit there and think things through. In the end, I came to a decision that I just couldn't go through with it, that I couldn't justify in my Christian conscience joining you to support your project Zero.'

There was a pause between them. Then David said 'you say "couldn't". That's past tense.'

The Priest stroked his greying beard and fumbled for his cigar box as he replied,

'Well spotted, David. You were always the sharp one. No, well, what happened was this. On my way home, I diverted to spend a couple of nights in Kigali, Rwanda. The Abbot has recently settled a new Mission there and he wanted a first-hand account of how things are going with them. A reasonable request which I couldn't refuse.'

He paused again and eventually David had to prod him. 'And?'

'Well, honestly, it's just desperate. Oh it's peaceful enough there now and there's a bit of economic recovery. There's a fair amount of local chaos of course, shanty dwellings, widespread begging, people looking seventy before they're thirty, general deprivation. But a lot of that is just Africa and you'll find it everywhere.'

David nodded his agreement and understanding, but Pente just kept talking.

'What's different and worse here is the underlying feeling

which is quite palpable. It's about three years on from the genocide and you still have the clear sense of every man jack looking over his shoulder and thinking "when's it going to start again? What's going to set if off this time". But you know, David, the worst of it is the way those guys speak to you and just make you feel guilty with their disappointment. There was one, an intelligent and well qualified lawyer who'd lost all but one of his immediate family and just didn't know the fate of many friends. He looked at me over a beer one evening and asked "why weren't you there for us?" Just that. No recriminating. No fulminating: just that simple, gentle question which carried for me such a weight of well justified accusation. It wasn't as if we Europeans turned the other cheek, you see. We didn't. We just ran for cover and let them get on with it: our performance and that of the UN, why it was simple disgraceful. So, in that single instant in the bar it came to me. I've got to do better than settle for a sinecure in Hexham. If my friend David thinks he can bring improvement to the wretched shambles which covers so much of black Africa, well, I must do what I can to help. As you put it, it's time to stand up to be counted. So here I am, yours for the taking.'

This was a moving moment which reduced them both to silence. Pente stayed overnight in a hotel and spent the following day in The Mansion House, much of it with Felix Maas from whom he learnt a good deal of the detail of Zero progress. Then he departed for Hexham, but thereafter kept in close contact, frequently on the phone and coming down to visit them every six weeks with a remorseless regularity.

Meanwhile, across the world in Hong Kong, big developments were taking place in the life of Alexa Bushell. There was no change in the situation of Hugh's wife Janey and therefore no opportunity for Alexa to move in with Hugh, much less to marry him. But that status seemed less significant these days. She was by now so much a partner to him, not just in bed and matters of the heart. She was also in business with him and there was so much to do that she had resigned from Ince and Co so that she could spend her full time in helping to administer Hugh's involvement in Zero. By now, he was full bore active in raising finance and he had started a new organisation, Dundas Securities, in order to keep the Project distant from his other business. He had known that they would need time to stock the war chest and how appropriate an expression was that. Hugh always thought big. Budget for champagne, he would say, if you need water. And, he argued, Zero was a project for which they simply could not have too much money. Of all the reasons for which they might fail, running out of funds would be the most unnecessary and ignominious. That wouldn't happen with him in charge but the demands made on him were considerable and the amounts were stepped up by Fergus Carradine with whom he developed a close relationship through frequent phone calls and the relative ease with which they could meet. Then there was the new charity which Hugh established as part of his grand financial plan. There was much detail here also, despite the recruitment of his old friend Ali Shuib to run it out of Kuala Lumpur. David Heaven was hugely happy when Hugh told him about Orphans of Africa, and that was because he immediately spotted a second benefit which would flow from the charity.

'What's the plural of Trojan Horse I wonder,' he had exclaimed to Hugh over an open line, and then, 'don't worry. It's brilliant and I'll explain when we're next together.'

Other aspects of Alexa's life were less happy during those months. Her father Joffrey died at home outside Limoges and her mother was hit hard by his loss. Alexa wanted to be there for Elizabeth and she was, but it entailed some frequent visits and thus many hours in the air between Hong Kong and Paris. At least this made it easy to keep up with Tepee and one day the two of them managed to meet up with Aischa for lunch outside Guildford. They were happy to have a girly chat, but before the end of their meal there were worries to exchange and the focus of their moans was David Heaven. Aischa was concerned from the moment David reported with pleasure that Connie had taken the brief to watch out for Ginger McCabe, only to vanish immediately afterwards to see Seb Mantel in Singapore.

'He told me,' she said, 'that he saw no reason to say anything about that trip and he was sure that Seb would have said nothing either. I told him that was barmy. Seb and Connie are two parts of the same business and of course they'll share everything. What's worse, I said, is that you didn't tell Connie yourself. You've chucked him a crumb and passed the cake to Seb even though Connie reckons it's a poisoned chalice,' and she finished with an apology for her mixed metaphor.

Tepee sought to give them all comfort by reporting that Connie had never mentioned the incident to her. She said he seemed better and more his old self these days but adamant on the few occasions when the subject arose that his strong disapproval of Project Zero had not diminished an iota. Alexa had less to say on this subject, but in her heart she was truly concerned. She had more experience than her friends as to the effects of stress and trauma and knew that blocking things out was one of them. Instead, she talked of the weird feeling of being somehow unfaithful to Connie through her commitment to Hugh and the close relationship, introduced by her, which had developed between him and David. Tepee and Aischa said that they could quite understand what she meant. They ordered another bottle of wine and agreed that men could be just so perverse, sometimes with all the sensitivity of a concrete block.

Alexa was entirely correct. Connie was soon aware that David had gone to Singapore and hired Fergus Carradine with Seb's help. It both hurt and infuriated him. Then the matter was made worse by hearing that Rory Trollope had transferred onto Carradine's staff. In his challenged state of mind, Conrad was able to overlook the fact that he had never told a soul about the events of Ndola and the brutal reprisal from Rory in 1992. He had sent Rory to Seb's office at the end of that year, to keep him out of Africa and hopefully to learn, but he had not revealed the horrors of his action: not to Seb and certainly not to Tepee. It was all part of the load he was carrying.

During the late summer, King Offenbach came to see David

at The Mansion House bringing news which pleased David very much indeed.

'I've been offered the chance to retire from the CIA. In Washington, they're fixing to devote way more resource to Africa and they want to beef up a couple of our offices down there — in Kenya and Cameroun. Both have a regional brief right now and operate out of the US Embassies. Well hell, that's OK and quite a compliment, I guess. The new outfits are to answer to Langley direct and no longer through me in London. That's OK again, except that supremo Stateside is to be a young schmuck with the brain of a peanut and an attitude a mile wide. It's their call of course, but they know I can't work like that. Also, would you believe I turn sixty years old in September '98 — just next year — and they've made me a generous offer to go while the going's good. I've already said yes and thank you kindly Uncle Sam. I'll be free come this Christmas and I figure to get myself an apartment somewhere in London and settle down where I can perhaps be a bit useful to you guys in making Zero fly. I'm in David.'

As the world move towards the close of 1997, David was pleased with the progress of Zero. He was delighted to have both Pente and King close at hand. He was mesmerised by the startling figures which Hugh Dundas bandied with such confidence.

'I'll feel comfortable with a total fund of five billion dollars,' he said, 'right now, we're halfway there and I can see where the other half's coming from.'

The reports from Fergus Carradine were regular and reassuring. He was getting his act together, satisfied with progress in establishing the human and materiel resources which they would need. He was now based at their training ground in PNG: it had all they needed and was comfortingly remote. He could also report that Rory Trollope had settled well and was proving of real value as his ADC.

Felix Maas continued to present David with impeccably presented project management information and this despite his increased workload which had resulted from the disappearance, almost overnight, of Ginger McCabe. It happened much as Felix himself had predicted. Ginger had done excellent, even inspired work for The Mansion House but after a year and more he had become bored with routine and his own achievements. According to his phone call on the Thursday of that week, there had been also the matter of his new friend, a long and lissom graphic designer who had been on assignment to a London agency but was now returning to his home in Brussels — or was it Paris? Honestly, Felix couldn't remember and now it didn't seem to matter. David agreed with him. They must concentrate on finding someone else.

All in all, David thought to himself on Christmas Eve, the only disappointment was the continued silence from his old friend Connie, who remained out of contact.

CONRAD AVELING — 1998

David's resolution for the New Year was to recover his relationship with Connie. He had been troubled about it all over the holiday period and had received no comfort from Aischa. Quite the reverse, in fact, and she had been very stern in her judgements. He had been thoughtless and unfeeling in the way he had used Seb Mantel to find his key new man, and if that wasn't enough, they had proceeded to pinch Rory Trollope as well, whom Connie had recruited in the first place. Was it really a surprise to him that his old friend had taken such serious umbrage?

David noted that he hadn't seen any olive branches coming his way from Conrad, but even so he was chastened by Aischa's observations. He was also hurt by the rift and he really did miss Connie for all his good company and especially now when he could really do with his expertise.

As soon as they were all back at work in the first week of January, David rang the Bastion office in Farnham and was put through to Conrad without difficulty. He didn't have to try hard to arrange a lunch together in London. They agreed on Connie's military club for that Friday and it all seemed to go very well. They both managed to stay away from the subject of Zero and instead updated each other on family news and gossip. David asked about Bastion business and Connie was keen to hear news of Pente, his relatively recent retirement from Africa and the reasons for it.

It was when they had moved to take coffee in a secluded corner that things went disastrously wrong. Conrad asked how matters were progressing at The Mansion House. David gave him a run down and concluded with a dig at himself.

'Honestly, Connie, I do feel a dinosaur when it comes to computers and so much revolves around them these days. I really struggle to keep up with what Felix is telling me, but still, I'll be out of it soon enough I suppose.'

Conrad looked up sharply.

'You are retiring then?'

'Well. Look, Connie, you know what I'm doing. We don't have to discuss it again.'

'I see. Well, I must say that's a disappointment, David. I was thinking you'd ask to meet so you could tell me that you've abandoned that idea.'

'No. No, I certainly haven't. In fact, we're doing pretty well with the detail plans.'

'We?'

'Well, Felix and I, plus Pente and King who are now with us. And Hugh Dundas of course.'

'Of course,' said Conrad with a curl to his lip, 'which means Alexa too.' He said it as a statement.

'Look, Connie,' said David trying to retrieve a situation which he felt slipping from him, 'would you let me tell you more of where we've got to. I think you'd be interested. I would certainly value your opinions and I would appreciate the chance to introduce you to Fergus Carradine, our military man. He's asked to meet you and says he has a great respect for your reputation. It was Seb who ...'

'Yes, I know well enough. Seb found him for you and Seb nicked young Trollope for you as well.'

'Connie, ...'

But Conrad cut him off again.

'David, you don't seem to have got the message from the two times I've told you already. I want absolutely nothing to do with this project of yours. So far as I'm concerned, it's mad, bad and barmy. It's also immoral. It's just fucking wrong.'

It was very unusual for Conrad to use such language and his state of upset was reinforced by the high colour in his face as he spoke and the clatter with which he set down his coffee cup.

He made an attempt to recover himself, apologising and then adding,

'We've just got to agree to differ on this, David, but not on everything. You're getting our reports on that contract.'

Again, he made it a statement and David, already distressed by the turn in the conversation, allowed himself to be riled by what he saw as a pretty high handed comment. He made a bad mistake, hearing himself say,

'Oh sure, I'm getting help from you on that one. But of course, you're being paid for it.'

Conrad went a mottled puce as he stared at him. Then he stood abruptly.

'I'll settle the bill here. I suggest you get on your way.'

He turned on his heel and stalked out.

David sighed deeply. He went through to the porter's desk and collected his coat and scarf. They called him a cab and he brooded on the short journey back to The Mansion House. He was not looking forward to recounting that grim incident to Aischa and knew she would be angry at his insensitivity. But he had been provoked, by God. He knew himself and he knew what he would do now. He'd stay angry for a while, then he would be maudlin sad. Then he'd put it behind him. Conrad was his first and special friend. But things change, and so do people.

In another cab on its way to Waterloo, Conrad was steaming. It wasn't just the arrogance of David which got to him, although that was bad enough. He remained hurt also at the way David had gone off to Sebastien behind his back, and the way Seb had accommodated him, not once but twice. There was something else which he kept to himself. He had taken payment from The Mansion House in the matter of Ginger McCabe and he arranged for regular billing thereafter. He even assigned a member of his staff to the file which was properly opened. And then put on hold. Connie told himself that if David Heaven was able to withhold information which he knew would wound, then he would do likewise.

DAVID HEAVEN — 1998

They met in the middle of October, a Thursday, and gathered in the dining room at The Mansion House. The time was twelve noon and there was a buffet lunch, set out against the back wall, leaving people to help themselves. Present were David and Aischa, Martin Kirchoff and Ruth, Hugh Dundas with Alexa, Pente Broke Smith, King Offenbach, Felix Maas and Fergus Carradine. There was no seating plan, no order of priority. Smiling around them all, David felt proud, happy, stimulated: also painfully conscious of who was not here, Connie Aveling, the one whom he had most expected to be with him this day.

David took a drink from his plain tonic water, cleared his throat and began to speak.

'This is a momentous day for us. It's time for me to tell you where we stand and you're going to peer over a precipice. You may not like all you see, so this is your last chance to pull back. It's the point of commitment. That's a lot to ask of you, but there's no need to hurry. We can sit here for as long as it takes and there's a big, fat folder to take away with you.'

He paused briefly. There was no hint of interruption so he continued.

'I'm going to start with a summary of Project Zero. It's brief and I'll set it out for you under a few headings.

'First, WHO? Who are we? Answer. We're close friends, some over many years, others more recent. We're like minded with a common interest and a shared objective. We travel the same road, but we won't all end up in the same place.

'WHAT? What's the mission? What's the purpose? It is to take control of an existing sovereign state on the continent of Africa, and therein found a new nation.

'WHERE? We've not been short of alternatives. We considered every prospect and our research has been meticulous thanks to the efforts of Felix. Our target has to be neither too small nor too large, and not too populous. It must not be landlocked. Our instinct preferred the West Coast and we compiled six possible targets from the nineteen countries which link the Mediterranean to the Cape. I have made our choice and I will reveal this to you in a few minutes.

'WHEN? The First of January 2000. What better day for a birth? And it provides the name for our new country and nation. It will be called Millennium.

'WHY? ... This is the heart's blood question. Why? Here's my answer, and I hope it speaks for all of you. We are all touched by Africa. Aischa was born there, Alexa blighted and Hugh impelled. Africa drives The Mansion House which is the way of life for Martin and Ruth. Pente and King have both devoted a working lifetime to this continent. Fergus is our committed professional, and Ursula is my valuable assistant and constant friend.

'And as for me? Well, I was captivated by Africa from my first visit and over the years, her countries have become my raison d'etre. But she has become also the nemesis of my spirit. I have watched from a grandstand view to see Africa's resources pillaged, her peoples impoverished, governance corrupted and prospects diminished. There have been reasons for the backwards slide, any number of them: but not an excuse, never a justification, not an imperative or a force majeure. Rather, we have suffered endless examples of bad luck, bad management and vicious greed.

'It's time for a change. Project Zero has developed into a clear strategy to reverse the tide of five decades. Saying that is not grandiloquence. We're going to prove our point and others will follow our lead. We're not going to waste more time and energy in fruitless debate. We won't take "no" for an answer: we won't be listening for an answer. We'll arrive in strife, but we'll settle in peace and growing harmony. Our new order will prove through demonstration rather than rhetoric the enormous capability of Africa, given leadership and opportunity. Over the last fifty years of so, the world has admired the achievements of Japan, then Korea, the Indians and the Chinese. Now it's the turn of Africa.

'Nevertheless, our motives will be impugned. We have no legitimacy for taking the action we plan and we will be branded as latter day pirates. Comparisons will be drawn with the invasion of the Falklands and Saddam's annexation of Kuwait. We will be condemned for brutality and profiteering. Global reaction will be instant and most of it ill considered, but we can't complain at that. It is we who are making a pre-emptive strike and we must expect to be judged. We can win a battle, but we can't sustain a war. If we are to succeed, we must win a welcome and as always, actions will speak louder than words.

'We have to strike fast and sure to take absolute control with minimum casualties. Then we must follow up with immediate help and succour. The city which is our first target is suffering. The inhabitants are not at starvation level, but they grind through a tough life on low incomes, intermittent power and water, an absence of healthcare, practically no transport, ramshackle housing, inadequate sanitation: the list goes on. Overarching this grim standard of life is an unforgiving dictatorship in which a few enjoy privilege and comforts while exerting iron control over the less fortunate through arrant corruption and a brutal police force.

'The capital is our first base but it's not our preoccupation. Because of the general deprivation, there's been urban drift with people flocking in from the bush and provincial towns. Paradoxically therefore, the faster we bring improvement to the city, the more of a problem we create in the hinterland. We have to roll out the benefits of our takeover clear across the country, and we are talking of a large land mass with dreadful road conditions.

'It's a huge task which requires people and equipment. Plus there's the need for speed and secrecy until the moment of our arrival. How do you conjure up such assets in place, on time and without warning?

'Before I answer that, does anyone want to question what I've covered so far?'

David moved round the room to pour himself a cup of coffee, conscious of the shifting and stirrings behind him. It was King who found words for all of them when he remarked,

'David, there's a helluva lot to absorb here. Of course there is. But you made the point earlier that we've time and more for talking and going over things which are not understood or which cause a problem. I suggest it's better for you to finish first, then we chew it all over again. Agreed?' He finished by looking around the table and there were answering nods.

David resumed his seat and said, 'OK and thanks King. Let's move to my final heading.

'HOW? For this, I'm going to get some help and let's start with you Felix. Tell us how you went about the research and preparation.'

Felix Maas began his commentary. He spoke precisely and without pause for nearly twenty minutes, drawing his audience into a fuller understanding of the complexity of the role he had been playing. He listed his sources of information, described the techniques he had used and invented to test facts, weigh probabilities and assess relative values. It was fascinating stuff, daunting in its scope and detail. As he concluded, Aischa asked Felix if he had included Angola in his marathon exercise and he affirmed. Her native land had been in David's gut feel list of fourteen to which were added two more at the suggestion of Felix before the analysis programme had reduced this to eleven, then to six and finally to the three from which David had made his final choice.

Felix Maas sat back then, warmed by the general murmurings of thanks and congratulations. He was followed by Fergus Carradine who was introduced by David.

'Fergus has been with us since May of last year, but he's based in the Far East. He's been establishing the Strike Force which he will lead. The role is critical. We have to acquire control before we can do anything else. We must quell any opposition, but we want to avoid bloodshed and mayhem. Fergus won my confidence at our first meeting and I believe he'll now do the same for you, but I'll let him speak for himself.'

'Thank you, David,' said Cogs Carradine and he steepled his hands in front of him as he started with a short resumé of his personal and career background. He looked from person to person as he spoke to them all. He had this brief opportunity to establish relationships and he wanted to make the most of it. Then he came to the meat of it.

'Since I joined, I've been occupied with establishing a base for Zero and starting recruitment. We have also been sourcing equipment and materiel — that's to say weapons and ammunition. I am quite happy with our progress to date: we are on schedule.

'I have no photographs to show you and few specifics to detail. That's because Zero Strike Force is a covert operation and it's wise to limit information. That applies also to those under my command. It's quite possible to make plans and dispositions without knowledge of the target or the full mission, but I can give you an overall brief.

'First, personnel. So far, I've engaged fifty men and women on generous terms and conditions. These are professional people, some experts in particular fields. They have their own contacts which will help our numbers to rise swiftly from June of next year. There will be a final few during the following quarter and we will be complete by the end of October 1999. We will then be at battalion strength, with 500 front line and 150 in reserve.'

Carradine gave himself a pause as he looked around the room, satisfied that his audience was hanging on his words.

'As the months pass and our numbers grow, there will inevitably be a small minority prone to speculation, but I'm not troubled by that prospect. I have the view that a little uninformed gossip provides effective disinformation.'

David felt the flow of confidence in the room. He noted King

Offenbach, who stretched out his long legs with a soft grunt of approval. Then Fergus was moving on.

'Secondly, equipment. I'm not going to set out a list of all we're buying, nor sources and delivery arrangements. We must have air power and transportation. As to the latter, it's relatively straightforward to buy Chinook helicopters which we need because the aircraft is produced in a civilian form. For attack, however, there's a greater challenge as we need Apache helicopters which is a fighting machine. We have to proceed carefully, but I believe we've identified our source and can take time to agree the price and delivery.

'Regarding less expensive equipment, we have no difficulty in acquiring personal arms and ammunition. It's quite straightforward to source the armoured cars, also the fleet of military Land Rovers which will give us mobility.

'One other word about personnel. We need engineers and technicians, some of them highly skilled. The most critical are for the aircraft and I'm recruiting them through Sebastien Mantel as part of the fighting force. For the remainder, to cover the vehicles, generators, bulldozers, forklifts and the like, we can find them quite easily on the open market and they'll be managed as part of the support team.

'Training. I have established a base in the Highlands of Papua New Guinea. This is a remote area and none too friendly in climate, culture or inhabitants. This is fine for Zero. We can look after ourselves and be left alone. The terrain and the heavy bush country give us ample scope for constructing buildings and city layout for assault practice. With the heat and humidity, it's a tough environment: become physically fit there and you'll be flying in West Africa. It can only add to our security that PNG is so far from our actual destination. It will be a discreet location at which to embark our force when the moment comes.

'This brings me to engagement. My force will travel by sea. We already own the vessel which is currently in Pakistan. Next July, she will leave her dry dock and proceed in ballast with a skeleton crew south and east, calling at ports in Indonesia and the Philippines at which she will be embarking fuel, aircraft and vehicles. All this will take time which is the best way of avoiding unwelcome attention. She will then steam on to New Guinea, to a very small harbour which I have identified. Loading will be slow and tricky, but worth the effort for security and we will be training for this part of the operation.

'In just over a year's time, we'll be slipping out of New Guinea waters, complete with crew and full complement of the Zero Strike Force. We'll steam south through the Coral Sea, then down the east coast of Australia, round past Tasmania and out across the Southern Ocean. As we pass the Cape of Good Hope and move into the South Atlantic, we will make contact with the other elements of the task force of which David will tell you more. I expect a final couple of days at sea with aircraft preparation and other details before we move in on the morning of 1st January 2000.'

David moved in quickly.

'I'm sure you'll have questions for Fergus but first, I'd like to bring in Hugh. He will talk to us about finance and his initiatives which have produced an additional benefit. Hugh.' Dundas pushed his chair back, rose onto his large feet and commenced a slow walk around the room, speaking as he went.

'Please excuse me. I'm just feeling a little cramped and a circuit or two will help.

'Now, money. Obviously, this is an expensive operation and like most budgets, ours has got bigger as time's gone by. It's difficult to quantify and we simply must not be underfunded. I can promise you all, that's not going to happen, but we've had to increase our valuation considerably since Fergus, Felix and I started to work it through. As a round figure, the total required for Zero, including a 20% reserve for contingencies, now stands at five billion US dollars.'

There were gasps around the table which coincided with Hugh regaining his seat. He sat at ease and let his gaze drift over them before he resumed.

'Please don't be alarmed. It is a large figure, but quite

possible to achieve. Let me explain. There are three elements to the finance plan and the first is the Zero cash account. We are already drawing down on this to meet the costs which Fergus has incurred to date, but it started with a fund of about 1.2 billion US. A quarter came through The Mansion House Charity which is in the personal control of David and Martin but really, it's David's money. The remainder is my own contribution which I have accrued over time through liquidating investments. I've moved slowly to avoid unwelcome interest in my activities. It helped that I was not only trading stocks and securities but also investments in kind, so for example, I've just sold two properties, one being a ranch in Wyoming. It's a fine place which I took in satisfaction of a debt but now the fortunes of the previous owner have recovered and he was pleased to buy it back in cash and at a decent profit.

'All this money was paid into my bank in the British Virgin Islands, and incidentally, it really is my bank which matters because I can guarantee absolute security of information.

'Now for the other two elements on which I am moving forward concurrently. The first is a charity which is entirely genuine in its endgame but also has a prior purpose. Having conceived the idea, I refined it through discussion with David and Martin. The end result my own charitable foundation and I have given it a name. It's called Orphans of Africa.

'I have brought with me copies of the prospectus. As you'll see later, the foundation targets the tragic circumstances of children and young people across Africa between the ages of five and twenty-five. Through war, refugee displacement, disease and especially AIDS, they are abandoned in their millions to struggle on alone except in each other's company, living perilously close to the breadline, quite unprepared and uneducated to take on the mantle of next generation Africans. They are reproducing themselves in numbers and circumstances which can only make matters worse.

'Orphans of Africa has been established to provide a framework of help with housing, sustenance, education and training. The plan is for Orphans to grow exponentially over the next twenty years so that the continent can reverse the tide of deprivation. We have set up a management operation to get things moving. A Malaysian is running it, an excellent man, and to suit him we've taken offices in Kuala Lumpur.

'The main effort, both his and mine, is to gain commitment for funding. I have started Orphans with $100 million, but we will soon start advertising for donors. We also need some serious investment from world organisations and we are now concentrating on two sources in particular. First, there's the United Nations in the form of several of its agencies such as UNICEF, the Children's Fund and UNDP which is concerned with infrastructure development. In addition, we are pushing hard for money from the European Union, specifically the European Development Fund or EDF: the former colonial powers are awash with cash and conscience. We can use the latter to get at the former.

'Fundraising from any source always takes time, but providing we keep plugging away at it, I'm confident we can swell the coffers of Orphans to 1.3 billion, including what's promised by international agencies. During the next year, we'll be starting to spend the money on Zero.'

Pente interrupted vigorously, 'but that's pure deception, Hugh, it's robbery!'

'You're right, Pente. It's exactly that. And there's worse to come, but hear me out and I believe you'll be satisfied.'

He did not wait for further comments before continuing.

'The third and most productive element goes under the name of Dundas Securities. This is a fund which I have created for international investments and I have chosen the title deliberately because I want to maximise the appeal of my name. Through track record and reputation, a fair proportion of the world's most wealthy have come to see me as a reliable guide to making the most of their money. I'm not mincing my words here and I make no apology. This is an asset of which I'm taking full advantage. I'm targeting here those around the globe with assets numbered in hundreds of millions, including individuals who have not generated their own wealth but are the beneficiaries of family fortunes.

'Dundas Securities is established in Hong Kong. I have invested in it some of my cash from the BVI Bank and I'm using this to pay a dividend which comfortably exceeds the performance of any competitor. The results are published, of course, their excellence has attracted a following. The target clientele is enthusiastic for this new Fund and is encouraging a second division of investors. Now this technique for attracting capital is a fraud. It's a Ponzi scheme, in this case using my money to pay dividends which could not, in reality, be achieved.

'It is true that we are acting dishonestly, but it is the only way in which we can meet our objectives within the required timescale. Please be reassured however. Investors in Dundas Securities will reap a very fair reward through the issue of government bonds from our new state and donors to Orphans of Africa will see their money spent as intended, although the process will be delayed.

'Finally, I make a commitment to you. Should disaster strike and Zero fail, then the financial burden will be mine to bear alone. That's the deal. I am Zero's banker, and I carry the can.'

David was not surprised to pick up the adverse body language around the table as Hugh concluded. Pente, King and Martin in particular, but Ruth also. Perhaps Hugh could have been more gentle with them, but the bulk of the money and all the commitment was his. If there was another way to do it, they didn't have the knowledge and they didn't have the time.

He needed to take control and said,

'Thank you Hugh. We'll come back to this, but I want you all to hear a final piece of scene setting from me. Do you remember that I posed the question earlier, how do you put a strike force in place without advertising its arrival?

'Well it's Hugh who found the solution while he was addressing a completely different problem. He created Orphans of Africa to give us funding, but Orphans will provide us also with Zero's coup de maître — our master stroke.

'Look. The genuine aspiration for Orphans is that it will grow to embrace all of Africa. It's a brilliant concept which will provide a life line to millions of young Africans. That's what will happen. But the first port of call for the charity will be the landing ground for Zero. That is a subterfuge. I acknowledge the fact but it carries great benefits. It helps us to prepare ourselves in secret and to arrive without warning. That will dramatically reduce opposition which will save lives and bloodshed. And in addition, we can start right now to advertise Orphans of Africa worldwide.

'I can sense your concerns and I know there's more to debate but let's look first at the rest of the plan. To win a welcome, Zero must make a difference to the people of the country, a total and mind zapping impact. We need to bring immediate benefits which can be recognised on the very day of our arrival.

'How do we do that? Felix and I wrestled with it. We need skills, therefore people. We need equipment, materials, stores. But we're not starting with nothing. There are assets already in place. There are drains and dams and roads and power stations and a municipal bus service. OK, they're in a bad state but they do exist. There are basics which operate. Our task is to repair and improve — quickly.

'For this, we want the basic skills. We need more builder than architect, more doctor than brain surgeon, we want cooks, mechanics and plumbers. We can get to poets and lecturers later. First priority is to get the show onto a better maintained road.

'So how do we get there with all our people and kit? Fergus has told you that Zero Strike Force will travel by sea and so will all the other elements of Zero. There will be three ships in total, plus one plane.

'Our principal vessel is now called "MV Orphans Angel". She was built in Germany in 1995. About 75000 gross tonnage, some 900 feet long and 110 wide. Ten decks. Constructed for the cruise market. She was to be mothballed for a couple of years because her owners had found a larger liner for their West Coast and Alaska business. Orphans has chartered her for a five year term. Under our contract, we are permitted to convert her, so the "Angel" is now docked in Korea with changes being made to her accommodation. She will emerge with fewer bars and restaurants, the most spacious cabins becoming workplaces, one cinema converted to a conference hall, the gymnasium much enlarged and better equipped, a huge supermarket and a complete hospital section. The "Angel" is a fine ship and she has come to us with an established skipper, an Australian, plus his officers and about half the required complement of crew.

'The other two vessels are container carriers built about twelve years ago, fifteen thousand tons each and both are roll on – roll off. We have bought them outright and we have a captain and crew for one, but not yet for the other. We have called them "Orphans Hope" and "Orphans Dawn", a bit schmaltzy but good for PR.

'"Orphans Hope" is currently under sub contract and doing work between Europe and Russia. She will come back to us next summer in July, and will get a thorough inspection in Rotterdam before proceeding to Felixstowe for loading in October 1999. She will carry all of our back up supplies: food, both dry and refrigerated, and a huge variety of other stores as well, everything from furniture to fireworks, medicines to metals, cookers to cradles.

'"Orphans Dawn" is different. As you've heard from Fergus, she will transport our strike force and the fuel reservoir which we'll need, particularly for the aircraft but also for the armoured cars, Land Rovers, trucks, forklifts, generators. She's now at a shipyard in Pakistan. They're making a form of flight deck on her, but it's hidden behind a wall of empty containers and they're adding a machine lift so there'll be access to the deck below. "Dawn" will emerge as a fighting ship in disguise and able to fly off the helicopters she carries.

'Now back to the big ship — "Orphans Angel". When her conversion is complete, "Angel" will leave Korea and make her way to Hong Kong, arriving there in about twelve months' time.

It's a very expensive place to berth but Hugh and I think it will be worth making a news splash. It will be at this destination that the recruits to Orphans of Africa will enrol and it will be from Hong Kong that "Angel" will sail with much publicity and cork popping.

'I have a little more detail for you on how this programme will progress. Felix is working to finalise the skills we want to hire. We've already started to interview locally in Europe, the States and Asia but the process of engaging people won't crank up until the middle of next year. The basic deal, however, will be the same for all to whom we offer a job. The contract of employment is for twelve months commencing 1st December 1999, including two months paid leave to be taken at the end. So you're paid 'till November 2000, free to go at the end of September. Salaries vary according to the post, but all to be paid by transfer from Hugh's Bank in Tortola, BVI. Follow on contracts available in principle, to be negotiated during year One. You are flown free to the ship in Hong Kong and at termination back to your airport of origin. No cost of living. Food and accommodation provided on the "Angel". No further perks or bonus. If you want health or life insurance, fix it for yourself.'

'I am quite sure,' said David, 'that this package is going to produce all the applicants we want. We'll need to weed them out carefully, but there are sure to be some rotten apples and we just have to deal with them as and when. But there's something further of course. All these people, from all around the world are essentially being engaged under false pretences. The business plan for Orphans is perfectly genuine and reflects all our aspirations. But we make no mention of the first part, the interregnum during which we are taking over a country and establishing a brand new nation. If that deception offends anyone, we don't argue. We simply pay them up and fly them home.'

It was Pente who interrupted him, 'how many are we talking about, David?'

'Round figures. The "Angel" carries three thousand. Say five hundred crew and the rest our recruits to the Orphans mission.'

There was the immediate expostulation around the table which he had anticipated. He held up his hands to gain some silence and went on.

'I know. These are big numbers, and so are the costs for them — win or lose. And of course, Zero Strike Force is on top and much more expensive per head. In addition, there's all the hardware and equipment. But we can't do things by halves: that way leads to frustration at best or disaster at worst.'

David paused briefly before moving towards his conclusion.

'There's no time limit to our discussion today and you can look at all our figures as closely as you like. But first, hear again from Hugh as to where we are on the money.'

On cue, Hugh came in.

'I've only one thing to add. We can get to the total five billion from the sources I've covered. I'm quite sure of that, but my confidence received a boost from news just a week ago when Dundas Securities received its single largest investment. It's for one billion dollars and it has reached us from a lawyer in Curacao, Netherlands Antilles. He's a man named Carl J Brogan and I know the identity of his largest client. Brogan has acted over the last twenty years for Mobutu Sese Seko, the deceased President of Zaire. Brogan continues to look after the estate for his inheritors. It's a fine irony that this contribution to Zero comes from an African ruler who was famously corrupt. Mobutu embezzled over five billion US dollars during his rule and now twenty per cent has come back to help with a new start on the continent.'

The participants in this crucial meeting were by now mostly slumped in their chairs, exhausted by the concepts and the figures. David acknowledged this by suggesting a break for them all and a chance for some individual conversations.

'You have listened to a great deal of detail,' he told them, 'but it's the whole of the grand plan which flays the senses. I know and I understand. I've been living with it for so long and I still peek over that precipice myself. You have every right to ask if this is a new dawn — or a perfect storm. All I ask is for your complete and honest reactions. Hold nothing back.'

By now, he was standing and starting to move towards the buffet, checking his watch and not surprised to find the time already past 4 pm. Outside, London's winter evening wrapped itself around them. There was an aura of detachment. Everybody moved from the table, some through the door towards the washrooms, others to the buffet. David's assistant Ursula bustled out in search of fresh coffee. David took another glass and returned to his seat. He sensed dejection amongst them, disappointment: or was it disbelief? Aischa came to sit with him and they whispered together as he described his feelings.

She shook her head.

'It's none of those, Darling one. It's exhaustion. There's a huge lot to take in and you've worn us out. But not completely: look at Hugh and Felix, all pumped up and raring to go.'

David glanced around and could see she was right. She spoke again, 'give us a good break. I'm just going to the loo, but I'll be right back.' They smiled at each other as she slipped away and David slouched back, sipping at his tonic water and feeling refreshed by her words.

There was more comfort to come from King Offenbach, who sat on one corner of the table swinging his leg as he began,

'I'd as soon keep this between ourselves, David. It's spooks territory and it won't help anyone else to know about it.'

David looked up at the familiar, quizzical smile and immediately felt invigorated. It was clear that King was coming from acceptance and embellishment rather than rejection.

'Go on,' he said.

'OK, my friend, I'll do just that. But first, a mite of reassurance for you. I've not changed my mind. I'm with you like I said before and I'll be staying that way. That's a promise, and I can add something to it now. I'm mighty impressed. You've done a whole lot of work to pull all this together, David. Of course, you've got the help of one powerful team what with Felix and this Fergus who looks damn good to me. To say nothing of Hugh Dundas,' and King shook his head in admiration, 'extraordinary guy. But with all of that, it's you who's taking the point and driving Zero forward. Congratulations.'

'Thank you, King.'

'They're well deserved. But now, here's my contribution. You're well prepared already and you'll sure as hell be doing a whole lot more during the next twelve months. I'm pretty confident that you'll steam right on in there, but my thinking is around what happens after. What's the rest of the world going to say? What's going to be international reaction and response even? Have you given that any thought, David?'

'Well yes, I have, King but maybe not enough. What's your point?'

'It's this. I reckon you're gonna stir up a helluva hornet's nest. Within a day or so, you'll have them table thumpin' in the capitals of Europe, there'll be preening and posin' in Washington and Downing Street. Outrage on all sides and you know why? Because the big hitters don't like to feel themselves outsmarted and they sure as hell will be feeling surprised. That means there's the danger of one or more of them saying "hold on now. Nobody told us about this. What the hell's going on?. We've gotta do something." And that would be real dangerous, David. It could start bringing you guys all the attention that you really do not want.'

David sat straighter in his chair. 'I'm with you King. So what do we do?'

'Distraction' was the immediate answer, 'Distraction and diversion. If anyone starts to get pushy with us, we need to have a counter punch ready which can at least buy us time 'cos that's what we'll need most. Leave it to me and I'll be ready if and when we need it.'

They were interrupted by Pente looking for some time with David, who moved on feeling contented by his conversation with King.

They were all back in the dining room now, but still in small groups or two together as animated discussion continued. After a while, David invited them to sit down again, saying that he had one further matter to present to them before bringing their session to a close.

'It's been a long day already,' he said, 'and I expect a part of you is asking questions. Why do this? Why try against all the odds and strive for the unthinkable? Why take such risks? My answer? Because there's the need, there's a clear purpose and because I've been given the opportunity to try. And that's what I'm going to do.'

He didn't wait for reaction. He built on his moment by rising to walk around the table, placing before each of his companions a leather bound folder. He returned to the end of the table and remained standing as he spoke to them.

'You will find here a résumé of the plan and facts we have considered. It concludes with our destination and the date of our arrival. On the first day of the new century, we will found here a new country which we will call Millennium and over its capital, Century City, we will raise the flag of a new nation in Africa.'

He did not need to issue a further invitation. They turned their pages to find the maps, the photographs and the depiction of a flag, a solid square of that azure blue, the cloudless sky of Africa and upon it, the thin outline of a rising crescent moon.

JOSH TROLLOPE — February 1999

On a cold afternoon, Josh took the train from London and in due course came home to his terrace house in Marlborough. He let himself into the loneliness, missing Moira as keenly as ever although it was nearly five years since the pneumonia had taken her. He made himself get on with it, to unpack his small case and make a cup of tea as he thought over the events of the last few days. He had enjoyed himself: the sense of involvement and of making contribution. The renewal of an old friendship.

It had started with a phone call from Rory, his son of whom he saw little these days. Not that Josh was complaining. Rory was now thirty-four, long grown and gone, but evidently fulfilled in his job with Bastion in the Far East. The quality of contact between father and son was good and better two days later when Rory flew in with his boss, a Mr Carradine who seemed to have the right cut about him to be the officer commanding. He had done most of the talking. They were planning a mercenary operation in Africa and needed to find a discreet advance party. Rory was pretty sure his Dad could help. Josh listened, liked the approach, made his contact and packed his small case. Then the three of them took a direct flight from London Gatwick to Lagos, Nigeria.

They arrived on a Friday evening, and joined the back of a long queue for immigration and customs, but it was at least a better ordered process now as a garrulous fellow traveller told them. He had been visiting Nigeria since the early oil boom years and entertained them with stories of getting through Murtala Mohammed Airport and on up north to Ibadan. Finally, they emerged from the airport building to find a cab and a slow drive to their hotel.

The traffic was no less intense the following morning as they were driven to Victoria Island. It took a further forty-five minutes before they found their destination and stood in the humid heat of midday as Carradine paid off their cab. Old Josh sniffed the air, the scent of Africa redolent with his memories of long gone days. They were in a cul-de-sac: at its end stood high steel gates, topped by rolls of razor wire. To the right of the gates was a substantial house on three floors, the windows and door on the ground floor shuttered, grilled and barred. They walked up to the gates. A personal entrance was set into one side. It bore no sign and there was neither handle nor bell in sight.

Rory gave the door a shove. It hardly moved, but they could hear it rattle against the locks which held it solid from the inside. Fergus glanced up and pointed out a CCTV camera mounted high on the corner of the house which would have seen them walk down the street. Rory turned to see an impressive figure. The black man approaching them was a colossus. Two metres in height and wide to match, he was moving with a sinuous motion which said he would also be quick on his feet, despite the huge boots. He had a baseball cap on the great head and Ray Ban glasses hid his eyes. He walked up and stood towering over them.

Josh Trollope took over. 'You must be Jonah,' he said, sticking out his right hand.

The black man didn't utter, but he shuffled one vast boot in front of the other and then they could all hear the pedestrian door in the gate behind them being unlocked. Through it stepped another black figure, trim and muscled, well dressed in collar and tie, neither hat nor glasses, a close crop of grey hair, mature, experienced, confident. He stepped up to Josh.

'Trollope,' he said, 'of Grenadier Guards.'

'Patrick Nugumu. Maiduguri Frontier Force.'

Josh spoke the words as he held out his hand, but Patrick brushed it aside and swept the Englishman into a great hug of greeting. It was many years since they had first met in the bush, when Josh had rescued Patrick from certain death. Rory and Fergus looked on in contentment, while Jonah continued with an impassive stare from his great height. They stayed in the compound on Victoria Island for three days. There was history to cover and plans to lay. Patrick insisted on moving his visitors from their hotel onto the top floor of his house. He lived with his family on the second and the ground level was devoted to his business.

Patrick Nugumu had been living here for fifteen years, and a further twelve before then at a variety of addresses in greater Lagos, since he had struggled into the city two years after the Biafra War. He had tried a number of jobs before putting his military training to best use by joining the army of private security guards which sprang up during the boom years of the seventies and eighties. Even after that frenzy had subsided and the focus had switched to the new federal capital of Abuja, there was good business for Sentinel Security which Patrick had founded and built up on his own. Along the way, he had married his Delphine, an illegal immigrant from Cameroun, and she had borne him three sons in quick succession. Then there was Jonah. Delphine had found him abandoned on a rubbish tip and they had given him a second shot at life. He was still only nineteen and had never stopped growing since they had taken him in. He was a gentle giant until roused in defence of his family and their home. He was also mute, having never spoken a word in his life.

Following their brief action together in Gabon, Josh and Patrick had clung to a spasmodic contact for eighteen months, but neither was a man of letters and then the civil war had put Patrick completely out of contact. It was not until after Josh was widowed that loneliness drove him to discover the possibilities of the computer age. He traced Patrick through his old regimental association and they started to communicate again.

That renewed contact led to the recruitment of Patrick and Sons to the team of Zero. Fergus found Patrick quick, intuitive and professional. He was over ten years younger than Josh and he relished the challenge of Zero.

'Delphine and I both have been refugees of a sort all our lives,

317

Suh,' he remarked to Carradine, refusing to address him by any other name or title, 'we both like the notion of a new start. My boys feel the same, but there's big Jonah too and he won't leave my side.'

'That's good,' Fergus smiled at him, 'and from our side there will be Rory and two more. Plus someone who's got pretty special skills,' he said with a wink to Rory and his father.

'OK,' Patrick beamed back at him, 'and do I get let in on this secret and what the guy does?'

Fergus was gathering papers together as he replied.

'Actually Patrick, it's not a guy but a girl. Her name is Verity Blades and she's the best explosives 'man' I've ever found. She's a Kiwi and I first met her when I was serving in Timor. She and Rory will travel in together as a couple, which makes for good disguise.'

Plus, hopefully, it makes for a future thought Josh to himself, as Rory had spoken much about this girl on the plane out from London.

They finished their planning. It was arranged that Rory and team would fly into Target as eco-tourists, arriving in the first week of December. Patrick and family would close the Sentinel business at the end of August and travel in by road, taking time to establish some safe houses in the capital. Patrick had a final question for Josh.

'Will you be coming in with the ships?'

'No, I won't. I'm too old, Patrick. I'll be more hindrance than help, but I'll be down a bit later when the dust has settled.'

The two old comrades gazed into each other's eyes, each knowing there was no more to be said.

THIERRY CESTAC — July 1999

Ginger McCabe was found dead in the first week of the month. His body was discovered in a corner end seat of a carriage on the Circle line of the London underground. It was early morning before peak hour when a fellow traveller thought that something about him looked wrong and pulled the emergency handle. There was a short report in the Evening Standard which said that the transport police were trying to establish where and when he had joined the train but made plain that this was a murder enquiry. A long, thin knife was still embedded in his chest and the blood loss had spoiled Ginger's favourite waistcoat.

The Mansion House PR Agency picked up the news item and passed it to human resources who informed Felix Maas. Felix was startled and distressed: he had liked Ginger and admired his ability. He had lived a rackety sort of life, but would never have hurt a fly and didn't deserve to go out this way. Perhaps it had been yet another love affair, this one gone badly wrong. Before dismissing the sad news from his hectic work schedule, Felix rang his boss. David was more brusque: these things do happen, plus it was now months since McCabe had left their employ and there had been no adverse comments from Bastion on his subsequent activities. They were now inside their final six months before Zero. They were flat out with no time for distractions and the subject was closed: but only for a few days.

It was mid-morning on a Wednesday when Felix took the call on his personal land line, a number available to only a very few. The voice and name were unknown to him, but he was chilled by a reference code which was quoted with familiarity. The code identified a summary file in one of his Zero Programs. Absolutely no one on the planet should have access to this information, but the voice spelt it out with perfect accuracy. It did not wait for a reaction which Felix would have been unable to articulate. The voice said that it required a meeting in The Mansion House that Saturday morning at 11 am precisely when terms would be laid down. Attempts at counter action between then and now would result in exposure of Plan Zero to the world media. 'Click' as the line was cut.

Felix felt he had been hit by a bus. He drank half a pint of black coffee laced with whisky and smoked two cigarettes as he clung to his discipline and wrote a note of all he had heard. Then he took the staircase three at a time to barge into David Heaven's office. David listened as he made his own scribble. He made Felix go over it all again. He kept calm as his innards churned over. He focussed his concentration. The threat was for a purpose. Someone out there wanted something in exchange for silence: a bargain, therefore, a trade, a bribe. Well OK, he could handle that. Not for nothing had he been dealing in Africa for thirty years. But how had it come to this?

David and Felix looked at each other and said simultaneously 'Ginger McCabe.'

Felix went on to say, 'It must have been Ginger. I should've worried more when I first suspected him. He's the only one I know who would have half the ability to crack my systems. And that was when he was working here. But the stuff I was hearing back is recent: it's current. It includes work from only last month. Which means that Ginger was hacking into me for all that time since he dumped us: right up to his'...

'Death.' David finished it as he thought furiously. The somebody somewhere had sent their message with murder, which could only mean that Ginger had become expendable. They already knew the lot: no need for further spying. They knew the plan, the destination, the timing. They had killed the messenger to make a chilling point and for all his knowledge of dark deeds in Africa in the past, David realised that he was now out of his depth.

'Felix,' he said with all the confidence he could muster, 'this is tragic, serious and dangerous. We need help and I know where to start. What you've got to do is to get back to work. That's tough but necessary. There's so much still to do and I'm not having us thrown off course now. I'll handle it urgently and I'll keep you posted, but you have to keep it quiet and leave it to me. Be here on Saturday in case I need you. Agreed?'

'Yes David. OK.' Felix looked relieved, as David expected, although the fear was still naked in his eyes. David sympathised. As Felix made for the door, he stopped him.

'The voice, Felix, you say you were speaking English but what about the accent? Foreign? European? What?'

Felix shook his head. 'No. The language was fluent but the guy was French, from down south somewhere I'd guess, and he seemed to have a slight lisp. Oh, and one other thing. He sounded, well an older man than you would expect.'

'And you're sure about the name?'

'Certain. But it means nothing to me.'

'Nor to me,' said David. Felix went out and David sat and thought and shivered before he reached for the telephone. He had no trouble in getting to Connie Aveling.

The two men exchanged a formal greeting and David laid out the reason for his call: the death of McCabe, the contact with Felix from out of the blue, the menacing demand to meet on Saturday. The voice of an older man, Felix had said, and definitely French in origin. David had never heard of him, but he gave his name — a Mr Thierry Cestac.

At his desk in Bastion HQ, Conrad was transfixed. He was also speechless and it took several bellows down the line from David before he became capable of reply.

'I heard you, David, but there was some break in the line. Sorry.'

There was a pause while Connie tried to pull himself further together and then he went on,

'I'll go over all our reports on McCabe, see what else I can piece together. I'll call back if I find anything. But also, David,

I think I'll come up to the meeting with this man. I may be needed.'

He rang off abruptly, leaving David staring at his dead phone and thinking that this bad day was getting worse. Connie had sounded to be in another universe, distracted, uninterested: but at least he would be here with us. It was good that he was so busy. He just had to get his head down and get on with it, ignoring for the moment all the horrors which might lie just around the corner. Saturday would come soon enough.

This was exactly the expression used by Conrad in a conversation with himself as he stayed barricaded in his office, the telephone barred, meetings cancelled, visits and visitors postponed. The overarching problem for him, which he had been wrestling to contain for a couple of years at least, was that he was sick and he couldn't find the cure. Sickness, for him, was something which you sorted with a course of pills or maybe an operation. It was all to do with a physical problem. Infirmity of mind or spirit, especially if brought on by that dreadful word 'stress', was not a condition to be recognised by an Aveling. Stress was for wimps. Pressure was something to be endured.

Connie told himself that he was winning, but he had to acknowledge that he was still suffering from sudden rage and torment, mood swings, forgetfulness and the inclination to be morose and grumpy. All this spelt worry which ate into the reserves of his energy and now he had to find enough of that to meet the challenge of this crisis. Could he do so? Admit it, he had been duplicitous. He had accepted The Mansion House contract to watch over McCabe, and then done absolutely nothing about it. He had allowed Bastion to be paid at full rates for a job which he, personally, had then ignored. Yes, he had been much wounded by David Heaven's actions but he should not have been playing personal pique against commercial standards. But that's done now. Whatever he might discover over the next couple of days, it won't bring back the brilliant geek with the easy morals and it won't undo the damage done.

Which is what? It seems pretty clear. McCabe was induced to

access and keep passing the total secrets of David's despicable Plan Zero. And the person to whom he has been giving this information is called Thierry Cestac. A Frenchman, sounding mature and with a slight lisp. Could this be the same man who had abducted Alexa in 1970? The year when he had flown out to his posting in Singapore?

Yes, Connie told himself, it's a huge coincidence, but it's just possible. Thirty years on and he might be about to meet the man who caused him to commit two acts of murder at Bahrain Airport: the Russian woman and the big Arab. Conrad spread his arms on his desk and clenched his fists as details of memory flashed before him. He saw again that sly little bastard Riaz, he visualised Alexa, standing her on the dead bodies to push her over the cubicles, sitting in his aircraft seat and willing Peter Bushell to get them into the air. And it made sense that 'Cestac' meant nothing to David Heaven. He knew about the abduction but had never heard the name, while Cestac himself would have neither known nor cared about the final outcome. Whatever, it would become clear on Saturday which gave him two full days to do some overdue research.

Conrad drove into London and reached The Mansion House fifteen minutes early. He hadn't entered the building since his abrupt departure over three years before. It felt longer to him, more like from another age and lifetime. The reception area was unattended for the weekend, but Bill Evans appeared immediately. Bill was Bow Bells cockney, retired through disability from the Police Flying Squad to manage security for The Mansion House with razor sharp efficiency. He had come in at David's request and was keeping a sharp look out for the arrivals. Bill gave Conrad a warm greeting and escorted him directly to the small conference room where Ursula was on hand to settle him with a cup of tea and left him to himself. He took a gulp to help wash down the couple of pills which were due about now and glanced around. The room was quiet, enclosed, with no windows: the temperature control gurgled softly in the background. There was a sideboard against one wall, flanked by two armchairs, but the room was dominated by an oval table which could seat maybe ten, but now there were half a dozen chairs drawn up. He took one of them. He didn't have long to wait. David came striding in with a mug of coffee in hand and on his heels was Rory Trollope looking overdressed in a suit and tie, carrying a smart briefcase. He was wearing heavy rimmed spectacles and looked like a fat cat accountant. David said simply, 'Rory happened to be around.'

He followed this curt announcement with, 'thanks for coming, Connie. I still don't know what the hell this is all about, but I'm bloody glad to have you with me. Now, how are we going to sit?'

He had no time to answer his own question as they heard footsteps outside. The door was opened by Bill Evans who stood aside to allow their visitors to enter the conference room.

There were three of them. In front and in charge was the man who must be Thierry Cestac. He was quite tall, a little stooped at the shoulders, very slim, over long hair which marched in pepper and salt waves over his ears. He stood for a second in the doorway, fixing Conrad with a piercing gaze from the clear grey eyes set wide to frame the long, aquiline nose. The face was clean shaven and heavily lined. He was immaculately presented in pure French fashion: an open necked shirt under a sports jacket of subdued pattern, flannel trousers, highly polished loafer shoes in deep brown. There was no denying the presence of the man but he was well into the autumn of his years. Sixty-five if he was a day, David decided, perhaps more.

Cestac advanced into the room to give space to his companions. The first was similarly slender, but a shorter man with a sallow complexion and oyster colouring. He was quiet, composed: his eyes moved constantly and his long, thin hands hung by his sides with ever flexing fingers. It was difficult to put an age to this man, but the third was obviously mid-forties, average height with a stocky, powerful build. He had a boxer's face with a broken nose beneath a bullet head with its light bristle of crew cut hair. His gaze lingered briefly on Bill Evans as he passed through the doorway.

David Heaven made no greeting and didn't rise from his seat. He simply gestured at the chairs opposite. The Frenchman took his time. When he had settled himself, he looked across the table into David's eyes.

'You are Mr David Heaven, I assume,' he said, and the suggestion of a lisp was in his voice with its slight accent, 'is one of these two gentlemen Felix Maas?'

David made no reply and Cestac continued,

'No matter, it is you, M'sieu Heaven to whom I wish to speak. With me are Toussaint,' and he nodded at the sallow face to his right, 'and Mr. Margolis from London.' The bullet head inclined. In the short silence which followed, David gave no reaction. He held Cestac's gaze and said simply, 'State your business.'

'Very well,' and the voice rose a notch in volume to assert an authority.

'My name is Thierry Cestac. I am entirely informed as to your Plan Zero. Your past employee Mr McCabe was able to provide me with the fullest detail through electronic access to the work of Mr Maas. I have followed your progress over the last two years and I know that you are now approaching your deadline. Mr McCabe was an extremely clever man, but with aberrant taste and quite unreliable. I decided to send him to carry a personal message to you. That is how we are together today.

'My requirement, M'sieu, is quite straightforward. I embrace your concept and admire what you have achieved. I do not wish to interrupt your activity. My interest is in power. I have now reached a maturity in years and I wish to exercise power for myself. You have provided me with the means of doing so. You can say that I am taking over your takeover. That is my demand.

'Now, Mr Heaven, why should you agree? In truth, M'sieu, you have no other choice. I have out manoeuvred you. I am in possession of your facts and your plans, all of them, and I can publish them across the world in an instant. But to be positive also, I can help you. I can guarantee your success. I have at my disposal large resources of manpower and armaments. We will have no need for make believe charities.'

Cestac curled his lip in disdain as he continued.

'Now Mr Heaven, I am a determined and ruthless man. I get what I want and now I want to acquire Plan Zero. The fate of McCabe gives you evidence of my ability. My people here today can provide further demonstration.'

Cestac let the threat hang in the air as he prepared to continue. David stayed motionless with his eyes locked on the Frenchman's face.

It was Conrad Aveling who spoke.

'Thierry Alphonse Cestac. Born Pau, France 1928. Left home as a teenager. Fled to Paris. Took up with ageing roué. Inherited his property and money. Commenced a discreet and successful career in international crime. Prostitution, drugs, brokering influence in Africa and Central Asia. Guarded by muscle, accompanied by this little wop of a knifeman.'

Cestac turned to face him with a pointing finger, saying 'and you are who?'

'My name is Aveling: a long time friend and colleague of Mr Heaven.'

'Ah yes, Monsieur Aveling. Mr Conrad Aveling. I am familiar with the name, but I think you are now less close in friendship to Mr Heaven? No? Perhaps that is because you failed to keep watch on McCabe as you had contracted to do. But you are trying to make amends, I see. Your summary of my background is correct as far as it goes and I commend you. Few people have been able to discover even as much as that.'

Cestac smiled. If Connie's revelations had disarmed him at all, he had made a remarkably swift recovery. By his side, Toussaint's eyes burned with barely suppressed fury: he did not suffer insult. Margolis appeared stolid and indifferent. David kept his silence, leaving the floor to Conrad who continued.

'My relationship with Mr Heaven is not your concern, Mr Cestac, and it has no bearing on your demands. But there is another matter of which you should be aware. You and I have not met before, but our paths have crossed — a long time ago. You will remember the occasion. Thirty years ago, January 1970, you seduced a French girl for sale to a deviant in Bahrain. She is', he emphasised the word, 'a friend of mine and of Mr Heaven from our university days. She was to be delivered by your colleague, a Mr Georges Eboli. She did not arrive and he did not return. I, myself, intervened.'

Cestac gave himself time to recover from the shock of genuine surprise and Connie pressed home his advantage by shifting forward in his seat and placing his meaty forearms on the table, stretching out his hands, palm down, as if to invade the Frenchman's territory.

Cestac rocked back on his chair and blew out his cheeks. He was giving signs of capitulation as he spoke.

'Well. That is indeed a revelation and a coincidence. I remember the incident very clearly. How unfortunate it was.'

He gave a wintry smile and smoothed his long hair back from his forehead before continuing.

'Of course I don't recall the girl. She was just one amongst so many as you will understand. But I do remember the result. I lost a great deal of money, and that mattered to me.'

As they were digesting the shock of his words, he added in a whisper —'Toussaint.'

The slight and sallow man moved in a blur. He half rose from his chair and leaned across the table, right arm supporting his weight while the left windmilled and shot forward with a glint appearing at its wrist as he plunged his killing knife into Conrad Aveling's right hand, to skewer it to the highly polished table.

Pandemonium ensued. Conrad screamed with the pain, clapping his left hand to his right wrist. Cestac was smiling, David was open mouthed, the thug Margolis was instantly on his feet and moving to give himself space. Rory Trollope was the surprise to which Toussaint should have been alert. He had assessed this bulky young man as they had entered and wondered if the average suit and spectacles aimed for disguise, but Conrad's jibe at the 'wop knifeman' had diverted him and he had been craving for Cestac's instruction to strike. He would not live long to regret it.

Rory started with Margolis, using the smart briefcase preloaded with a couple of house bricks to attack the broken nose, smashing into it with such force that the former boxer collapsed in a struggle to draw breath into his lungs.

Toussaint lunged for him with a fresh knife shaken from his wrist, but you can't use a rifle against a tank. Rory caught the first thrust with his case, then pushing it back into the olive face as he attacked with a salvo of kicks to the groin and the slight body, ignoring the slashing blade to grind his opponent into the plush carpet, one foot to the belly, the other to the head. Toussaint lay writhing.

Meanwhile, there was a scene which would remain with David all his days. Connie didn't try to free his hand. Crouching on the edge of his chair, he stretched across the table and grabbed Cestac by his shirt front. By brute strength, he pulled the Frenchman across the width of the table using his one available arm. He sat back then, cradling Cestac in his left arm which he slipped up around the chest while he wrapped his legs around the struggling body. He shifted himself further to work his left hand round Cestac's throat.

It was a primeval scene and David was able only to sit and watch. Nevertheless, he could understand. Conrad had always exhibited extraordinary strength in his upper body. He was much older now and his power diminished, but older also was this adversary from so long ago. The years fell away. The veins in Connie's temples and neck stood out like whipcords. He grunted and groaned like a beast from the deep. Cestac flailed and thrashed to escape. He could not. The struggle seemed to last an eternity.

Elsewhere in the room, Margolis lay like a stranded fish, whooping for breath. Toussaint lay terminally still. For David Heaven, this was a world beyond his ability and understanding. He sat motionless and awaited the outcome.

Finally came conclusion. Cestac lay stretched, his feet drumming on the table, his neck in the grasp of Conrad's left hand. The seventy year old Frenchman became quieter and then ceased his struggle. It was over. He was gone and dead. Conrad let the body slide off him and onto the floor. He was himself a dreadful sight, mottled and puce from the effort. Rory moved in to release his hand from Toussaint's knife and Connie gasped from the pain. In spite of it, he managed to look at David and say 'for Alexa.' His voice was slurring. The eyes were glazing.

David was conscious that Bill Evans had entered the room and was speaking to him.

'I'll clear up here, Boss. Danny Margolis isn't a problem. I know him. He'll just want out of here. We'll give the other two the burial of St Luke.'

He saw David's expression, 'That's not the Bible, Guv. It's Met. Police speak from when Lord Lucan vanished. We'll slip them over the side of a cross Channel ferry. No traces and no questions.'

David was incapable of speech, but he nodded vaguely before turning back, twisting in his chair to look at Connie who was still slumped beside him with Rory on his other side, fumbling to release Conrad's tie and collar. David wanted to talk a while to his old mate, to use this moment to bridge the gap which had opened between them and to rebuild their friendship, starting with some words of thanks for the supreme effort which Conrad had made. But his mood was changed in an instant by the look in Rory's eye and David sprang up to bend over Connie's recumbent form.

'What is it?' he demanded.

'Not sure exactly, but he's out of it and I can't find a pulse. We're in trouble here. Need a medic. Could be a heart attack. He's not conscious.'

David was galvanised into action. He could do crisis management and he swept from the room bellowing for help from The Mansion House weekend staff. Within thirty minutes, the room was empty: Conrad Aveling in an ambulance bound for Emergency, Bill Evans in a dark van bearing a macabre load out of London, with Danny Margolis back on the streets heading for anonymity.

DAVID HEAVEN & AISCHA GOMES —
September 1999

They were stalked by death during those summer months. Cestac and Toussaint were buried at sea and they left not a trace behind: no word of enquiry, no acquaintance of either to mourn.

Connie Aveling had suffered not a heart attack, but a stroke and it was very severe. He was paralysed down the left side of his body and he lost the power of speech. They did their very best for him, but he had lost the will to live. He died in hospital at the end of August, over the Bank Holiday weekend. Tepee was with him at the end and his three children, Peter, Oscar and Camilla. Pente Broke Smith took his funeral service at which all who had mattered to him were present in the small Hampshire Church in which he had worshipped. Alexa and Hugh from Hong Kong, David and Aischa, Kingston Offenbach, Martin and Ruth Kirchoff, Sebastien and Izzy together with Rory Trollope and a contingent from the business which Connie had nurtured.

The Oxford Five were reduced to Four. David was distraught. Tepee did not reproach him. She was simply sad and lost and inconsolable. Alexa was shattered for her. Connie had gone to his grave in defence of her for a second time and his sacrifice had cost her dearest friend Tepee the companionship on which she depended. Talking about it later, David said to Aischa,

'I'm haunted by that last look he gave me when he said he'd done it for Alexa. He meant more than that I'm sure. He was also confirming his rejection of me and my philosophy and the whole Zero concept. And, no doubt, ramming it home that if I could conceive of such a thing, so could a villain like Cestac with no motive except his self satisfaction. Connie will have died mighty disappointed in me, that's for sure.'

David shook his head in sadness as he reached for his whisky glass, but Aischa was having none of it.

'You're not attractive when you're wallowing,' she said sharply, 'and you're not looking at the facts. Poor Connie was already a sick man before this tragedy. He had worked too hard for too long. He was depressed by the world in which he worked and anyway, he refused to recognise depression. He barely listened to your proposal before rejecting it out of hand. Tepee knows all this and it tortures her now. She saw him withdrawing into his moods and now she wishes she had done more to change his lifestyle. Oscar thinks the same. He and Anna have talked it over endlessly and she has told me of course. Alexa understands it best of all, not surprising after all she went through. So for God's sake, David, don't you start mooning around in recriminations. It's not right and it's not fair to the memory of a great guy who just lost his way a bit, but who certainly pulled your walnuts out of the fire at the very end.'

David was startled by her words and her tone, but properly rebuked.

'I think you mean chestnuts, Darling, but otherwise I take your points.'

He continued to brood over ensuing days but kept his thoughts to himself. Aischa was right and he knew it, but the memory of Connie and his friendship burned bright. David had always believed that their relationship would return in full strength, but now it was gone forever.

Then life moved them on again and brought another departure. Aischa returned to Lisbon at the beginning of September and a week later, she called David to say that Alves was in a hospice in Lisbon and slipping away. Anna was already on her way there and David jumped for the first plane. They were both too late. With a lack of drama and a self effacement which was the style of the man, Alves Gomes went on his way, happy to leave the party of life while he was still enjoying it. He and Aischa had shared some precious conversations during his last couple of days. He had some final words of advice and they had both been smiling as he said,

'Don't delay now. Get on and get married properly. You're like me and not getting any younger.'

Anna endorsed this advice, but Aischa was still amazed to find that it was already on David's mind. He proposed to her on the day they buried Alves and they married in Lisbon before the weekend. Anna stood as witness and the Mori's at the restaurant baked a cake. They all sensed that Alves was beaming down on them.

'We will honeymoon,' said David, 'in a new century and on another shore.'

DAVID HEAVEN — December 1999

At midday on Christmas Eve, David and Aischa walked out of the apartment above The Mansion House and descended the building to find his car waiting outside in a quiet Piccadilly. They didn't linger and as the driver took them away, David wondered if and when he would come back.

The previous evening had been a subdued occasion touched with apprehension. They had gathered together for a final report, a last hurrah, some quiet time of reflective conversation before the pandemonium of their own making swept over them. As he walked into the dining room of The Mansion House, David saw that it was set for fourteen which set him wondering until he saw that Ursula had included places for Conrad and Tepee — one who could not join them and the other who would not. He was touched, and more so when he noted that they would have made the total thirteen, a number for bad luck, and so she had put the bust of old Sol in front of a chair. She was right: he would certainly be with them in spirit.

They enjoyed a glass or two of champagne before they sat down. Then Pente recited a special grace of his own creation, looking around as he did so to embrace them all. The food was excellent and the wines peerless. Ursula administered and Bill Evans assured their privacy from his watching post in reception. When coffee and liqueurs had been circulated, David called for a moment's silence while he brought them up to date.

'Our fleet has sailed. The "Orphans Angel" left Hong Kong on schedule with her full complement of crew and passengers, nearly three thousand in total. We attracted some outstanding press coverage as you will have seen. Her voyage, which some journalistic bright spark has dubbed "Mission of Mercy", seems to have caught the global imagination and getting under way just before Christmas has given a further boost. We have published the schedule and the dates, so the world is informed that "Orphans" will be putting into five different ports and countries down the West coast of Africa over the next nine months and we have got correspondence with all five to prove she is expected. Only we know that she'll be delayed into all but one.

'Her journey is uneventful so far and the captain told me earlier today that they have all settled down together. The ship is now in the Pacific and closing on Cape Town where Fergus will join her by helicopter. He will be flying out to Cape Town tomorrow and can tell you this evening that the embarkation of the Strike Force was complicated, but no worse than anticipated.

'The "Hope" did have some problems which delayed her arrival into Felixstowe and had us sweating a bit. But they managed to make up time in loading her there and she's made a good passage since. We know that she'll make the rendezvous with the others.

'So far, so good. Now for the rest of us, the original plan is unchanged. Martin and Ruth are staying here of course. Fergus goes tomorrow which leaves me and Aischa, Alexa and Hugh, Felix, Pente, King and Ursula. The eight of us fly out of London Stansted on New Year's Eve. We'll have plenty of space. Hugh has bought us a Boeing 747. It's not new and it's unusual as it's a short bodied model designed for both passengers and cargo. That will be useful as we have a bit of kit to take with us, a couple of vehicles and a whole lot of medical supplies in particular. The aircraft came fitted out with a cabin full of sophisticated communications gear which will be useful to us. Also with a flight crew, led by an experienced chief pilot called Arnie Schwartz, a South African who is quite a character. Hugh and I had no choice but to tell him what we're about. It was a risk, but he had to know and we think we've struck lucky. Arnie is delighted and now, so am I.'

David paused to sip at his port and his silence denoted that he was ready for questions. But overall, the prevailing mood was of a weary resolution: let's get on with it for all that we're scared of what the future holds. That goes for me also, thought David to himself.

They broke up before midnight, going their separate ways and conscious that they were now bound together, for better or worse. In the back of the company Range Rover the following day, Aischa took his hand and squeezed in comfort as the chauffeur piloted them through Knightsbridge ablaze with the Christmas lights, over Hammersmith flyover and onto the motorway to Heathrow. They were going home to Lisbon for a few days before returning to spend a night with Oscar and Anna in their draughty old house outside Hereford.

And then.

FERGUS CARRADINE — New Year's Day 2000

Fergus spent a sleepless New Year's Eve because one of the two lifts from hold to flight deck on the 'Dawn' went unserviceable and the engineer who could fix it was being carried on the 'Angel'. Typically of Carradine, he didn't waste time wondering at the cause of this cock up, but concentrated on sorting it out. And they did, but only just before daybreak after the technician had been trying to give advice over a mobile phone whilst in an inflatable ploughing through heavy swell from ship to ship. Then the omens got worse. The first aircraft away was a Chinook, perhaps a little overloaded for the flight conditions. It crabbed off the deck and clipped a container in passing. The container was pushed over the side of 'Dawn' and the chopper had to ditch a mile away. All the guys on board were saved, but only at the cost of time and effort. The machine and its load went down of course, so all this meant that they were behind schedule with some loss of assets.

After this poor start, he was mighty relieved that everything went exactly to plan. They were lucky in some things, but Fergus held to the belief that you make your own luck and he had ensured this through nit-picking planning and rigorous, repeated training until all his people were as near perfect in their roles as could be achieved.

There were others outside his immediate control. Patrick Nugumu and the advance team had been in place for weeks and were careful to draw no attention to themselves. They were thorough also, refining their observations to identify the hard targets which the Strike Force needed to hit first. The docks, so the three ships could come in to unload. The large barracks just out of town. The Presidential Palace, for obvious reasons but also because it was so near the base for the praetorian guard, the regime's best troops, who were quartered just half a kilometre distant. Then there was City Hall, both radio stations, the main bus depot and the single TV transmitter. There was also the airport, but that was to come in for attention a little later.

Fergus had been preoccupied with how to get himself from ship to shore. He wanted to direct matters from the quayside, but was reluctant to leave his command and it was essential that 'Dawn', with the Strike Force, and 'Hope' remained out of sight over the horizon until 'Orphans Angel' had received her welcome to enter harbour. He cudgelled his brain for alternatives and his best hopes were rewarded. As the first light of a new century was brushing the waves, Alec Singleton, Master of the 'Angel' sent a message announcing their arrival to the authorities. He received a polite response saying he was expected, but please to wait an hour until the pilot boat from the harbour could come out to greet him. This gave Fergus ample time to gather a small team and transfer to the 'Angel', so it was from her deck that he saw his first view of the city which was to become Century before that day was out.

It was also from the 'Angel' that he called in the first wave of Apaches, followed as fast as they could get airborne by the Chinooks carrying his fighting troops. The helicopters were screaming in as Verity Blades, the ace Kiwi girl, executed her brilliant, brave idea that called for all her demolition skills. She blew the overpass bridge which took an access road from the main highway up to the Palace. The effect was to box in both the President and his crack guards. It wouldn't hold them for long, not with byways around, but for long enough to cause confusion and to disrupt command. It was a subject for much debate during planning, but Verity proved her expertise, taking out a three metre strip to leave a clean gap too wide to jump but easy to close again with temporary roadway.

By 1000 hours, Fergus was in position on the quay. His command post was formed by two small containers, pre prepared with communications and lifted in by the first Chinook. He was accompanied by his personal staff including Rory Trollope as his ADC and they were ringed by troops flown in to provide protection. By the same time, the 'Angel' had berthed and Strike Force personnel had taken over the Harbour office to give guidance to the 'Dawn' and the 'Hope', both vessels being now in view from land and approaching fast. On board the 'Angel', a carefully phrased announcement in the cinema, on radio and in print was being circulated amongst the Orphans personnel to inform and to advise that no one was yet permitted to leave the ship. There was dramatic noise all around, but little opposition. The truth was that most of the invaders and more of the residents had no idea of what was taking place. It was exactly this confusion on which Fergus was counting to encourage take over without bloody confrontation, but he knew it couldn't last. The first news of fighting reached him when Patrick screeched to a halt and hopped out of a scruffy old van which he had commandeered. Patrick had been watching the main barracks, just out of town, while his son was observing activity around the Palace from a safe distance.

Their news was not surprising, but not good either. Despite Verity's bomb, at least a hundred troops from the Palace Guard had made their exit via the bush tracks which ran north off the hill to link up with the City ring Road. They must have organised themselves, because he had seen them link with a much larger group in a convoy of trucks driving from the direction of the barracks. Patrick took over to describe what he had seen.

Oswanje Camp, the barracks, was hard hit by the Apaches in their first attack, using rockets to create maximum mayhem and drama. They were followed immediately by Chinooks, dropping the Strike Force as the machines hovered and returning to the Dawn for more. Patrick reported that the scene was chaotic and Fergus was not surprised. Oswanje was the camp for enlisted men, largely untrained and ill-disciplined who would be panicked by the crash and thunder of the Apaches, and easily contained by the far smaller number of his own, professional force. The greater worry was posed by a smaller number of men who moved off smartly, forming themselves into sections and climbing into their transport.

Patrick had his adopted son Jonah with him. They had arrived before first light at a minor, back gate into the camp, driving in a truck loaded with baulks of timber. They had retreated higher and further back into the bush from where Patrick could watch the action through his field glasses. As matters progressed, he manoeuvred their vehicle closer, planning to drop the timber over this camp exit. He had not expected to confront any of the President's elite soldiers but now it was plain that those organising themselves were just that. He watched them through the glasses. Perhaps they made up a relief detachment which slept at Oswanje for want of space at the Palace. Whatever, they moved surely and calmly, and there were not a few: he counted a hundred plus.

Time was pressing. Patrick abandoned his plan for barricading the gate. He retreated to hide in the bush, but since that was low and skimpy, he reckoned Jonah would be better concealed by the baulks of wood. He shouted at him to get in the truck and poor Jonah, young man mountain but pretty simple with it, did precisely what he was told.

The first vehicle carrying the President's Guard came barrelling up the rough track from the camp and burst through the light mesh gate without stopping. Outside, however, it found Jonah standing with his thumb out. The driver took him for one of their own as in all the chaos there were few of them in uniform and he slowed up just enough for Jonah to jump for the tailboard and be hauled inside before the vehicle took off followed by five others with soldiers packed in and hanging on however. Jonah had done as he was told: 'Get in the truck!'

At that point, there was nothing which Fergus could do about Jonah. His hands were full with matters of moment and he couldn't allow himself to be distracted. One look told him that Patrick understood, despite his personal anguish. Fergus asked for any further detail on the escapees and Patrick remembered a sixth truck at the tail of the column, closed in and down on its axles: weapons and ammunition. Fergus worried. It now looked that there were close to two hundred of their best fighting men on the loose and he couldn't afford too many of his own to go in search. He needed them to keep the hundreds of riff raff soldiers pinned down. He asked about Patrick's other two sons: one was at the television station, the other well out of the city at Bolongula, where the power station was located. Both were waiting to guide in Strike Force teams.

'Stay with me, Patrick', Fergus instructed before turning to Rory, 'time you were on your way. Hook up with Simon and get going.'

They were just entering the next and critical phase. Hugh's Bertie the Boeing was carrying David Heaven and party as well as a section of twenty-four from the Strike Force. There was cargo on board as well and young Arnie Schwartz at the controls. They left London Stansted as late as permitted by CAA rules, but that was still going to put them in too early, so Arnie filed a flight plan for N'Djamena, Chad and they laid over there for a few hours. They were timed to arrive overhead the airport at noon and to land after that.

Simon Goring was their most experienced commando. Backed up by Rory Trollope and three more, he travelled out to the airport in one of the Force Land Rovers which had rolled off the 'Dawn', by now in harbour. They worked fast, leaving their vehicle, cutting the perimeter fence and moving quietly in on their target. The management at the airport had no idea that the control tower was in enemy hands as the Boeing was cleared to land and rolled down the runway onto the apron.

Then things changed. From the Captain's seat, Arnie Schwartz saw activity all around the terminal building and three trucks drove onto the apron, jerking to a halt and spilling out armed troops who started to surround his aeroplane. He reported to Goring in the Tower and alerted the leader of the Strike section on board. The word had got out and someone out there was competent to respond. Arnie left the cockpit to tell his passengers to stay put. He couldn't see the action but guessed that his soldiers were jumping from the cargo access door at the rear, engaging as they hit the ground with support coming from Simon Goring's team way up in the tower.

Arnie urged David Heaven and party onto the floor of the aisles and they huddled together as the plane took sporadic hits from the fire fight which was blazing all around, continuing for what seemed like eternity. David lay there with his arm around Aischa, wondering if it was all going to end here. They had Hugh's great feet in their faces. Then suddenly, there was silence, followed by the appearance of Goring who had swung himself through the cargo hatch and came padding through to them. He had lost two, with three lightly wounded. They had killed many more and the remainder had run. The entire airport was now under Strike Force control.

David Heaven's party arrived at the Presidential Palace — immediately renamed Founder's Hill — at dead on 1400 hours as scheduled.

By then it was clear that the city was taken. There was little more resistance. The 'Orphans Angel' was berthed, the 'Dawn' and the 'Hope' both tied up. The utilities were secure, communications were under control and the helicopter base was established. The good news was that the provisions and the helping hands were rolling out and starting to win a welcome. There was much evidence that the former President and his coterie had left in a rush: doors left open, furniture awry, cupboards half full of abandoned possessions, an empty safe and papers everywhere — including those which had survived the half-hearted fire which someone had tried to light in front of the garage block. David had no idea why they had panicked, how they had travelled or to where. It really didn't matter.

As planned, they deployed the Strike Force contingent which had arrived with them to clear and check the large mansion and its outbuildings, then to provide personal protection as they settled to work, cathartic after the shock of the gun battle at the airport. Felix Maas took over the dining room and started to assemble information on progress, Hugh Dundas went down to the harbour to confer with the Captain of the 'Angel', Aischa went with Pente to visit the city hospital, King stayed with David who found himself a position within the grand entrance hall from which to work. Alexa toured the main building with Ursula, noting what was where, deciding that it was well named as Founder's Hill, and finding some members of the staff who had been left behind and were amenable to instruction from a new management: she was reminded of Aischa's prediction.

David's first imperative was to make contact with Martin Kirchoff in London. He was relieved to get through to him immediately.

'You've been reported on the news, David,' Martin told him, 'The BBC, but radio only so far: nothing on the TV. I guess it's as you expected. Now we're in the new century, all anyone wants to hear about is if the world's computers are still working, so a coup in West Africa isn't attracting much attention.'

David smiled at King who was listening in at his side. It was what they had hoped to hear. David broke the connection and turned to congratulate Fergus who had just arrived with Patrick to join them. Fergus looked grim, grabbing a seat while he briefed them on the situation at Oswanje Camp. As he finished a terse account, David looked towards King and spoke to them all.

'Add in those who got away from the Palace fighting and that could mean nearly three hundred armed men, drawn from the best they ever had here. We don't know where they've gone and we don't know what they'll do next. Am I right?'

'Plus they have their boss in charge. This is their Guard of Honour, right?' it was a statement from King.

Patrick chipped in, 'They'll go home, Suh, to the place they call Panje. They'll be there now.'

'Where the hell is Panje?' David asked, bellowing for Felix to join them. He arrived at the run and didn't need his notes to supply the answer.

'Panje is the name for both a place and a tribe or sect, 'he told them, 'It's a large group of rocks about 170 kilometres north east of here in the foothills which climb towards the central plateau. Panje was the meeting point over hundreds of years for the hard fighting men from the mountains who used to come together for some bonding and witchcraft before raids into the fertile country stretching down the coastline. Panje came to mean not just the place, but also the people, a name to identify the most feared and violent of the warrior class. From the mid 1960's, succeeding Presidents here — only three as you know — encouraged a myth to grow up around Panje, fermenting the superstition that true Panje are a breed apart, with invincible strength and a sort of inner eye for divining the truth. They are an elite, ideal to provide the classic Praetorian Guard, a bit like the Tonton Macoutes in Haiti. This type of voodoo cult is extremely effective in a poorly educated and down trodden society. All it needs is to be rigidly disciplined and given enough leash to ensure that the general population rolls its eyes in collective terror of attracting the wrong sort of attention.'

'This is great,' said David bitterly, 'and we've let them escape. It would've been the best and brightest who grabbed their chance.' He smacked a fist on his knee in frustration.

'And they've taken my Jonah with them,' Patrick added.

David whirled round on him, saying, 'How had you heard of the place?'

'Anyone living here a while hears of it, Suh, can't avoid the name. But the place too, well that was one of my sons. He went up there to have a look one day back a couple of months. Didn't get too close: got frightened off, but he knows where it is.'

David sat back with his arms folded and looked at them all for maybe thirty seconds. Then he stood and asked Felix to take Patrick with him and mark up a couple of maps with the best location guide to Pange which they could manage. Left alone with King and Fergus, he didn't mince words.

'Fergus. I want you to go after them. Take who and what you need. Don't give me the detail.

Return with Jonah if you can, but bring me the evidence that you've got all the others. And be quick.'

King raised his eyebrows but said not a word. He'd always figured David could be ruthless and single minded when he saw his opportunity. He'd first seen it so long ago with the protection thugs in Westbourne Grove. Here it was again, but big time. A punitive expedition, nominally to rescue one mute boy, but really to rub out any remaining opposition to 'winning the welcome'. David had made an instant decision, taken it himself without debate. It was certainly ruthless and probably right. It was not a move which King could have made himself.

Fergus Carradine set out at 2100 that New Year's Day. He took their five SAS converted Land Rovers and his pick of the best men they could carry, including Simon Goring and Rory Trollope. He took Patrick's son for his knowledge of the route. They made reasonable time, all on dirt road and using just convoy lights. They were in position before dawn, with just enough time for each man to have a few rations and check his weaponry. They left the vehicles and force marched the last two kilometres. They found Pange easily. The camp was impossible to miss and there were only three guards out who were expecting nothing and looked surprised as they died.

The site among the rocks and surrounding acacia trees looked shambolic under the fading moon and was it lit by several camp fires. The country had started to undulate for some distance back so Fergus and his party could lie up behind a ridge and look down on the scene. He didn't need night vision equipment. In the light of the fires and the waning moon, binoculars were enough.

At a quick count, there were over three hundred down there, but including camp followers, women and girls amongst them. Most were sitting on the ground with their backs to Fergus as they gazed towards the main grouping of boulders which made for a stage, particularly one long, flat rock which looked like a giant coffin lid. On top of it a figure was cavorting, dressed in just a breech clout. He was prancing about, gesticulating with an evil skinning knife which was streaked with blood and attracting glints from the moon. Behind the coffin rock was a dark pile of something. Fergus shifted focus and could make out an untidy heap of bodies, maybe five or six and all men from the size of them. It made a gruesome sight. Fergus realised that the dancing figure with his weird incantations was the Pange Man. That made him not the boss here, not even a senior lieutenant, but every bit as powerful in this setting because he was the ju-ju figure, the bogeyman and the executioner.

It wasn't hard to interpret the scene. They'd spent the night weeding out interlopers, men who had escaped fighting in the city, but who were not recognised Pange. They had moved from frying pan to fire and it was impossible to know if Jonah had already perished amongst them. Being mute, large and of the wrong tribe, he wouldn't have lasted long.

As they looked on from their ridge, Fergus saw a tall man with a large head rise from his position at the front of the crowd and recognised him as the former President of the Republic. He wielded a long staff, a sign of his office, and bawled an instruction. The crowd subsided and voices fell, but for seconds only. Fergus caught a movement from off stage right and saw a huge figure, shambling in a docile fashion as he was being led in to confront the Pange Man. Here was Jonah, and he was going like a lamb to the slaughter.

Fergus dropped his glasses and looking left, gave a thumbs up to his sharp shooter, Kenny Crowe, an Aussie from the Northern Territory and an artist with the sniper's rifle. Kenny had already prepared his position and started to lay his cheek along the scope in an awkward looking angle which apparently worked best for him. But he was to be delayed. Big Jonah had worked out a plan for himself.

As he reached the edge of the coffin lid, Jonah seemed to stumble and he looked a cowed and abject figure. His escort jabbed him in the back with the butt of an AK47. Jonah leaned forward and placed his massive hands, loosely tied together in front of him, onto the rock as if in preparation for heaving himself up and onto it. Then he struck.

A muffled grunt of appreciation came from Patrick's other son beside him as he watched young Jonah sweep his hands wide and break his bonds as if they'd been rice paper. He whirled around in a tight circle. He swept up the guard, plucking the AK from his hands and hurling it high and far into the acacia trees behind the coffin. Then Jonah leapt onto the rock to confront the drooling dervish, setting about him with an unusual weapon. In his mighty arms, he carried the guard who was screaming and struggling. Jonah dumped the man head first onto the rock with a sickening thud to his skull which could be heard in the sudden silence of a stunned audience. He picked up the man by his ankles and used the inert body to club the Pange Man. Blow one might have killed him and the skinning knife went flying from his grasp. The Pange Man slumped onto his execution rock and Jonah rained another couple of mighty blows upon him, skull to skull with a force which made for vengeful retribution and a bloody mess.

The onlookers were past shock and on their feet, grabbing their weapons. One was quicker than the others and had a machine pistol in his hand. Fergus watched through his glasses as Kenny Crowe took him with a clear head shot. Two or three others followed before the shouting body worked out the direction of fire and turned, bellowing their message of fury and attack.

Fergus and his team had cover, quickly improving light and good weapons, but they were hugely outnumbered. They were happy to hear the faint whump whump which announced the arrival of the support which Fergus had put in place before leaving the city. Two Apache gunships popped up from ground skimming behind the ridge. They came in to hover just above the commando group and opened up their hellish firepower. The Pange fell like flies and any that managed to break out were picked off by Kenny and the rest of the team. Very soon, it was all over and Fergus walked down with his men to sweep the area and far into the trees beyond to ensure that all had perished, every last one. It was there and then that they found Jonah, still mute but alive.

Fergus himself attended to the corpse of the Pange Man, cutting off the head. It was a gruesome business, made worse by Jonah's attentions. With his ravaged features, almost toothless mouth and the long, matted hair bloodied from his splintered skull, it made for a nightmare sight. The Pange Man, who had lurked and menaced and killed, was now very damn dead himself. That was the message which David Heaven wanted to put out and he did so with photographs of this ghoulish horror which were posted up around the city. It was a graphic illustration that the threat of the past was gone and a new era had arrived.

MARTIN KIRCHOFF — March 2000

From the BBC's Today Programme on Radio Four. An interview with Mr Martin Kirchoff, (MK) Chief Executive, The Mansion House, London. Interview conducted at 0809 hours, Wed 29 March 2000 by John Humphrys. (JH)

JH: I am speaking now to Mr Martin Kirchoff who is the chief executive of The Mansion House, the substantial British conglomerate. Mr Kirchoff is in our radio car outside the company's corporate headquarters in Piccadilly, London. Good morning, Mr Kirchoff.

MK: Good morning.

JH: Thank you for joining us today. I want to ask you about your colleague Mr David Heaven who is the self-styled leader of the illegal regime in West Africa currently referred to as Millennium.
PAUSE

JH: Can you hear me Mr Kirchoff?

MK: Perfectly, thank you. I was waiting for the question.

JH: Very good. Let me start by asking you what connection, if any, Mr Heaven still has with your organisation?

MK: Mr Heaven is a shareholder, but he has no further interest or position. Together with myself and my late father, Mr Heaven was instrumental in developing our business over a period of some thirty years and it is in large measure due to his efforts that The Mansion House now deals with 493 suppliers and we sell to over 70 countries worldwide. Our major operating divisions include mining, manufacturing, agric.....

JH: Yes, Yes, Mr Kirchoff. Forgive me interrupting but a commercial for The Mansion House is not the requirement here. What I would prefer to ask is why your organisation is retaining any sort of contact with a man who is now widely regarded as a latter-day pirate?

MK: Well, that is of course your characterisation but it certainly isn't mine. As I understand matters and from what I read in the international press, the citizens of that country are already pretty content with all that Millennium has come to offer them. Order to replace corruption, hugely improved public services, advances in health care and the supermarket shelves bec...

JH: Yes indeed. But that's just one point of view isn't it? There are a host of other informed commentators who report with equal conviction that this is a colonial land grab. Am I not right?

MK: You are right in what you quote, but surely neither of us knows all the truth of it. We all wait with growing interest to be given facts, and I am not personally privy to details which have been denied to the rest of the world.

JH: You are surely not expecting us to be satisfied with that Mr Kirchoff. After all, this is a man whom you have known and worked with for over thirty years. You must have some continuing contact with David Heaven?

MK: To the extent that I may do, Mr Humphrys, it's private and that is how I shall keep it.

JH: So you do admit that you retain contact with Mr Heaven?

MK: Well ... yes I do, but it's infrequent.

JH: Perhaps. Now Mr Kirchoff, let me ask you about another member of the so called Millennium mob. Do you have connections to Mr Hugh Dundas, the financier?

MK: I know him, certainly. But Mr Dundas is in no way involved with The Mansion House.

JH: Quite so. But your company's past public statements have confirmed, have they not, that The Mansion House has donated funds to Mr Dundas' charity 'Orphans of Africa' which is currently under investigation by both the United Nations Fraud Investigation team in Geneva as well as equivalent authorities within the European Development Fund?

MK: Yes. I confirm that our company did donate and yes, I do understand that enquiries into the Dundas Charity are on-going.

JH: And this makes you uneasy?

MK: No. I wouldn't say that. I have confidence in the skills and the probity of Mr Dundas. I welcome the exercise of investigation as the best means of proving the good intent and the effective operation of all that Mr Dundas has put in place.

JH: And can you confirm also that it was Mr Dundas who funded the invasion of this West African State?

MK: I believe that is provocative. I have no knowledge — and neither should I have — as to the funding for the development of Millennium. If such an arrangement exists, you would need to ask either or both of Mr Heaven and Mr Dundas for clarification on the matter.

JH: I wish we could do just that, Mr Kirchoff, but as you know, neither is available for comment. But let me ask you a final question. If you were a peaceful citizen of background and established means, how would you react to an undemocratic assumption of power by an incoming force? An illegal invasion by any other name?

PAUSE

JH: Mr Kirchoff? I must press you for a response if you have one. Time is against us.

MK: Very well. I would say that it would depend upon the circumstances.

JH: Yes of course. But do I take your answer as meaning that you would prefer to avoid a direct answer?

MK: By no means. I mean just as I have said, and I might illustrate my point. My father was just such a citizen in Germany before the outbreak of the Second World War. He was also a Jew. I believe that he would have welcomed an invasion some time before it happened to release him from his concentration camp.

JH: Just so. Mr Kirchoff, thank you for speaking to us.

And now, what is to happen to the visitor centre at Stonehenge? We have a special report ...

KINGSTON OFFENBACH — May 2000

King was worried. Mostly, he was worried about where he was. He had agreed to come on down to Millennium with David and had been very pleased to witness a successful arrival followed by some pretty dramatic progress. Five months on, you could feel throughout Century City that the welcome had been won. But joy at their results was not unconfined. Just as King had feared, there were pressures building elsewhere in the world for action against the makers of Millennium. What they had done was simply not proper by 21st century rules of international diplomacy. It was different, which was bad enough and apparently successful which was worse. Something must be done — and soon.

King could pick up all those vibes by reading the news or tuning in to international stations and they were getting them all in Century now. He could flick between CNN and Sky but he preferred BBC World, and for reading, the Wall Street Journal and the Economist. What he could not do was to pick up the phone and talk to his buddies of working days. He was now regarded as a maverick who had gone seriously bush in his retirement, opting out to join the renegades. Folks didn't want to know him right now, especially not stuck in Century City and unable to travel. He had his US passport, of course, and it was an entirely legal laissez-passer. But in practice, if he tried to enter the USA, they would pick him up and process him straight through to Langley without his elegant feet touching the ground. The CIA did not care for a retiree giving them cause for embarrassment. If he flew into Europe someplace, the reports would go back and he would become a watched man, compromising his ability to help in the one area in which he had promised to deliver.

King spent a long night in deep contemplation, looking out

over the peaceful Millennium Ocean, which greeted the view from his balcony. The task in hand was not that hard for him and he should have finished by midnight, but he kept getting distracted by memory. It was all about just one day a long time back, but it had been significant and it had combined jungle action with bullshit diplomacy — just the mixture he was wrestling with now. So he took his time and sipped at his rye and water as the memories marched through the night hours.

As a new day dawned, King assembled the pages of notes which he had been compiling in his spare, neat hand. He took them to the shredder which stood in the corner of the kitchen. All that remained of his labours was the single sheet entitled 'Analysis and Action Plan'. The concise summary read:

AA) Millennium is established, but not accepted.

BB) There is evidence, drawn from published facts and informed speculation, that the prominent governments of the European Union are preparing a political intervention with military support. The British, the French, the Germans and the Portuguese are all in favour. The Dutch and the Spanish are against.

CC) The thesis advanced is that Millennium has resulted from an illegal act of aggression. The world, led by the former colonial powers, should take steps to dissolve the unelected government in Century and simultaneously appoint the former President's son, who is in exile in Estonia.

DD) The Organisation of African Unity (OAU) endorses the principle, but will commit neither funds nor forces, professing greater priorities. South Africa likewise. Russia has 'no comment to make'. The USA believes that 'this is a matter for Africa, those living there and those who formed her as she is today'. Shorthand saying that Bill Clinton has no wish to get involved during the last months of his Presidency.

EE) The British are leading the charge. Prime Minister Tony Blair and Foreign Secretary Robin Cook are making a rare common cause, Blair being flushed with success in Sierra Leone and Cook seeing an opportunity to practice his ethical dimension. Civil Servants are, however, very sceptical and the

Whitehall mandarins seek to cool the passions of their political masters.

FF) This background serves to justify the advice I gave you at our dinner in October 1998. We need to influence a delay. A quick punch on the nose to encourage more reflection before action.

King read this over and drove himself to Founder's Hill for breakfast with David Heaven. Their accompanying conversation was brief. David was in full agreement.

'We need more time, King, more breathing space. Can you give us that — even a few months more?'

King then described his plan which David heard with a grunt of admiration. Short, sharp and simple. But also sweet and sour. They would get in two separate and very different blows. Neither would be very wounding except perhaps to pride, but taken together they might well do enough to bring that bit of respite.

'Go for it,' David said, 'and don't worry about the money. It's really not much and God knows, we've got enough. You've done well with this King, I wonder where you get the ideas.'

King departed in deep and rich reflection. Africa had left its scars on him. The pain of this dark cruel continent made him wonder how there could be found a better way, which influenced his support for David's Zero from the moment he heard of it. He'd won his victory in Liberia through a mixture of thump and thought. By clobbering the guard, he'd diverted Andrade's attention and conned him into accepting half price and the loss of his own life, a fate richly deserved. It was the combination punch which worked, sweet and sour as David said. It was time to try that again.

David was also pondering as he went to his office. It really did frustrate him. Things were going better than he had dared hope. The infrastructure of the city had improved dramatically and they had pushed out into the provinces with all possible speed, so that the reports which he received daily from Felix Maas were telling the tale of people now choosing to leave Century to resettle in their home towns and villages. The newly constituted National police force was making flying progress under the Inspector General who had come to them from Ethiopia, the healthcare benefits to all were spectacularly apparent and they had built and/or renovated no less than forty-three schools — all in less than five months. Best of all, a mere five per cent of the artisans and experts who had arrived on the 'Angel' had chosen to leave. Why did the bloody Europeans have to be so blind and mealy mouthed?

King lost no time in getting on with it. He returned straight to his apartment and called Bill Evans at The Mansion House. It was a simple conversation because he'd been through the detail with Bill before leaving London. They talked for an evening in a quiet pub and King had been impressed by the range of Bill Evans' contacts. As his final word to conclude this phone call, King said to Bill 'housemartin', this being the prearranged code that he should now go to Martin Kirchoff to access the £50,000 in cash which he would need to deliver the goods.

Bill Evans went to work. At 0233 in the morning of Wednesday 10th May, a large Scania truck with a 40 foot box trailer made its quiet way around London's Embankment past the Tate Gallery, heading for the Houses of Parliament. It bore Dutch registration plates and was identified by graphics and logo as an intercontinental transporter. One of the leviathan travellers which operate at all times of the clock, it carried a full load, but with a single occupant of the cab. He was English, a character and a bit of a rogue with a record of making mischief. He answered to the sobriquet of Shorty Driver, but he was born with neither name. He was 'Shorty' because he stood only just over 5'2" and 'Driver' because he was outstandingly good at that function.

Shorty was well known to Bill Evans who had felt his collar more than once during his policing years. Bill had no difficulty in recruiting Shorty for this mission. The whole idea appealed to the little man's sense of fun and then there was the reward — £10,000 paid in cash and up front. Shorty had wondered about the end objective but he knew better then to ask and much better than to take the money and run. Nobody risked that with Bill Evans. Shorty had good contacts in the international trucking community and quickly found his mark in a Turk who drove for a haulage company in Rotterdam which carried machined goods between the UK and the Balkans. For some serious money, the Turk had agreed to be sandbagged in a layby outside Ramsgate on the Monday evening and he was still lodged in a dingy B&B making reports to his employers and the Kent Police. Meanwhile, Shorty had taken over the vehicle and made his untroubled way to a warehouse in the London suburb of Mitcham where the trailer was repacked and he had time to ensure that the Scania was set up to his liking. Shorty seemed childlike in his stature beside the towering cab of the vehicle, but once inside it and behind the wheel, his legs helpfully stretched by his Cuban heeled boots, Shorty was in his element and a virtuoso with the controls of any truck, whether they be set to the left or to the right.

He didn't need to check his watch to know that he was bang on time as he slipped idly around Parliament Square and turned left into Whitehall, heading towards Trafalgar Square. There was no one around at that hour to confirm that his vehicle was authorised to be in the heart of London, and he drew scarcely a glance from the duty police officers watching over the closed gates from Whitehall into Downing Street, from within which the lights of the Prime Minister's Office at Number 10 burned constantly. Shorty let the huge Scania potter past on low revs and with minimum engine noise. The whole rig felt balanced and poised, precisely to his exacting standards. He slid closer to the kerb and stopped. He released his seat belt, lit a cigarette and let it dangle from the corner of his mouth.

A few minutes later, at 0246, the policemen at the Downing Street Gate heard the throaty bellow of a heavy engine powering up. By then, Shorty had engaged reverse and was on the move. His hands on the steering wheel and his right foot on the accelerator were moving in a coordinated blur, his head remained fixed forward but his eyes flicked constantly from mirror to mirror. He built up his speed as he moved his vehicle much further out into the middle of this prime London thoroughfare, dominated by the Cenotaph. Shorty was changing his lock, changing his direction, maintaining his engine revs and further increasing his speed.

The astonished guardians at the gates could do more than shout a warning to each other as the massive trailer back swung in at them and Shorty gave himself a snort of satisfaction at the precision of his manoeuvre. With tyres screaming their protest, the tail of his trailer, so far behind his seat in the cab, was only a degree or so off square as it met the low pedestrian railing across the entrance to Downing Street and it punched straight through. Immediately behind the railing, shut firm and bolted, stood the infinitely stronger construction of heavy, wrought iron gates. Shorty Driver was as prepared for them as he could be. A last glance in his mirrors told him that he was on target. He whipped his steering back from full lock to dead centre. He lifted himself slightly from his seat back as the shock of collision travelled up the length of his trailer and through the fifth wheel coupling into his cab. The noise of the impact was shocking in the still of the summer night. His entire rig was brought to an instant halt but he kept his foot to the floor for a final couple more seconds and swung the steering wheel from one extreme lock to the other. There was renewed crunching as the trailer skewed a further inch or so through the gates to stick finally and firm.

Shorty was instantly on the move. Like a whippet, he was out of his cab, door left open, engine running, lights on. He slithered down the handholds, hitting the tarmac of Whitehall and scuttering across to the shadows of the far pavement, his little boots ringing as he ran. And ran. Shorty was clean away up Whitehall before anyone could see him, much less lay hands on him. He skipped across Trafalgar Square, running up past St Martin in the Fields and on eventually to a safe burrow somewhere in Soho.

He left pandemonium behind him. To supplement the police on duty, night workers from buildings in Whitehall and Downing Street started to gather on either side of the cork, stuck in its bottle. The few residents of the locality, amongst them the most influential in the land, were startled from their sleep by the noise and the shouting which followed. Successively senior national security figures were alerted and summoned by urgent call. There was one concern on the minds of all.

Bomb.

By 0330 an avalanche of emergency vehicles had descended on Whitehall — fire engines, ambulances, innumerable police cars and vans, one or two with dogs and handlers. Leading them all was a bomb disposal team which left their colleagues to clear the area, evacuate the buildings and close the roads while they went methodically to work on Shorty's Scania and trailer.

It took them until midday to find what was not there. The commander of the team had started with the truck, suspicious that engine shut down would trigger whatever lay in the box container behind. But they could find nothing, and after an hour of painstaking investigation, the vehicle lay silent. By then, they had daylight to help them as they moved to the trailer, the team still convinced that they were to be challenged by an explosive device of some sort. Why else would someone perpetrate this outrage?

In nearby Police Headquarters at Scotland Yard, significant figures had gathered, The Commissioner, Head of Counter Terrorism, senior heads from both MI5 and MI6, scientists from Aldershot, communications experts from GCHQ Cheltenham: all powerless to act without further information.

Then came the news that the disposal team had the trailer loading doors open and were confronted by a solid wall of breeze blocks, neatly arranged from side to side and from top to bottom. It was 9 am before they had removed them all without incident, to find a second wall of the same behind. And then another. And another.

As the morning wore on and the waiting became more irksome, the mystery was intensified by the absolute absence of demand or threat or communication of any sort. And the pile of discarded breeze blocks on Downing Street grew ever larger.

At 12 noon precisely, the disposal team commander had worked his way to the very front of the trailer and there at last, he found something different. He checked it over with infinite care before he decided. This might be a message of some sort, but it was not going to explode. He removed his protective headgear and studied the plain square clock, set into a wooden frame which was secured dead centre in the final wall of blocks. The hands now stood at 1232 and ticked over to 1233 beneath his gaze. The face of the clock was plain and unmarked by numerals or symbols. Its colour was the azure blue of a cloudless sky, overlaid with the thin white outline of a rising crescent moon.

Since the early hours, there had been a media frenzy which went on mounting during the day. Parliament Square and all Whitehall was cordoned off behind police barricades, Westminster Bridge was accessible only from the Embankment. There were endless radio interviews with the informed and the less so, television crews demonstrated their ingenuity in finding even a remote vantage point from which they could present the scene. Such pictures were immediately beamed around the world, and King Offenbach enjoyed seeing them in his Century apartment. He sent a one word text to Bill Evans, but Bill was too busy to read it, being at the time engaged in passing another hefty sized briefcase stuffed with cash to his second contractor.

The first Millennium message and flag was delivered by buffalo. The second was as subtle as silk. Since it was a Wednesday, Prime Minister's Questions were to take place in the House of Commons, and the PM was not prepared to cry off this commitment. He and his family had been spirited out of Downing Street into St James's Park and he had gone from there to his office in the House. He had no comment for the Press on what was happening in Whitehall. That would follow when the Security Services had completed their work and their assessment. For himself, he wanted somebody, somewhere to have the gumption to explain what the hell as going on. All he knew so far was that an audacious and irritating effort had been made to wave the National flag of this tin pot regime right under his nose. The buggers down there deserved to get poleaxed if only for that effrontery, but London definitely needed to keep this quiet. It would not make them look too clever to the moaners in Europe who were dragging their feet over setting up the task force to go in there. Quite how they were going to make a public explanation of the truck was something else. That would take vivid imagination and some lively work with the Press, but they were well equipped to do that.

When it was time for PMQ's, the Prime Minister went into the Chamber with his briefing book under his arm. His staff had put together some suggestions as well as background on those questions which he knew to expect that day. The first was from a Birmingham MP, Richard Burden, who wanted to pose something random but designed to shine a glowing spotlight on the efforts of the newly formed MG Rover car company. The Prime Minister heard him out and then rose to approach the Despatch Box to provide his reply and he opened the folder to have the relevant briefing note in front of him.

The PM was too accomplished a performer to be thrown off course, nevertheless those present who knew him best did note an untypical delay before he turned a page in his folder and commenced a fluent comment. He carried this off well, whilst simultaneously asking himself how a sheet displaying in full colour the flag of Millennium had been placed at the front of his briefing book.

Much later, right at the end of a very long day, there was a well attended conference at No 10 under the chairmanship of the Prime Minister. By then, the truck had been towed away, the mangled gates had been removed for repair or replacement and a tripled strength police detachment installed in their place. The Home Secretary had appeared on television to explain that a displaced and disgruntled Armenian had been responsible for this morning's incident. The authorities had a name, but had not yet managed an arrest.

The PM demanded the views of his phalanx of advisors. What were the day's strange events intended to signify, and how should they respond? Of the twenty or so of the great and the good sitting round the table, it was Jonathon Powell, the Prime Minister's aide and Chief of Staff who produced a succinct reply which he knew to be the clear majority view of those attending. He had taken trouble to ask them.

'Prime Minister. We should take these incidents as a single message. The people managing Millennium have delivered their calling cards which are intended to inform us that they are neither fools nor incompetents and that they have capabilities greater than we have assumed. There is no commentary here on the political element and neither do I wish to address that now. We have an abundantly clear British Government position that a former sovereign state has been illegally annexed and that in consequence, the correct international policy should be a restoration of the status quo. The only issue which I put before you now is the question of timing. As has been already agreed, we need an initiative, and critically one which calls for a military force of intervention, to be multilateral and thus to enjoy the unequivocal support of our partners in Europe. I believe that requirement may now be seen to be all the greater because these people in Millennium are better resourced and equipped than we had supposed them to be. My advice is therefore that we should make haste more slowly. Let's back off a little and give ourselves a break during this summer season. We can afford to move Millennium back up our agenda after the recess as we move into autumn.'

'And what happens meanwhile? We allow them to take advantage of the respite?'

Powell raised his hands from the table in an expressive gesture.

'That may be so, Prime Minister, but whatever. I still say that we have greater fish to fry.'

The PM looked around the table.

'And this is the view of you all?'

There was no vote, of course, but a general murmur of assent. The PM looked suddenly weary of the subject.

'OK,' he said with a sigh, 'put Millennium on the back burner for now. But there is one thing we can do right now, Jonathon. Cancel the passport of that bastard Heaven. He's persona non grata here now.

PENTE BROKE SMITH — December 2000

Pente was standing in the warm mid morning sunshine at Acacia Grove, his own choice of a new name for Panje. The prolific trees all around supplied a little shade as they rustled in the light breeze of an exceptionally beautiful day. Behind him rose tall and straight the recently finished National Monument and before him was gathered a large crowd, standing silent and patient all over the killing field which had followed their arrival a little less than a year ago. Pente was leading a simple service which he had created to mark the Day of Gratitude, a name he had chosen to devote to the memory of all those, without discrimination, who had died to bring Millennium into being.

He finished a closing prayer which he had composed for the occasion and then the Combined Services band, supported by two choirs from Century City, struck up the newly created National Anthem. Out on his own at the front of this great assembly, Pente felt his heart lift and as the stirring music rang out, he felt a tear escape from one eye and run down into the cover of his copious beard. 'Sloppy old fool', he told himself, 'but this is a great day'.

The congregation started to break up, a few slipping away but the majority in their various groups wandering to find a spot to set up a picnic. Pente meandered through the crowd, stopping for a word here and a handshake there. As he made progress, he had an eye for the surroundings and was well pleased with how Acacia Grove was developing. It still looked raw of course, but so much work had been done. A handsome wrought iron railing fence enclosed the entire site and within it, their arboreal specialists, one of whom had come to Millennium from Kew Gardens in London, had been busy with felling, lopping, pruning and planting. Meanwhile, a master stonemason of

Russian descent had crafted the elegantly simple monument from locally quarried material. Acacia Grove was a fitting symbol of progress which looked good now, and would weather and settle to become superb.

Pente gave himself a moment to wonder how other things and people would settle. At the top of his list were David and Aischa. David had stepped down from his position as President of Millennium at the end of November, handing over to Hugh Dundas who was to take them through to June 2001, during which, it had been announced, there would be an election, with international observers invited, to seek consensus on a Constitution for the country. David had taken the toothless title of 'Father of the Nation' which was fair enough but a bit overblown for Pente's taste. He'd been given a life tenancy to the former Presidential Palace, now renamed Founder's Hill. He and Aischa were settled there with her now busier than he was.

Pente knew that David would never have agreed to this demotion without the influence of Aischa. He'd discussed it with King who agreed that she had been the power to reallocate the throne. She had told him that he had to give up. Millennium's future depended on being accepted into the international community and he, David Heaven personally, was standing in the way of that accomplishment. Pente and King had been present when Aischa had delivered the firm, gently expressed lecture to her husband.

'Millennium would not have happened without you, David. It has been your dream, your drive, your determination. Don't spoil that now by refusing to allow your baby to grow in its own way. I know this is happening sooner than any of us wanted, but you know Darling, that's because of your success and not in spite of it. The major powers around the world, especially the States and in Europe, are about ready to recognise us as a new, legitimate country but they won't do that with you in charge. You're the bogeyman and you've just got to go. But if you concentrate hard and let your logic rule your heart, you'll see it as I do: it's a compliment.'

Aischa had a second and a knockout argument but she didn't produce it until she and David were alone together. It was to do with Aischa herself and with her health. She had breast cancer. Her first fears had been raised in Lisbon around the time of Alves' death and she had consulted a London specialist before they left the UK. For now, Millennium and Century City were short of oncologists. That was not a surprise: it was the whole point and the whole plan. They needed plumbers before piano tuners. But Aischa had assumed that she would be able to travel at will to seek advice and treatment and it had been a shock to discover that she could not do so. As Mrs David Heaven, she was not welcome and she could not appeal for sympathetic consideration without telling David the whole story. So she did just that, sitting him down after dinner one evening in Founder's Hill.

The following day, David had summoned Hugh, Pente and King to put them all in the picture. Pente remembered it as a very painful occasion. He had never seen a David Heaven quite like this. The man looked bereft already — shocked, shattered and frightened. But the crisis did produce results and they seemed to be positive, at least so far.

David had announced his retirement from public life, his impending handover to Hugh and the plan for a national referendum on the Constitution. Matters went further than that. At Hugh's instigation, they brought forward plans to delegate more widely the management of the fledgling nation, appointing men and women who had come in with the First Fleet, but including some who had been nationals under the previous regime. There was a form of democracy here which the European Union had been relieved to acknowledge as it would enable Millennium to be removed from the 'worry list'. The United Kingdom remained obdurate and continued to refuse both David and Aischa permission to enter the country, but Hugh managed to persuade her specialist from London to visit them in Century and thereafter she flew to Lisbon for treatment.

As he meandered through Acacia Grove, Pente reflected that things were not perfect, but they could be a great deal worse.

He paused to savour his well loved scent of Africa, then drove it from his nostrils as he lit one of his noxious cigars. He turned his thoughts to the Musketeers Club, his own initiative which sought to establish social centres in town and country where the growing number of new arrivals from a huge variety of countries could mingle with those who were locally born. He was interrupted by a familiar shout and saw King Offenbach waving him over to the location in which their group was encamping. Pente modified his direction and increased his pace towards them.

They had been hoping that Martin and Ruth Kirchoff would fly down and stay over Christmas. David had been disappointed but had to accept Martin's judgement that he remained the subject of interest and speculation in both Downing Street and the City. It was just too soon for him to be observed travelling to Millennium, although he was confident they would make it next year.

Bill and Tina Fullerton were there. They had moved from Hong Kong to Shanghai, but Hugh was hoping to persuade his old friend to move to Millennium and start working for him in Century. Hugh wanted to start a stock exchange during the next eighteen months and he needed Bill around.

'It'll be mostly to carry his bags,' Bill remarked to Pente over drinks on the evening of their arrival, 'I'm really too simple to be of use for much more'.

They had laughed together but it was well known how Hugh valued the relaxed friendship of his buddy from schooldays.

'And you know the other reason, doncha darlin', Tina said to Alexa when the girls were alone together.

'I do, Tina. We've talked it over, Hugh and I. He wants to bring Janey down here to live. Perhaps not really wants, but needs to, and that's alright with me. So long as he comes home to me at night.'

Tina Fullerton shook her head in exasperation and reached for her cigarettes.

'She's sure as hell lucky to have him, that broad, and she's just as lucky to have you. She had a shit of a time with that accident — a life ruined and all that. But I do still wish that she'd try a little harder. She's got all that can be done for her in Hong Kong and he'll make that happen here too won't he. Waal, if you can stand it, Alexa honey, I guess I can too.'

The picnic lunch was under the trees, with some of them on folding chairs, some perched on the benches scattered about and others lying on rugs spread on the ground. It brought back to David their first gathering at the time of the Queen's Silver Jubilee when they had met under the eaves of 100 Piccadilly, an address then new to Kirchoff and Son. Sol had been there of course, and Martin and Ruth but he had been without Aischa which now seemed unimaginable to him. And there had been no Hugh either. He happened to catch Alexa's eye just then and they exchanged a secret smile, perhaps both remembering for a fleeting moment how they had consoled each other on that occasion. Much worse for them both was the absence of Connie and Tepee. David sighed to himself. He would never stop missing the man, but at least the girls remained in close touch and they had the promise from Tepee that she would fly down in the New Year.

There was just one topic of serious conversation during that happy picnic lunch.

Hugh remarked, 'Now we know George Bush has been declared the winner in Florida and will be going to the White House in January, we can start to work on our contacts with the incoming administration. Right, King?'

King was propped on one elbow as he reclined languidly on the close cropped grass. He put down his sandwich and replied.

'Mebbe, Hugh and I sure as hell hope so. Trouble is, no one seems to know much about where George W wants to head — probably doesn't know himself yet. We can be sure that little ole Millennium will be well down his list come January, and that's good. But I hear also that he can be one tough hombre, so we'd better not count on a warm welcome.'

Tina Fullerton chipped in to say,

'My folks back home in Dakota reckon Bush is just mad to make America great again but he's also said that he doesn't think our boys in khaki should be used for nation building. I dunno if that's supposed to cover nation grabbin'.

'Well, I'm certainly worried that Bush doesn't like me,' said

Hugh, 'he was one of the first investors in Dundas Securities and he brought in some others. Of course, he wanted out last January 2nd as soon as he made the connection and I can't blame him. He had an election to fight and I gave him back his money and no arguing. But he still felt scammed and he doesn't like that. Makes him feel he's been bested. So there's no love lost.'

David Heaven stepped in then. He didn't care for general chatter at a public occasion and anyway, he wanted to preserve the happy spirit of the day.

'Let's leave it there. We just have to wait and see. But the European diplomacy is all good news. By this time next year, we could be in the Commonwealth.'

There were smiles all round, and Felix Maas took the cue for to change the conversation.

'Now Tina,' he asked, 'how long are you and Bill staying?'

'Depends on Alexa, Felix. She's got me a date!'

'More like a place,' said Alexa joining in the laughter. Since their arrival in January, Alexa had involved herself in the Orphans of Africa programme and liked to show off what they had achieved so far. The track record in healthcare and jobs training was impressive and her latest project was situated in the small town of Singahala. She had promised to give Tina a personal tour and the day's journey each way from Century would give them some good gossip time.

'When do we go back, honey?' Tina asked Bill who looked to Hugh for the answer.

'Whenever you want. Bertie the Boeing remains on standby for you, a few others and a whole load of cargo.'

Tina wagged her finger at him as she said,

'Hugh, sweetheart, you've gotta get rid of that fuckin' plane, terrific as it is. It makes no sense to own something that size. Besides, my Bill says the best advice you ever gave him was that if it flies, floats or fucks, then rent it.'

It was Pente who led the guffaws at this outrageous humour and Alexa extended it by remarking with a mischievous twinkle, 'I suppose that applies to me too?'

AISCHA HEAVEN — May 2003

It was the first weekend of the month, just a few days before David's birthday. He wouldn't be doing any dancing that year. Having become increasingly troubled by arthritis in his hip, Aischa had persuaded him to have a replacement. David was taken into All Hope hospital and the operation was performed without complication, resulting in an excellent prognosis. Now, hardly a week later, he was feeling unreasonably pleased with himself. He was so delighted that the procedure was complete, having confided to Aischa in advance that his greatest dread was to go under an anaesthetic, something which he had never previously experienced. She hadn't laughed at him, but gave him a wry smile which shamed him as he was immediately reminded of the many operations she had been through in order to keep her body going.

Aischa was not a well lady and had to live a life of constant pain, ordered and controlled by endless medications. Despite these privations, she managed to remain a marvellously attractive and feminine figure. She was always poised, immaculately presented, beautifully dressed and still retaining her come hither sexiness when her mood was right and the hurting reduced. She remained as active as she could and her programme of visits and involvement in her many causes was as committed as ever.

Both of them delighted in the fast developing world of Millennium. During the last three years, things had gone from strength to strength. There was all the evidence that the country was becoming a nation in its own right. They were well past the point of being accepted on the international stage and were now respected for welding together a dynamic and homogeneous society, celebrating almost daily advances in every aspect of life, from medicine to music and from science to sport.

It is a function of the human condition that characteristics harden with the passing years. David Heaven remained sharp in his intellect but his perceptiveness in matters of the heart did not improve. He was more dependent on Aischa's guidance and company than he liked to admit and this led him into a failure to acknowledge her deteriorating condition. He did not want to accept it. Worse, he knew it was beyond his capability to arrest which amounted to an impotence which he hated to recognise.

Aischa was badly affected by the news of her father's death. Jonas Savimbi perished in a bloody little fire fight in February 2002. He was then a less than significant figure and a by note to history. He had never ceased to struggle, but that state of permanent warfare had become for him an end in itself. As Aischa had predicted, he battled for most of his life and never came within sight of his goal which had become progressively more illusory with the passage of time. This judgement was confirmed by Rafa, who came over from his home in California to visit them later in the year of their father's death. He stayed for two weeks and was of comfort and good company to them both, but when he left, David saw the extinguishing of some light from behind Aischa's eyes. A vital chapter of her life was closed.

Hardly a year later, David was still able to persuade himself that his Aischa was a constant in his life. For a man so accustomed to his own success by dint of ability, effort and single bloody mindedness, he couldn't accept that the most important achievement for him might be beyond his influence. His own responsibility made the matter far worse. It was true that he hadn't known of the diagnosis of a malignancy back in 1999. She had not told him, but he had been aware of a change in her — a tiredness, a hurting and being a little remote from time to time. Typically for him, he had put this down to other things. She would get over it and he would help her: but a bit later when he had more time. Right then, he was completely absorbed in Zero to the exclusion of any other subject. The same was true for Conrad Aveling as he now reminded himself bitterly. He had ignored Connie when he might have been able to help. Pray God he could do better by Aischa.

That Saturday morning, they left the house to walk in the gardens of Founder's Hill. David was in a powered wheelchair which he had been ordered to use for two weeks after his operation. He piloted the damn thing while Aischa walked haltingly beside him, breathing heavily and using a light cane stick. They went slowly, heading up the gradual incline towards the outcrop of rock which gave them their favourite view out over the Atlantic Ocean.

Aischa remarked to him, 'We're a right old couple of crocks, you and me!'

He had given a gruff laugh and replied 'We'll get by.'

They were both silent for a while as they continued their painful progress. Then Aischa started to speak to him and he knew that he couldn't interrupt her.

She was giving him one of her lectures. She spoke of all their time together, their unlikely meeting and still less expected reunion. She talked of the family members and of precious friends. Of happenings which had been so significant to them both. She discussed her father and her brother. She dwelt on the girl who was a daughter to them both and who had mothered their grandchildren.

They reached the vantage point which gave them full sight of the restless ocean — constantly moving, always the same. They were silent for a while. Aischa stood tall and unbowed beside him. She hooked her cane over the back of his chair. She put her hand on his neck and moved it to squeeze his shoulder. David felt the tears come into his eyes, and he was powerless to hold them back.

Aischa spoke to him.

'Most of us leave not a stone to mark our passage here. You have done much and you will leave a monument. I'm happy to have been with you and to have brought you help and comfort.

But we must finish our journeys alone and hope for another time and place to be together. For now, just remember how much I have loved you.'

Aischa paused then, and David was quite incapable of speech or gesture. She was in control and in charge. She moved in front of him. In a lithe movement which belied her years and condition, she dropped onto one knee and took his right hand between both of hers as she looked into his face which was already ravaged by his grief.

She spoke for the last time. 'Harisha, my darling David.'

Then she stood gracefully and moved on and away from him around the Point. In a moment, she was lost to his view and he knew that he would never see her again. A little further on, she slipped over the cliff and was gone. No trace of her body was found. The ocean does not give back those who were greatly loved.

They came in their hundreds to her memorial service. They came in thousands, thronging the Cathedral Square, and within the fine old building, people crammed themselves into every nook and crevice. It was a Service of Thanksgiving, a theme reflected in the music which Aischa loved and in a congregation which did its best to ensure that she would hear it. There were thundering crescendos, the great organ teaming with the massed choirs and the platoons of trumpets. In contrast, a hushed silence respected the delicate interpretation of a Chopin nocturne which had been a particular favourite. There were readings, a poem recital and an anthem.

David had asked Pente Broke Smith to lead the service and to give an address. It was a challenge to which Pente rose magnificently. Standing on the wide altar steps, Pente resembled most people's imagination of the prophet Abraham, his huge figure isolated and dominant, the cascade of beard spilling down his chest, his voice deep and powerful over the PA system.

He captured a perfect image of Aischa. He spoke of her courage in life and her dignity in departure. He placed her accurately in the position which she had made her own. She was, he said, the First Lady of Millennium. It was in every sense that she merited this title, but it was most deserved in recognition of her boundless generosity to the people of our country and her efforts did not falter in spirit even when her physical strength was diminishing.

'We are all familiar', boomed Pente, 'with her work on behalf of our charities, our schools and the university, our literary festival and the hospital concerts. But I say that her most precious gift was to those countless individuals whom we don't know. But Aischa did. Aischa was ours. She was here for all of us and there are so many whom she met along life's way who will bless the memory of her loving kindness. She was our First Lady of Grace.'

They were all there. Alexa and Hugh. Tepee Aveling. King Offenbach. Martin and Ruth flew down from London. Fergus Carradine and his wife, Ursula Hampton of course, Rory and Verity Trollope. From further afield came Mark Bushell, also Sebastien and Izzy Mantel from Singapore. Rafa arrived from California with his family, and from Lisbon, Mario and Isabella Mori, from their favourite restaurant in Lisbon, at David's special request.

David had met Anna Aveling on the tarmac two days earlier when her plane from London touched down in Century City. They had not seen each other for some years but he carried in his head a picture of Anna, always calm and welcoming but with the slight air of harassment which goes with the territory of managing a boisterous household.

It thrilled and shocked and saddened him to see her emerge from the plane, which had halted by special arrangement on the apron, well short of the terminal so that this VIP for the day family could be welcomed by David with a small entourage. The sight which greeted him might have been of Aischa just a few years ago. Anna struck a poised and glamorous figure as she stood at the top of the aircraft steps, very smart in a tailored tropical suit which heightened the contours of her excellent

371

figure, her long chestnut hair about her shoulders, stirring in the light breeze. She waited just long enough for effect, not so long as to give exhibition, and then she turned to usher her two sons in front of her while Oscar, as always smart but subdued in English country style, brought up the rear. As he watched her graceful descent from the aircraft, David gasped at the similarity to her mother and the effect of it caught in his throat.

After Aischa's Service, it took almost two hours for the congregation to file past David with a nod of respect or a handshake as he stood at the top of the Cathedral steps. Beside him stood Anna, and beside her was her elder son Oliver, now fifteen and showing all the signs of a developing young man. He stood motionless, holding himself erect, standing a little taller than his mother, very conscious of the solemnity of the occasion.

When the final visitors had filed past and said their farewells, David turned to smile at both Anna and Olty, his careworn expression hinting at the gratitude which he felt for their presence with him. He found it impossible to speak in those few seconds, and Anna was discreetly brushing a tear from her eye. It was a moment for distraction and he used it to reach into his pocket and withdraw a buff, hard backed envelope. From this, he pulled two copies of a black and white photograph. The setting was a dockyard of some sort. A small forest of masts showed in the right hand middle distance. In front, there was a iron railing which guarded the edge of a wharf and behind was a type of deep sea trawler, tied up to await departure.

In the foreground, two young girls were leaning on the railing facing the trawler. They had turned their faces in head and shoulder profile to look back at the camera. They were beautiful, their faces full of laughter, life and fun. They looked so happy and relaxed in this pose as to suggest that they spent almost every waking minute with each other. They were obviously twins, very closely alike, with just some tiny differences of expression which would be unobserved except by standing this close and staring.

Neither Anna nor her son needed to be told that this was a photograph of Aischa and Ouye, with Ouye on the right of her sister.

David told them, 'I took this myself, very many years ago. I was about to leave on the trawler you see there. It's not a brilliant photograph but it's the only one I've ever seen of the two girls together. They did love each other so, and I thought that you would like to have a copy.'

They smiled together and Anna rose to kiss David on his cheek.

'Thank you,' she said. There was no more to add, but then she used the privacy of the moment, standing there with only Olty as witness.

'May I ask you David, before she left you, did she say — anything?'

David's eyes clouded with instant tears as the moment returned to him with piercing clarity.

'Yes, Anna, she did. Just one word. She said Harisha.'

He turned away, more abruptly than he intended. Anna restrained him with a light touch on his arm, but didn't wait for him to turn back towards her as she told him in a soft tone which was inaudible to her son,

'That's good to hear, David, and you should be comforted. It means that she went in her own time and as she planned.'

Later that evening, David hosted an extended family supper at Founder's Hill. They had set out long tables on the wide terrace and the meal was served as a buffet with everyone able and encouraged to move around and exchange neighbours from time to time. Only later did the poignancy of the arrangement strike him. It was so like the evening in the restaurant when he had first met Aischa and Ouye, along with Rafa and Benoit and so many others.

Before then, he had started his dinner by inviting Olty and Edward to sit by him on either side. They had a good and lively conversation which ranged predictably over school and games and hobbies. There was a thoughtfulness about Olty which impressed him, especially when the boy asked, 'Mr Heaven. Can you tell me please. What exactly does "Harisha" mean?'

David was startled but determined to give him a straight answer, and so he replied,

'The best I can do, Olty, is to repeat to you what your grandmother told me. She explained it this way. Harisha means literally "I see you". It is a salutation and an expression of farewell with honour and affection. It is used only by a woman speaking to a man and may sometimes be used as greeting to recognise an outstanding achievement, but that would be very rare.'

Olty nodded, rather wide eyed, and thanked him. Quite soon afterwards, David moved around the table and the boys went off to play snooker.

ALEXA DUNDAS — August 2004

Alexa had never felt such happiness in her private life, nor as fulfilled in her work. She refused to feel guilty at her satisfaction that Janey Dundas had died about six months previously, a case of simple heart failure which took her on a summer day in the specially adapted villa which had been built for her down the coast. By then she had seemed more like a decrepit old aunt to Hugh than his wife. Pente comforted them all with his pronouncement that the Almighty had acted as much for Janey herself as for anyone else.

Very shortly afterwards, Alexa and Hugh married and there was a celebration in Century which lasted a week and included rousing toasts to both Aischa and to Connie Aveling.

Hugh himself was busy as ever with a good deal of travel. These days, he flew commercial, having taken Tina Fullerton's advice and sold Bertie the Boeing to the national airline which was using it for cargo work within the country and on international routes. This week in August, Hugh was again overseas, back in the States. One of the American oil companies had title to a block off shore in Millennium waters. They were producing and believed there were good prospects for discovering more, maybe even much more, but they were being greedy in their demands.

Whatever. Hugh remained bright and tough. He would work it out and Alexa would continue here for him in every sense when he came home to relax with her and to talk it all through. Meanwhile, she had her own timetable. The Orphans of Africa programme had expanded enormously and they were now getting close to rolling out into two neighbouring countries. This was not only good for the people they could help, but it was good for their politics also. She had involved Tina in this work and loved the stimulus of her company as well as her risqué humour.

There had been a great bonus earlier in the year when Tepee came to stay for nearly a month. Alexa had shown her around Century and a fair bit of the country while they looked at some of the projects, but mostly they'd just talked and talked. A lot of it was about Connie. There were tears and recriminations, but overall, Alexa was impressed by how Tepee was getting on with her life. She had enough money and was making some more from the sale of her painting which had developed to find several admirers. One of these was a widower who lived in Cornwall and they had started a modest affair.

'It's not going to go much further,' Tepee confided, 'Gavin is a lovely man but he's too far away and — well he's not Connie. But he is a comfort from time to time and it's nice to be wanted.'

Alexa was sorry to see her go, but there was consolation when she received a surprise visit to Century from Mark Bushell, who had flown all the way from Sydney via South Africa. It was years since they'd last seen each other and Alexa was thrilled to find him quite unchanged. Still the great, gruff, shambling bear of a man with the woolly mane of hair and the slightly dishevelled beard, still the huge horn rimmed spectacles, still the razor brain which he sometimes hid behind an 'Ocker Oz' humour and still the irrepressible sense of fun. She had thought he would be exhausted from travel on the evening of his arrival, but found that he was still flying. Mark and Hugh had never previously met, and Alexa was thrilled to see how well they got on from the first, all the better as Hugh had to depart the following morning. They asked the Fullertons to dinner and were reduced to tears of laughter by the American/Australian banter.

There was another purpose to Mark's visit. Alexa was responsible for a special programme within the agenda of Orphans of Africa. It had been created to give a sanctuary of assistance to those who suffered mental trauma for whatever reason. It appalled Alexa to see how many people throughout

Millennium fell into this broad category and they were the ones prepared to volunteer a problem. Alexa shuddered to think of the numbers which would be produced from under the repressive regimes throughout Africa. Mark had been encouraging by an email from Sydney, providing many helpful directions, but he said that he must see for himself, and he did so, giving her a bare week's warning of his arrival.

During his time there, they remained in Century and Alexa set up a number of appointments with patients whom Mark could meet at her office in the downtown Orphans building. They were sitting there together on his last day, awaiting the final visit. There was a light tap on the door and in came a man of more than medium height and slight build. He was dressed in very smart, but casual clothing. He was more chocolate than black in colour. He was well into the autumn of his life and the curls on his head were more grey than black. He made for an elegant figure and he bent his head over Alexa's hand before shaking Mark's, then carefully adjusting his trousers to preserve their razor crease before he took the proffered seat.

Mark noticed that he supported his left hand in his right, and the visitor followed his gaze. Unprompted, he said,

'Too many years as a musician. Playing the double bass.' His smile was charming.

Alexa said nothing. A strange feeling of anticipation mixed with disquiet was invading her. Their visitor started to introduce himself.

'I thank you both for seeing me,' he began. His English was excellent but clearly not his mother tongue. 'I apologise that I'm here under false pretences. I'm not in need of counsel and I don't seek help, except perhaps from a priest. I'm here to make a confession. My name is Paulus and I believe that it was your brother, Madame, whom I condemned to death over forty years ago.'

Alexa felt the onrush of shakes, was in that split second transported back to those long gone years of inner terror as she struggled with her demons. By the grace of God, she had as her companion the one person who could help her through,

Mark who should be on the other side of the world, but whose hand she now felt take her own with the unspoken message. Whatever this is, we will face it together. And now he spoke for them both.

'OK, Paulus, would you tell us more please.'

'Oui. I will. In 1963, I was in Niamey, Niger with my band. We played at a modest dive named La Chatte. To supplement our fees, I looked out for young men who could be seduced into a danger from which others would pay to release them,' he shrugged, 'a form of blackmail, pure and simple. I was then thirty years old. Today, I am seventy. A little slower, and very much wiser.

'That evening, we played the club and a young French boy appeared who could play the guitar a bit. Nothing special, but not bad. He carried his hormones on his forehead as we all did at that age. I introduced my honey trap girl who hooked him and brought him back for more. We grabbed him for ransom, all was arranged and then my little whore and her strong arm man decided to go independent. They killed the boy, but I kept the money. I do not know where they laid his body.

'You will want to know why I'm here now. I was born in this city but moved away, working as a musician. I have led an itinerant life, but last year I returned home by coming to Century City for the first time. I met a man from Nigeria of about my age. His name is Patrick. He's good company and he likes jazz which is what I play best. We have come to know and to like each other, and at our age, that is a process which happens gradually over time. It's only recently that he's had the confidence to tell me about his background. He described his childhood and spoke of his career in the Nigeria Army, of which he is rightly proud. He dwelt on his experiences in the Biafra War. He talked about his time as a soldier of fortune, a mercenary, and how he was befriended by the father of Mr Rory Trollope, who lives here today, of course, and is I suppose known to us all?'

Paulus let this question hang in the air. Mark shook his head and said,

'Not me, but I'm just a visitor. Been here less than a week.'

Under the table, Mark squeezed Alexa's hand and she managed to nod her head in an affirmative message. Paulus nodded in return as he resumed.

'Patrick Nugumu mentioned other names to me, drawn from that period of his life, and particularly those he had met in DRC. Zaire as it used to be or even further back, the Belgian Congo. One of these names was a Frenchman, Luc Courty, who was certainly known to me: a formidable man whom I respected and feared. Courty was a tough French soldier who retired young and went out on his own as an investigator. He worked from Paris but combed through all the hotspots of French and Belgian colonial Africa. In 1964, Courty tracked me down when I was living in Kinshasa. He was hunting down the story of a young French guy who had gone missing in Niamey. Courty had found his way to la Chatte, heard the rumours of other such abductions from there, and they were well founded by the way. That got him my name, and eventually he found me. It was not a pleasant experience. Courty gave me a very hard time indeed. But I was pretty tough myself. I knew he had no proof. I just had to sit out the pressure until he gave up. And eventually, he did. End of that story, which I have never told before, not even to Patrick.'

Paulus stopped to give Alexa a self deprecating smile of great charm. Alexa felt frozen in time. Mark hung on to her hand. Paulus continued.

'Now for another coincidence. Two nights ago, I was playing at our club down in the Spanish Quarter. During a break, I wander across to say bonsoir to a Moroccan couple who like to listen to our music. They are called Maurice and Petronile. She is a psychiatric nurse and I believe that she works with you Madame?'

Alexa could only nod again.

'We exchanged pleasantries and Petronile said they were out to relax as she was having a tough, but interesting week. I enquired further, and she explained it was on account of your visit and work, Monsieur Bushell. You are clearly much respected in your field. She added that you had been introduced as Madame's brother-in-law and Petronile asked if you were Australian born.

'No, Petronile reports you as saying, my mother was English and my father was French, an army officer and a farmer. We lived in the country near Limoges in a house now owned by my brother. I was born Alexandra Labarre.

'This casual conversation hit me hard,' said Paulus, 'especially after my talks with Patrick which brought back old times and had resurrected in my mind the name of Labarre. When that Luc Courty found me in Kinshasa, he hurt me very much indeed. As he kicked and punched and threw me around my dingy attic, he would intersperse his blows with the same warning: tell me, Paulus, tell me so that I can tell le Colonel Labarre. Tell me what you did with his son and tell me where is the money which you took from Labarre.

I could not concentrate on my music for the rest of that evening and when I got home, I went straight to my computer. A wonderful thing, the Internet, is it not. I found quite easily the reference to the small family Chateau, the history, the names of Colonel Joffrey and his wife Elizabeth, now both deceased, their three offspring — Alexandra, Bernard the current owner of the property and finally, mention of an older brother Michel who died many years ago.'

There was a very long silence. The men held each other's gaze. Alexa shivered as she looked down at her feet. Finally, Paulus gave a long sigh, and commenced his conclusion.

'I could not keep silent. I have been guilty of many things during a long life which has included too much crime and foolishness. But I have never maimed, nor tortured, nor killed. I did not kill your brother, Madame, but I did arrange his kidnap and I did set a price upon his life. It is not much now to say sorry, although I do offer that apology. Anyway, I am here to accept whatever you may wish to exact from me in retribution. I am yours Madame.'

And Paulus sat back a little in his upright chair.

There was no further delay. Mark Bushell felt the hand between his lose its tremors as it was withdrawn from his grasp. He could feel Alexa's strength return, could sense her resolve and determination. A kaleidoscope of memories marched through his head as he recalled all the struggles that he and she had been through together in Sydney as he had fought to pull her back from a mental brink, a catastrophic precipice towards which this man before them had propelled her first steps. He might not have known, but he was guilty nonetheless.

Alexa acted. She rose from her chair and moved to the centre of the room. She turned and looked down at Paulus.

'Stand up and come here,' she instructed calmly.

He looked uncertain, but he did as she asked. Then she stepped closer to him, opened her arms and enfolded Paulus in her embrace. The seconds ticked by, turning into a minute and longer. Mark kept his silence and his seat. Finally, Alexa stepped back: she looked calm — serene even. Mark could see the catharsis seep through her. She had reached the end of a painful road and was finally able to lay the ghost which had troubled so much of her life.

Paulus just stood there, a slight and diffident smile on his face. He said nothing but he raised his weaker hand in a gesture of salute to them as he turned to leave. As he reached the door, Alexa stopped him with a gentle question.

'I must hear you play one evening, Paulus. How do I find you?'

'You will have no difficulty with that Madame, and you will be most welcome. My club here in Century is well known and the name is over the door. I call it"Michel's".'

DAVID HEAVEN — May 2013

Ten long years since Aischa's death, David thought to himself as he sat in his study after breakfast. For an old and cynical independent such as him, it was remarkable how much he still missed her. He was not, however, sloppy about it. He didn't sit weeping into his whisky every evening. He was not especially lonely and was often out and about, happy to be entertained or joining in some activity. He certainly did not wallow in self sympathy. He just bloody well missed her — missed the sound of her footfall, the choice of her words, the delicacy of her accent remaining from childhood. He missed her shrewd judgement, missed her encouragement and even, he had to admit, her firm correction to his wandering path. He missed being able to check if he had chosen the right clothes to wear, missed being reminded of who was related to whom and how. Just missed her. And even today, ten years on, he might come home from a dinner, get inside the door and call out to her before being hit by the consciousness that she was beyond the compass of his voice.

May was not a good month for sloughing off the memories, but he could distract himself with a little review of what else had happened during these past years, and he could not help but hug to himself the recognition of achievements.

Millennium was now a country far removed from the place they had come storming into at the turn of the century. Not everything was perfect of course. There was and would forever remain more to be done and to plan for, but there were times when it was so good to sit back and reflect on the story so far.

It was the politics which fascinated him the most. David relinquished the President's office to Hugh Dundas who held the position for just a matter of months. During that time, Hugh concentrated on their finances. He was tireless in effort, impeccable in judgement, inspired in innovation. When he gave up day to day control at the Treasury, he left behind an apparently perfect machine of management which promised to run for a thousand years without much adjustment.

Concurrently, they worked as a team on creating a new Constitution and looking back on it, David had to admit that his own contribution was of better quality because he didn't have an executive role to distract him. Hugh was replaced as President by an impressive lawyer, born in Vietnam and thereafter a Canadian citizen before he emigrated to Millennium in the second wave of arrivals. He took over under the new Constitution to head a Presidential executive with seven members who voted their choice of President. Beneath the executive was a form of parliament with two hundred members who were voted in by their electorate. The parliament elected the members of the Executive who were full time, salaried officers of the state. The parliamentarians were obliged to demonstrate a profession or business which would engage and reward them for the majority of their time. They were not permitted to be full time politicians. The Constitution called for national elections every four years. A President could serve only one term but a member of the executive was permitted two consecutive terms and thus each succeeding President was identified four years before he or she took up the top job.

They created a new style of fixed civil service which drew on aspects of the colonial services which had operated so long ago. The detail of all of this was complex to devise and install, but it worked well enough in practice and it did much to earn legitimacy for Millennium in the eyes of the international community.

By this time, of course, David was long departed from any sort of official office but that did not prevent him from maintaining his close interest, his contacts and occasionally his influence. He was surprised to find how well the arrangement suited him although he should have known better. Aischa had always told him that he had done his bit: much better to quit at the top and leave others to build on his foundations.

And how well it had gone. Earlier this year, Millennium had succeeded in joining the Commonwealth and now there was even talk of a State visit from the Monarch. Everywhere, there was an acknowledgement that Millennium was bringing a new style of nationality to Africa. It would have been impossible for the world to ignore, much less deny, the success which the formula as created by David Heaven and his colleagues had brought to the country. The opportunities for personal success and fulfilment in a land blest with space and natural resources were self evident and proved on a daily basis by the track record of those who had been encouraged to come from the four corners of the world to practice their skills and diligence. This in turn meant that standards and facilities were constantly improving against the backdrop of a rapidly developing economy.

Once rolling, this bandwagon had hardly slowed in its progress and had never checked, hardly even during the world financial crisis of 2009. There had of course been problems, scandals, dishonesty and mismanagement, but successive governments had used a heavy hand to deal with transgressions. Overall, the enthusiasm and commitment had been such that Millennium could point to outstanding results in just about any area — in manufacturing and trading business, in agriculture, in mining and in oil, in forestry and ecology, in tourism, in the arts. In support of these developments were outstanding examples of citizen care — health, education, transport, policing and a legal system free to all.

I'm a fortunate man, thought David Heaven to himself as he gazed out of his study window across the immaculate gardens of Founder's Hill. It may be that we make our own luck in this world, but by God I've been lucky with my friends and my opportunities: all the people, all the things I've seen and the places I've been. It's best of all to be able to look out over a plan, a dream, a vision and see that it has become a reality.

What of regrets? The absence of Aischa to share the twilight years which we planned to have together. That's the haunting sadness, made far worse by my responsibility for her illness and premature death. The same applies to Connie Aveling, my greatest friend. I wasn't there for him when he needed me and I was too busy with my own life to notice it. But then there's Anna and her children, all my descendants although they don't know it and it's too late now for lifetime confessions: still it will all come out one day. The memoir is done. I know it's merely adequate and certainly not inspired but I've done my best and I'll give it to young Olty one day when I think he's ready: I've got high hopes for that boy.

With that thought, David rose from his chair and walked over to the long wall in his study which displayed his rogues' gallery, a hundred and more photographs hanging on the wall of his study in an arrangement which was impressive if not artistic. There were few occupations these days which gave him so much pleasure as to muse over this record of the places in which he had set foot, and the people who had populated his varied life. And he never failed to look longest at the original of that snapshot of the twin sisters in Mocamedes in 1970. It was the least expert record of all on his wall, but it carried the most meaning for him.

He pulled himself from his reverie and went to fetch the light set of steps which were stored inside a cupboard. He put them in place, returned to collect a couple of empty frames which he used for sizing up which of his latest acquisitions should hang where. With a soft grunt of appreciation, he approached the steps. This was his favourite past time, and it seemed reasonable to enjoy it to the full on this rather special day, his seventieth birthday.

David Heaven was standing near the top of his vantage point on the steps when he had the presentiment that he was to be as lucky in death as he had been lucky in life. The sudden pain in his chest was briefly excruciating. He dropped a frame to the carpet and clutched at a photograph which skewed in its mount. He lost consciousness and he had lost life before his body hit the floor.

OLIVER AVELING — 2021

It's Christmas Eve and working up to the hottest time of our year. I'm in my apartment in Century and staring at my screen. I should finish the writing today and I'm going to feel quite lonely with this project complete.

It's now nearly two years since Guy Labarre came to visit me in New York. We had our business meeting and then we went off to lunch with Guy carrying that small suitcase which has since come to dominate my life.

We started with a news roundup on our families. Guy sympathised with the trouble I have in keeping up with everyone. I've been living in Millennium since I graduated from university in Century nearly seven years ago. I've never regretted the decision to make the country my home, but a downside is that I get to see my parents and siblings only once or twice a year. My brother Edward went into shipping and is now doing a couple of years based in Korea, Christina my elder sister is through Uni in the UK and training to be a vet and Charlotte is having a ball at Durham reading English. My Dad, Oscar, continues a hard working pillar of Hereford and my mother is non-stop busy and into everything. It's not easy to get any of them to come here, so when I go to Europe I don't usually get further than Hereford, plus Hampshire to see my grandmother Tepee.

Over coffee, Guy got down to business

'I have to give you this suitcase Olty,' Guy spoke excellent English with a lovely Clouzot accent, 'and there's a letter of authority which goes with it. I understand that it contains a form of memoire left to you personally by David Heaven. He left it in his will to my Aunt Alexa for safekeeping and she thinks it's high time for you to receive your legacy. She asked me to deliver it by hand, so here am I; and here it is.'

Guy pushed across the case under our table and I grasped the worn old leather handle for the first time. I must have looked pretty perplexed. He smiled at me and said,

'It seems that David finished his work on the manuscript a year or so after Aischa died. Then he packed everything up in that old case and left it to Alexa. With your grandfather Conrad gone so long ago, I guess she was his greatest friend from Oxford days which is where life really began for him it seems.'

'Perhaps,' I replied uncertainly, 'but I'd have thought he would have chosen Pente Broke Smith for something like this.'

'I don't know, Olty, but my guess is that maybe Alexa and David had a thing going in days long past.'

He gave a Gallic shrug as he continued, 'Who can say? My aunt would never say and I wouldn't ask, but she was insistent that I should make the handover at the earliest opportunity. To be honest, I think she had forgotten all about it, but she's over seventy-five now and wants to conclude her responsibility for it. What's more, as she said to me, you yourself are full grown and established. Whatever it is that David wanted to leave to you is overdue for delivery.'

I thanked him warmly for his candour and for taking this trouble. Then we talked of other things until we left the restaurant to go our separate ways. I haven't seen Guy since then, but I'll send him a copy of this account. There will be things which he'll want to read about.

I took the case home to Millennium with me. I started to browse through it here in my apartment in Century and as I've said, I was fascinated from the start. But I didn't have time to do much more right then because we were manically busy at work and the reason for that was Joe Kaba.

He's a wonderful man, my boss: Armenian born but no one could pronounce his name so he made up another. He's been in Millennium for seventeen years, arriving with his wife and three children, their hand luggage and a bit of cash: nothing else. They were evicted from Minsk where Joe had been well established until he fell foul of the authorities and he was lucky to get slung out on his ear.

He's an absolute powerhouse, is Joe: a brilliant linguist and a superb manager. He comes from humble origins but he mixes easily at any level. He's strong on detail with an inspirational style about him. Thinking of the characters I've been discovering over the last year, I guess he's a bit of a mixture of Sol Kirchoff and Felix Maas, but he's got also my grandfather's sense of strategy. Joe's weak point is figures. He can make money OK and has proved it. But he has no grasp of high level finance and that's why he absolutely idolises Hugh Dundas and still picks his brains whenever he gets the chance.

From New York and my meeting with Guy in December 2019, I went first to the UK and spent Christmas freezing with my parents in Hereford. I didn't mention the legacy to my mother. I'd hardly opened the case by then and felt that I needed to know more before I started in on it. I got back to Century, celebrated my birthday with a bit of mischief, and went off to work again.

Joe Kaba got stuck in straightaway to tell all of us in International Affairs about his latest brainwave. In a year's time, he said, Millennium would turn twenty-one and if that was a coming of age for a person, why not a nation also? He had already cleared it with President Menendez. We were going to organise a great shindig in Century at the end of January 2021. Nominally, it would be a conference based around Orphans of Africa and the plans to extend the Charity. In addition, we would have a setting to showcase everything about Millennium — the people, the progress, the productivity. We were going to invite the world for a week or so to see at first-hand how our country had become the standard bearer for Africa.

All this was heady and exciting stuff, but it was a huge project with only a year for preparation. Joe was ready for that. We would do what we could do, but not attempt the impossible. So there was only one building project, which was to be an upgrade to the airport. Otherwise, he was planning a myriad of trips and demonstrations all around the country to provide a real flavour of what we had achieved under the auspices of Orphans. He had a key task programme for the twelve of us who worked directly for him and we went away to get stuck in to arranging our own staff and timetables to make sure that we delivered for him.

Looking back on things, I can understand that Joe's vision always risked being seen as propaganda. We were extolling Orphans which is an international charity, but the second agenda was to trumpet the success of Millennium itself. Not every country round the globe liked that, but the reasons for disapproval varied. To explain why, I have to give you a few facts and figures.

Millennium has posted some impressive statistics over the last twenty years. Our GDP world ranking has moved up from 121 to 68. The per capita income has quadrupled. Our exports now exceed $25bn a year, but the contribution from oil has declined from 50% to just over 15%. That's not because we have fewer reserves, as we have discovered much more offshore. The reason is that we make a lot of goods here which the rest of the world wants to buy. Our population has shot up from about 5 million to 13.76 at the last census in 2018 and the reason is that some eight million people, nearly 60% of our nation, have chosen to emigrate from forty different countries around the world to live amongst us and to contribute to Millennium's success. Considering that my grandfather arrived with three thousand odd, that's some result.

Our literacy rate has gone from 15% to 85% and our life expectancy from 45 to 73 years. Our political system gives every adult over eighteen a vote every four years. Tertiary and university education is free to all. You can travel where you want on decent roads by scheduled services any tick of the clock and your security is assured by our Combined Services and National police force which are so efficient that they are now contributing to our export figures through the sale of training to other countries.

All this is good news, and I could go much further in listing results and measurements. The trouble and the paradox is that our development is not universally well regarded. Why not? Well, of course, the cynic can always say that good news is no news and for sure, there's some dog in the manger attitude out there. But the truth of it goes much deeper than that. For starters, we have benefited from some outstanding people who came to Millennium because they were outcast from the nations of their birth or previous existence: my own boss today is a good example. And the countries from which they fled don't like to acknowledge that they got it wrong.

Then you have the Great Powers. The US of A still claims the title of the land of opportunity. The descendants of European colonisers of two centuries back can't decide whether to be ashamed or patronising. The Chinese and the Indians are happy to grab what they can with whatever it takes. But having said all of that, Millennium remains a small plot of real estate on the map. Whatever we're doing or achieving, however different the style and quality of life which we are building, none of this should be of too much account on the world stage. That's true until you come to South Africa.

The problem here is the Republic's direction, because South Africa is going backwards. It's not been easy for them, of course. Since apartheid ended with a new beginning under Mandela in 1994, there have been huge issues for them to confront — really grotesque in size and complexity. The tough bottom line is not that they haven't succeeded; it's more that things have got worse. During the first decade of this century, whilst we were lucky enough to be starting afresh, South Africa struggled with a prolonged hangover of celebration followed by a protracted 'where do we go from here?' There were disasters of crumbling infrastructure, diminishing wealth, deteriorating governance and soaring crime. Meanwhile, the whole world wanted to believe that new roses really were springing up in the garden.

During the last ten years, things started to change. About eighty per cent of native born South Africans are black with the remainder white, coloured or of Asian descent. They make a small minority, but that's still a powerful lot of people and many of them became completely disillusioned by the 'new' South Africa. They felt condemned for the sins of their forefathers, disenfranchised by the majority rule. In a country with a quarter of workers unemployed, they were still the powerhouse of the economy and yet — and this was the worst of it — they felt increasingly threatened. Throughout the Republic, in cities and rural communities, violent crime continued to grow with the have's being constantly menaced by the have-nots. This was the prime reason for so many applying to come to Millennium. But a much greater number said 'No. I was born and bred in South Africa and my forebears have been here for generations. Whatever the colour of my skin, this is my place and I'm staying even if I do have to build a fortress around my home, my family and my business.'

There was another influence on this group. Around that time in '11 or '12, the world witnessed what was dubbed at the time as being the Arab Spring. There was uprising and regime change in all sorts of spots in the Middle East — Egypt, Tunisia, Syria and Libya, even a bit going on in Jordan. Incoming new governance didn't work so well for all of them and there were problems which made even American-invaded Iraq look mild. But each country worked it out over a while, although at great cost. Meanwhile, all those minority South Africans were looking at what happened in the Middle East and were saying to themselves that maybe you've just got to shake the cage a bit to see what drops out. It can't be worse than it is now. After a while, they began to talk to each other and in late 2015, they formed an organisation which they called simply 'Future', claiming with reason that's what it's all about.

The Future Group took a big gamble. Their leader, Henrik de Vries, made a speech in Durban over Easter 2016 in which he said to the ANC-descended Government of South Africa, 'Look. We need each other. On our side, we don't want to leave the Republic and we acknowledge that you guys are the elected Government and there's no chance of you being voted out.

From your side, you can't afford to lose us or ignore us. You're in enough shit already and it's we Whites, Coloureds and Asians who make the economy work, bad as it may be. But a lot of us have had enough of working our balls off only to worry if ours is the next business to be pillaged or if we're going to get home and find our women raped and our houses trashed — secure compounds or not. So here's the deal. We'll stay put and keep putting money in your coffers. In return, you give us a place of our own. More than one. At least three tracts of land which we can enclose, protect and develop as our own communities with our own security. Without that, what's the point of living even if we get to do so? And anyway, this is not such a radical idea. Look at Lesotho: self governing up to a point, but still an enclave surrounded by the Republic.'

The Government of the day simply could not see its way past this one. It was a weird proposal because it implied a sort of reverse apartheid. Future's promise — guarantee even — was to produce the money, the technical and management skills in return for living in isolation, taking no part in politics but leaving Pretoria financed to sort out the shambles into which the Republic's health, education, housing and policing systems had degenerated. So they agreed eventually and in 2018 the first Dedicated Territory was opened in Cape Province with the next being prepared in the Karoo for the following year.

Meanwhile on the world stage, all this was seen as a seriously retrograde step. The great and the good of global statesmen were complaining that the maturity of civilisation had been diminished during the preceding thirty years. Exploitation in the former USSR, carnage in Iraq and Afghanistan, thuggery in the Middle East and now turning back the clock in Southern Africa. Not to mention the outright piracy which had brought Millennium into being. This was disingenuous talk of course, mentioning nothing of the desire in established quarters to maintain the status quo.

That's enough of a lecture. I know that it's a point of view but the fundamental truths are there and verifiable. And here's another. One of the facts of life with which we struggled in Millennium was the persona of Hugh Dundas. Not the person and not the character. But the perception and the manner in which others wanted to portray him. No one on the planet could deny that Hugh was a toweringly successful man. Whatever his personal wealth, it was immeasurable and with hardly a bean of it inherited. He was quite simply a very clever guy with the additional talent of knowing how best to employ his abilities. And this made him a target for jealousy, all the more so because he was so straightforward and open. He never sought to hide his long term relationship with Alexa while maintaining his marriage to Janey and he never denied or excused his activities to fund Zero. Perhaps this was a mistake although he would never have played it differently. Whatever, the result in later years and long after he had given up the Millennium Presidency was that he continued to be shot at from all sides. Nobody, the world decided, could be both that successful and simultaneously that honest. The net result was that whenever a world figure chose to have a go at Millennium, they would include Hugh Dundas personally as part of the target. He was fair game for all.

Back to Joe Kaba and his Aurora Programme. That's what he called it: Aurora as in dawn. He wanted us to create not a new beginning but a new chapter, a new day. The name fitted well enough. Joe's strategy was clear. Millennium was to host a conference in Century City, inviting chosen Heads of State from around the world. The main item was to be Orphans of Africa: what it meant, how it worked, what it had achieved both in our country and across this continent. That it was ready now for roll out across the rest of the globe as Orphans of the World.

Joe had a second agenda. The event would serve to showcase Millennium — everything about us: who we are, where we've come from, what we stand for and where we're going. It would be the opportunity to show the doubters and the cynics that we're not colonisers and we're not pirates. Millennium is an established sovereign state and there's no comparison to be drawn with the breakaway enclaves further south. And that we've risen from a fresh start, not struggled out of some internal strife. Communicating this message would also give Joe the opportunity to bury Hugh Dundas. Much as he admired Hugh, Joe told us, it was time for him to depart the scene. Hugh was the last link with the controversies of the past. He had been a pivotal figure without whom there would have been no Chapter One in the Millennium story. But he has no place in Chapter Two and that, Joe assured us, is precisely how he feels himself. Hugh is about to turn eighty and he wants to retire from any form of public life.

So then we all went to work. There was a lot of it and all the practical stuff was demanding enough: the building at the airport, a couple of roads and then all the detail of the programme, where to go, what to see, who to meet.

The less predictable revolved around the guest list and I guess I was flattered that Joe involved me in this. It was crucial that we got it right. No point in a flash theatre with a great new show if nobody comes to watch. In this case, there was never going to be a problem in getting an audience. The Chinese were immediately up for it and probably looking to get a further piece of our action. India also was keen. The Japanese accepted and so did the Koreans. Australasia said 'yes please' and we included everyone from our home continent. We were more picky with the South Americans but we asked Brazil, of course and Argentina plus a few more. We included Russia for sure, also Kazakhstan and Azerbaijan. With tongue in cheek I asked Joe about Armenia and he almost exploded before he saw me grinning. The Middle East was a minefield except for the obvious — the Saudis and UAE. And Israel. We asked a couple from the Balkans and from South East Asia too. Joe was particularly anxious to attract the Thais. We rounded off the guest list with some international big hitters — the UN, the World Bank, WHO and the like.

The real challenge was to get people — but the right people — to come from Western Europe and the USA. To be fair to the Yanks, it was difficult timing for them because 2020 was an Election year in the States. They couldn't be sure who'd be in power after November and our week the following January would be very close to Inauguration date. Sorting this out and making sure that we could count on a representative of sufficient stature was a delicate business for Joe Kaba and had me travelling to and from Washington to present his suggestions. It was on one of these trips that I side tracked to see King Offenbach.

The greatest problem was in Europe. Not with the French or the Germans who were as keen as mustard. So was the EU and the European Development Bank. The problem lay with the Brits. There was yet another coalition in Downing Street, this one a patchwork between Labour and the LibDems. The Foreign Secretary was a particularly mousy individual and the PM highly distracted by domestic matters. After Parliament's summer recess, we finally got a breakthrough. If Joe Kaba could get himself to London at the start of November, the Prime Minister would fit in a meeting and they could get the matter settled. The PM was, in principle, willing to lend support.

This was great news and Joe was determined to take full advantage. Of course he would go to the UK but he would also take in France and Germany plus a flying visit to the Portuguese. He set aside a week in all to include three days in London for Downing Street, the City, a parliamentary group which backed us and a couple of charities. He was delighted at the whole prospect and so was I as he was sending me over ten days in advance to get his schedule set up to the minute. I'd be busy, but still have the time to see all my family. Before I flew out, Joe was on a charge and working all hours, partly to pull forward other work which he was doing on behalf of Helen Menendez. Our President's health had been very bad and although she was improving, her time was limited under strict medical orders and she was aiming to be completely fit for Aurora.

There was only one evening free in Joe's week in England, the Thursday, and then he filled that too. He received an invitation to speak at the Oxford Union, to take the lead in opposing the Motion 'This House deplores neo-colonialism in all its forms'. Joe expostulated with excitement as I was leaving the office for the Airport.

'I can't miss out on this one Olty. It's a great chance to tell it like it is.'

I was rushed off my feet in Europe but the adrenalin was flowing and I loved every minute. I did the other capitals first, especially enjoying a day in Lisbon where I had never been and which holds obvious significance for me. In London, Martin Kirchoff gave discreet but vital advice on those whom Joe Kaba should meet. Martin was looking ten years younger than his seventy-seven and Ruth even better as she mothered me in their house from which they had never moved. Martin was pretty much retired although he still went to The Mansion House once a fortnight. He wouldn't let me go there.

'Don't do anything to resurrect old connections,' he advised, 'it wouldn't be helpful.'

The day before Joe Kaba's arrival, I was ready, waiting and excited. I had everything arranged and he had approved the tight timetable over the phone. We had many phone conversations and I thought it was him again when my mobile went off that afternoon. It wasn't. It was his aide in Century, Jerome, ringing to tell me that Joe had suffered a heart attack.

Apparently it was not too serious and the medics were confident of his full recovery. But it would take some time. Joe had been working flat out for months and he had exhausted himself. This was his body telling him to slow down and take a break. Yes, probably he'll be OK for Aurora in January, but as for flying tonight? Forget it.

I was horrified but I started to unpick the arrangements immediately. I wanted my contacts in Europe and London to hear from me personally rather than getting the news via the media or social sites. It took me almost twenty-four hours to reach everybody — the conversation with the Prime Minister's office was pretty testing — and at the end of it I realised that I had forgotten about Oxford. Before I could get to dial again, my phone rang with Mrs Menendez herself calling. I gave her a rundown and finished with the one thing I had left to do. There was silence for a few seconds and then the President spoke again in her mellifluous tone.

'You know, Olty, I believe you should carry out that engagement on Joe's behalf. You should at least make that offer. You won't mind me saying this, but it's the one appearance which you could take on and I'd like everyone to see that Millennium is doing all it possibly can under these difficult circumstances. Would you do this for me please?'

'Of course.'

'You've got his notes? What he planned to say?'

'I've got the speech in detail. He mailed it to me.'

'Alright then. Just do your best for us, Olty, and good luck.'

I took the train to Oxford on the Wednesday, arriving in the early evening. I had booked a room at the Randolph hotel for two nights, thinking that I may as well do this in some style. There was no pressure of time on me now and I wanted to take the opportunity to see something of this city and the university which had been, in a sense, the birthplace for my country. I gave myself a brief walk around before having dinner in the hotel, and a far more extended tour during the daylight of the following morning. I was captivated by the place.

There is a timeless peace to Oxford which wraps you to its bosom, insisting that you appreciate the past and block out for a while the frantic hurrying of the world around you. Guided only by my tourist map, I meandered through the streets and market places and courtyards. My inclination was to absorb the atmosphere rather than to take instruction on the specifics. So I wandered past the Bodleian and the Ashmolean, I flirted with the Cathedral at Christ Church, I nodded at the Pitt Rivers Museum and paraded down Broad Walk and around the Botanical Gardens. I pottered past a fair number of the colleges, lingering outside the entrance to Brasenose which had sheltered my grandfather during his time here. Instinctively, I was projecting myself back through two generations to days of sixty years ago when the Oxford Five would have been indistinguishable from the undergraduates who crossed my path today in their scruffy clothes on their clapped out bikes. And when I stopped for a sandwich and a pint of bitter in a pub steeped in history, I could not help but wonder if it had been there that King Offenbach had first been introduced into their gathering. And the underlying message which sprang from those majestic buildings and ancient thoroughfares was unchanging: forget about sixty years, try six hundred and more.

I finally returned to the hotel at tea time and gave myself some time to change and prepare for the evening. I was looking forward to it, more surroundings of ancient history in the location and the practice of the Union and without any onerous responsibility for me. I simply had to make a reasonable job of reading the script. Thursday debates commence at 8.30 in the evening and there was a drink and a light dinner arranged beforehand for the Officers of the Union and their invited guest speakers. It gave us a chance to meet each other before debating battle was joined.

I knew already that the Oxford Union Society, to give it the full and proper title, was founded in 1823 and its home is in Frewin Court off St Michaels Street in the heart of Oxford, just around the corner from the Randolph Hotel. The President for the year was an affable guy, a citizen of Afghanistan and probably a bit of a fan of Millennium judging by his informed and enthusiastic comments. But he was also mindful of protocol and manners and he moved on swiftly with his duties as host for the evening.

For every Union Debate, one student and two guest speakers are fielded both for and against the Motion of the day. Mary Clovelly was from Belfast, in her third year at Jesus College, a bright and bubbly girl and a passionate debater, she confided, as she took me under her wing. She would open the argument for us in Opposition. Mishaal Rahman was to lead the speeches for the Motion. He was a second year student from Chittagong, Bangladesh. A bit older than most, Mary told me, good on his feet with a fiery disposition reflected in the dreadlocks which hung to the shoulders of his gangling frame.

The first guest speaker on our side was a burly, bearded man called Kurt Kruger. Born of German parents, Kruger had been brought up in Zimbabwe and farmed outside Bulawayo until the Mugabe regime banished him. For the last twenty years he had lived in Johannesburg, managing his fast developing business which offered 'resettlement advice'. He was closely connected to the Future Group and a strong advocate for the principle of the Dedicated Territories. In the Debate, I was to follow Kurt as the final speaker against the Motion, quoting the pre prepared thoughts of Joe Kaba. I wondered and worried if Joe had ever met or spoken to Kruger. It didn't sound as if their views would be complementary. But then again, one little evening in Oxford was hardly going to be life changing.

Ranged against us were a couple of big names, but at least I knew a bit about the first of them. Trevor Mullen was in his late sixties, a United Nations man only just retired at the most senior level. He had a blue chip background. He was worthy but dull. He was overweight and overblown, inclined to patronise and very sure of the excellence of his opinions. I thought of him as a bit of a dinosaur but still with a punch to throw.

The senior member of their team was a different proposition and I don't mind admitting that I quailed at the thought of her. Marion Albermarle — aka Marble Mo — was the US Ambassador to Britain. She was only mid-forties and already something of a legend. She was extremely good looking, immaculately presented. No husband, no partner, no children. Thought to be lesbian but without evidence. Diamond hard and sharp as nails. Fiercely ambitious. Publically stated aim to become President of the United States. Understood to have stepped aside in the race for this year's nominees because she has so much time on her side. They say she took this key diplomatic post as her reward for not rocking the US domestic boat. Not yet anyway. A tough customer by any standard. We exchanged a brief handshake when introduced before dinner and later I heard her aside to Mullen about 'a boy for a man's job'.

Thinking back, it's strange that I didn't feel more nervous as we were all escorted through to the debate. I was being pushed into the lion's den, yet it didn't seem such a big deal. I had Joe's speech in my pocket — it certainly sounded good to me — and anyway, this was simply a provincial event. What's to worry about?

The Oxford Union still lays claim to being 'the world's most prestigious debating society' and there's no denying the number of quality figures who have appeared there over many years past. They won't have been there for the surroundings. It's of a good size, seating several hundred when the gallery is full, but the decoration is drab, the seating basic and the acoustics poor. But none of that matters. It's the atmosphere which is everything and from the moment you enter, you feel the hand of history on your shoulder. And there is the dynamism. There is brain power and the skill of expression permanently at work here. There's a charge which runs through the whole chamber and it invades your soul from the outset.

We ran to expectation that evening. Mishaal Rahman opened with a diatribe against the exploitation of the world's down trodden. It wasn't completely relevant, but he had powerful language and a great gift of timing: a supreme orator in the making.

Mary Clovelly countered with a well prepared speech which concentrated on the need to learn from the past and to adapt for the circumstances of today. She articulated all the body of argument but on the way, she lost some of the soul of passion.

Trevor Mullen was as boring as I had hoped. He quoted an endless stream of statistics which confused his listeners and distracted them from grasping his essential points. I was happy to hear the scraping feet and shifting bodies in the audience which signalled a lack of attention. This also made me look around to see how the numbers in the chamber had been steadily increasing. We were getting to be a packed house.

Kurt Kruger was then invited by the President to speak and I was cringing at some of his words. His views were completely at odds with Joe Kaba's aspirations. Kruger was all about South Africa and nowhere else. He was obsessed with the disadvantages which 'his' people were suffering. If there was a larger picture , he was quite unable to see it. Then he finished with emphasis on the need for 'a reverse apartheid'. He couldn't have conjured up a more damaging image and I felt Marble Mo licking her lips.

My despair was soon increased. Ms Albemarle rose to conclude the case for the Motion and she was devastating. She stood there, tall, elegant, domineering and confident in her ability to destroy the opposition. She started with a reminder of the Motion — this House deplores neo-colonialism in all its form — and she emphasised the 'all'. Then she offered a definition of 'neo colonialism'.

'It means,' she said, 'the use of economic, political or cultural pressures to control or influence other countries.' She paused to good effect as she swept her eyes over her audience before continuing.

'It is precisely this which we in the United States deplore and that's why I'm here to argue for this Motion. From all that we have heard from the advertising of the Future Group this evening, it's clear this activity is their entire intent in South Africa. That honourable Republic, which is striving every sinew to serve its population and to improve the lot of its citizens, is being held to ransom by the greedy and grasping business people of the Future Group who, despite being citizens of the same country, are placing a steep price on their availability to help. Mr Kruger has made that abundantly clear and he has even stooped to describe their policy in a word which encapsulates infamy.

'But there's still worse. Look at the history of the last twenty years and you'll see that towering example which is encouraging the followers of Future to believe they can flout the law in their own land and break faith with their own people, feathering a new nest for themselves while letting their fellow citizens fester in misery.'

Whatever your view, this was language to raise the temperature and I could feel the whole chamber stir with renewed interest. Marble Mo stood tall and poised and perfect, occasionally wagging a finger at me as she tore into Millennium, ripping at our past, denigrating our achievements and pouring scorn on the plan for Aurora.

'This isn't about charity,' she said, her voice dripping acid, 'it's all about buying legitimacy and international respect. It's time that even the fabulous Mr Hugh Dundas should learn he can't buy that status. It has to be earned, and that will never happen. Millennium should never have happened. It arrived by stealth, was established by piracy and continues to exist through bribery and cunning. The whole place is a blot on the world's landscape, created by the cupidity of vipers who sprang from this very heart of learning and I am glad to be here to denounce them. I would like to be addressing their President elect Joe Kaba, but I won't kill his messenger,' and she paused to curl her lip at me, 'I don't need to. I'm sure he will give us whatever it was that Mr Kaba intended to contribute to this debate, and when he's finished, I'm just as sure that this House will support the Motion. It's the only way forward for our modern world.'

Wow. This was not going to plan. When working up Joe's speech before I left Century, we had been confident of a relatively easy ride. We had not anticipated such venom. We had not expected a vicious and sustained attack and I could see the shock on Mary's face beside me while Kurt Kruger had his head in his hands.

Perhaps we hadn't done our homework, but there was no time now for recrimination.

I was on and I stood up to the Secretary's table, holding Joe Kaba's script in both hands like it was a lifeline. And then the world stood still, my head cleared and my hands stopped shaking.

Bugger this, I thought. I'm not taking this lying down. So I chucked Joe's papers on the table and started speaking for myself.

'Ms Albermarle accuses us of grandstanding,' I said, 'well she should know!'

This opening sally drew laughter and better still, it had Mo's face snapping up and staring at me. I had her concentration and that of our audience as well. My confidence grew. I went on.

'It's nonsense to compare the Dedicated Territories in South Africa with the sovereign State of Millennium. My nation has been in existence for years and I am proud to be a citizen of the country. Let me tell you some reasons why.'

Then I set out some of the statistics and the track record. Not too much though. I had just watched Trevor Mullen bore them into fidgets, but equally, I knew how little was really understood about Millennium and it was time to make a few things clear. I finished my short summary with a conclusion.

'Does that sound to you like a place which is using pressures of any sort to influence events outside our borders? I don't think so. I think it's the reverse. Millennium concentrates on its own. We're successful and America doesn't like to see a success for which it can claim no credit.'

I stepped up the attack. 'The USA is well represented here today by Ms Albemarle. Listen to the language from the world's leader and the global nanny. But it's all 'do as we say', not 'do as we do'. Look at the history. About two hundred years ago, the first Americans, the '49ers, were setting out from Council Grove in their wagon trains to spread across that vast land. Was it empty at the time? No it wasn't, and many Indian tribes like the Sioux, the Cheyenne, and the Apache were ground beneath the wagon wheels of the settlers' progress. It was those local people was who paid the price of establishing the Land of Liberty. Wasn't this the very sort of piracy of which we in Millennium now stand accused?

'America claims to carry the standard for enlightened civilization. The American people stand proud in recognition by the world community that it's you who set the example and force the pace. It's you who get things done. Everything is possible in America. So during the hard and troubled history of the continent of Africa, what help and comfort have you given to us? What initiatives? What guidance? What support?

'Where were you in the 1960's when the Nigerian Civil War choked the life out of Biafra?

'Where were you in the Rwanda genocide of 1994 which killed almost one million people?

'Why did you pay court to Mobutu of Zaire for over thirty years while he plundered enough to fill the Grand Canyon?

'Why did you stand aside whilst Mugabe of Zimbabwe wreaked havoc in a model economy?

'Where were you during the Sudan war of 2015?'

I gave myself a break here. I was happy to note that I had a captive audience. You could have heard a pin drop. I continued.

'Can it be that there is one simple answer to all these questions? Is it that the United States of America felt too self important to care?

'And yet now, Ms Albermarle is claiming that it's Millennium which is wallowing in selfishness: that we are, how did she put it? "a blot on the world's landscape". She should think again and examine the facts, for which there is an early opportunity waiting. Millennium does not yet have an American of high stature to visit us for Aurora, and surely Ms Albermarle is the ideal candidate. Marble Mo's just gotta go!'

There was uproar at this, the speakers opposite springing to their feet in protest and the President rang his bell for order and silence before rebuking me for my intemperate language which risked being slanderous.

'Please moderate your language and move to conclude. You have only a minute left of your allotted time.'

I inclined my head in apology, but inside, my blood was zinging.

'Millennium is different,' I said, 'we are an established nation, made up of many peoples and backgrounds and cultures. We work and live in harmony and we are succeeding. We are the new face of Africa and we are proud to say so. And finally, I am personally moved to be in Oxford where the men and woman who turned a dream into reality first came to know each other. And the memory of one of them, our founding President David Heaven, means still more to me because he was also my grandfather, the father of my mother.'

We lost the vote which followed, but narrowly, and it didn't seem to matter much. We had given a good account of ourselves. The experience had been dramatic and fulfilling but the debate had always been the sideshow to Joe's week. I caught a final glimpse of Marble Mo as she swept out of the Union's courtyard with her minder from the Embassy. I had a quick drink before leaving. Mary Clovelly was excited and friendly. The President thanked me and said that he was pleased, adding,

'We had a big crowd in tonight. People like to hear a good scrap and you guys certainly gave them that.'

Soon after, it was time to go. I shook hands all round and walked back to the Randolph. As I got into bed, I was still buzzing and my imaginings were all about Oxford in days of long ago. I would be thinking of other things in the morning.

As I was shaving, I was startled to hear my name mentioned in a short news bulletin on the TV which had moved to other things before I could get in front of it. I grabbed the newspaper pushed under my door and reached for my watch to tune into the Net. An enterprising Oxford newsman had been in the audience at the Union and made the most of his opportunity during the night. It was a quiet Friday morning for world events so there was an international appetite for this entertaining snippet and a fair bit of coverage.

'Millennium founder grandson attacks the US', was the prominent inside page headline in one paper and this was also the theme used by the TV reports. I was horrified. In no profession, especially not in diplomacy, should you step out of line in public. I had done just that — but big time. I'd chucked away the brief and put in my own. I'd probably given poor Joe Kaba another heart attack. I'd surely be for the high jump myself and God knows what would happen to Aurora. And there was the President herself.

'Do your best for us, Olty' had been her final words to me. I doubted that this sort of publicity was what she'd had in mind.

But I had to get on with it and face the music, and to do that I had to go home which had been the plan anyway. I was due out of Heathrow on that evening's flight to Century so I had plenty of time. I rang Hereford and spoke to my father who was sympathetic but guarded. I pushed down a small breakfast, checked out of the hotel but leaving my luggage there as I went and wandered the streets of Oxford, very much distracted by my worries. I must have walked miles and was glad that it was a fine day. I read all the papers I could find and kept checking news on the Internet. To my relief, they moved to other things as the day wore on.

In the late afternoon, I collected my things from the hotel and found my way to pick up a bus which went to the airport direct. It was a huge electric thing with three floors and was much less than full. I had plenty of space to myself, to look at the passing countryside and to chew over my worries.

I arrived at the busy airport and went straight from security to check in at the departure gate, carrying my hand luggage. I was sitting there when a ground staff member approached and asked me to wait until called. I wasn't surprised. I was no doubt an embarrassment and they would prefer to slip me on at the last minute. Eventually, the girl came back and asked me to follow her. I did as I was told. She paused to check my boarding card and passport and then we were walking again and turning the corner to pass onto the air bridge.

It was then that I came up short with a gasp of surprise. I didn't count the numbers but it seemed that half the aircrew were lined up there, and in front, my old chum Arnie Schwartz, immaculate in full Millennium Airways uniform, complete with jacket and cap, standing there with his hand out in greeting.

'Welcome aboard, Olty,' he said in his guttural Afrikaans accent, 'you and I both may be close to our last flight, so let's make it a good one together. And Olty. Everyone here and many more beside just want to say thank you for what you said last night. We're proud of you for giving us pride in ourselves.'

Arnie never hangs about, and he turned sharply to go back to work. There were smiles and a little ripple of applause. I felt unbearably embarrassed and a bit tearful with the emotion of it all. But then I was being ushered onto the plane, straight through the front entrance, into first class and to a seat which I had been lucky enough to occupy many times before. I can't remember much about the flight until the end of it. I certainly had a few drinks with dinner, and I'm sure that I slept a bit. That's my pattern. But I do remember everything about our arrival into Millennium the next morning. I will never forget it.

Arnie's voice came over the PA to say we were on time and due to land in Century at 0800 local. The familiar movements to make ready were everywhere around me. I accepted a cup of coffee and sat sipping at it, wondering what life would bring next. I felt calmed by the background of my family and my antecedents. I felt the spirit and comfort of my grandfather around me and my thoughts played over others who had gone before, Aischa and Conrad especially.

The screen in front of me flicked on and I heard Arnie's voice again, giving us more details of our arrival and speaking of a special welcome. Suddenly there was a clear image of the scene, quite a crowd on the apron in front of the terminal building, the huge sign above announcing 'Heaven International Airport', and then I could see Pente Broke Smith, a vast compelling figure on the tarmac and probably scrabbling for a cigar in violation of all the rules.

I could see the camera vans now, clearly marked with the logo of Century Seven, my favourite News Channel, and I flicked over to see the image they were beaming. I could see and feel the aircraft move as Arnie flipped us to port and we moved around onto final approach. The bright sun of Africa caught the Millennium flag on our tail plane and it flashed on the wings of our morning as the Dreamliner snapped sharply into level descent. Arnie was determined on a smart and perfect landing. We were on target with just a few minutes to go.

I was tired from travel, emotionally charged by recent experience and no doubt fired by imagination. But the vision which then appeared remains crystal clear to me and I know that it will never diminish.

I saw it first on the screen in front of my seat, a small cloud marooned by itself against the embracing blue of Millennium skies. As we drew closer, the cloud seemed to reform itself into two figures enjoined, two head and shoulder profiles which startled me with the reminder of that precious photograph of Aischa and Ouye, captured in Mocamedes so many years ago.

I looked out of my window then, and as this feathery image drifted past, the faces seemed to turn towards me, blowing a single word of greeting, and the salutation of our people came sighing down the generations in welcome to a warrior, returning home.

—